# the UNHAPPY MEDIUM

# the UNHAPPY MEDIUM

# T. J. BROWN

## CHAPTER 1

# MUSEUM

The curator of the Langton Hadlow village museum paused as he crossed the quiet market square and squinted up into the intense blue of the morning sky. Already, the air was filling with thin white contrails, trailing behind scores of charter jets heading south to the cheap beaches and predictable weather of the Mediterranean. He let out a long weary sigh of frustration and scurried on past the dusty, dead shops.

In its heyday, Langton Hadlow had been everything you would have expected from an old English village. Beneath moss-covered slates, drunken half-timbered cottages leant sleepily against each other under the fragmented ruins of the castle, their weathered façades draped in wisteria, the gardens kept impossibly picturesque by the mostly retired population. The now-wild flower baskets, wobbly doors and panelled windows still defiantly lent the place the vision of a rural idyll, but the silent shops and closed, shuttered pubs told of a newer, more unfortunate era.

As the old curator walked bow-backed down the High Street towards his small museum, he looked sadly up at the growing number of estate agent signs and narrowed his eyes; everything seemed to be changing. There were no market days anymore. The big supermarkets in Weymouth and Swanage had long since starved out the butcher, baker and greengrocer, while online shopping had comprehensively killed off the antique shop and the second-hand bookstore. The young families had all drifted off to Dorchester and Bournemouth in search of employment and homes in which you could stand upright. Langton Hadlow had begun to die.

The village's rather unspectacular castle only added to the general air of neglect. It had probably looked pretty shabby when it was first built; the foundations were lousy and it had leant to the west from the very beginning. One whole wing had fallen clean away during the reign of Edward the Third, taking with it half of what had had up until that point been quite a successful banquet. It had been partially rebuilt during the reign of Henry the Fifth, but it was never really quite right

5

and visiting noblemen were not infrequently killed by falling masonry and loose crenellations.

Its sole attempt at being a real castle came during the English Civil War, when supporters of the King were forced to dash inside to avoid a rampaging parliamentarian army coming up the road from Swanage. The defending Royalists were well stocked with cakes, pastries and a range of complementary table wines, enough to keep them from surrender for a good day and a half. And so, after a last cathartic binge in the great hall, they walked out with crumbs in their beards and their hands in the air.

The victors elected then to deny the castle to future tourist guide books, and with a pathetically small amount of explosives – one or two kegs at most – they blew it up. The modest blast eviscerated the shoddy structure in one fell swoop, leaving nothing but a toothy inebriated ruin perched upon an unstable mound. This spectacular result astounded the sappers to such an extent that they excitedly rushed in to inspect their efforts, only to lose fourteen of their number when the master bedroom fell on them.

In addition to its castle, Langton Hadlow once boasted five public houses around its beautiful old centre – not bad for a village with only forty six buildings. The ivy-covered Tugger's Arms had been the biggest of the pubs, and every inch the picture-perfect English country inn. The Green Man was a more formal affair, its elegant rooms once frequented by visiting squires and traders. The Old Cock, by contrast, was a classic spit-and-sawdust pub, which the old curator could remember from his first youthful ales. Back then it had been jammed to the rafters with ruddy-faced farmers and sheepdogs. Then there was the oddly named The Piece of String, which had been unique amongst the county's pubs for being very, very small. Its three notoriously rude staff normally outnumbered the customers, and on market days they once served burnt sausages and thin watery ales out of a hatch direct onto the pavement of Duck Street. Finally, there was The Turk's Head, nestling into the castle wall itself. It had been a mass of flowers and justifiably famous for ploughman's lunches with pickled onions so strong that once you'd even just smelt them, you'd cry for days afterwards. Sadly however, The Turk's Head spent more than half its time closed, falling masonry from the castle above rendering the premises too dangerous even for the most hardened of Langton Hadlow's drinkers.

These grand old pubs had survived virtually intact into the 20th century, and as a result, in their time they had seen many passing faces: Tudor bowmen practising on the heathlands to the north, Georgian wool traders heading to London from Devon and Cornwall to the west, and British and American tank crews, billeted in the area in the lead-up to the D-Day invasion.

Post-war, the market square played host to beaming day trippers, sports cars containing spivs and cocktail waitresses, and healthy young couples on bicycles. Coach parties would briefly swamp the small post office for postcards and ice cream then tear away again towards the coast.

Due to the fresh sea breezes, ill-informed Victorian medical theorists had also deemed the local climate convivial to the insane and, as a result of their endorsement, a series of large institutes sprung up in the surrounding landscape. The mad, deluded and just plain misunderstood had been shipped down wholesale from London, where they had until then been deemed a source of entertainment in a strange foretaste of modern television.

Not that any of this really impacted much upon old Langton Hadlow itself. For the most part, the village remained a quiet unchanging place, beloved of painters and ramblers, but still retaining its old beating heart in agriculture, community and ale.

'Nothing lasts forever,' thought the curator as he turned the corner into Mire Street, the empty, boarded-up shell of The Old Cock to his left and the dusty windows of the Langton tearooms to his right, dead wasps hanging despondently in the webs between the curtains. With a plastic clatter, a sudden breeze fluttered the estate agent signs, their brash typography clashing unsympathetically with the rural aesthetic still limping on around them.

Of course, it hadn't helped when the castle started falling down again, this time on top of its own gift shop. Luckily it had been empty at the time due to staff illness, but all the same, it was hardly good publicity. Then the big stores opened in the county towns and suddenly you could get Dorset clotted cream flown in from Peru in two-litre tubs for half the price of the local stuff. Cheap flights carted sun-loving holidaymakers out of England and away to where there was never any rain, the hotels were brand new and you could eat all the paella you could stomach for five Euros.

Pretty soon the old village just withered. The quaint post office went to the wall first. Then, one by one, the pubs went belly up. Eventually, following accusations of malpractice, even the Gothic psychiatric institute nearby at Hadlow Grange shut down, its inmates released back into the community by reforming politicians, with mixed results, and the vast bleak building sold to developers.

Only the little museum kept going.

Langton Hadlow's village museum had never been a big affair. The curator's grandfather had founded the collection way back in the 1890s when he'd finally come home to his family after an eternity criss-crossing the British Empire, spreading the doctrine of administration at the point of a quill pen. With him he'd brought back five huge shipping cases packed close to bursting with relics collected during a lifetime in the service to the Crown. There were masks from the jungles of Sumatra, spears from the Naga Hills and animal skins from the bazaars of Marrakech. These formed the nucleus of a collection that grew in time to take in many European curiosities and odd little trinkets from the Americas.

The grandfather had been given an empty milliner's shop to house the objects by the local old Earl, a one-time major in the Royal Tank Regiment. It was a surprisingly spacious series of rooms just opposite the recently created memorial to the dead of the Great War, which even in tiny Langton Hadlow had honoured some thirty five dead, mostly from the newly formed tank corps. Later, this simple cross had been replaced by the huge lozenge shape of a genuine World War One tank, donated from a regiment up the road at Bovington Camp. The Earl was a soft and sentimental old chap who'd done a fair bit of travelling himself, much of it in pursuit of argumentative indigenous peoples. Through him, the collection finally had a permanent home and the right to declare itself proudly a proper museum. No actual deeds had been signed, admittedly, but in those gentlemanly days, well, quite often people couldn't be bothered. The arrangement had been duly toasted in ale at The Old Cock, which was the important thing. And so, in 1920, the museum opened for business.

It was a great success.

Old spinsters down from Salisbury for the air and touring clergymen from the Home Counties would poke gleefully about the glass cases, perfectly content that the items were grouped in no logical pattern whatsoever and none was accurately labelled. Inspired by the attention, the locals soon started turning up with curios they had acquired themselves and these were enthusiastically added to the collection. There were flint tools from the caves at Banghampton, arrowheads from Juggin's Lump and oddly shaped fruit and vegetables fresh from the village allotments. Stuffed birds flew in through the door in flocks, followed immediately by the small moths that enjoyed eating them.

The curator's father inherited the museum when the old boy finally died, succumbing to something exotic he'd been carrying since he'd played truth or dare on a packet steamer bound for Madagascar in 1879. However, the curator's father had never been that keen on his own father's obsessions, preferring to think of himself as a bit of a playboy and spending much of his time away from Langton Hadlow in London. He'd squandered his days drinking gallons of Pimms with a notable 'someone' called Bunty, something that his long-suffering wife seemed to find perpetually annoying. Weighed down by these issues, she had let her young son play unsupervised in the museum while she sat seething on the front desk, selling tickets and reading *Madame Bovary*. The young boy, oblivious to these adult dramas, drew the stuffed birds, wore the dusty helmets and memorised every detail of every object with a child's intensity. Although there was a gap where his philandering father ought to be, the boy filled it with history, nature and the collection of strange vegetables on the first floor.

His father died in the Second World War, blown to atoms by the Luftwaffe in a nightclub just off Pall Mall. The curator, however, was lucky enough to have come of age in the immediate post-war generation that could enjoy the great universities, undisturbed by mechanised total warfare. He took a degree in history and passed with decent grades that should have seen him heading for a future in academia and corduroy.

But the pull of the old village of Langton Hadlow was strong. With his mother ailing, his decision was made, and in 1949 he returned to the museum and settled down for a modest life as its curator, untroubled by the modern age.

The years had flown gently past the curator like clouds. The 1960s, all self and sex, had barely imposed their tie-dyed fabrics upon his consciousness. In 1972 he'd finally sewn elbow patches on his old university jacket and in 1983, for the fourth time in ten years, he'd fully catalogued the museum on index cards. The decades passed, each as uneventful as the one preceding it.

The curator had always been too shy to ask for state funding for the little establishment, but, with a small sum bequeathed by a neighbour in 2006, he bought a computer and learnt enough code to build the museum a modest website, turning the chaotic collection into an online gallery for who knows who, somewhere out there on the web.

By now Langton Hadlow had begun its sad decline, however, and the curator had his first ominous thoughts about the future – a niggling sense of unease that left him sleepless way into the small hours. The old folk of the village had started to die off leaving vacant properties behind them. Inevitably, these were attracting flashy estate agents like blowflies, sniffing the scent of second-home bonanzas on the same ill wind that was killing poor Langton Hadlow.

Nearing the tiny museum, the curator looked down the old street back towards the castle. The 'Sold' boards were dominating the scene so much that he barely recognised the street of his happy distant childhood. The same obnoxious name seemed to occur again and again.

'Another purchase by McCauley Bros, developers. We sell – we buy – we change lives.'

'Well you are not going to change mine,' thought the curator, huffing, knowing at the same time that it was probably already too late. He fumbled sadly for his keys as he neared the small museum's door. The floor behind the letterbox was as always a slippery mass of junk mail. The curator sighed and began flicking through the envelopes.

All but one was from the McCauley Bros group, the local property developers who for months had been prowling all over the village like hyenas. The curator knew the contents off by heart – he'd been getting the letters for a year or so, offering him just enough to give up and call it a day. But how could he? The museum had been his life, his grandfather's wonderful old things, such treasures. Why didn't people care anymore? It was as if they only valued property and electronic gadgets; the whole world seemed to beep like a robot. Langton Hadlow used to be free from all that.

He binned the letters one by one without opening a single one of them. He wasn't sure if there was any fight left in his gentle heart, or so much anger he couldn't hold it in; he just wasn't sure anymore. Sighing, he sat back in his chair and looked up at the old tin signs and muskets above the butterfly case and remembered quietly for a while.

Whatever happened, he'd have the memories – maybe that would be enough. But then, realistically, he knew he'd no idea about life outside in the big bad world and he began to breathe hard and fast. A sense of panic and vertigo washed over him.

He was busy hyperventilating like this when he noticed a rattling noise from the far room, almost as if an electric razor was lying switched on in one of the cases. Not having turned the lights on for the day, the room was still dark and as he edged around the corner of the door, he was struck at once by an odd purple glow. The light was emanating from inside a small glass case, the one housing peculiar Gothic curios that his grandfather had brought back from Germany after the First World War. Several medieval carvings, goblets and crosses sat in a corner case and every one of them was frankly a bit of a monstrosity – ugly faces, crude carvings and primitive metalwork. One particular object, the one now rattling in the case, was downright creepy.

It was a caped figure the size of an ostrich egg, with claw-like hands held clenched and angry before it. A dark red painted hood hung fully over the face, revealing only a sharp diabolic chin. It knelt, twisting and agonised, above a dark octagonal box, a silver lock sealing its heavy base. There was a large letter 'V' on this box, carved deep and painted blood red and gold. The curator didn't know what on earth it signified; sure, his playful grandfather had made up all sorts of scary stories about the contents of the box and the identity of the figure, but the curator himself had never got round to properly researching the horrid thing. But now, there it was, glowing like a bedside lamp and rattling like wind-up plastic teeth. A sulphurous smell began to fill the small room as the air noticeably chilled. The few remaining hairs on the curator's coot-bald head started to rise, almost as if he was holding a Van de Graaff generator. He stared transfixed, his gaze locked upon the object as it danced and hopped in its case, the other curios falling and breaking as it bounced and whirled amongst them.

Abruptly, it stopped.

CHAPTER 2

# CHRISTOPHER BAXTER

Chris Baxter, senior sales director for the West Midlands area and a growing force in Henderson Applied Plastic Solutions, was in typically buoyant mood. His spotless Lexus GS executive-performance saloon in arctic pearl finish hummed and purred just like the advertising had said it would, pounding the sales beat down the M4 corridor, burning the tarmac from the Westway into the wild frontiers of England's industrial estates and office parks.

Chris Baxter liked what he did. He loved the way his suit hung behind him on the elegant fold-down hanger; he loved the way he effortlessly overtook hatchbacks and plumbers' vans with only the lightest touch on the accelerator. He loved the morning light on the feeder road at junction 6 near Maidenhead and he simply adored the orange glow of the streetlamps as they announced the proximity of the London orbital at the end of each epic day.

But above everything, Chris Baxter loved selling. He was awesomely good at it, each new deal an orgasmic climax to a complex, intimate seduction. The wipe boards at head office said it all. He was head and shoulders above any other rep by such a margin that his rivals would often gape at him with admiration at the monthly sales meeting, heads tilted and jaws slightly ajar as the latest figures came pouring in.

This morning he'd done it yet again. Bang on 9.30 as he was feeding the Lexus, the call came in from the office – confirmation of a juicy 300k from those ditherers over in Swindon. Nice one. Henderson Applied Plastic Solutions had been after those guys for months. They'd all had a go. Sexy Debbie, all cleavage and legs, had flirted like a Bond girl but not sold so much as a shower curtain. Then that new Asian guy offered a raft of incentives, took the directors to Stringfellows, all the classic stuff. Nothing.

Chris Baxter, though, he was in a different league. People in the trade claimed he could sell clouds to the Welsh, pork scratchings to Mossad and nipple clamps to the Archbishop of Canterbury. Baxter was different, Baxter was special. He could engage, barter, cajole, press

12

and convince. Difficult clients would end up inviting him to family weddings. Chris was a star, no question about it.

He was also obsessively tidy – the inside of Baxter's Lexus was as sterile as his soul and as organised as his itinerary. He lived his life totally in control, and as a result, there was so little left to chance in his working day that sometimes even the biggest and most spectacular deals seemed a mere formality.

Alone in his wheeled nerve centre, the Baxter wagon, he would allow himself brief moments of triumphalism, punching the air and giving himself high-fives. Then he'd select a suitably heroic piece of music on the car's over-complicated entertainment system. This morning, straight after the call, he'd pulled off the motorway and whooped for a good two minutes before popping on 'Don't You Forget About Me' and singing along, his top button undone and his tie neatly rolled on the seat beside him. Sometimes it would be 'Where the Streets Have No Name', despite the fact that his sat-nav not only knew the names of the streets but could advise on how to get to them without running into congestion caused by ongoing roadworks.

Chris Baxter didn't like having passengers in his Lexus. He even refused point blank to take his mother to the shops in it, just in case stray hairs from her moth-eaten cat came along for the ride. No, the wagon was strictly off limits unless there were genuine benefits to be gained. He'd been horrified to hear that fellow reps had picked up hitchhikers or rescued broken-down motorists. Anyone ragged and failed enough to stick their thumb out was never going to wheedle their way into the Lexus. No way, no how.

At 10.55, Chris Baxter glided off the motorway and into Membury services for his scheduled piss stop and 11 o'clock mocha and cranberry muffin. 'Must be a bloody festival on,' he muttered, casting a critical glance at a crowd of studiously ragged twenty-somethings cluttering up the entrance, their wiry bodies piled high with camping gear and music magazines, a million miles from Chris Baxter at the same age. He'd spent his twenties refining his patter at business school, reciting commercial theory as if he had been at a madrassa. He'd had no time for festivals, music or clubbing. Even for girls he was willing to wait, to wait for a time when the sweet smell of his success would bring the ladies to Chris Baxter like wasps to a picnic.

He'd time for clothes, though. Chris Baxter especially loved suits.

As a child he'd never felt right in jeans and T-shirts. What he'd dreamed of were crisp pink and white striped shirts, designer ties and charcoal-grey bespoke suits with a silk lining. As soon as he'd been old enough and his frame sufficient, he'd haunted Next whenever he had the time, trying on all the styles and materials, longing for a time when he'd be wearing nothing else.

Baxter also had a liking for motorway food. He liked the way the heat lamps reflected on the top of the lasagne. You could trust these places, he thought, as he entered the cafeteria. The standards were universal – it didn't matter which arterial road you were travelling on. The chips were piping, the toilets cleaned in a strict rota and you could count on a good selection of motivating compilation CDs in the well-stocked shop. Chris took comfort from this consistency. He sat his refreshments down on the formica table top then gazed contentedly out of the window, over the neat shrubs to the truck park.

He took a sip from his coffee, broke open the muffin then deftly rummaged through the emails on his iPhone with one hand. Couple of congrats from the office, one the now-obligatory soft-porn affirmation from sexy Debbie, a heady mix of innuendo and thinly veiled jealousy. 'Might just do you again,' seemed to be the gist of it. It sounded like lust, but she was probably chancing her arm at finding out over a bottle of piña-colada lubricant exactly how he consistently hit his targets.

'Gonna have to try harder than that sweetheart,' thought Christopher Baxter.

And then he began to notice the smell.

Some smells contain more nail-biting drama than a whole bookshop full of novels. They are so pungent it is surprising they are not visible, like smoke. They drift heavily across places and spaces where they don't belong and with them they bring panic, unease and horror. This was such a smell. It was both musty and acidic, like a filthy body rotting at an ammonia factory. It was as if the nameless detritus that had accumulated at the bottom of all of Cairo's lift shafts had been skilfully blended with the aftermath of a thousand medieval massacres.

The unwelcome reek had an immediate effect on the chronically dirt-averse Christopher Baxter. He dropped his cranberry muffin onto his lap, and as he violently gagged, he inadvertently forwarded sexy Debbie's lurid email to his personal trainer, an aggressive former

Serbian commando who was unlikely to write it off as an error. As he instinctively covered his nose with his napkin, Baxter's eyes darted around him from seat to seat across the tables until finally they came to rest upon the undeniable source of the stench, a hunched darkened mass of old clothing and string, piled up like a bear beneath a wide-brimmed leather fedora, pierced with a filthy black feather. The bastard was huge. The shadow from the hat may have hidden the man's eyes, but Chris Baxter knew he was being scrutinised intently by this grim vision who sat a mere four tables away, with no food or drink in front of him. Sitting stock still and with his body clearly facing the salesman, the figure rested its huge forearms upon the shiny table top.

Baxter looked around him for a sympathetic face, but for some inexplicable reason only he seemed to have identified or even registered the source of the appalling smell. At a table just to the left, a truck driver was busily ramming what appeared to be two all-day breakfasts into his face, seemingly oblivious to the hideous odour that had just put paid to Baxter's elevenses.

Unnerved by the rancid vagrant, Baxter decided to ignore his rock-steady gaze and self-consciously busied himself by scrolling aimlessly around his iPhone while planning his exit from the corners of his eyes. Curiosity soon forced him to look up. The figure opposite had vanished.

'I nud a luft.'

The voice was deep, deeper than the deepest deep pipes on a deep church organ. Baxter both heard it and felt it at the same time. With it came a stream of breath so vile that the sales rep began to taste his cranberry muffin for a second time, tainted with the acid tang of bile. Beside him sat the massive figure, his filthy form looming over Baxter till he filled the salesman's entire field of vision.

'I'm ... sorry?' he stammered, looking around for a member of staff.

'I nud a luft,' repeated the tramp in an unrecognisable, ancient accent. 'Yu will take mu ... in yer cur.'

'Now look here pal, I er ... look, I ...' he began to protest. But already, as the foul breath of the monstrous hitcher seeped into him, he began to waver. A clammy mush of confusion washed over and into him, a stream of chaotic images. Memories that were clearly not his own began to cascade haphazardly through his mind – burning castles, Gothic church interiors, black rites, massacres, mighty and everlasting storms of light and fire.

'I hope you like Coldplay,' Baxter muttered.

******

Chris Baxter, always so pleased with his own legendary powers of persuasion, was having some trouble working out just how he had come to allow a huge, stinking vagrant into his pristine Lexus. Somewhere between the encounter in the eatery and the present awkward silence of their journey together, he must have agreed to the stranger's request. The very thought of this unlikely transaction made Baxter's mind once again succumb to a veil-like porridge that left him wondering in misty confusion what he had been trying to remember in the first place. He glanced towards the passenger seat and caught a glimpse of a centipede appearing from one of the hitcher's pockets. It scurried across a greasy sleeve before re-entering the dark, damp interior of his coat through a ragged buttonhole.

'You've er ... got something on you,' Baxter motioned to the giant next to him, his finger hovering over the temperature controls as he pondered switching on the air con to try to alleviate the must and decay. The figure did not respond, but continued to look straight ahead at the motorway from under its wide-brimmed hat. 'Music?' Chris found himself suggesting. The bulk beside him exhaled a long-drawn mix of grunt and sigh, which Baxter decided to take as a yes, and he began to scroll through his collection. What do tramps like to listen to? He used to have 'Another Day in Paradise' by Phil Collins, and didn't Sporty Spice write something about the homeless? Sadly neither had made the progression from CD to MP3. 'You'll like this,' he said, and the car's Nakamichi surround-sound system began pounding out something life-affirming by Snow Patrol. 'Oh yeah,' Baxter drummed on the wheel.

The figure stirred uncomfortably and tilted its hidden eyes towards the display screen. Baxter's eyes flitted from the road to the stranger, aware that he now had the ghastly old man's attention.

'You like this?' he said, anticipating common ground with the looming mass beside him. But the figure offered no reply, continuing instead to look directly at the display as its complex flashing characters pulsed manically along with the rhythm. 'This your kind of thing?' Baxter asked, hoping to break the ice as the figure sat immobile, seemingly transfixed by the music centre glowing blue on the dashboard.

Abruptly, the hitcher lifted up one of his vast shovel-like hands, the equivalent of three grow bags lurking beneath his torn and stained fingernails. Baxter glanced at the road then back to the grizzled claw hovering a few inches from the screen. 'Sorry, bit loud for you mate?'

Without replying, the stranger rammed his hand hard into the display and there was a flash of sparks. Fatally injured, the in-car entertainment stuttered wounded for a second before fading terminally. Baxter, alarmed by the sudden violence, leapt in his seat. The Lexus veered savagely from side to side across three lanes of traffic before the rep, his arms pulling at the wheel, regained control and surged away from the barrage of horns blaring at them from behind. 'Why did you do that?' he screamed hysterically. The figure, having rid himself of the annoyance, had lowered his huge hand again and resumed his silent vigil on the road ahead. Strangely, the smell of burning electronics mingling with the whiff of rotting cabbage from the bizarre passenger soon pacified Baxter, and they continued on up the motorway. 'OK,' he offered awkwardly, not a little terrified, 'maybe we can talk for a bit.'

\*\*\*\*\*\*

Hours may have passed. Chris Baxter couldn't get his head around the strange course of the day. It had all started so well, but now he was trapped alone in a cheap road movie with an eight-foot-tall, 25-stone cross between Grendel and a compost heap. The figure beside him was dropping mildew, spores and cobwebs onto the beautiful cream trim, leaving more unmentionable stains on the seat covers than two teams of Eastern European car valets could remove, even if they worked through the night. His obsessive cleanliness wailed muted despair through his slackening jaw as they sped on, the once-bright day turning a brooding blue grey. His white-knuckled hands remained locked to the steering wheel as the miles passed unmeasured. Dimly he noticed a family of earwigs chasing each other joyfully in and out of the car's stylish air vents.

'Airwags,' he mumbled to no one in particular. How long had they been driving? The sun was low, hovering dull and weak between gathering steel-grey clouds.

'We near,' finally rumbled the voice beside him. 'You will draw

17

frum this rud when nuxt we aspy a hostelry.'

Baxter dimly wondered whether he should ask what kind of hostelry the stranger hoped to be aspying, but as the thought fragmented and became lost in the rumble of the road, he found himself steering involuntarily into a service station. The Lexus glided to a halt in front of the service area, slowing too late to avoid knocking over a sign advertising a meal deal. Baxter robotically switched off the engine. In the silence that followed, the two of them stared ahead for a long minute, until finally and abruptly the bulk beside Baxter opened the door and heaved himself from the car, the long black crow's feather following. The saloon wobbled with relief as the mass lifted from the suspension, a blast of cold, damp but mercifully fresh air filling the stale void behind him.

'Du nut follow,' boomed the hitcher as the door slammed violently behind him. He lumbered away, only partly visible to Baxter through the steamed-up windows. Baxter sat still for a long confused minute, his mashed and suppressed thoughts struggling to re-orientate themselves. He looked in despair at the crushed and polluted passenger seat beside him, which only that morning had been as fresh and neat as the day he'd picked the car up. Now it looked as if it had been used to ferry dead jungle animals over a long weekend. Small invertebrates that Baxter could never have identified scurried confusedly or lay flattened to the upholstery, their liquid interiors staining the weave alongside woodland fungi.

'Nurrggghhhhhhh,' he wailed as his poor head began to clear. From what seemed a great distance, the ring tone of his iPhone oozed insistently into his mind. Finally, and with great effort, he was able to answer. 'Hewooo?' he dribbled.

'Chris? Chris? It's Jenny from the office ... we've been trying to reach you all day.' Chris Baxter lowered the window and took a long deep breath from outside then lent mushily forward towards the Tom Tom, as it slipped back into focus on the dashboard. 'Chris ... are you there? Where the hell are you?'

'I flink I'm in Norlthomberlard,' he said.

****** 

In the sanitised open-plan service station, the shambling mass of Baxter's unwanted hitchhiker moved purposefully but seemingly unseen by the families and lorry drivers around him. He lurched into the central concourse and stopped dead. Lifting his head up from hunched shoulders, the blunt and flattened nose, textured from a millennium of bramble scars, began sniffing the air.

Behind him, a party of Goths came in from the car park, the swish of a long leather coat and squeal of oversized boots on the smooth marble floor announcing their arrival. The alpha Goth of the group led his pale and blackened harem into the food hall, his movements followed intently by the hitcher. His nostrils began flaring and twitching as he scrutinised the slightly bloated male, his dark eyes darting around the collection of trinkets and rings adorning the Goth's black leather attire and chubby fingers. He was pierced to an insane degree in an attempt to emphasise a sense of the sinister, which, like all Goths, he simply didn't possess. At times the Goth himself worried that he might snag on a door handle and tear himself in half like a book of postage stamps. His wannabe Satanist crowd certainly worked hard to elevate themselves above their humdrum reality, taking every possible opportunity to hang around near ruined abbeys and overgrown churchyards, even taking an annual trip to Prague to act all medieval in the old city. It was here that the Goth had acquired the interesting little charm now dangling amongst the crosses and skulls around his fat neck – the charm that the genuinely scary stranger watching him had travelled so far to intercept.

Intent on his toilet stop, the Goth was blissfully unaware at first of the bulk sliding in beside him as he entered the washroom. Despite his enthusiasm for the dark and the sinister, it came as something of a shock when a genuine sense of unease and dread overtook him, just as he sat down heavily on a worn toilet seat. It was even more of a shock when the toilet door abruptly swung open to reveal the stark outline of the vast terrifying figure, its silhouette throwing him into near darkness. As the door swung shut behind it, the Goth had cause to be grateful for his current sitting arrangements, as he suddenly overcame the constipation he'd been cursed with for the past four days. The dark mass loomed forward, its eyes visible beneath the wide-brimmed hat. The poor Goth was horrified. Dead, dead eyes; pale yellows, deep, dark blacks, spidery veins and an ancient physical tiredness – eyes that had seen things for real that the Goth and his kind could only imagine with the aid of badly written horror novels and teen slasher movies.

Then the stranger's gnarled fingers began to move steadily towards his sweaty pale neck and once again, quite unplanned, he lost a few pounds of unwelcome weight into the potty.

'Don't kill me, please don't kill me,' he found himself pleading, suddenly convinced that Hell had caught up with him. 'Tell Jesus I didn't mean it,' he whimpered.

But the horrific figure was not interested in the boy. His lumpy hand instead lifted up a single piece of the Goth's ungodly bling and regarded it fixedly with his cold eyes. Though fitted with a cheap modern chain, the fine silverwork and ingrained tarnish pre-dated the tawdry Camden tat that hung alongside it. It had been fashioned in the shape of a small lantern complete with tiny glass panels and a locked latch that the Goth, despite much effort from his podgy fingers, had been unable to open. Inside lay the object of the monstrous figure's unyielding attention – a tiny shard of yellowed, part-carbonised bone.

'Take it! Take it man, you want it? Take it ... just don't kill me!' blubbered the Goth, whose bowel movements were now near continuous. Deaf to the boy, the figure merely closed the gigantic fingers of his right hand around the tiny relic and slapped his other hand like a filthy mop across the Goth's sweaty, make-up splattered face. As he prepared himself for death there was a sudden movement above him, fast for such a huge, cumbersome body. With it the cheap chain parted noisily, and the silver and glass relic was taken. Leaning back from the whimpering boy, the monster opened the vast drapes of his overcoat to reveal a foul wasteland of ragged, filthy undergarments and an ancient leather bag slung under the right armpit. Deftly, the trinket disappeared into the satchel's damp interior.

With that, his mission complete, suddenly the monster left, leaving the toilet door swinging on its hinges and the terrified Goth exposed to the washbasins and a curious general public. He was genuinely pale for the first time in his life and at least one stone lighter. His trembling hand slowly reached out and tugged the flush.

Ignored by the crowds on the concourse and drivers milling around the car park, the lumbering presence moved straight to the edge of the service station and hopped with surprising grace over the perimeter wall and away into the scrubland beyond. Above him, gathering darkness had brought with it a sudden squall, rain falling in sheets across the neglected agricultural land. Soon the sound of traffic from the busy motorway gave way to the sodden hiss of the downpour as the dark figure pushed on towards the Northumberland hills. Darkness closed around him as he climbed. Finally, he reached a stony depression in the hillside, a small hollow offering some meagre protection from the lashing wind. Here, he built a small fire, which sputtered and danced in the storm. In its puny light, the man in the wide-brimmed hat with the greasy crow's feather began his incantations.

The Latin mantras were learnt so long ago and repeated so many times that he knew every complex stanza by his heavy heart, even if he didn't understand a single word of them.

He didn't need to. Laying a filthy rag on a flat stone, he reached into his bag for the Goth's trinket and dropped it beside a small pestle and mortar. As the rain slammed down, driven by a hard easterly wind, he brought up his huge fist, the hard granite pestle balled up between his monstrous fingers. With staggering violence he brought it crashing down upon the ornate artefact. Its remarkable 300-year survival ended there in a wreck of splinters.

The trinket that the Bonetaker had shattered contained the sole remaining fragment of one-time fraudster, bully, abuser of children and serial torturer of women, Billy 'The Knife' Hamilton – the last remnant of a man who'd burned the innocent and abducted girls from hundreds of hamlets across the British Empire and who, even after his public execution, had still hung his foul shadow over the living. In the rain-haggard hollow, mumbling his ancient ramblings, the Bonetaker dropped the shattered 300-year-old bone into the mortar and with his voice rising against the howling gale, he added dried herbs and complex powders. Finally, he dropped in blood from a fresh gash upon his scarred hand and mixed them all together into a paste.

Far away, in an entirely different kind of place, a whirling being radiating malice and sickly purple light spasmed suddenly in its incandescent cage, its face sharpened by a life of constant spite and hatred but now filled with a shock realisation of its new vulnerability. Back in the world of men, the Bonetaker was ritualistically destroying Hamilton's final surviving manifestation upon the good earth. As the giant mouthed his incantations, the murderer in this other world realised in a flash that his second time had come – his final time. There would be no more hauntings, no more possessions. The spirit of Hamilton, in a deep and maniacal panic, flew raging at his restraints, surges of purple plasma swimming around him within the cell in which he had for so long been contained.

To no avail.

For as the Bonetaker's massive hand ground remorselessly, the raging fury began to abate, and in time, the tendrils of hatred, anger and malevolence that had made the spirit such a danger lost their ghastly purchase. The vile wraith watched aghast as the evil light flowed out of him like an ebbing tide.

Then all at once, the light, and with it all traces of one Billy 'The Knife' Hamilton – in this world or in any other – vanished for good.

The Bonetaker, his work at an end for now, buried the mangled trinket deep in the moorland soil and diligently folded away his otherworldly toolkit.

CHAPTER 3

# NEWTON BARLOW

There was nothing fantastical, paranormal or superstitious about Dr Newton Barlow. Dr Barlow was extremely black and white. He carefully trod the logical path of scientific reasoning and if it couldn't be measured, observed, duplicated and peer reviewed, then Newton was having none of it.

Not that he was a walking talking real-life Mr Spock. On the contrary, Newton had deliberately gone out of his way to buck the cliché of the geeky academic and in time he became about as cool as an internationally renowned physicist can be, hanging around with rock bands, featuring in men's fashion magazines and cracking smart and occasionally edgy jokes on panel shows. Good looking in a tall, gangly way, Newton was popular with the ladies, the envy of the academic male and a gift to the media. His sharp sideburns, Buddy Holly quiff and trademark black schmutter marked him out from his contemporaries resulting in a certain sniping resentment, especially when he popped up on prime-time TV spouting forth on everything from CERN to the paranormal. But the majority of criticism ended up looking an awful lot like professional jealousy, which of course most of it was.

It didn't help that Newton came from a dynasty of scientific high-achievers. His grandfather had been right there at Los Alamos with Oppenheimer during the Manhattan Project, high on theoretical physics as the bomb took its first baby steps towards Hiroshima and Nagasaki. Like so many who had been on this theoretical roller coaster, Richard D. Barlow had been too deep in equations to foresee the horror that the terrible weapon could actually inflict. The devastating results shocked the sensitive Richard Barlow so much that he found it impossible to settle into the routines of the Cold War, with its paranoia and nuclear arms racing. So he had decided to up sticks from the desert laboratories and married a beautiful, gifted research student he'd met on a visit to England in 1947. She had turned the physicist's head so comprehensively that it wasn't a difficult decision to make the move, a neat transition from Los Alamos to the leafy cloisters of old Cambridge where he took a senior teaching position in the university's prestigious physics department. Settled into a reassuringly theoretical environment, he thrived, and with his wife had a son, Graham.

Graham Barlow had been only ten years old when his father died in a car crash, killed outright in a collision with a truckload of sugar beet on the London road. But already Graham had enough exposure to the rarefied scientific environment of the university campus to steer him into theoretical physics. He never questioned following his father's footsteps for a precisely measured nanosecond. In fact, the echoes of his father's brilliance perhaps drove him beyond immersion to a form of scientific zealotry, his ambition evolving in time to border on the absurd.

Graham Barlow's theoretical work at Oxford University in the 1970s was nothing less than magnificent. His theory of as-yet-undiscovered quarks had all the mathematical elegance, beauty even, that was needed to finally persuade the doubters that these elusive nuclear particles must exist. Several colleagues quipped that Graham Barlow would surely bag himself a Nobel Prize and that possibility hovered constantly in the back of Graham's mind as he reached the prime of his career. Then, unwittingly, he and his wife Germaine found themselves with a son, Newton.

Germaine had been her husband's professional confidant, ally and in many ways a scientific equal. So it was with some trepidation that the parents elected for Germaine to step back from her own career to bring up young Newton almost alone, giving Professor Graham Barlow distance from the nursery and the freedom to continue his research unobstructed.

In fairness, Germaine was in many ways relieved to finally have a reason to detach herself from the intensity of her husband's ambitious programmes. His obsessive drive for success was becoming increasingly divisive at home. Science for breakfast, physics for lunch and a bedtime reading from Darwin; there would be little time in the Barlow household for basic childhood fun if Germaine had not dug her heels in. As the father pushed, so the mother increasingly pushed back.

All the same, Newton was genuinely bitten with the science bug. The house had been full of scientific curiosities, journals and papers, and most visitors were luminaries from the global scientific community. Newton had so many fond memories of playing games in the garden with assorted academics, or helping out with fun experiments organised by some of his father's more light-hearted colleagues, keeping the lad entertained while the father sweated himself thin in his study.

Newton especially enjoyed it when one physicist in particular visited. Dr Alex Sixsmith had an irresistibly cheeky sense of humour and often, Newton had noticed, seemed to find more time for the young boy than his increasingly driven father. With no children of his own, the jolly, bespectacled and portly Dr Sixsmith couldn't resist playing the fun uncle whenever he dropped by. Pathologically mischievous, he'd have Newton in stitches over his mother's dinners in an atmosphere of homeliness the unmarried doctor clearly relished. And while they giggled helplessly at Sixsmith's banter, Newton's father would huff in frustration, the serious discussions he had intended to impose upon his colleague utterly side-showed. In later years, it was this same intensity that finally destroyed his marriage, just as Newton neared his eleventh birthday.

After their sudden but restrained separation, Germaine rented a small terraced house within easy walking distance of Graham. Newton's father continued his work, but it was in a softer, almost apologetic manner. Belatedly, he realised how much his ambitions had cost the family and his own state of mind.

But it was all too late. The punishing research finally caught up with the learned Professor Graham Barlow and in the small hours of a humid July evening, he had a massive, fatal heart attack. He was found slumped inert over his desk, his bifocals askew on his lined and colourless face, his head resting on a pile of half-read research papers. That early-morning call from Stockholm had never come, and now it never would.

Ironically, the obituaries rewarded the dead physicist with all the plaudits he had never received in life. There was a sad paradox in this posthumous eminence. Although Professor Graham Barlow had never achieved the recognition he felt he deserved, his work had touched many. He had opened stuck doors across whole swathes of complex enquiry and while he may not have bagged the big prize, his work had enabled many others to find the right path. All this was apparent at the funeral, where the list of luminaries attending read as comprehensively as any *Who's Who*.

Newton, never comfortable in a church himself, was baffled that his father had opted to have a church funeral. He'd always been such a devout atheist, but here they were anyway. Despite the religious teaching obligatory in his school, Newton had made the leap from belief via agnosticism to hardened atheism in the space of an afternoon in his first term. As he solemnly but reluctantly followed the funeral service, Newton resolved never to back down from his own well-honed beliefs, even if mortally terrified by his own imminent death.

After the service, Dr Sixsmith sought Newton out. True to form, the teenager was avoiding the cloying sympathies and trying to engage the gathered scientists in detailed conversation. Sixsmith ruffled the boy's hair affectionately and led him away into the churchyard where they sat down together on a neat wooden bench.

'How are you doing then young Newton?' Sixsmith asked, his trademark irreverence restrained somewhat by the occasion.

'I'm fine thank you, Dr Sixsmith,' he replied earnestly. 'It's sad, of course, but I plan to get back to work as soon as I can.'

'Work?' Sixsmith narrowed his eyes briefly in puzzled amusement. 'Are you talking about your schoolwork or have you a secret laboratory somewhere I don't know about?'

Newton blushed at his own seriousness. 'Sorry, er ... I just meant that I'm looking forward to getting all this over with. Can't say I like funerals.'

'No, not much fun,' Sixsmith smiled knowingly, peering over his half-moon spectacles. 'I tell you Newton, when it's my time I'd rather get fossilised or something. Fired into space maybe.' Newton laughed, and Sixsmith leant forward conspiratorially. 'To be honest old boy, I find all this ...' he gestured at the sombre graves around the churchyard, '... it's all so ritualistic and silly. Don't you think? Why we have to treat death in this po-faced way is beyond me. You live, you die and that's that. Your atoms mingle back into the same cosmos they came from. Why do we need to dress it all up with fairy tales and solemnity?' He pointed at the hearse. 'I mean look at that thing, ridiculous! I'd rather get carted off to the crematorium in a milk float.'

'Or a taxi!' said Newton.

'That would be good,' said Sixsmith. 'I'd like to see what they'd do when you failed to tip them. Anyway Newton, your mother tells me you're doing well at school, especially the sciences. Not that I'm surprised of course! But any idea what you have in mind for when you leave?'

'Well, I thought I'd try theoretical physics – there's some fantastic research going on in superstring theory. That would be good. I'm also dreadfully keen on languages so I'll probably do a couple of those on the side, Latin and French for starters, probably some German when I get the chance.' Sixsmith pulled a teasingly reproachful expression.

'Er ... hello? What about girls, music and clubbing? What about hanging out and generally having fun? Any time for all of that in your career map Newton, old chap?' He smirked as Newton blushed.

'Uh ... I guess, I mean I expect so,' he stammered. 'I haven't really thought much about that kind of thing.'

'Look Newton,' Sixsmith elaborated, 'I love science, I really do. But you can't let it dictate everything you do. Not everything in life is quantifiable; some things just have to be done because they make you happy. That's all. Leave some space in your life that's free from all this hard logic.' Newton sat silent for a second, confused. Free from logic? What on earth did he mean by that? He was fumbling for a considered reply when Dr Sixsmith cut him short again. 'Come on Newton me old mucker, let's stop that enormous brain of yours from reaching meltdown, we'd better get back – they'll be wondering where we've got to.'

The mourners were spilling out of the chapel and back towards their cars. As Newton and his mother prepared to leave, Sixsmith leant into the car to say his goodbyes.

'Stay in touch Newton. I'll always be here if you need me.' And with a wink he walked away.

\*\*\*\*\*\*

And so, Newton passed his exams, with the straightest of A's, and departed at last for university. He opted for King's College London, every bit as good as Oxford and Cambridge but with the added advantage of the capital's social sophistication. Newton, mindful of Dr Sixsmith's cryptic advice, enjoyed the city beyond the university to its full. He mixed with a more varied and hip circle than the students around him and predictably it set him apart from some of his more conservative fellows. Newton was determined to be more Carl Sagan than Professor Brainstorm and took the resulting disapproval in his stride. All the same, the science came first and he was careful not to allow his social life to thrive at the expense of his studies.

Newton stayed on at King's until he had a PhD in nuclear physics tucked neatly under his belt, and then turned his attention to his postdoctorate. He secured one at the Joint European Torus on a windswept aerodrome in Oxfordshire, lured by youthful optimism that this giant experiment in nuclear fusion would fulfil its much-anticipated promise and deliver a new clean energy source, the holy grail of all nuclear development. Unlike dirty, problematic fission reactors, fusion reactors would be exceptionally safe, not generating mountains of horrendously long-lived radioactive garbage. A noble enough desire one would have thought, but whenever he told acquaintances about his project, they recoiled as though nothing with the word 'nuclear' could ever describe anything but pure evil. People were so wedded to their ignorance, Newton observed, frustrated not for the first time by the yawning gulf between fact and assumption. In the pub, he started to say he was a mathematician, which was sure to stop the conversation dead and save him from what was becoming a repetitive and defensive series of arguments.

But gradually, even his own enthusiasm dulled. He was insightful enough to realise that the project wasn't going anywhere. The fusion reactor, if it was to have any chance of success, had to operate at temperatures hotter even than the core of the sun and making the concept work in practice was sadly the longest of long-shots. The undertaking was going to drag on at the pace of continental drift, and Newton, being Newton, wanted more excitement.

Besides, he'd become distracted and perhaps a little obsessed by another hobbyhorse. Trawling through the archives on fusion research, he'd come across a strange phenomenon called 'bubble fusion', an unusual series of observations that had sparked some excitement back in the 1970s. Experiments had hinted that sound waves could force small bubbles in a liquid to collapse incredibly quickly upon themselves, heating the gas inside to extreme temperatures hot enough to melt steel – and maybe as hot as the sun's core. There were vague signs even that the hot gas had prompted nuclear fusion, the same holy grail that Newton's earlier studies had so notably failed to achieve. But then the case went cold – until now, two decades later, when some small research groups were pursuing bubble fusion once again, hoping that this time they could test its potential rigorously with the new technologies available. Newton was intrigued. This interesting frontier appealed greatly to his sense of the arcane and problematic. It was a real challenge with possibly world-changing potential. It was controversial too, of course, and possibly pointless, but if true, it could be sensational. He couldn't resist it.

So after only a year in Oxfordshire, he headed back to King's and persuaded the department head to let him revisit bubble fusion – providing he could raise some commercial sponsorship. Newton threw his soul into a presentation that would snare some of the more progressive venture capitalists, keen to hedge their bets on esoteric frontiers in green energies. But even he was surprised at just how quickly he managed to secure funding. Three days after presenting his plans at the smart London offices of alternative-energy investors Havotech, they called him to offer sponsorship for a full three years.

A few days later, still skipping on air, Newton ran into Dr Sixsmith in the street outside the university. However, his delight in seeing his old mentor was soon tempered somewhat by Sixsmith's less-than-subtle scepticism.

'Are you sure you want to do this Newton – isn't it a bit flaky?' Sixsmith asked, his normal joviality replaced with something more restrained. 'It might not be the best thing for you to be seen doing, have you thought about that?'

Newton, who was growing a little weary of explaining his choice to his colleagues and contemporaries, stuck to his guns. 'Of course, I've thought it all through. I just want to get stuck into something that's really out there, something that's got a real mystery to solve. What's wrong with that?'

'Trouble with being really *out there*, Newton,' said Sixsmith sagely, 'is that you can't always *come back*.'

'Science should be about risks, shouldn't it?' answered Newton, a little too cockily.

'Tell me about your sponsors,' Sixsmith asked, affecting not to have heard Newton's mission statement.

'Havotech?' Newton was not sure if he appreciated the questioning. 'Big outfit, lots of cash and they're willing to back a long race.' Sixsmith left a silence that Newton felt obliged to fill awkwardly. 'It's pretty unconditional, pure research stuff – I'm not going to promise anything in return, if that's what you're implying.'

'Business is business Newton,' said Sixsmith wearily. 'No investor fires cash into a blue-sky project without some promise of a return. The problem with your funky little bubbles is that they offer a lot of promise to the greedy but ill-informed. Free, clean energy, we've been there before Newton – you don't want to muddle up pure science and hard business, it's not a good mix.'

'I can keep my head,' Newton replied, prickling. 'The postdoc is not under their control, they have no influence.'

'Just watch your step is all I'm saying,' Sixsmith persisted, his face uncharacteristically serious. They looked at each other awkwardly for a second, neither enjoying the atmosphere. 'Look, I hate to cut and run old chap, but I'm going to be late,' said Sixsmith, relaxing back into his more usual grinning self. 'Let's catch up properly soon, have lunch or something.'

'Absolutely,' answered Newton uncomfortably, 'of course.' Sixsmith shook his hand, winked over his spectacles then scurried through the university's entrance and was gone.

Newton stood quietly for a second, stewing. He had inherited much of his father's bloody-mindedness and far from considering the advice he had just been given, he found himself dismissing it, his determination to cut a maverick dash in the scientific community more powerful than a sense of self-preservation or caution.

This same lack of caution may have been the reason that soon after, Newton met, and then very quickly married, Rowena Posset.

\*\*\*\*\*\*

Steadily growing his circle of influential and fashionable acquaintances, Newton had studied by day and partied by night, brushing shoulders with the potpourri of London's elite. One thing led to another, and after a few select parties and gallery openings, he began to ease into the cooler and rather flashier world of the media. Picked up as a handy science voice on a few panel shows, he'd found himself suddenly in a very different environment. For the somewhat scientifically challenged commissioning fraternity in publishing and television, the cool-scientist aura of Newton was an absolute gift. Consequently, though he was still relatively young and far from established, he began to start getting the gigs that normally passed to older steadier hands. Book deals, TV appearances and radio interviews came thick and fast, and Newton soon began to float closer and closer to the tent pegs of the celebrity circus. He'd be at a fringe conference on neutron detectors one day and then partying at a guest-list-only gig by Gorillaz the next.

Somewhere between the two, Dr Newton Barlow had been pinned to the wall by a vivacious blond biologist. A taxi ride later and Newton's hormones had been activated so expertly that he had trouble working for several days, his normally steely concentration interrupted by frequent X-rated images of Rowena sipping red wine for breakfast, giggling as they lived only for the moment on nothing but Shiraz, dark chocolate and sex.

Ms Posset was clearly proud of her conquest. Newton had become a regular in magazines and TV shows, and although her own career was underway, she seemed oddly disinterested by it, a warning sign that Newton was only going to recognise when it was far too late.

Newton started leaving his brain in the laboratory and spending dizzy afternoons in bed with Rowena, listening without any reservations to her self-aggrandising tales of conquest amongst an unsuspecting scientific community. Rowena liked scientists; she told Newton that the wonderful Carl Sagan had been her first true crush and that she'd written his name, including all his qualifications, all over her pencil case after seeing him presenting *Cosmos*. Being too loved-up to think clearly, Newton was not really sure what he made of such revelations, especially the claim that she'd bedded five eminent physicists in the past three years, two at the same time. He felt both excited and alarmed by Rowena, and chastised himself for being conservative one minute and vaguely dirty the next. So, he answered this unease and concern over the young woman in the time-honoured fashion for a chap in his late twenties – he married her.

Initially, Rowena relished being on Newton's arm as he flitted through the mix of academic and cultural occasions in the capital. Then suddenly, after two summers together in Newton's small apartment in Crouch End, she announced that she wanted a baby. Her old school friends, who'd almost imperceptibly grown to be a strong third force in the relationship, had begun hitting the maternity ward in ever greater numbers and so, Rowena persistently reasoned, this was the best time to have a child of her own. Gabriella was born less than a year later and within two weeks of the nursery being painted and stencilled in sickly pink and yellow animals, Rowena was bitching incessantly about the pokiness of the flat. Three years later and the flat, Rowena and the rapidly growing child had built up into something a little more pressing.

Newton, distracted by his research, the TV appearances and book projects, had not seen the crisis approaching. But abruptly he could see that his academic life was no longer his own. Now there was a very real threat to a career path he had always taken for granted. The science was hardly top paying, even on the TV front, and time was limited. With Rowena opting out of paid employment to bring up little Gabby, Newton woke up one dark and cold November morning in something of a panic.

Rowena had been dropping large city-shaped hints for the whole of the last evening, citing seemingly hundreds of friends of friends who'd given up the sciences to work in finance.

'You've got to look to the future Newton,' Rowena lobbied relentlessly, as Newton struggled to catch up on some research reports. 'It's great that you love what you do, darling, but really, where's the incentive financially?' She let it hang for a while for maximum effect. 'What about your daughter? Do you want her to grow up in … this?' She waved her spindly fingers at the walls of the flat.

'What's wrong with this?' Newton waved his own thin fingers more affectionately back at the walls.

'Newton!' she snapped impatiently, turning to face him reproachfully. 'It's not all about you, you and your *science*. You can't go on like this forever. Suzie's husband opted out of science and went into big business. Have you any idea what he earns? Why you can't see sense and do the same thing is beyond me.' She huffed and turned back to the television, her cold shoulders broadcasting considerably more tension than the finale of *Britain's Got Talent*, flickering aimlessly on the other side of the lounge.

Business? The city? That was the last thing Newton wanted. He'd rather work as a cartoon animal in a theme park or dance naked for sex tourists than don a pinstripe and sell his mortal soul in Canary Wharf. But the more he tried to explain this to his wife, the more she seemed to harden. Gone was the giggling sex kitten who'd lit up Newton's lounge a few years earlier; now she was moody, manipulative and seemingly indifferent to her husband as an actual person. He looked at the small bundle of child around which their arguments had begun orbiting and knew he would be hard-pressed to win her over.

He was three years into his postdoctorate work and more engrossed in it than ever, despite the pressures building at home. Newton's team was getting intriguing results from an experiment using sound waves to generate and collapse tiny bubbles in specially prepared acetone, the key ingredient in nail polish remover amongst other things. Their detectors were registering heavy isotopes of hydrogen in the liquid, hinting, just *hinting*, that fusion might actually have occurred. Newton was waiting to hear if his paper on the topic would be accepted by the journal *Nature*. He daydreamed of the stir the paper could cause, and knew that publication would likely guarantee increased funding from Havotech. But the editors at *Nature* were making sceptical noises about his paper's claims – so it wasn't a done deal. So it seemed fortuitous when a director of Havotech turned up to make Newton an offer, just when relations between him and his wife were hitting rock bottom.

On a cold wet Wednesday, one Peter Carnatt arrived at the King's College research lab where Newton had spent the weekend with his lab assistant, rigging up a small demonstration. Carnatt's slick manner took him by surprise. The late-thirties city boy exuded a sense of quiet dynamism that Newton found both energising and difficult to tune into. He persistently left awkward gaping silences and when Newton asked leading questions about Havotech or Carnatt himself, he fielded them obliquely, taking the conversation off at strange tangents. Though Carnatt smiled incessantly, Newton soon realised he was not even close to communicating with the man on a human level. They stuck to the bubbles and Carnatt followed the science intently. His detailed enquiries implied an impressive grasp of the physics – Carnatt had clearly done his homework.

'This is great Newton,' he said suddenly from behind his protective glasses. 'You've done a lot with your ... *limited* resources.'

'Limited? Well, every scientist would like better gear, sure.'

'Still, it would be nice if you could take all this ...' Carnatt gestured to the apparatus still humming away as it cooled, '... take it up a gear or two.'

Newton had a sudden sense of vertigo. Was he about to have his funding axed – had Carnatt rehearsed some disingenuous spiel about how Havotech would be doing him a favour by letting him move on to a bigger player? 'I can achieve a lot with this little rig though, really I can,' Newton said defensively.

Carnatt smiled. 'I'm sure you can Newton. In fact we *know*

you can, we've been following your work quite closely.' He looked around the lab to ensure that the assistant was out of earshot. 'Look, let's not talk here. There's a good bar round the corner, let me buy you lunch.'

So they crossed the road to the chic Beluga Bar. Carnatt led Newton to a tall table where he sat with his legs dangling foolishly, increasing his sense of poor relation as the businessman went to the bar to order food. He came back with drinks and a numbered wooden spoon then let Newton take a long sip of his bitter before continuing with his pitch.

'I gather you and your wife have a baby now,' said Carnatt, as he opened his laptop.

'Baby? Oh yes, well not a baby anymore, a girl, Gabriella,' Newton blurted awkwardly, the sudden familiarity a little unsettling. 'Do you have children Peter?' he replied. Peter looked at him, the smile staying identically both warm and cold.

'No,' he replied, and without missing a beat he turned the laptop towards Newton. 'This is the website of Havotech Futures, your primary source of funding.' He took a sip of beer. 'You'll notice that the majority of our projects are energy based, or at least pointing meaningfully in that direction. Green, clean and on the scene, that's the idea Newton. Things are changing. Global warming, oil conflict, financial upheaval – it's all a bit of a mess. Everybody is looking for something else to fire up the pretty lights. And that, Dr Barlow, is why we like your little bubbles.'

Newton rushed quickly to cut Carnatt off – he wasn't close to anything concrete and was determined to keep things in perspective, even if there was cash in the air. 'No. No, wait, you have to understand, this is a long way from that kind of breakthrough. It's still at the early research stage, you know. You can't bank on this kind of thing, it might be decades away from anything that can have a commercial application – it might be never.'

'Newton, please, you do us a disservice. Havotech is very used to the realities of scientific work. We deal with many people in your ...' he paused, '... shall I say, limiting circumstances.' Carnatt took another sip, his eyes staying unnervingly on Newton's. 'We are well aware that your bubbles might go nowhere. On the other hand, they also might go somewhere very interesting, interesting enough for our investment to pay off, and pay off handsomely. That's the business we're in Newton, and we're in it for the long haul. There's a race to find new technologies. Politicians are finally waking up and they want something fast – a kind of Manhattan Project for power if you want, and sure, they'll throw money at the problem, lots and lots of big juicy grants. Our job is to take their demand for a breakthrough and turn it into a viable frontline of research.'

'But like I said,' Newton insisted, 'there's no guarantee my work has any possible applications in terms of energy creation.'

'It doesn't have to, Newton,' Carnatt continued. 'The important thing is that our business finances a very wide portfolio of projects out there on the margins, because it will be out there somewhere on the margins that the really important stuff will be found. We aren't interested in your common-or-garden hydrogen cells, solar power, wind power or any of that old stuff. We believe that the best stuff, the really mind-blowing stuff, is yet to come.'

Newton frowned. 'So what are you saying then? That you'll continue my funding for what, another year?' Carnatt's smile widened.

'Oh, we can do better than that Newton.'

Carnatt was about to elaborate when their food arrived, leaving Newton balanced like a high diver on the edge of his bar stool. The barman seemed to endlessly fuss over the food, the cutlery and the napkins, and he delayed the financier's next point by what felt to Newton like a geological time period. Finally they were left alone again. 'Go on,' said Newton, leaving his food well alone.

'That's actually not bad,' said Carnatt to his tuna and olive wrap, ostentatiously chewing and enjoying the suspense he was manufacturing. 'Let me ask you a question first. How far are you into your postdoc, Dr Barlow?'

'It's the last year,' said Newton earnestly.

'Well, how would you feel about stopping the postdoc right now, today even, and taking your research up to our state-of-the-art labs in Cambridge?' Peter Carnatt let the words hang and took another bite. Newton looked stunned for a second, but characteristically countered with a question.

'The same research? You mean I just stop here one day and start with you the next?'

'Yup, no interruptions, no deviation and no interference,' Carnatt continued, dabbing his mouth with a napkin, the smile changing imperceptibly towards the smug.

'Really?' Newton's scepticism was fading way too fast and he knew it; he was forcing out more questions almost out of duty. 'What about my research team? And I'd have to bring the family up to Cambridge too, that might cause problems.'

Carnatt waved the issues away in a tight shake of the head. 'Not a problem, you can bring anyone you really need from your team. They'll get the going rate – more if they need the incentive. And the house, well, we can rent you a big detached house in some nice leafy suburb while you're looking for something of your own. And considering the rise in salary, I'd imagine it would be a tad bigger than the current place.'

Newton's sense of relief and excitement was strong enough to make him overlook any sense of discomfort at having been researched a little too much. The carrot was now far chunkier than the stick, and given the state of things at home, Newton felt like he was witnessing something akin to divine intervention. He slipped with ease upon the hook.

'Tell me a bit more about the money,' he said, biting into his brie and cranberry baguette.

## CHAPTER 4

# LANDFILL

The history of England is a history of battles. Even a cursory look at the map will reveal a mass of little crossed swords, testament to the bloody tendency of one Englishman to have a crack at another with whatever weapons they have to hand. From the Roman conquest to the Second World War, these savage altercations have left their mark upon the land. Not every battle has been recorded, of course. Some skirmishes were too small or too remote to be noted by chroniclers, while some were just one in a sea of other troubles, historians far too busy saving their own skins to write down the details.

Such a period of trouble descended on England during the twelfth century and when it came, it came in big steaming piles.

In what has become known as the 'Anarchy' or the 'Nineteen-Year Winter', from 1135 to 1153, the realm was ravaged by civil war, crime and persecution in a wave of mean-spiritedness and frightfulness that drove the normally restrained editorial team at *The Anglo-Saxon Chronicle* to declare the era as the time 'when Christ and his saints slept'.

Sleeping through the Anarchy may have seemed a good strategy at first, but most likely you'd have just woken up to find your underwear had been stolen or that you'd been bundled into a sack, bartered as a hostage and then thrown down a well.

It was more than sixty five years since the Normans had conquered the land following the punch-up at Hastings. Subjugated, taxed and pacified, the country had calmed under William the Conqueror and his eventual successor Henry the First. From his coronation in 1100, Henry had ruled harshly, nothing unusual for the time, of course, but he had also proven to be skilled and rational in the affairs of state. Taxes were organised and laws were passed, bringing the nation finally under something approaching common sense and fair play. For thirty five years he reformed and organised until in 1135 he suddenly croaked.

It was not your average demise. To quote a contemporary account, Henry died from eating 'a surfeit of lampreys', a river fish very popular at the time. None loved them more than Henry and his passion for this dish was so intense that it killed him. Sadly Henry left more than a bad smell of fish behind him; his succession was terribly ambiguous and as the saying goes, where there's a will, there's a relative. Even as he lay belching to death, the family began bickering about who would take over the number-one spot.

Having lost his only legitimate son William in a boating accident in 1120, Henry had decided that his daughter Matilda, a feisty young woman if ever there was one, should therefore have the crown. But England was not ready for a female monarch, no matter how feisty, and there were many, mostly men, who were therefore quite happy when Henry's nephew Stephen of Blois stole the throne. The usurper had rushed over from France claiming that King Henry had changed his mind as he lay dying, apparently finding it possible to explain in some detail that he would prefer Stephen to have the job instead. Not a bad achievement for a man stuffed end to end with eels at the time. It was a cheap move, but it worked. On 26th December 1135, Stephen was crowned at Westminster Abbey.

This was a very big mistake.

You may expect that the reason things were to go so wrong was that Stephen was yet another historical bad guy, but in fact, the opposite was the case. Stephen was actually a very nice bloke, in fact he was far *too* nice – that was the problem. The barons had been kept under strict control by King Henry, their natural tendency to steal, loot, fight and murder curbed by punitive justice and instant retribution. Well, Stephen was no Henry. He was affable, eager to please and about as assertive as a ballet dancer on a rugby pitch. He was a good listener, prepared to say he was sorry and reluctant to punish. As a King he was all but useless. He'd only been allowed to have the job because he was A, not a woman, and B, a pushover, given the throne by the very people who were about to run the kingdom into the ground.

The tax system that Henry had spent so long perfecting fell into immediate ruin. Ditto the law, and with nothing to curb them, the robber barons enjoyed a field day. With self-interest sweeping the court like head lice at a primary school, things spun out of control at an alarming rate. As always, it was the hapless general public that got the worst of it in the form of arbitrary, withering taxes and outright theft.

Things went from bad to worse, then to terrible and eventually, bloody awful. Stephen belatedly understood why his uncle had been so good at his job. Frantically, but ineffectually as ever, he tried to put the brakes on, but with no one listening, he found regaining control of the wayward aristocracy far beyond him. As the barons became richer, the state became poorer and what little power King Stephen may have had withered pathetically upon the vine.

Desperate for cash, the hapless Stephen tried to sell off the churches and abbeys, only to find that the barons had got there first, stripping them of all the gold and silver and rendering them worthless empty shells.

For these barons, however, it was a wonderful, golden time. Free from the former King's governance, they could do pretty much what they felt like, so seizing the opportunity with both chain-mailed hands, they plunged the towns and villages into abject misery and heaped ruin upon the peasantry. Unrestrained by Stephen's apologetic interventions, they grew rapidly in power, evolving all the classic warlord stereotypes – fighting with each other at the drop of a hat, raiding the shires for food and women, taxing the locals stupid money and murdering anyone rash enough to raise the issue of justice.

It was two minor barons such as these that were to act out one of the lesser-known military engagements in British history, the Battle of Juggin's Lump.

Lionel, Earl of Weymouth (Lionel the Ugly) and Keith of Swanage (Keith the Small-Minded) were two marginal figures in the unfolding national drama. Their fiefdoms were fairly piss-poor as fiefdoms go, with lousy agricultural land, pestilent marshes and vast tracts of useless acidic heathland, shunned by both wild game and farmers alike. Whereas the huge dark forests to the east had long before been nabbed by William the Conqueror as his personal game reserve, the lands of Lionel and Keith were to remain neglected and unloved, right up until the modern era when they were recognised as a rare, fragile wildlife habitat and an ideal tank training range, though not by the same people and not at the same time. But during the Anarchy, a mess of badly constructed hovels, haunted by a few sickly peasants eking out their sparse living amongst the bogs and gorse, were all that the land could sustain. The paltry manors of the two would-be despots abutted each other along the margins of the far-from-mighty River Snelt, not so much a river as a series of fetid swamps hanging together in a line in an attempt to appear on the map.

At first, the two barons had little reason to fight amongst themselves. In fact, as the fashion for uncontrolled nastiness swept the nation, they had watched together jealously as the bigger landowners had no end of mindless fun with their manors. The wealth of even the smallest of these large-scale estates simply dwarfed the possessions of the two small-scale barons combined and they clung to each other, their chronic bitterness bringing them closer together.

The big players hardly even noticed Lionel and Keith though, unless it was to wince over a banquet as Lionel – Ugly by name and especially ugly by manners – sucked the grey meat off a scrag end of cheval. And while Lionel was pig ugly, Keith was mindlessly petty. His whining nasal voice and unending bitching ensured that, together with his grotesque neighbour, he was never going to be invited to any of the really interesting social events. As a result, the two noblemen hung listlessly together on the margins of the increasingly anarchic court, their bitterness growing as they watched England fall to pieces without them.

Events took a turn in their favour, however, when together they gatecrashed a lavish subjugation organised by Giles, Earl of Lewisham, a first-class robber baron and big hitter in more senses than one. They were both paid a handsome lump sum by the Earl just to go away, a sum that turned out to be enough for both barons to finally upgrade to a more warlordy status, albeit on a somewhat modest scale. Thus financed, the two barons jumped upon their horses and rode back to their respective manors to recruit personal armies from the feckless peasantry. Waving their groats at the men folk, they soon denuded local agriculture of its workforce, and many a wife, mother and daughter soon had cause to curse the barons as they arrogantly led their men away from their homes. Unable to feed the growing ranks of their peasant armies, the two despots were then forced into raiding the self-same hamlets and villages in a bid to stave off starvation, something that went down rather badly with the hard-pressed ladies.

Unhealthy competition soon developed between the two barons. They trailed their armies along the border between the two shires or practised martial skills upon the heathlands, each in full view of the other. It was only a matter of time before the two warlords began to eye each other's rancid lands with a degree of territorial ambition.

They had foolishly used their private armies to bespoil what little value had existed in the meagre countryside. They'd wantonly burned the churches, selling the gold and silver they contained to buy second-hand siege engines that neither army knew how to operate. The fish and game, such as there had been, were now utterly extinct, and nothing bigger than a rabbit was willing to come above ground in daylight. The crops had all been ravaged and spoiled, generations of inept farming gone in one year of ill-organised pillage.

Famine stalked the land.

In the late spring of 1143, the crops having comprehensively failed before they'd even been planted, Lionel and Keith inevitably found themselves facing each other in battle order across the fetid trickle of the River Snelt. Clouds of flies, perhaps sensing the feast to come, swirled in the humid air, biting at the bare feet of the ramshackle armies and making the men hop and scratch in an unsoldierly manner. Because they'd both started with the same meagre defence budgets, the two armies were evenly matched at some 700 soldiers, archers and general nasties apiece. But these were not the elite formations cast in other epic medieval clashes. The archers would never have made the grade at Agincourt; most would have been hard-pressed to hit a twice-life-sized wood pigeon from two yards, even if it had been tied to a chair. There were no noble knights among the ranks, just a disease-ridden reluctant mob of hunchbacks, cripples and other misshapen military rejects. They did, however, represent the sour cream of local manhood and as the formations closed within hacking distance, the wives and maidens back home had cause to contemplate the imminent collapse of the local gene pool, which had never really been big enough to swim lengths in.

Following the traditions of knightly chivalry, Lionel and Keith sat astride sickly nags on high ground to the rear of their armies. From his vantage point on Gorse Hill, Keith could easily make out his opposite number on the heights of the feature known locally as Juggin's Lump. Both commanders had mulled their battle plans, the total adding up to a combined strategic preparation of 36 seconds, essentially a vague muddle of inept, ill-informed wishful thinking. There could be no going back. As the weak morning mists began to lift from the scraggy wasteland, the messy little battle commenced.

It fell to the archers on both sides to open the batting, sending a cloud of badly made arrows in all directions, arrows that were soon felling friend and foe alike. They instantly halved the forward echelons, caught fair and square in the back of the head by their own lousy bowmen. A terrible screaming and wailing filled the morning air.

Ignoring the poor start, the warlords urged their remaining men forward over the dead and into close-quarter combat. As the hodgepodge of ragged infantry finally mingled, both formations realised, belatedly, the practical benefits of a decent uniform. Confused and frightened men randomly lashed out at the figures around them, totally in the dark as to where one army ended and the other began. Friend killed foe and friend killed friend in a feckless skirmish more reminiscent of a fight outside a nightclub than the opening minutes of Crécy or Thermopylae.

The confusion over identity greatly compounded the difficulties of battling knee-deep in a foul stream, while the universal lack of soldierly skills across the battlefield made the fight drawn out and at times strangely boring. Having commenced just after sunrise, the hacking, drowning and flailing was still going at teatime. The last hundred or so combatants, drained by hours of aimless slaughter, stumbled wearily towards each other through the slime and gore in one last attempt to resolve the issue in time for dinner. But their fatigue was such a serious impediment to the slaughter that some soldiers found themselves too knackered, even with a prostrate foe at bay beneath them, to deliver that final, lethal stab. In fact, most of the final casualties succumbed to a pitiful death by drowning in the mire of the Snelt, the one exception being Leofrick the Immortal who discovered, unexpectedly, that he had an allergy to wasp stings.

And so, as the sun slowly set on the carnage, the two warlords sat aimlessly upon their ponies, looking down at the slaughter and then over at each other, wondering what on earth to do next.

In so many wars, the sheer pointlessness of the horror and destruction finally dawns upon the hardened warrior, bringing with it a sudden desire to end the suffering – to end the violence once and for all, and extend a hand of peace and reconciliation towards their former foe. And so it was with Keith and Lionel. As they surveyed the carnage in the valley below, it struck both men that the wanton killing must stop and that they must learn to work together in a bid to create a new, kinder world, a bright new upland, where man can finally live in harmony with his fellow man. More importantly, they also had no intention of actually fighting each other with swords because they were both shit-scared. Tentatively, they began to wave at each other across the killing field.

They knew in their dirty little hearts that they were probably going to have to hang out together again at court because, frankly, no one else would have them. They rode slowly towards each other, picking their way past mangled arms and legs. As befitted their class, they feigned not to hear the last desperate pleas from the maimed, dying pathetically on their behalf in the mire around them. Eventually, they faced each other directly across the bloody river.

'I guess we'd better be friends again,' said Lionel the Ugly. Keith mulled this sad inevitability briefly, but before he could answer his rival, he had cause to pause. They were both aware of a thin dark line of figures appearing Zulu-like on the gnarly heights of Juggin's Lump. Avenging womenfolk gathered menacingly above the two barons, their anger and indignation evident even at this distance. Enraged, the furious wave began to tear down the hillsides towards the two noblemen, an eerie banshee-like wail of vengeance filling the air. Lionel and Keith could clearly see the corn threshers and razor-sharp scythes.

'Uh oh,' said Keith.

No one is sure anymore what the women actually did to the two warlords. There had been a contemporary illustration of the executions on the wall of the parish church of St Furley, but a badly driven Vickers infantry tank had destroyed that in 1937, sadly before any photographs had been taken. Local legend has it that Keith and Lionel took some considerable time to die, and before doing so, had the rare opportunity so few of us are granted, of seeing ourselves from behind.

With law and order non-existent, and the men's low standing at court, there would be no retribution for these avenging angels. Quietly and with great dignity, the wives and girlfriends left their mangled menfolk where they were for the dogs and the crows. The piles of savaged skulls and torn limbs sloshed in the filthy brook, soon hidden from view in the mud. In time, they sank deep into the acid soil.

Memory of the battle persisted only in a curious local song, still sung occasionally by Open University lecturers with thick beards and an unhealthy interest in folk music.

*Twas sad the day the numpties died,*
*Fold de roll de roll,*
*But they had it coming frankly,*
*Flum de do da dey.*
*Now they is buried in slime up by Juggin's Lump,*
*Flum de bump de dung,*
*Food for the worm and the river fluke,*
*Janglo rang de dar.*

And so the little battle passed into obscurity. Stephen was finally booted from the throne and Matilda's son Henry ended up with the Crown, finally a king with a bit of a brain. Henry immediately embarked on a cleanup of the British Isles, which after all the malarkey that had been going on was something of a bloody mess.

People understandably wanted to put the troubles of the Anarchy behind them and as a result, the Battle of Juggin's Lump was all but forgotten. Centuries later, the heathlands would be a barren playground only to the tanks of the British Army as they practised their clanking manoeuvres amongst the heather and bracken. Then in 2013, as part of a package of swingeing government cutbacks, a diminished Ministry of Defence sold off the land to developers in a futile bid to help reduce the budget deficit.

It was around the same time that a historian from the Battlefields Trust, a charity that endeavours to preserve sites of historic military interest, chanced upon an account of this minor engagement in an ancient church ledger. This yellowed manuscript, together with the lyrics of the obscure old song, gave a very clear indication as to the precise location of the skirmish. An exploratory trench was dug into the bleak heath to see if any evidence of the battle remained.

Thanks to the acid soil and the waterlogged conditions, it transpired that there was still much to be found. Like the bog men of Ireland, some bodies had remained remarkably intact, at least as intact as the battle had left them. Their bewildered leathery faces and flattened grimaces were still as pathetic as they must have been on that sad day in 1143.

But it was also around this time that the site was earmarked for another project – construction of yet more badly designed urban overspill. Legendary estate agents and developers, the McCauley Brothers, had arrived on the scene. Even by their competitors' standards, the brothers were generally considered the most cold-blooded and insensitive developers in the long, dirty history of real estate. They had developed many a controversial location, building theme parks on the grounds of ancient massacres, schools on plague pits and chemical plants in sites of special scientific interest. They'd caused no end of protest along the way. Looking at the majesty of the former battlefield's windblown trees and wild purple heathers, they could quickly see that by draining the site and employing bulldozers, they could create some four hundred box-like dwellings with all the personality and charm of a filing cabinet.

As they had successfully done countless times before, the McCauley Brothers began a battle for control of the site using every corrupt ruse in their considerable arsenal.

The charities did their charitable best. Public opinion was firmly on their side and there were even questions in parliament, but behind the scenes, the funny handshakes and backhanders worked their unjust magic. So the inevitable day finally came when the McCauleys took possession.

On the bleak heath, security guards had arrived long before dawn, their yellow high-visibility jackets and hard hats defining a protective phalanx for the advancing diggers. Protestors, their faces wild with indignation, screamed hoarsely through their loudhailers at the show of force deploying towards them across the historic battlefield. Old gentlemen threw themselves pointlessly in front of bulldozers. With the local TV crew filming, scuffles ebbed and flowed for many hours. But by midday it was clear to all that the developers, equipped as they were with considerable hired muscle, could not be deflected from carrying out their planned desecration of the site. The protestors were kept at arm's length from the gathering workmen as they erected a screen around the full extent of the battlefield, the stony-faced security men returning the demoralised insults from the protestors with practised indifference.

Around 4pm a convoy of vehicles drove onto the site led by the shiny black Land Rover Discovery of Ascot McCauley, spokesman for the McCauley family, provoking the TV crew to rush through the security cordon in anticipation of a statement. As the vehicle pulled to a halt, the passenger door opened revealing Ascot McCauley himself, his spindly Savile-Row-besuited body topped by an affected twirl of foppish dark hair. His sharp cynical features quickly dropped the sneer of victory as the camera caught him; seamlessly, he replaced it with a priest-like countenance. He surveyed the ragged line of protestors and paused briefly before placing his wellington boots upon the sticky soil. With that a wave of protest erupted from the gathered crowd.

'Shame on you! Shame on you!' they chanted aggressively. An empty bottle of Welsh spring water sailed close overhead.

'Mr McCauley,' asked the young female reporter, 'can you give us a statement?' The developer looked back to the Range Rover and winked knowingly to his siblings, intently following the proceedings from behind the tinted windows.

'Of course young lady,' he replied, his sharp face oozing sincerity and dark charm. 'McCauley Developments have nothing to hide.'

'Well,' continued the insistent reporter, 'what have you to say to the hundreds of people here today who have come to try and prevent your development of this sensitive site?' Ascot closed his eyes briefly and folded his hands together, the forefingers extended to his lips to imply pensive deliberation.

'Well firstly,' he began, deploying a holier-than-thou manner with well-rehearsed panache. 'I would like to reassure everyone here today, and all your many viewers at home, that with this development, as with every other domestic, industrial and leisure initiative undertaken by McCauley Developments, every possible effort has been made to approach the sometimes opposing issues of a growing housing shortage, the pressure on the environment and the respect of this country's wonderful heritage with great sensitivity.'

'Bollocks!' announced a loudhailer.

'Great sensitivity,' repeated Ascot McCauley, smiling through his perfectly white but oddly small and uniform teeth. 'And this development will be no different. We shall be ensuring that, in order to serve the needs of the wider public and save the environment and history of England for future generations, we will be employing every means at our disposal in the pursuit of a harmonious balance. Indeed, this is why we have engaged a team of professional archaeologists to be present at every stage of this exciting project, ensuring that a proper scientific record of this unique site ...'

'Leave the dead in peace!' bellowed the protestor's loudhailer again before it was rendered mute with pepper spray.

'Please, please ...' continued Ascot, waving away the accusations with his dangly hands, his pink shirt and cufflinks popping out from under the pinstripe. 'Rest assured that we will be paying the utmost respect to any human remains we may happen to discover during the course of development.' He gestured back towards a minibus and beckoned its occupants to come out for the cameras. 'Why, here is our team of archaeologists now,' he declared to the camera, and with that a dozen unusually beefy men sidled awkwardly out into the weak light. Superficially they resembled archaeologists but the bushy beards were in most cases probably false. While the exaggerated shorts, checked shirts and caterpillar boots lent a certain *Time Team* air to the gathering, the cauliflower ears, broken noses and violence-themed tattoos hinted at a different specialism altogether.

'Are you sure these men are archaeologists?' asked the reporter, watching the men gesturing obscenely towards the protestors from behind the cordon of luminous yellow.

'Certainly, these men are the finest in this field,' replied Ascot. 'You can rest assured that they will see to it that the dead of Juggin's Lump shall find a new and peaceful place of burial and dignity, entirely at the expense of McCauley Developments.' Ascot looked reverently up to the clouds in religious affectation. As he let the words hang, there was a last murmur of abuse from the demoralised protestors. 'Now please, if you will excuse me, we will need to begin our sensitive work immediately.'

'But Mr McCauley,' pushed the reporter, to no avail, and Ascot McCauley walked briskly away signalling to his team. 'Surely ...' But the words were lost in the din of a huge bulldozer as it started its engine and lumbered relentlessly towards its desecrating duties behind the now-complete screens.

The protestors, knowing beyond any doubt that the second battle of Juggin's Lump was at an end, began slowly to drift off into the early evening. They trudged sadly away as the large arc lights surrounding the site began to crackle, one by one, into life. The diggers and faux archaeologists were left to their dubious devices.

Hidden behind the screens, the excavators began without ceremony to scoop the damp and fetid soil from the ground, their mechanical shovels heaving the rags and bones from the ground and dropping them with zero dignity into dump trucks. The depressing little bundles of cloth and leather, many still holding pathetic weapons in their skeletal grips, tumbled worthless into the lorries, mixing messily together when they had once been intact within the preserving bog.

The powerful machines took no time to complete their sacrilegious work. Night had only just fallen by the time the last bodies had been dragged from their resting place and dropped like mere root vegetables into the trucks. Ascot McCauley sipped from his hip flask as he watched the proceedings and wiped the moisture from his lips with his pink, initialled handkerchief. Smiling with satisfaction at yet another dirty rotten job done, he turned and stuck up a spindly thumb of triumphalism to his brothers, still behind the Land Rover's darkened glass.

'OK,' he shouted to the foreman as the last of the lorries pulled away into the darkness carrying their sad cargoes, 'you can tell them all to go home now, nice work.' He reached into his pocket and pulled out a roll of notes held together with a rubber band. 'Here you go, there's an extra four hundred in there – make sure they keep their mouths shut.'

CHAPTER 5

# NEEDS MUST

After months of bad atmospheres, stress and arguments, Newton was delighted by his wife's response to the news. The move to Cambridge presented no obvious friction, and she even leapt slightly off the ground when she saw the size of the temporary house that Havotech had made available. The rapidly growing Gabriella was immediately at home in the extensive and verdant garden.

They'd felt confident enough of their new circumstances to become a two-car family. Rowena chose a sleek dark Audi and Newton, indulging a lifetime weakness for the classics, splashed out on a 1972 Citroën DS. The DS was by anyone's standards an impressive car. True, it wasn't fast and had to be treated like a sensitive elderly relative, but its shark-like lines and technical eccentricities meant that Newton often found himself talking to interested blokes whenever he pulled over. He delighted in demonstrating the headlamps that followed the turn of the steering and the wonderfully eccentric hydromatic suspension that lifted the old car up off the ground as if it was hovering.

Rowena threw herself immediately into the Cambridge scene while Newton busied himself with the impressive new laboratory. Peter Carnatt was pleasantly attentive as Newton made requests for new equipment, encouraging him that anything would be considered and usually procured. Soon the old rig back in London seemed pitifully quaint and inadequate.

It took Newton's team some five months to assemble, test and calibrate the experiment before they could finally start to harvest scientific data. To celebrate the occasion, Carnatt and the management assembled awkwardly and expressionless in lab coats and goggles as Newton talked them through the apparatus, conscious of the odd way in which they blankly listened devoid of any real warmth or interest. Between them, Peter Carnatt floated almost as an interpreter, switching chameleon-like between the vernacular of business and the lab floor. There was a pronounced gulf between the two worlds. The CEO and his top team had their own entrance to the building with its own hedge-shielded car parking and they could usually only be seen distantly through the walls of glass from which the entire complex had been built. On one occasion, Newton found himself in a corridor near what may or may not have been a board meeting. Through the glass, Peter Carnatt caught his eyes and then turned, activating the blinds to deny Newton his line of sight. Not that there had been anything to see – just energy figures and graphs. Clearly, the distance between the lab and the company executives was there for a reason and it was there to stay.

Mingling with visiting scientists from some of Havotech's other projects, Newton also found that much of the usual cross-pollination he had enjoyed in his academic environment was curiously lacking. Many seemed positively loathed to divulge any sense of progress or detail, and after a while, Newton stopped even asking. He was also slightly put out after a year in the lab to find himself and his team slapped with a raft of non-disclosure agreements, effectively cutting them off from the wider scientific establishment. They seethed and cursed for days, turning the laboratory air blue as they waved the documents around with contempt. This placed Newton in uncomfortable and unfamiliar territory, and his inability to defend his team in this new atmosphere began to nag and unsettle him.

At least Havotech was understanding about his television and publishing work. During his second year in Cambridge, the BBC approached him to write and present a series of six programmes exploring the history and application of scientific thought. Newton threw himself wholeheartedly into the project, seeing it as a prime opportunity to make the case for scientific rationality in the face of growing superstition and mysticism, a trend that troubled and irritated him on a daily basis. Newton's series was predictably measured and well considered, but it did not hold back its punches. The paranormal, religion and the full menu of irrational thought came in for the Barlow treatment in a series that ranged far and wide both in its scope and in air miles. Filming took Newton all around the world and though he was gone from the lab for several months, his paymasters at Havotech seemed pleased with the reflected kudos that Newton brought to their profile.

The series did very well, pulling in surprisingly high viewing figures from a British population driven half mad by two decades of reality television. Part of this no doubt came from Newton's effective on-screen persona, a cool, smart young man as opposed to the tired old cliché of the nutty professor; soon he became used to being recognised as he walked the streets. He even had the embarrassing yet flattering accolade of being voted one of the top ten sexy men in Britain by one of the very same glossy magazines that Rowena seemed to be reading every time he saw her. This won Newton a much-improved domestic environment but he found himself the constant centre of attention at Rowena's less-than-comfortable supper parties, introduced to endless fawning couples like some kind of performing sea lion.

But now he seemed to start attracting criticism as well. First came a muttering from the scientific community, white-coat academics less than comfortable with his dapper on-screen image. His TV work was consistently belittled in some learned circles, but Newton, on the crest of a wave, refused to be fazed. In a world that seemed hobbled and traumatised by superstition, Newton felt he was duty-bound to promote the alternative logical message. This he did with tactics that some were beginning to consider overkill. His big TV series ended with a barely disguised attack on religion and superstition, Newton declaring that: 'Belief, a notion that is advertised as bringing comfort and calm, instead brings uncertainty, conflict and mistrust. Our inability to move forward from this construct into an era of logic, where we can face reality and our own future with objectivity, lies at the centre of all mankind's great dilemmas. If we continue to abdicate responsibility for our actions to a higher being, then in the chaos and fear that follows, we will have no one to blame but ourselves.' Citing suicide bombers, the Spanish Inquisition and the Salem witch trials, Newton made his case firmly. Needless to say, it created something of a fuss in the papers the following day with one critic describing Newton's attitude as arrogance of the highest order.

'Barlow's dogmatic atheism is nothing new, of course. It is driven by smugness and a desire to look down at people far more than it's driven by any desire to uncover truths.'

Looking for some good old-fashioned on-screen bloodshed, programme controllers soon had Newton debating with disgruntled theologians in a series of TV debates. Angry and on the defensive after Newton's prime-time atheism, there were several heated encounters with Newton holding the line coolly against sustained counter attacks from various faith groups. Not being in the least faint-hearted, Newton waded in with relish, giving both his fans and detractors a treasury of sound-bites that could rally or enrage depending on your orientation.

'Dr Barlow has clearly forgotten the difference between debate and bullying,' said the *London Standard* following a lively slugfest in which Newton had told an archbishop that Jesus Christ, should he happen against the odds to return to the earth, would in all likelihood hang out with the atheists. As if this wasn't enough, he crowned the evening by stating that 'common sense is just God's way of telling us he doesn't exist'.

'Let this be the last time this odious cynic is allowed to parade his ill-judged conceit on prime-time television,' said the *Sunday Express* after Newton declared that the notion of God hampered human development.

And it wasn't just religion that came in for the Barlow treatment. Even as he was swatting away the devout, Newton was invited to participate in a series of somewhat lighter programmes designed to test a number of paranormal phenomena and self-declared 'gifted' individuals.

It was an offer Newton couldn't refuse. He had always loathed the irrational, superstitious and fraudulent. UFOs, ghosts, clairvoyance and alternative medicine – as far as Newton was concerned, each one of them constituted something beyond mere harmless fun or an over-active imagination. Weren't the natural wonders of the real world stunning enough? Most of all he was horrified at how far pragmatism had diverged from public life and influence, society seemingly drowning under the weight of religion, bigotry and political dogma.

Although Newton was generally careful to avoid playing the evangelistic role too hard, on this occasion, he entered into the spirit of the programmes with gusto, spending most of each episode fighting an irresistible smirk in the presence of self-proclaimed ghost hunters, diviners, conduits to the cosmos and spoon benders. Some episodes of *Ghost Show* were hilariously silly, and Newton's wit and dryly delivered analytical cynicism soon became an unmissable weekly treat for the scientifically minded viewer. Faced with the seemingly limitless public appetite for the spooky, Newton felt he was doing his small part to keep the charlatans at bay, but inevitably, it led to yet another wave of criticism, this time from the mediums, the believers and the superstitious themselves. Their attacks ranged from ill-prepared attempts at pseudoscience to charges of Newton being a general killjoy. But he calmly pointed out that 'contacting' the dead on behalf of the lonely and bereaved, or claiming to rid houses of the tortured souls of murder victims, could hardly be described as 'just a bit of harmless fun'.

Soon he was the focus of a pro-paranormal backlash as an army of mediums and ghost busters, licking their wounds from yet another Barlow tongue lashing, fought for an opportunity to silence Newton's cool and dismissive message. His blood up, Newton was drawing a line in the sand, a bulkhead against a growing tide of mysticism and mumbo jumbo.

It irked him somewhat that other scientists tried to put him off his sceptical activities, warning him that even slight contact with the 'crazies' might rub off on him – as if you could somehow catch superstition like an unpleasant skin infection. Undeterred, Newton continued his campaigning media presence with gusto, merrily unmasking the odd fraudulent séance here and debunking a miracle there. With his face now familiar and frankly over-exposed on both sides of the rational divide, clouds that Newton chose to ignore were gathering.

Dr Barlow was starting to accumulate his enemies.

CHAPTER 6

# IDOL

Islington residents Juliet and Piers Layhard had been preparing their dinner party since 5pm. Piers had come home early from his architectural practice by way of the posh gastromarket on Liverpool Street, where he'd parked the vintage Saab and grabbed the wine and cheese. Juliet was something of a perfectionist – she'd be the first to admit it – and had been agitatedly marinating the prime Angus beef since the morning, fretting and huffing, cursing the kitchen they currently had neither the time nor the designer to upgrade.

Piers dropped the shopping bags onto the table. Wisely, he kept his distance from his wife as she flashed a wicked looking knife in his direction, a little too close to his bow tie for comfort.

'Pour me a glass of Pinot will you darling,' she said, sniffing, trying to avoid tainting her pointy nose with her flour-covered hands. 'The kids went off OK – Beckie says they're not playing up this time so, so far so good.'

'That's excellent darling,' replied Piers distractedly, enjoying the lack of the children. 'You OK here for a bit? I need to contact the office.' With her nodded approval, he climbed the neat white staircase up to his study.

Piers Layhard was a collector of sorts; they both were. They liked their house to be a blank canvas with pockets of interest, lit beautifully – classical sculpture, carvings from Africa and old Chinese chests, spotlit above utilitarian carpets. The only thing that spoiled the effect was the children, of course, who didn't share their parents' taste for retro wooden toys and antique train sets. Piers shuddered as he remembered when Toby had run riot with a marker pen and his own waste products, and wrote 'poo potty bum poo' all over the dining room, missing an expensive abstract by mere millimetres. Tonight, though, their muddy bikes had been neatly stowed on the patio. Juliet had erased all evidence of their scruffiness by 8.30 that morning, when her sister had taken the kids away to the suburbs.

Piers checked his emails and upped a bid for a period statue of Josephine Baker on eBay. His study was scrupulously Scandinavian, with smart angled lamps and an over-complicated chair he'd bought in an exclusive showroom in Shoreditch. On his odd 1970s office desk, there was little out of place, the Mac laptop at perfect right angles, a framed picture of Piers accepting an award at the design museum and a die-cast model of a Saab 96 convertible in white. He poured himself a cold mineral water from the miniature fridge and made a few business calls, playing with the thick black hair of the Oriental wooden figurine on the mantelpiece as he did so, its exaggerated bottom and wide staring eyes a source of some amusement to the children on those rare occasions when Piers had let them through the door.

At 7pm, Juliet asked Piers to lay the table. The guests arrived and by 8.30 sharp, dinner had been served. Sarah and Daniel had popped up from Hoxton and the other two were singles, set up awkwardly by Juliet. They tried frantically to break the ice in the embarrassing spotlight of Juliet's clumsy matchmaking. Lulu was not quite as ready to move on from her divorce as Juliet thought she was, especially as it had only been finalised a day earlier, and Edward, the new junior partner from Piers's architectural practice, was not exactly in the mood for a long-term commitment either, given his studiously concealed fixation for men in leather hats.

Juliet served the food as Piers uncorked the wine and eventually they adjourned to the sitting room with cheese and biscuits. Piers, stressed, had refilled himself a little liberally and was fighting an urge to release a loud, manly 'who gives a shit' fart when they heard the restored Victorian doorbell. 'Who's that at this time?' he asked Juliet.

'Well I don't know, do I! You might find out if you answer the door,' she said sarcastically. Piers rolled his eyes, put down his goblet and ambled off down the long hallway, his cotton socks slipping slightly on the varnished floor.

He opened the door.

The Bonetaker, immobile and literally breathtaking in the blue of the twilight, was staring back at him. 'Oh crap,' said Piers, quickly trying to shut the old door, but the Bonetaker's vast shoe had jammed it wide open.

Piers made to cry out, but as the pungent odour from the giant steamed over him, he instantly lost track of his instinct.

'Hewoooo, clam I hurp you?' he burbled, opening the door and leaning back against an antique map of Anatolia.

'Innnnn,' said the Bonetaker's deep resonating voice, and with that he lurched heavily into the hallway past the architect, scattering the children's spotless wellington boots lined up beneath the coat rack. 'In nah. Idul, guv me idul.'

In the sitting room, the polite conversation carried on oblivious, Juliet retelling the mind-numbing story of how they'd all been stranded in Umbria by the Icelandic ash cloud, unaware that an eight-foot nightmare had just gained entry to her house and was ascending the staircase.

Piers was a trifle confused. He'd had a lot of Chilean Cabernet Sauvignon over the years and it had never done this to him before. His legs had all the strength of rolled towels and his manicured hands hung useless at his sides. He stumbled in the vast shadow of the stranger as they climbed the neat stairs to the study, trying vaguely to work out how long they'd been friends. The guy was huge, and that smell – somewhere between strong Italian cheese and smoked mackerel. They entered the study, a daft smile flicking on and off Piers's face as he struggled to regain control. A damp patch had appeared on his linen trousers.

'Idul,' boomed the stranger, his giant fist rising up like a leg of ham to point at the mantelpiece. 'I wull huv.'

Robotically, Piers handed the figure over then flopped down heavily on his £5,000 chair, watching as the Bonetaker held the curious little carving up to his massive face, tilting his head as he scrutinised it in the light of the Anglepoise. The big hands grabbed the figurine's hair and he let the ten-inch body hang beneath it for a moment, sniffing and watching as a faint glow flushed upon the dark wood. Piers, struggling to focus, watched as the figure began, subtly, to emit an indistinct purple brightness. The Bonetaker, confident he had successfully tracked down his quarry, opened his long filthy coat and placed the long-haired idol in his tired leather bag, fragments of dead moss and ivy falling away onto the spotless laminate flooring. Piers closed his heavy eyelids, a wave of extreme fatigue engulfing him as if he'd taken three of his sleeping tablets in one go, and by the time the Bonetaker had unlocked the large French windows and stepped out onto the roof of the kitchen extension, he was out for the count.

His target in his possession, the Bonetaker dropped silently into the immaculate paved garden and lurched away. Unnoticed, he passed through gardens and alleyways until he broke out suddenly into a modern estate, and finding some graffiti-ridden garages behind a block of flats, he crouched unseen and began to assess the small figurine.

The Bonetaker's tired yellow eyes stared into the face of the idol. Its pearl and bead eyes glared back at him in mute defiance as far away, in some other place, its connected spirit sensed in horror that the moment of oblivion was imminent.

The tribal leader that the idol represented meant nothing to recorded Western history. He'd wreaked terror beneath distant tree canopies in Indonesia and Sumatra long before white men had passed that way, but the horror of his reign had ranked as wantonly evil as that of Hitler or Stalin. He'd visited much suffering upon many peaceful peoples, inflicting a terrifying wave of expansionist attacks across the islands of Oceania. In doing so, this all-destroying raider had proclaimed himself a God, a deity beyond the control of mortal men, free to pursue his cruelties and rank sadism unbound by humane considerations or common decency.

Here in this peculiar Purgatory, he never aged and never died, kept alive in one world and the next by the folk memory of his savagery and a slowly diminishing collection of vile little idols. Or at least he never seemed to die as he had died before, hunted and killed by tribes keen for revenge and peace. Now he floated, held firm in a cell by arms he could not see or understand, spitting and hissing at the bright white beings that hovered beyond his secure perimeter. Their benign faces looked concerned and puzzled as the intense purple light began its mad swirl about him. He raged at their taming of him, he bellowed and spat, but he remained tightly held in place.

In the light of a vandalised streetlamp, the Bonetaker cursed a cat that had foolishly come to investigate, its tabby hackles raised high as it sniffed his foul scent. It scurried hysterically away into the estate and the Bonetaker began once again to chant his incantations, his big fist yanking away the ancient black hair from the idol, which he flung into the mortar. It flared suddenly as it caught the flame then sizzled and spat as the big hands bled into the mixture.

In Purgatory, the confused angelic figures hovered close to the edge of the tribesman's room, watching intensely as he writhed spasmodically in a torment of fear and despair. His evil force flowing away, he began to chant in an ancient tongue, calling for the assistance of the same forest spirits who had failed to help his own victims in their torments. Now they equally would fail to assist the God King as he died his second death. The bright figures could only look on in bewilderment as the ghastly gyrating wraith dissipated and faded before them.

'Here we go again!' one of the white beings shouted above the screams, and then, suddenly, it was over. The Bonetaker had finished his work and was carefully folding away his paraphernalia beneath the streetlights. The holding cell was silent now. Cautiously, the white beings entered the empty chamber, its glowing restraints floating free.

'Excellent,' said one of the councillors, hovering majestically at a 45 degree angle. 'There goes another one.'

## CHAPTER 7

# BURST

Back in Dr Newton Barlow's lab in Cambridge, things were going from strength to strength. Using impressive new equipment, Newton and his team were able to strengthen the evidence of nuclear fusion within their enigmatic bubbles, and despite the secrecy in which the team was forced to operate, rumours of a breakthrough had begun to circulate amongst the universities. The rumours may have been hugely exaggerated, but nonetheless they were starting to receive credence in some of the more sensationalist chat rooms. The more sensitive antennae in the investment market had also started to twitch; pretty soon Havotech's share price was on the up. Peter Carnatt told Newton the good news in the canteen, almost as an aside, but rather than sharing his corporate excitement, Newton was uneasy. He sensed the need to calm things down and proposed a well-written report on the project, something that spelled out the facts and the limitations to dampen any ill-founded speculation. Carnatt, with a notable absence of charm, shot this down almost before it was airborne, making his excuses before leaving Newton and his frustration at the table.

Newton felt his unease slipping towards alarm. It didn't help when the following weekend, he was unpacking shopping from the car with Rowena when a persistent reporter appeared out of the rhododendrons and started pressing Newton for an inside story. He gave no comment to the irritating little man, but was wearily conscious that his evasion was more likely to fuel speculation than to end it. Newton phoned Carnatt straight away, but he seemed annoyingly unconcerned, merely pacifying Newton with some glib comments about 'show business' before cutting the call short. Newton knew he had to act. He would distribute a lay-reader report whether Carnatt sanctioned it or not, a summary of their findings so far, something that could and would quash all the hype. That would work ... surely?

So, over a bank holiday weekend, Dr Newton Barlow locked himself away in his study and hammered the bloody thing out. He flagged the limitations, lit up the pitfalls, highlighted the dead ends and studiously tempered the causes for optimism, choosing the most universal, non-technical language he could muster, almost as if he were writing a script for one of his TV shows. When it was finally finished, he stared out the window at the rambling garden and as the dawn cast its warm light on the high hedges, he was suddenly struck by how cut-off and isolated he had become.

The next morning he sought out Carnatt and presented his material to the bemused manager as he stepped defensively from his black BMW in the car park.

'Look,' said Newton, breathless and wide-eyed, 'this, this ... report ... it explains the real, the actual real, state of play. Please Peter, I'm asking you, you've got to make sure that people know. I need you to help calm things down. Science isn't like a pizza delivery; you can't just order whatever you want whenever you want it.' Carnatt, alarmed, backed away.

'Woahhhhhh, steady Dr Barlow, let's keep things professional here,' he countered, moving away like a banker from a harmonica-playing junkie. 'Look, there's a lot of cash swimming around in this thing right now. This is no time to go all mushy on everyone.'

'Mushy?' Newton snapped back. '*Mushy*? This isn't a question of what *I* think, or what *you* think, or what all the investors out there may *want* to think. We're not even sure yet ourselves that this experiment is right, logical, hell I don't know – we can't say anything till we get independent confirmation, please!' Carnatt tried to interject but Newton wasn't to be stopped. 'When we started here you told me this was going to be a pure research programme. Now I'm getting the distinct impression that the opposite is the case. Dammit, why is no one talking to me! Well, that report you have there in your hand is the basic, simple *truth* about what we've been doing. No spin, no marketing, no wishful thinking, just the hard facts. For God's sake Peter, get the bloody thing circulated, please!' Far from being noticeably moved by Newton's uncharacteristic outburst, Carnatt merely rolled his robotic eyes dismissively, snatched the report and stormed inside.

Newton, queasy from his toes to his quiff, could feel the ground moving beneath him like an escalator.

That evening, seriously unnerved, he made the mistake of confiding his concerns to his wife. Far from offering any support, Rowena accused Newton of being a purist who cared more about his ego than he did about his family. Newton, weary of stress and confrontation, recoiled ineffectually across the kitchen as his wife railed against him. Young Gabby screamed hysterically at the two of them and ran sobbing to her bedroom. With Newton's alarm climbing hourly like a bikini alert, he even considered calling Dr Sixsmith and pouring his confused heart out. He could now see, only too clearly, that he was in danger of fulfilling every single one of the concerns the old family friend and mentor had raised a few years earlier.

Newton's supersized pride stopped him lifting the receiver.

Suddenly, as if life wasn't complicated enough, along came the global financial meltdown. Havotech, like so many other companies, woke up to a new era of low confidence. Several other programmes in the Havotech scientific complex were axed overnight and Newton found himself even more under pressure to bring his bubbles to the boil. No amount of backtracking and alarm calling from Newton seemed to slow the mounting pressure and so, when ordered to deliver a series of press releases about the project, Newton's already substantial unease grew to epic proportions.

On paper, the bubble fusion experiments had shown a glimmer of promise. Newton's detectors had registered telltale patterns of neutrons emerging from sonoluminescent bubbles – hinting at fusion – but he couldn't rule out some other effect at work. The results needed confirmation by another team in another lab. Wishful thinking was no substitute for thorough good science. What Newton was being pressured towards lay not in science but in business, and a panicked desperate business at that. Havotech's stock was dropping like a broken elevator as the investors started ducking out – it was going to take something sensational to make them stay.

The meeting with the public relations department would haunt Newton all his life. It flowed back and forth for eight long hours, the two parties almost speaking in two different languages. The frustration directed at Newton bordered frequently on ridicule, with Carnatt making a show of mediation but failing to hide his own preference for the company line. Newton was worn relentlessly down. He was dog-tired, tired of the company, tired of his isolation and tired of the entire issue. Late in the day, they reached something laughingly called a compromise in the form of an embargoed press release to be dispatched ahead of a media conference the following Tuesday. Like a condemned French aristocrat, Newton stepped up to the guillotine.

The press conference drew an unnervingly large crowd of suited journalists to a hired meeting room on the Strand. Seeing the hacks massed before him, Newton's guts lurched. He opened with a five-minute talk that he hoped would counteract at least some of the hyperbole, whilst still appeasing his masters at Havotech itself. Following up, a PR assistant guided a microphone round the assembled reporters.

'Jonathan Redmond, *The London Post*. Dr Barlow, could you clarify how long you think it will take for bubble fusion to become a working technology for clean energy?'

'We don't know that it ever *will* be,' Newton quickly countered. 'We're really just at the early stages here, so I'm not going to predict a timescale. It could go nowhere, but it's important to explore every possible lead that might, just *might*, get us out of our looming energy problems.'

'But thinking optimistically,' Redmond persisted, 'if your wildest dreams came true, when's the earliest this could happen?' Newton shuffled uneasily.

'Well, *if* the results are confirmed and *if* the technology scales up easily, well, then it could be within a decade – although that really would be in the wildest of my wildest dreams. The likelihood is that it will go nowhere within the next 20 or even 30 years. And even that's a maybe ...'

At that point, Carnatt urgently stood up from the front row to address the audience. 'On behalf of Havotech,' he blurted, working to bypass Newton's pragmatism, 'I'd just like to emphasise that we'll be aiming to push this research ahead as fast as possible. All being well, we're hoping to get the loose ends tied up and seek substantial cash injection later this year.' A wave of surprised murmurs washed through the room. 'Dr Barlow and his team are very modest,' Carnatt continued. 'Yes, there are uncertainties, but these dedicated, skilled scientists are doing some truly revolutionary stuff, absolutely first class. We can't disclose the exact details, of course, for commercial reasons, but let's just say, watch this space!'

Newton's eyes rolled in despair. Other questions followed in a blur and he found himself talking and thinking at the same time, not completely about the same things. He really knew the runaway train was well out of the station and heading for disaster. His nervous attempts to backtrack were barely noticed. They went unreported, all of Newton's prepared caveats lost beneath the sound-bites and hype in the resulting news stories. Free clean energy 'within a decade'.

Major scientific breakthrough, British science achieves the glittering prize. Not only did Havotech's share price jump – it leapt. Newton was horrified, and his adversaries, at long last, scented blood.

As other laboratories rushed to duplicate Havotech's exaggerated findings, the noose tightened around Newton Barlow. The final disastrous moment came in a TV interview where he was asked to speculate on the potential for the world if bubble fusion could be made to work. Newton resisted the angle of questioning repeatedly but with such indigestibly hard science that it was chopped wholesale from the broadcast. Once again, the message came sailing inappropriately out to the waiting audience; free clean energy, an end to oil wars and fuel poverty. The audience lapped it up. Sadly, so did the massed ranks of Newton's detractors. Inevitably, bemused and dismissive responses came back from the rival laboratories. Newton's misreported optimism made him the perfect target for a backlash, not just from the science community and his enemies in the mystical world, but also from the business community as Havotech's inflated share price came in for scrutiny. Now the only bubble generating heat for Newton Barlow was the one bursting around him.

The attacks came thick and fast – accusations of improper business practice, poor scientific safeguards, and even outright fraud. Newton, already a familiar figure and poster boy for scientific reason, was now a sitting target for accusations of hypocrisy. Damning articles appeared in such diverse publications as *The Sun*, *The Economist* and *Nature*. Newton found himself hounded. Rowena, far from standing firm with her embattled husband, departed with their grumpy daughter for her mother's.

Within Havotech, things moved very, very quickly. Newton's team vanished within days, their identity cards left hanging in reception while Newton dodged the journalists camped outside the now-empty family house. Returning to Havotech, the atmosphere in the corridors was downright sinister, like a walk to the gallows past a silent mob. Carnatt had seen to it that the door to the lab itself was locked, and Newton was still rattling it pointlessly when Carnatt and a security guard arrived to escort him protesting from the building. Pushed out into the car park, Newton turned to face Carnatt, whose pink striped shirt was now only vaguely visible behind the locked smoked-glass doors.

'Peter, Peter, for Christ's sake!' Newton blurted, wrought with frustration and anger. But Carnatt, his face blank and impassive, simply watched his former colleague raging on the tarmac then silently turned away.

Though near mortally wounded, Havotech was soon on the defensive, heaping blame upon Newton in his enforced absence. Branded internationally as the 'rogue physicist', he found events swirling around him faster than protons in an accelerator. Old colleagues distanced Newton en masse and as a final humiliation, the family was evicted from the large rambling house in Cambridge. Rowena, inevitably, asked for a divorce.

## CHAPTER 8

# SOMETHING WICKED

The curator of the Langton Hadlow village museum returned hastily to his lodgings in the small rooms above The Tugger's Arms, the strange hooded carving tucked firmly under his arm. It was cold and blustery, and as he hobbled urgently past the looming war memorial, the fresh wind whipped the ivy around on the façade of the old inn, making a near-continuous rustling noise. As the leaves fluttered, they beat a frantic rhythm with the old streetlight as it flickered near the foliage.

The curator let himself in through the warped and darkly aged side door into the pub's silent interior. Weak daylight from the greasy windows caught whirling motes of dust as they danced in the empty bar. Once, the curator would have been hard pressed to make it across the crowded and boisterous pub without numerous welcoming pints being thrust into his hand by ruddy-faced locals. Now there was no one in the entire building but the old curator himself, and he shivered at the brooding interior as he climbed the rickety staircase to his lodgings.

Once in his modest kitchen, he scrutinised the unpleasant little figure closely under the glare of a rusty old desk lamp. It was hardly a triumph of sensitive carving. The chisel had clearly been used in a frenzy, the wood ripped and torn to reveal the demonic figure, crouched and angry. Clawed hands emerging from the cloak suggested a ferocious defiance that the old curator had never really noticed until now. It had a darkened lacquer-like sheen giving it an almost waxy feel.

Below the crouching presence of the figure lay its secured box, locked with an ancient mechanism for which the curator had no key. He held the carving up to the light and regarded it from different angles. Scratching his hairless scalp, he placed it on the table and opened the cutlery drawer. He rattled the tray of old knives and forks from side to side before finally lifting out an aged little fruit knife. He began, tentatively at first, to poke and pick at the box and its rusted old lock.

Sometimes he seemed to make progress. A small opening on one side of the tiny door would reluctantly open but then, as he prepared to use a spoon to widen the fissure, it would return to its original position making him increasingly frustrated. He took a deep breath to overcome the urge to set about the figure with a meat tenderiser and lifting his fruit knife once more, he wedged its sharp point back into the thin crack beside the crusted lock. Carefully, he applied an increasing pressure, the blade gradually forcing itself deeper into the widening gap as his elbow shook with the effort.

Without warning, the old blade shattered in two as the box finally cracked open. The curator's hand, still pushing, rushed in a flash down the handle and he let out a high-pitched yelp as the knife took a neat chunk of his hand. Shocked by the sudden pain, he leapt from his seat and began to hop and curse around the room, his bloody hand tucked under his armpit in an instinctive effort to relieve the stabbing agony. After a minute or so he pulled out his hand tentatively to check the damage, and being a sensitive soul, he nearly passed out as he watched the thick dark blood ooze from the ripped flesh, cascading down onto the old lace tablecloth.

'Oh dear me, oh dear me,' he muttered anxiously to himself. Leaving the figure where it had fallen next to the sauce bottles, he dashed breathlessly to the bathroom cabinet and struggled to self-medicate with his left hand. Eventually, he emerged from the bathroom with his right hand looking like a red and white boxing glove, his injury throbbing and stinging beneath a mess of lint and sticking plasters.

The curator couldn't dwell on this too long, however, because when he came back down the corridor from the bathroom he was greeted once again by the weird and peculiar purple light he had seen before in the museum. This time, it was emanating from the kitchen. Peering round the corner, he witnessed the now-intensified light as it pulsated from the crack where the fruit knife had finally shattered the box. As he watched, the light grew still more powerful until, almost imperceptibly at first, it began to reach menacingly out from the artefact, solidifying ribbons of intense purple feeling across the table.

His lined eyes widened. The tendrils caressed and nudged the ketchup bottle, first testing and then, deciding it unrewarding, flicking dismissively away so that the bottle rolled and fell onto the lino with a loud smash. The curator was rooted to the spot as the stream of purple fingers spread relentlessly out across the small kitchen, their focus doorward as they washed purposefully towards him like high-speed film of weed growth. His breath staccato and shallow, he seemed unable to either move or scream as they climbed with dark purpose over his tattered brogues and up his corduroy trousers, individual limbs of purple poking and prising their way into his pockets and his more intimate spaces. At his throat and face, they picked and played with his ageing features, pulling at his loose old skin before prising open his lips to explore his mouth cavity. As though he was a slave in a market, they examined his yellowed false teeth then reared back in perceptible repugnance at his dental failings.

Suddenly, the glowing vines left the curator in an abrupt surge of purple, rearing up before him into a waving ball of rippling glowing spaghetti, one single thick string of light leading back to the cracked carving on the kitchen table. It turned purposefully towards the staircase and to the bar below. Finding himself able to move again, the old curator nervously pursued the strands of magenta and mauve as they separated and washed like treacle down the stairs. He felt drawn to follow, but as he did, he kept his back glued firmly to the walls and the banisters, his curiosity and alarm fighting each other for control of his common sense as he pursued just out of reach.

The entire lounge bar was bathed in the evil purple glow as it assembled itself into near-human form, static electricity and a smell of burning filling the air. Packets of crisps, left when the bar suddenly closed a few years earlier, began popping and jumping off the shelves and the old fruit machine lit up and whirled madly, bells sounding off in the increasing chaos.

Startled, the curator was wondering where all this was going to end. His eyes darted from exit to exit as he planned his escape. The spirit – it was the only suitable word the curator could think of – started testing the doors and windows with intense violet wisps of plasma. But most of the doors and windows of the shuttered pub were locked and secured. Frustrated, it tugged and battered at them, pausing only to smash an old Guinness mirror and fling dirty pint glasses across the bar. The violent barrage came close to hitting the old man, showers of glass erupting around him, but they abated abruptly when, to his horror, the blob of plasma solidified into the hideous figure upon the carving. It gradually turned, menacingly, towards the curator as he stood in a mess of broken glassware on the stairs, his hands locked for dear life to the banister.

'Oh dear, oh dear me,' he muttered again to himself, almost as a protective incantation as the unambiguous glowing figure of a 15th-century clergyman began floating towards him over the pool table. The curator closed his eyes, too old to run, timidly awaiting the ghastly finale to his foolish curiosity.

At that very moment, far away in some other place, the holding room of the spectacularly evil Cardinal Balthazar De La Senza was flagged up as matter of concern by a group of alarmed ethereal beings. They pulsed with gold as they frantically tested the perimeters of the old medieval monster's glowing prison. Clearly the demonic spirit within the cell was highly active again, its purple malevolence flailing against the walls with vile intent. But unlike the occasional, seemingly random assassinations visited upon the inmates of these celestial cells, La Senza was clearly *not* under attack. Instead, the beings correctly sensed they were witnessing an attempted breakout and it filled them with horror. As his beady spiteful eyes glared with defiance at his jailors, his ectoplasmic radiance pierced new tears and fissures in the translucent walls around him and passed invisibly away into the land of the living.

And so, the councillors of this other place and their ethereal assistants all gathered around the edges of La Senza's restraining cell, working frantically to cut off the dark Cardinal's escape before his evil presence could regain a foothold in the human realm. They chanted, they wailed. They used small oily things with lights at the end and they made trumpet-like noises with some sort of trumpet. One particular figure of radiance with bright golden dreadlocks sang a pleasant and not un-danceable song while playing a harp. Bit by bit, the cracks and fissures through which La Senza had sought to escape began to close.

Unaware of these developments, the curator was still very much face to face with the ectoplasmic visage of the demonic Inquisitor La Senza, unbeknown to him, the killer and destroyer of both the living and the dead. Cardinal Balthazar De La Senza, the self-proclaimed judge of heaven and earth, reared cobra-like before him.

'Oh my goodness!' muttered the curator, somewhat understating the horror of the moment.

The monster seemed initially reluctant to possess the clapped out arthritic body of the curator with his feeble teeth and anything but

20-20 vision; it seemed to hesitate. But this was La Senza's only hope of striking out from The Tugger's Arms into the wider community of Langton Hadlow, and beyond it, the world.

'Any port in a storm,' hissed the apparition, just inches from the old man, and it then pulled back to begin releasing many new probing tendrils that crept with demonic purpose towards the curator's hairy ears.

However, just as the curator was about to become lost forever to the evil Inquisitor, the entity widened its glowing violet eyes. Belatedly, La Senza sensed the threat from his cell on the other side and he pulled back instantly in alarm. All around the curator, the evil wisps began to recede as the frantic incantations back in this strange other world sucked the Inquisitor savagely toward his nasty little box just as if someone had switched on an extractor fan. Like noodles down a kitchen sink, the box drew La Senza back towards Purgatory, his apparition fruitlessly attempting to grab both the staircase and the curator's lapels in a desperate bid to stave off the inevitable. Appalled yet fascinated, the curator followed the spirit of the Cardinal up the staircase as he was pulled relentlessly back into the kitchen. The shrinking human form broke up once again into a seething mass of glowing tree roots, each making last frantic attempts to resist before flipping back into the box like spaghetti into the mouth of a small child. The salt, pepper and sauces scattered with a clatter as the last wisps reached out desperately for purchase on the table, but in a chaos of glass and seasoning, the last tendrils were gone and the purple light extinguished.

Back in his cell, La Senza wailed and screamed in fury and frustration. His bitterness welled up into foul blobs of jellyfish-like plasmas; welts popped and sizzled all around his thrashing cloaked form. To add to his indignity, an open bottle of HP sauce was rotating about him, its brown contents smearing him with each revolution.

'Oh my,' said the curator. Dazed, he looked at the mess in the kitchen for a while before finally fetching a dustpan and brush.

Somewhere else entirely, benign beings with good hearts were breathing long sighs of relief and spinning long lazy cartwheels of self-satisfaction in the air as La Senza, menacingly silent now, brooded and schemed in his bonds.

CHAPTER 9

# Viv1234

After his fall from scientific and public grace, interest in Dr Newton Barlow waned almost as fast as his career and lifestyle. It felt long enough at the time, though. It may have been a year, maybe even two; he'd stopped counting the more he explored the pleasures of increasingly cheap whisky. In fact, Newton had been out in the dark cold for near to three long years, the butt of anyone out for a cheap shot. The parodies, the incessant mocking media enquiries and the awkward or hostile encounters with the general public had been an almighty kick to the last shreds of his dignity.

In retrospect those awful, humiliating reality TV invitations were a symptom that the trauma was entering its final, lurid phase. Gradually, thankfully, public recognition began to fade, helped in part by Newton's abandonment of his trademark image. The rockabilly quiff was gone, so too the leather jacket and pointy shoes. Now he passed unnoticed by the population in the blandest of supermarket jeans and jumpers, thankful for the anonymity that was enveloping him. The mocking stares were getting rarer, just the odd science graduate in the wine shop chancing a second glance or an old acquaintance thinking better of saying hello on a crowded tube train.

Nonetheless, Newton had to finally face the challenge of making something close to a living out of the wreckage of his once-glittering career. There could be no question of a return to academia. To any self-respecting university, Newton Barlow was the very definition of soiled goods, his mere presence on campus likely to undermine the international standing of the establishment, his pariah status ensuring that he'd bring doubt and excessive scrutiny to any project before it had even begun. With ruthless efficiency, Havotech had seen to it that they'd escaped the worst of the whole bubble fiasco by wantonly sacrificing Newton's reputation. Though Newton had played with the idea of taking legal action, it was clear very quickly that Carnatt and his paymasters would have run rings around the out-gunned and weary Dr Barlow.

So Newton had opted to lay low. Bucking the trend of his

collapsing fortunes, at least he'd been lucky over the apartment back in London. It had been rented out when he and Rowena moved to Cambridge and he was able to slip back into the old place with minimal outlay, rather important now that his wife had systematically cleaned out every single account that Newton had his name on. As he languished in London, she'd stayed in Cambridge with Gabriella, buying a picturesque terraced house outright. The divorce had been fast and furious, and Newton, utterly drained in every sense of the word, couldn't muster a defence from financial evisceration in any meaningful sense whatsoever. Contact with his ex-wife was now sparse, Antarctically cold and centred solely on occasional contacts with his daughter, usually timed, Newton suspected, to coincide with Rowena's blossoming social engagements. Visiting her pristine new house, he was invariably confronted by Rowena's decorative girlfriends, a phalanx of haughty disapproving looks greeting him from the kitchen table as he waited awkwardly in the hallway. He'd stand there silently, rebuked en masse, waiting for a reluctant daughter to slouch out to the rapidly degrading Citroën. The classic old French car was the one thing Rowena had not felt the urge to prise off him. Pleased as Newton was to still have any form of transport, no matter how eccentric, it was becoming something of a battle to keep the museum piece on the road.

Income, once of little meaning, became Newton's greatest daily concern. The Barlow family, though never filthy rich upon their academic triumphs, had never been short of a bob or two either, so Newton's experience of edge-of-the-seat economics was patchy to say the least. It took an age before he adjusted to stretching his meagre resources and doing without. Even then he was woefully bad at taking care of himself. For some of his wilderness years he'd resembled a mad wino, rambling bitter mumblings in one of his five languages amidst the empty cans and bottles. He'd bounced back to some extent, but he was still far from on the ball when after years of self-pity he started allowing a few select old pals to know where he was. So when Newton was offered some freelance editorial work for *Living Physics* magazine, he felt obliged to jump weakly forward.

*Living Physics* was on the fringe end of the science rags, and to Newton's mind, always hard-line in such matters, one of the most flaky. The editors had been inclined to run every offbeat theory on the shape of the universe that was offered to them and were therefore seen by the elite, to which Newton once proudly belonged, as more geek than academic. An old friend from college, Denise Garrand, had been its managing editor for years. She took pity on Newton and sought him out, holed up in his Crouch End flat, unshaven and dabbling with a badly written account of his downfall.

'Bloody hell Newton,' she'd exclaimed as he opened the door, his just-out-of-bed eyes and bleary stubble at odds with the 3pm chimes of the nearby clock tower. 'Mind if I come in?' Newton fumbled for a suitable escape line but Denise pushed past him into the darkened flat. 'Ewwww nice,' she muttered as she stepped over the socks, newspaper cuttings and empty supermarket whisky bottles. 'I love what you haven't done with the place.'

'Sorry, bit of a mess,' Newton awkwardly admitted. He tried to kick one of the more offending items behind a chair but it became stuck to his sock, making him shake his foot as if there was a small dog on the end of it.

'Just a bit,' Denise agreed, wincing. 'Come on, look, get yourself buffed up and I'll buy you a coffee.' She went to sit down then very quickly changed her mind. 'Right away though, if you don't mind. I'm not sure I can be in the same room as your last five breakfasts for much longer.'

'No, sorry, right,' Newton said apologetically, and he backed away towards the bedroom wondering if he had any clothes that were stain-free and less than catastrophically creased. 'I'll be right back.'

'It's good to see you Newton,' said Denise over a cappuccino a little later. 'I've been wondering how you've been.' She tilted her head to one side leaving a yawning gap in the conversation for Newton to fill. 'So ... how have you been?'

'Oh you know,' he answered, knowing full well that she probably didn't know the half of it but could probably guess the rest.

'That good eh?' she said, causing Newton to shrug in a lame attempt to appear positive. 'Well ... it's high time you pulled yourself out of this thing,' said Denise, narrowing her eyes. She had always been a good friend. Newton couldn't deny it was nice to see her.

'I don't want to be ... like this,' he said, staring at his spoon as he aimlessly spun the froth. 'I guess I'm a bit ...'

'Yes, you are,' Denise interjected, without waiting for a full verdict. 'Look Newton, I know what happened isn't fair, lots of us thought it was awful, really bad, but it's in the past now.'

'She left me you know,' Newton muttered. 'Fancy a proper drink?'

'No,' said Denise, pushing his coffee back towards him. 'Yes I know. It's terribly unfair. But Newton, you have to move on.' She sat back and looked hard at him for a second. 'Are you working?'

'Working ... er ...,' he shuffled uncomfortably. 'Well I am playing with the idea of writing a book actually.' Denise sighed.

'It wouldn't be about you and Havotech by any chance, would it?'

'Yes it would,' replied Newton enthusiastically before he realised that Denise was several steps ahead of him. 'I suppose you think that's a bit obsessive?'

'Yup. Also it's pointless because you won't finish it, futile because it wouldn't get published and useless because even if it did, you'd be sued into atoms.'

'You've got a point there,' Newton sighed. Denise's point-blank observations echoed the lingering feeling of ennui that had niggled him since he first had the book idea. He sagged. 'Well what the hell am I meant to do though, really?' His frustrated finger flicked a sachet of brown sugar across the table and down the back of a radiator. 'I can't sit here and just take it!'

'Well that's exactly what you *have* been doing, isn't it? Stuck up there in less than glorious isolation letting the whole thing eat you up.'

'True,' said Newton flatly, admitting defeat. 'I'm tired Denise. Look, I've no idea what to do next, absolutely no idea.' He dropped his head into his folded arms and let out a long weary sigh.

'Well in that case Newton, if you can't do something for yourself, then you can do something for me.' Denise nudged him and his head gradually rose back to the horizontal.

'And what would that be then?' he huffed.

'We need writers, how about it?' She let the offer hang in the air. Newton winced awkwardly.

'*Living Physics*? Me? Is that really a good idea?'

'Yes you,' Denise said. 'And if you're worried about your "dark" reputation then you don't need to be, we can fix you up with a pen name.'

'Oh I don't know Denise, look I'm grateful and everything, really, but I don't know. I'm a bit out of the loop.' He dodged her eyes and shrugged again, rubbing his stubble and gritting his teeth to transmit his lack of motivation.

'Don't be silly, bright young man like you. You know the subjects back to front and upside down. Are you going to just sit there and rot, or are you going to stand up and get your life going again?' She looked him steadily in the eye as he tried to disappear into his jacket. 'There's some money in it, you know ... wonga.'

'Well I could certainly use a bit of cash,' admitted Newton. He sighed again and let his gaze drift through the window. 'Oh what a bloody mess. I was far too cocky,' Newton reflected. 'I should have listened to Alex Sixsmith – if anyone predicted all this then it was him.'

'Alex Sixsmith?' asked Denise. 'Oh yes, he worked with your father didn't he?'

'That's the one, a family friend really, used to look out for me.' He sat silent for a second, regret washing over him like steam. 'I owe him a visit really, say I'm sorry.'

'Well you'd better hurry up then,' she said. 'I heard he's very ill, terminal I think.' Newton looked stunned for a long second then quickly put on his coat. 'Sorry,' said Denise, 'I thought you'd have known.'

'I'm going to have to go.' There was urgency in his voice and purpose in his step for the first time in years. Denise shouted after him as he ran from the cafe.

'I'll see you on Monday then, yeah?' Newton's affirmative answer merged with the sounds of the buses crawling past the clock tower. Denise pondered the wisdom of her offer for a second and then signalled a waiter for the bill. The young man watched as the frantic figure dashed off to his flat.

'Isn't that that bogus science dude?' he asked.

'That was Dr Newton Barlow,' said Denise, and she paid for the coffees and headed back into town.

\*\*\*\*\*\*

Newton spent most of the afternoon ringing round, furious with himself for his reclusiveness and isolation now that his mentor and friend was shuffling up to the mortal coil. He had always intended to catch up with the old boy, but Newton's colossal pride, savaged and bruised by his downfall and subsequent decline, had prevented him from lifting the receiver. The futility of such misplaced dignity was now apparent and Newton's urgency reflected his desperate longing to see Sixsmith and obtain something akin to absolution.

After prolonged enquiries, he finally located Sixsmith in a hospital in Eastbourne, where he had moved to be close to his sister Jennifer. Newton finally reached her, and she confirmed that Alex was indeed gravely ill, an aggressive cancer having done its worst over the last few months. Newton caught the next train.

The wait for the first visiting hours was interminable. Finally he made his way hesitantly down the corridors of the old hospital. Pausing occasionally either out of nerves or out of remorse, he wasn't sure, he stood awkwardly as the staff and visiting families moved around him. It was almost as if he had to force himself forward. Eventually he rediscovered his locomotion and catching Sixsmith's name on a wipe board, he prepared himself for their first meeting in many years. He was composing himself when he felt a hand on his shoulder. He turned to see a small woman, her lined face looking sadly into his eyes.

'You must be Newton,' she said gently and with composure. He caught his breath.

'Yes, yes I am. You must be Alex's sister,' he replied, tripping awkwardly on the words.

'Yes dear,' she continued, 'but I'm so very sorry, you've arrived a bit too late. Alex passed away about an hour ago.' She smiled sweetly. In her frail hands she was holding Sixsmith's half-moon spectacles. 'And he was so looking forward to seeing you again.'

'Oh,' said Newton, winded. 'Ohhh.' He sat down heavily in a wheelchair. For the first time in the long sad saga of his decline and fall, Newton Barlow began to cry.

******

The funeral of Dr Sixsmith back in London a week later was a no-nonsense affair, the non-descript suburban crematorium echoing Alex's lifetime avoidance of pretention and drama. The humanist service was devoid of any of the religious trappings the scientist had found so irritating and pointless. He had wanted to die sure in the knowledge that his existence would be firmly at an end, something he had always declared as a perfectly acceptable state of affairs.

Newton hung back at the service and cremation, keen to avoid any awkward encounters with the gathered luminaries. Alex's sister smiled warmly at Newton, too old and realistic to be emotional at her brother's passing despite the apparent absence of any other family members to offer condolences.

Outside, the rain slanted near horizontal as the early evening arrived and Newton, realising that his car was nearly as close to collapse as he was, began to dread the journey home. True to form, the dear old Citroën refused to start. Newton trudged wearily home on public transport, his mood as black as the evening. Through the rain-streaked windows, he watched the houses slowly passing as the bus fought its way back through rush-hour traffic. Back in his flat, he looked at himself in the bathroom mirror. The sad, wet scarecrow staring back finally got too much and Newton, sick of himself, sick of his problems and sick of his reputation, took out his electric razor, erected the ironing board and put on a wash. He took his old leather jacket out of the wardrobe. Dusting off the epaulets, he decided that the time had come to pull himself together.

******

The Monday morning editorial meeting at *Living Physics* was a quiet affair, less *Washington Post* and more parish magazine. Its somewhat fringe status ensured that its editors and writers were quirky, cynical or resigned. They were keeping Newton at a certain distance, well aware of his recent past and complex status. Newton, still deeply pragmatic at heart, struggled with the whacky stories and geeky takes on his beloved physics and struggled even harder to prevent himself from snorting cynically at the stories under discussion. So he was soon put in his place in no short order by the hacks and enthusiasts around the table, none too keen to be cross-questioned or belittled by the new arrival. He made an easy target, of course, and stung for hours after each meeting.

In time, though, he settled down to the extent that he started to lose himself in the fluffy stories and forget his old zealotry. He began to enjoy representing himself with a pen name, the lofty sounding 'Kenton Sussex', and even started to receive a trickle of mail from his audience, some complimentary, some critical and a large proportion utterly and bafflingly weird: men who could communicate with other worlds via talking squirrels, an Aztec spaceman living quietly in Barnes and a charming lady from Leyton Buzzard who sent Newton small framed pictures of her buttocks.

Inevitably, his return to his old style meant that he was starting to get recognised again, but the old horrors seemed remote enough that it was a price worth paying. Gradually he was getting back some semblance of self-respect, and Denise, who'd done so much to resurrect her old friend, decided that the time was right to bring up the thorny subject of dating.

'Oh hell, I don't know Denise, I don't know if I'm ready,' he said over a pint after work. 'It's still too soon.'

'Too soon? It's been years Newton, don't be soft.' With characteristic ease, she'd put Newton on the back foot once again.

'What do you suggest then? I take it you have a long list of frustrated thirty-somethings up your sleeve?'

'What my lot?' Denise replied laughing. 'You've got to be kidding, they're bonkers, all of them. Besides you're hardly what they'd have in mind either, much too complicated. They don't mind being complex and insane themselves, they just don't want to see any of that in anyone else.' She smiled conspiratorially. 'No, I reckon you should do your dating online.' Newton let out another weary sigh. He shook his head slowly and obviously in the hope Denise would drop the subject. She was having none of it. 'Sure, why not? Everyone's doing it now.'

'My point entirely,' said Newton, visualising a seething mass of crazies, fingers twitching above mouse buttons waiting for fresh meat. 'I think I'm happy to just wait until I bump into someone I like.'

'Yeah right, like that's going to happen,' said Denise. 'At least by doing the whole online dating thing you can get to meet someone you genuinely get on with. Someone who shares a lot in common with you.'

'Ah divorced!' Newton snorted.

'No not that,' Denise corrected firmly. 'Although you do need to be realistic – you are in your late thirties, and anyone without baggage at that age has probably never lived.' She looked into Newton's tired eyes, looking to see past his current avalanche of defeatism. 'You don't *really* want to spend the rest of your life on your own do you Newton?' He would have loved to have said yes, but he couldn't. The empty flat and the lack of companionship were wearing very thin. Whether he wanted to admit it or not, he was longing for something – maybe romance, or maybe something more physical. It might have just been having someone around who made him wash his socks before putting them back on again.

'OK,' he sighed. 'What do I have to do?'

\*\*\*\*\*\*

Having signed himself up to Denise's recommended singles site, the tragically named Onehandclapping.com, Newton uploaded a somewhat ageing picture of himself he'd grabbed from a website about scientific scandals. In the absence of anything better to do on a winter's evening, he sat back and waited for a response. It wasn't long in coming. Around 20 minutes later some two hundred prowling singles had scent-marked his personal details, trailing their coats with a wave of 'Hi you', 'Well hello!' or the evergreen 'Are you new here?' Newton wasn't sure how to respond, so he ran out to the supermarket and bought himself a large bottle of Merlot.

When he got back, the nudges, prods and pokes had risen to somewhere in the low thousands. Quickly loosing perspective under the corrosive effect of a litre of red, he tentatively replied to a few of the messages to see what would happen. Back came the responses: a long account of a break-up with an insurance negotiator called Carl; a series of mercifully out-of-focus underwear shots; a list of dirty, cheap hotel rooms in the greater Manchester conurbation (weekdays, 11am to 3pm, no baldies, must be clean). It was a disappointing first encounter but as the night stretched on, he decided to make his own approaches rather than sit there waiting. He began to make better headway. For a start, there were a large number of professional women, probably waking up in a good position at work and a lonely flat at home after years of dedicated and fruitful employment. Doctors, architects, publishing directors ... Newton felt drawn more to these independent women than the initial surge of wallet-watchers and needy frumps who had got their oar in first.

Sometimes, he had moments of vertigo and ran off to read a book or listen to loud boyish music on his iPod. But each time he'd felt compelled to drift back to the keyboard to see if anything new had happened, which of course, most of the time, it had. But he kept his romantic firewall up to its maximum, resisting contacting some of the more managerial faces, who, despite their best efforts, could not look kittenish unless someone had staple-gunned a young Siamese cat to their foreheads.

He wavered back and forth. Too scientific, not scientific enough. Too kind looking, not kindly enough. Lives too close, lives too far away. He finally conked out about three in the morning, too tired even to block yet another approach from Sylvia in Woking who had amassed a valuable collection of Garfield ephemera in her one-bedroom flat and who needed a good seeing-to.

The morning produced a mass of new responses that made Newton inexcusably late for the production meeting.

'Said you'd enjoy it!' Denise teased. 'Any dates yet?'

'God no,' he said. 'There's a lot of nuts out there.' But he was already stuck on the conveyer belt, just as Denise knew he would be.

'Then you should fit in nicely,' Denise laughed. 'Seriously though Newton, don't be so judgemental. They're just people like you, all having their ups and downs. Cut them some slack.'

That evening, he kept her words in mind as he sat, more soberly this time, promising to commit to setting up a few dates to test the water. Keeping a typically scientific approach, he decided to hedge his bets on a spread of types: scientific, not scientific; vampish or down to earth; over and under confident.

At 2am, with several dates arranged, Newton crawled into bed filled with a strange mixture of teenage excitement and adult apprehension.

\*\*\*\*\*\*

Seeing Samantha, Belinda, Jane, Tabby, Jo, Julie and Sarah proved something of an assault course. Samantha was confident, independent, a distinguished biochemist. She was nice at first, but increasingly dismissive as she twigged Newton's circumstances. She was old-school enough, though, to expect him to pay for the moules marinière.

Belinda was pleasant, but she started every sentence with a self-dismissing put-down. Newton's academic credentials made it even worse, so that towards the end of the evening, she seemed compelled to declare that she 'didn't know anything about salt' and despite Newton's heroic efforts to dumb himself down, she'd then burst into tears of self-loathing.

Jane had been all front, ready for a fight from the moment they met outside *Les Miserables*, aggressively deconstructing Newton's suggested venues and culinary choices. Most of the evening felt like an argument so Newton nearly complied when she suggested he went back to her flat, if only to keep the peace. 'I'm not sure it's a good idea,' he'd started saying, but he was cut short by a barrage of expletives as she stormed off into the late evening crowds.

Tabby called herself Tabby because deep down, she wanted to be petted and cosseted, preferably around the clock, by a team of Hugh-Grant-a-likes armed with 'yummy' chocolates. She had endless stories about assorted dirty rotters who had failed to sufficiently pamper the scarf-and-jumper-coated sofa monkey. He introduced physics into the conversation mainly as a last-ditch attempt to stay awake after a mindless thirty-minute sermon on the merits of scented candles. Her destiny seemed to be to make more room for herself, a twenty-year plan of 'me time' that was set to last until presumably a future husband drowned her in her own essential oils.

Jo was a vamp, no question about it. She shimmered in her Superdrug splendour beneath the flickering lamps of the Steakhouse, her harsh trilling voice competing with the back-catalogue of boy-band masterpieces dribbling out of the cheap speakers. It seemed that Jo was wishing to better herself by dating upwards. She'd had enough of kickboxers, nightclub owners and time-share salesmen, and she wanted something else. By the end of the evening it was obvious to both of them that it wasn't Newton. She kissed him goodbye, giving him a complimentary sheen of cheap glitter, and he went home on the train convinced he must look like Brian Eno back in his Roxy Music days.

Julie was certainly vulnerable. Ten minutes of date, a short abridged tale of perpetual abuse and mental illness, and then a sudden tearful exit that left Newton feeling userous and clumsy, a guilt that seemed to hang around for days although he'd not in any way acted in anything but good faith. He awkwardly tried to contact her by email afterwards but after no replies he thought better of the whole issue and left it.

So that left Sarah. Sarah got Newton spectacularly drunk before they'd even got through the basics and he, dropping his guard in favour of Sarah's finger-clicking drink orders, lost all track of himself. He woke up next day in distant Harrow with an award-winning headache and no underpants. She was quite nice about it, but as Newton was urged out onto the street outside, he almost felt remiss that he had not signed a visitors book.

It was not exactly a good first run. Newton was determined to end the whole process there and then, but on his return to his computer he found he had a message from an altogether different kind of respondent.

'It's a right load of cobblers all this online dating don't you reckon,' it said. 'I think I'm going to throw it in … it's driving me banjo.' It was signed by one Viv1234.

The cynicism was refreshing. After weeks of raking his way past old wedding pictures, GSOHs and a vast army of women who liked to swim with turtles, Newton was taken aback by the change in tone. He replied there and then. 'You're not kidding, I got nagged into it by a friend.'

Viv1234 came back instantly, clearly idling away on her PC somewhere in the suburbs. 'Oh that old chestnut,' came the reply, 'we all say that!' Newton smarted strangely, the simple digital message cutting through his desire to portray a measured aloofness. 'No really,' he pinged back.

'Well me, I was getting a bit bored of my own company, to be honest,' Viv1234 went on regardless. 'But I'm not sure that I prefer the inmates of the medieval jail I've been out with. You need to be accommodating, sure … but bloody hell! One guy smelt like a flood-damaged charity shop, another ate cockles with his mouth open and one got thrown out of the pub for vandalising a condom machine. And those were the good ones.'

'I thought it was just me,' replied Newton

'What? Who vandalises condom machines?' pinged Viv1234 with commendable speed.

'No, I mean the lousy dates. Mine have been a bit of a washout too.'

'The important thing, the really vital thing,' Viv1234 announced grandly.

'Yes?'

'Is never, ever to sleep with them.'

Newton's lack of a quick answer soon drew her attention. 'Oh no, you didn't!'

'I'm afraid I did,' he typed, not really feeling the need to hide anything from so tenuous a contact.

'Yup me too. Bloody awful,' she quickly replied. 'Woke up with his mother bringing us breakfast in bed.' Newton nearly spat out his wine.

'You're kidding me? Really?'

'Yup ... Quite nice as it happens, sausage was undercooked, but then that was hardly her fault.'

'Bloody hell Viv1234, that's mad – has he stayed in touch?'

'Nope, his mum sent a nice text though. I think she hoped we'd get married.'

'You are funny Viv1234,' Newton pinged.

'Please, call me 1234,' she replied quickly. 'So what do I call you then, Darwin456?'

'Call me Kenton,' Newton replied.

'Pity, I'd rather call you by your real name.'

'That is my real name,' he persisted.

'No it isn't, Newton,' she replied after a short delay. Alarmed, Newton opened an almost empty bottle of Budgen's own-brand vodka.

'???????' he typed, trying to buy some time to think.

'It's not rocket science,' she typed back. 'I recognised your photo because I used to watch your shows, I was a bit of a fan.'

'I'm surprised you want to talk to me now then. I'm persona-non-grata these days.' He decided to air the issue quickly, to see if she'd back off.

'Oh that, that was nonsense wasn't it? I didn't take that seriously at all.'

'You didn't ...' replied Newton, somewhat relieved by the tone.

'Nah, that's big business for you. Happens all the time.'

'It does?' Newton asked doubtfully.

'Well no, probably not, but who cares?'

'That makes a change, most people would prefer to avoid me I think, soiled goods and all that.'

'Really? That's a bit harsh. Pity, you were good on TV. Do you still look like that?'

'Like what,' Newton asked.

'You know, that kind of Jeff Goldblum Jurassic Park thing, Buddy Holly meets Harold Pinter.'

'Is that what I looked like? Wow, that's a bit worrying,'

Newton typed.

'Why?' asked Viv1234.

'Because I've just started dressing like that again,' Newton replied.

'Cool,' said Viv1234 both in type and out loud. 'Wanna meet up?'

\*\*\*\*\*\*

Newton Barlow and Viv1234 met up on London's Southbank on a crisp and bright Saturday, bitterly cold, the sun unable to warm much beyond their faces. She turned out to be a pleasantly down-to-earth woman in her late thirties, independent of spirit, but in no way territorial about her private thoughts or feelings. Her instinctive honesty and casual good looks charmed Newton enormously. She was certainly no clothes horse like his ex-wife. She was clearly more at home in jeans and jumpers, and her hair was more casual than couture. She had a buoyant air that Newton felt instantly drawn to and her relaxed informality came over like a breath of fresh air.

'I've had the usual round of chaps coming and going,' she explained over a large glass of red. 'But I think I've got a really low threshold for all the game playing and complexities that people insist on bringing with them. I wouldn't say I'm difficult myself at all, just can't deal with those who are.'

'You live alone then?' asked Newton.

'Yeah, afraid so. Not a thing I thought would happen really, but it's not something I'd exchange for a life of endless stress ending in a pointless messy divorce.'

'Amen to that.' Newton raised his glass and Viv smiled kindly.

'I get the impression you had the whole world fall on you after that bubble thing,' she said. A sensitivity in her voice let Newton relax and he found himself comfortable enough to be truthful.

'Yes, it's been pretty ghastly. To be honest, the broken marriage bothers me less than the fact I let myself get caught out so badly. I should have seen it coming and put a stop to it. Too late now, but I was a fool.'

'Oh don't beat yourself up, I can see why it happened. Some things just have a way of unravelling all by themselves.'

'It really doesn't bother you that I'm such an instantly recognisable walking talking cock-up then?' asked Newton, keen to test her tolerance to destruction.

'Nah, I'm not judgemental about stuff like that. I like you, and I think I can trust you, you sound like a friend to me.'

'Just a friend then?' Newton asked, worried that he'd already lost his chance to take things further.

'First date Newton, first date. Got to be a good girl or I can never look my mother in the eye again.' She smiled sweetly but firmly.

'Ah OK, gotcha,' said Newton, laughing and blushing in equal measure. 'What do you do for a living then Viv?'

'Not much is the answer at the moment. I've been in and out of publishing, did a lot of picture research for a while, used to quite enjoy that. But right now, I'm temping half-heartedly till I get my act together and decide what I want to do next. I'm up for anything most of the time, though I get bored easily.' Viv smiled, shrugged and quaffed the wine.

Newton and Viv spent a gentle happy day by the river, jolly but not drunk by the time the sun started to dip down below the skyline. Unsure what to do, Newton hesitated as they finally neared the station.

'It's been a lot of fun Viv,' he found himself saying.

'Yeah, me too,' she replied, giving Newton one of the most honest smiles he'd ever seen. 'Tell you what, give me a kiss and go away?'

'Go away?' Newton asked, puzzled. 'What? Er why?'

'Just do as I say.' She winked conspiratorially. 'Go on.'

'OK, er ... here goes then.' He lent forward and kissed her gently and deliberately on the cheek. As he reluctantly drew back she smiled again. 'Bye then,' Newton said as he turned, somewhat confused, and walked away.

'Newton ... Hey Newton,' Viv called after him, then beckoned to him to come back to her at the second-hand bookstands.

'Sorry, Viv, I'm confused ... what's happening?' Viv brushed back her hair, put her arms around him and gave him a long passionate kiss. As the moment washed over him, Newton felt a sense of calm smother him like warm foam. Months of tension and ennui floated away. She pulled back just enough to look him directly in his widened soppy eyes. She had looked attractive to Newton before, but now, frankly, she looked irresistible.

'This, Newton, is our second date.'

CHAPTER 10

# SENSITIVE DEVELOPMENT

The morning mists had cleared from the surrounding scrubland as Ascot McCauley's black Land Rover Discovery entered Langton Hadlow. Ominously, it circled the square twice before finally pulling up next to the war memorial. In the last occupied homes there was a fearful twitching in the net curtains.

After a small delay, the car door swung open. Ascot McCauley stepped purposefully out onto the flagstones, a light breeze flicking his foppish locks as he scented the air like a hungry hyena. Casting his beady black eyes around the village square, he smiled with satisfaction; it was very near the ghost town he had intended it to be, the chipboard panels rendering the once-lively village centre blind and dead. His dark gaze followed the many empty properties around the square until finally, it settled upon the mess of protest signs and graffiti outside a solitary cottage. Ascot narrowed his eyes. Fresh signs insulted his lineage, his business acumen and his sense of fair play in badly spelt black letters, and his trimmed eyebrow twitched by way of reply. From an upstairs window, a shadowy ball of hatred stared back defiantly and Ascot, relishing the conflict, sneered with a Billy Idol lip curl to reveal several small snow-white teeth. Waving his hand dismissively towards the protest, he turned and sniffed the air again, then shifted his attention back to the war memorial. Gazing up at the slab of trapezoid metal, he flared his nostrils, sensing. On his right hand, the long thin fingers danced with each other as if rolling particles of sand, his gold signet ring catching the winter sunlight in dull flashes. He walked up to the plinth and climbed. McCauley's eyes focused somewhere in the middle distance as he cautiously extended his thin bony hand and touched the cold metal, gently, with a single exploratory finger tip. As if shocked, stunned or on the verge of a climax, Ascot's eyes closed like electric garage doors. He took a sharp, deep intake of breath, which he held for a long second before letting it go in a jet of condensation. Something akin to ecstasy flitted across his sharp features. As if he were using his hands to seduce a sexually frustrated duchess, he then placed all five fingers

86

onto the tank and confident he was unobserved, he rubbed it furtively in a lingering caress. Then another breath, this one sharper and more sensual. His eyes rolled upwards in their sockets as the eyelids flickered orgasmically.

A flash of images poured through the developer's mind. A tumble of savage disjointed snapshots: barbed wire, clouds of rolling choking green mist, wicked machine-guns whipping into never-ending lines of figures struggling hopelessly through seas of cloying, hideous mud. Then, above the cacophony, the jarring crash of the artillery, bursting amongst the rounded shoulders of screaming terrified men, the blasts creeping nearer, nearer, ever nearer until ...

'And just what the bloody hell do you think you're doing?' said a voice from inside the tank. Ascot wheeled around guiltily, like a pervert caught at a widow's clothesline. After spinning on the spot to find the source of the interruption, Ascot's eyes fell upon a small opening in the metalwork through which an eyeball and a wild eyebrow were staring straight back at him.

'Who's there?' he hissed back defiantly. 'What are you doing in there? Isn't this meant to be a monument?'

'It's a *living* monument,' came the clipped ex-military tones, which were followed by a series of clangs and bangs as the man inside put down his monkey wrench and fumbled for the exit. Still mildly away with his visions, Ascot quickly composed himself, pulling his cuffs out from beneath his blazer and straightening his tie as the mechanic stepped out onto the plinth, his oily blue overalls instantly at odds with Ascot McCauley's market-town chic. He wiped his hands on a rag.

'I'm Mr McCauley,' began Ascot haughtily, more of a boast than an introduction.

'I know who you are,' said the mechanic coldly. 'Come in search of more carrion have you?'

'Carrion? I'm not a vulture Mr ...'

'Brigadier,' corrected the mechanic, 'Brigadier Gerald Baldwin, 5th RTR.'

'RTR?'

'Royal Tank Regiment, British Army. Though probably you'll know me better as one third of Langton Motors.'

'Ah yes,' said Ascot, looking towards the distant ramshackle garage. 'The petrol station. A charming throwback, quite old school. How on earth do you make any money?'

'Yes, a good question,' said the Brigadier, his eyes narrowed, 'considering you've driven out 99 per cent of our customers.'

'Driven out?' said Ascot, feigning hurt. 'Oh but it's nothing personal Brigadier, I assure you. Just market forces. I'm quite certain they've all gone to better places. Anyway, you can hardly blame us for providing them with such keen incentives.'

'Incentives? We both know your idea of incentives McCauley. You drove these people mad with noise, irritation and veiled threats. You ought to be ashamed of yourself. You insensitive cock.'

'Insensitive?' asked Ascot, as he ran his hand back along the camouflaged metal and closed his eyes, smiling knowingly to himself. 'You have no idea just *how* sensitive I can really be.'

The mechanic eyed Ascot with distaste as the developer took another sharp, near-orgasmic breath and rolled his eyes upward. 'You're a creepy bastard McCauley, you do know that, don't you.'

Ascot reluctantly drew his hand away and brushed past the mechanic along the plinth before dropping like an upper-class ninja to the pavement below. 'You have my most recent letter Mr Baldwin?'

'Not selling.'

'Ah. You require more inducements?'

'Not selling.'

'A pity. Just you, the museum and the village idiot in the fortress opposite,' said Ascot, sneering. 'Such a pity. Of course, you'll have to sell in time, trust me. Such a lovely village, a shame you feel compelled to hold back its future.'

'It had a future once, you took it. And anyway, a village like this is not just the buildings, you soulless parasite. It is defined by who lives in it. I don't expect you to understand.'

'Well that's convenient Brigadier, because I don't, and I won't. We shall just have to agree to differ,' said Ascot, looking back up at the tank. 'A wonderful machine – brutal, simplistic and utterly savage. It has seen so much pain and suffering. How much would you like for it?'

'Go away.'

'As you wish, Brigadier, as you wish.' Ascot turned and strolled nonchalantly away as if he owned the whole place, which of course with the exception of The Tugger's Arms, the museum, Langton Motors and the strongpoint opposite, he did. Behind him a stream

THE UNHAPPY MEDIUM

of military oaths caught the breeze and floated towards the ruins
of the castle, rearing up above the morning mist like broken false
teeth. Ignoring the insults, Ascot smiled a sleazy smile to himself
and crossed the square. He turned the corner into the street towards
the museum.

On full alert, the tattered remains of the village network had
warned the old curator of Ascot's arrival and he was more than
prepared for whatever the property developer could throw at him.
He sat impassive in reception, his dancing fingers the sole outside
manifestation of his deep agitation.

The old bell rattled as the door swung open, revealing Ascot
McCauley in thin silhouette against the weak winter sunlight. He
entered, motes of dust and stray cobwebs falling gently around him.

'Admission is 50 pence,' said the curator curtly.

'Fifty pence!' said Ascot disdainfully. 'Oh I shall have to dig deep
for that!'

'It's not about money,' said the curator defensively.

'Good job it isn't,' said Ascot cackling. 'A bloody good job
it isn't.'

'What do you want,' said the curator, sharply handing Ascot a
doctored bus ticket.

'I've come to see the museum.'

'No you haven't McCauley,' said the curator, peering over his
glasses. 'I'm not an idiot. I presume this is yet another attempt to buy
me out?'

'Buy ... you ... out?' said Ascot, slowly and deliberately. 'You make
it sound like a bad thing.'

'It is. I'm not selling.'

'Not *now* maybe, but you will.'

'Not now and not ever. You will never get this building. Never.'

'The building? Oh dear me, you don't understand, do you? It's not
just the building I'm interested in. That would be toooo simple. Too
dull by half.'

'Then what *do* you want?'

Ascot waved his hand theatrically up the stairs past the Zulu
shields and the moth-eaten battle standards. 'Why all this of course.
The relics ...'

'*Relics*? What do you mean relics?'

'Did I say relics, I'm so sorry, I meant ... exhibits.'

89

'Don't waste your time, this is a collection. It can't be broken up.'

'Who said it would be broken up? I'm going to have it all.'

'It's for public display, for the education and enlightenment of the masses.'

Ascot snorted.

'Ha! And just how many of the masses have you had in this week then? Shall I check the visitors book?' He leant forward and jabbed his sharp index finger onto the paper before the curator could slam the ledger shut. 'Well look at that!' mocked Ascot. 'The masses you've been enlightening can be summed up thus: one entry from four months ago. Oh the British Museum would be just blown away with footfall like that.'

'I'm here when they need me. I'm a public service.'

'Oh are you? Are you really?' laughed Ascot. 'It's a pity none of them needs you then isn't it? Oh go on, sell it to me! With the money I give you, you could visit a real museum.'

'How dare you, this *is* a real museum.'

'Is it buggery. I doubt you even know what you have in here you old fool. This for instance ... this spear.' Ascot put his hand out to a primitive feather lance, its tip holding a rusted oval point. The long fingers closed around the shaft with a vile relish. His eyes closed and he inhaled again, sensuously.

'This weapon ...' He spoke the words as part of a long-drawn-out sigh. 'This weapon has killed many men, many of them white men in fact. Missionaries. Some of them were begging quite pitifully by the end.'

'What are you talking about?' blurted the curator. 'Stop touching the exhibits.'

'Why? Isn't it a hands-on exhibition?' snorted Ascot, and with indifference to the curator's protests, he reached out to rub an old life preserver, the name SS Gurdon written in faded letters around the loop. 'Ahhhhhhhhhh, nice,' said Ascot, his eyes closing once again as if he were savouring a fine wine. 'This witnessed a few nasty little moments I can tell you. Oh yes, I can see it all quite clearly: the Irish Sea, a dark November night, the ship floundering in a force twelve. The storms broke her back in the end and when they all ended up in the freezing black water there was only one survivor. Pity he didn't tell anyone he'd grabbed this life ring from a woman and child. And why would he? Dreadful. His own wife and child I think, judging by the guilt,' said Ascot, adding the last detail matter of factly as if it were of little importance.

'You don't know that ... you can't know that,' said the curator, somewhat rattled.

'Oh you'd be surprised what you can pick up along the way,' said Ascot, rummaging through the exhibits. 'Oh these knives ... These are particularly nice, I've got a real *feel* for blades you know.'

'You're mad.'

'Mad? Maybe,' Ascot answered nonchalantly, 'but successfully mad, and that's the important thing. Money is so wonderful, don't you think? When you have money, well, there's nothing you can't have ... eventually.'

'Well you can't have this museum,' snapped the curator angrily.

'I admire your defiance. I really do. But you see, I'm also very, very patient,' said Ascot, as he turned back with a pantomime villain's grin spreading across his chops. However, before he could fully elaborate on his many vile attributes, he abruptly stopped.

His dark senses tingling, there was something on the edge of his awareness asking for his attention. It was somewhat stronger than the background grimness drifting off the main exhibits and he raised himself up upon his toes like a meerkat, feeling for the vibrations.

'What is *that*?'

'What is what?'

'There's something here ... something unusual, I can sense it!' Ascot's head rotated close to 360 degrees and then spun back elastically, the nostrils shotgun wide.

'Sense it? What are you talking about?'

Ascot sniffed the air again, eyes closed and his body swaying gently like a cobra. Like a compass, he gradually rotated on his brogues until he pointed towards the far room where until recently, the carved figure had sat malevolently in its case. 'There's something here – I can't quite fix it.'

'The museum is closing now,' said the curator, impatiently cutting Ascot short in mid flow.

'Closing ... what?' said Ascot, angrily snapping out of his fixation. 'But it's only 10.30!'

'Staff holiday. I'm going to have to ask you to leave.' The curator slammed the visitors book shut and a storm of dust exploded towards

Ascot through the weak light.

'How dare you!' barked Ascot, coughing. 'I've paid to see this museum! I demand to see it! I could get you for consumer rights violations!'

'Take it up with head office,' said the curator. 'Off you go.'

'But I haven't had a chance to talk business with you!'

'Well we've both saved time then, haven't we? I was going to say no anyway. Goodbye.'

For emphasis, the curator fished out a caribou jaw from under the counter, where it had been kept for emergencies. He let it fall repeatedly into his hand like a cosh.

Ascot sighed wearily. 'OK I'm going, I'm going.' He jangled noisily back through the old door into the street. Turning, he saw the 'closed' sign slam hard against the glass. He walked back to his car where the Brigadier was still banging away on the tank with his tools.

'Don't know what you're smiling about,' he shouted down at Ascot. 'I'm sure he told you to sling yer hook.'

'He did,' said Ascot smugly. 'It was no more than I expected though. He'll come round eventually.' He waved his thin hand arrogantly around the empty square. 'They all do ... in the end.'

He was still gesturing to the dead village when he was hit by an egg, thrown with commendable accuracy from the barricaded cottage opposite. It smashed messily upon Ascot McCauley's navy blue blazer in a spectacular explosion of yolk and albumen. Infuriated, Ascot pulled at the mess, strings of shiny glob stretching like webs from his fingers to his lapels.

'Not all of them McCauley,' said the Brigadier. 'Not all of them.'

## CHAPTER 11

# GHOST WALKING

The past few weeks with Viv had been a long-overdue departure from the omnipresent horrors of Newton's troublesome past, and already he was feeling the benefits. They had spent wonderfully daft afternoons in bed talking the world to rights, planning over-complicated driving holidays costing way more money than either of them possessed and, when they weren't stark naked, they had haunted the bars and restaurants of Greenwich where Viv had a modest but pleasant enough little flat.

In his newfound bliss, Newton had to fight hard not to neglect work or his residual parenting duties with his daughter. Gabby was every inch the sulky teen, dabbling endlessly with ever-darker clothing and engaging in a running battle with the outside world, the frontline being her reluctant interaction with her estranged parents. Newton's ex-wife loathed Gabby's blossoming Gothic fantasies and sniped endlessly at her poor daughter with barbed digs about femininity. So Gabby lurked like her own shadow up in her blacked-out room, only venturing forth to eat. What soulmates she had were kept firmly out of view as she increasingly revelled in being an outsider, a loner or a tragic heroine.

Gabby hadn't inherited her father's attitudes. Instead, she sank herself in a world of Gothic novels and dark dreary music. On the black walls of her bedroom, a rogues' gallery of sunken-cheeked teenage vampires brooded and smoked with dead-eyed sexuality. Her modest IKEA shelves began to amass a small library of books featuring the supernatural, the paranormal and the plain weird; deep into the night she soaked up tales of wraiths, tarot and death.

It was the only thing that seemed to make her happy.

Rowena had ripped spectacularly into Newton on the phone when, due to an unaccustomed state of relaxation, he overlooked his monthly visit to Gabby. His ex-wife's voice was so loud and sharp that Viv heard the shrill barking even as she was showering.

'What a bitch,' gasped Viv as she dried her hair. 'What are you going to do?'

'I'd probably best get going,' said Newton, dressing. His recent euphoria had been swiped off him like chalk on a blackboard. Viv turned off the dryer and put her arms sympathetically around him.

'See you soon, yeah?'

'Ooooh yes,' said Newton with feeling. 'Try and stop me.' He kissed her gently on her forehead.

\*\*\*\*\*\*

For once, the Citroën was behaving, content with mere grating noises and a trail of oily smoke on the motorway. In a record-breaking three hours, Newton was pulling gingerly up at Rowena's Cambridge town house. The slab-like Chelsea tractors parked haphazardly up and down the street were a sure sign that Rowena's coven was gathered on site. Plucking up courage, Newton rang the bell.

'What time do you call this?' hissed Rowena.

'I'm sorry,' he grovelled, flattened under the weight of six cold shoulders as he entered the kitchen. The air was heavy with a cocktail of Estée Lauder, Chanel and loathing. 'I'm really sorry.' Rowena looked Newton dismissively in the eye for a long, long moment. Her nostrils flaring in disgust, she called upstairs for their daughter.

'Gabriella dear ... your ... father has arrived, finally.' She snarled the last word in his face and there was a bubble of tsks from the kitchen table. Eventually, and with every muscle of her black velvet body oozing reluctance, Gabby stumbled blinking down the stairs from the darkness of her bedroom.

'Hi Gabby,' said Newton, sheepishly.

'Snorf,' mumbled Gabby from under her white foundation, as she flounced melodramatically through the door.

'Back lunchtime tomorrow Newton, I mean it,' Rowena warned, playing to her tribe in the kitchen.

'Yup, lunchtime ... for sure,' said Newton. As he turned to go, he awkwardly waved and smiled at the ladies and immediately the temperature dropped even further. He was hustled outside onto the street to where Gabby, her face like thunder, slouched against the Citroën.

'Can we go now?' she huffed.

With Rowena's eyes burning neat laser-like holes in his back, Newton inched the car slowly down the street and away towards

London, his sullen daughter folded up like a deckchair in the passenger seat.

'Sorry Gabby,' he offered, 'I'm a bit distracted at the moment.'

'Whatever,' came the predictable reply.

\*\*\*\*\*\*

'What would you like to do then?' Newton said, after twenty minutes of teenage silence.

'Dunno,' Gabby replied, pulling her hood up.

'You can do anything you want. Well, within reason,' he said. Sensing her father's eagerness to please, Gabby thought hard for a second and cautiously lowered her hoodie.

'What? Literally anything?'

'Er ... yes, I guess.'

'OK ... I'll have a think then,' said Gabby, and she plonked her Dr Marten boots up on the dashboard.

As they drove along the leafy roads leading to Crouch End, Gabby suddenly exploded with a burst of enthusiasm.

'Got it!' she shouted sitting upright, animated in a way her father hadn't witnessed since she'd been five or six.

'What ... what!' he answered as he checked all the mirrors. 'Got what?'

'What we're going to do while I'm here!'

'Err ... yes?' asked Newton, sensing it was likely to be painful, expensive or humiliating.

'A ghost walk,' said Gabby, 'I want to go on a ghost walk.'

'Oh terrific,' sighed Newton, realising it would be all three.

\*\*\*\*\*\*

For Dr Newton Barlow, one-time scourge of all things irrational, there were some things he simply couldn't be seen to do. But times had changed. With his reputation first eviscerated and then widely forgotten, he faced the stark realisation that there were few enemies, if any, still interested in him enough to point the finger, should he be caught in the wrong place at the wrong time. It comforted and smarted in equal measures. Keen to build bridges with his sulking Gothic daughter, he acquiesced. So that evening they found themselves in the heart of old London, waiting patiently outside a pub for a guide.

In a city with as much grisly backlog as London, it's not hard to weave a theatrical yarn or two for the benefit of paying tourists. After all, London has always produced more history than it could locally consume. Its plagues, riots, wars and disasters give it a million stories, most of them horrific and messy to clean up afterwards. Ghost walks tap into this dark underbelly, and as you wind your way between London's haphazard mix of the old and the new, you can spook yourself up and either enjoy yourself before finishing up in a pub or scare yourself so much you need to return to your hotel urgently for clean underwear.

Newton didn't object to the theatre of these walks, but he couldn't ignore what he felt to be their utter failure of logic. Gabby, knowing this about her father, felt the need to state the rules of the evening from the outset.

'Look Dad,' she hissed through her clenched teeth as they waited for the guide. 'I hope you're not going to spoil this.'

'I promise I'll enter into the spirit of things, no pun intended.'

'I don't care whether you intend a pun or not,' sneered Gabby. 'Why can't you just drop all that science stuff and have fun for once?'

Newton winced, recognising the faint echoes of some of his wife's criticisms.

'Sorry, look, OK, I promise,' he said, holding up his palms. 'I'll be good, let's have fun. I promise, really.'

'Really?'

'Yes really, honest. Cross my heart.'

'No sarcasm? No analysis?' She narrowed her eyes and the threat of an award-winning sulk hovered above Newton like a kestrel.

'Yup, really honest.'

But keeping this promise as they followed the guide through the cobbled back streets was never going to be easy. The group, some twelve or so, lapped up the theatrical tales with obvious delight while the guide, almost certainly a major player in amateur dramatics, turned all Shakespearean beneath the streetlights. Despite the cape and top hat, he was no Vincent Price. As Newton endured his fanciful tales of phantoms, ghouls and apparitions, he had to bite ever harder into his already lacerated lip.

'Imagine if you dare!' the guide pronounced with a flourish outside The Two Hands pub in Goiter Street. 'Picture that late night in 1806 when there was a knock on the old pub's door, the very same door you see before you tonight!' The cameras began to flash wildly. 'Picture the landlord, one Frederick H. Hodgkin. He's in his nightshirt and holding a candle, his hand cautiously fumbling with the locks in the flickering light. As the door creaks open, there is a sudden ... sickening ...' He went silent for a badly timed second of suspense. 'CRASH!' With the guide's shout, all the tourists except Newton obediently jumped. Newton merely raised a sceptical eyebrow.

'Yes my friends,' continued the guide, 'an unknown assassin rushes forward with a sharpened knife! He lashes poor Frederick, not once, but twice across the throat, then, with cruel deliberation ... he thrusts the blade deep into the publican's heart!' The crowd around Newton all visibly shivered, a wave of suggestibility washing over them with lamentable ease. Newton rolled his eyes and tutted beneath his breath. 'And yet,' the guide continued, holding up his index finger like a TV lawyer, 'the assailant was not finished. Oh dear me no! He rushed on up the stairs to the rooms at the top. It was there, friends, there in those very rooms, that the landlord's wife and daughter lay sleeping. And then ...' He looked up and took a deep and sorry breath for emphasis before blurting out his macabre prose. 'Then, in a frenzy of blood, bone and mangled mucous membranes, he slashed and stabbed the poor women until they lay blood-soaked and still upon their beds.'

'Oh gosh,' whimpered a middle-aged Canadian woman, visibly shaken. Newton looked over at his daughter who seemed to be smiling for the first time that day. She stopped abruptly when she caught her father's eye.

'So who was it that brutally killed these poor innocent people that cold November night?' The guide scrutinised the surrounding faces, hesitating slightly when he met the unconvinced sneer of Dr Barlow. 'We may never know,' he went on. 'But what we do know is that to this very day, these grizzly events still play out in this pub late at night. When the drinkers have gone and the bar falls silent, something stirs. Bar staff tell of cold hands on their shoulders, steps upon the flagstones and creaks on the old staircase. But when they search ... there's no one to be seen!'

'That's original,' said Newton, forgetting his promise. The guide pretended not to hear him and carried on regardless.

'In the night, strange, eerie sounds echo down the narrow stairwell. And no one can sleep in the master bedroom, where the poor wife was ripped and violated by the maniac's savage blade.' The guide was clearly enjoying the sound of his own voice. 'So friends, spare a thought for the soul of the fair daughter. Some said she was a rare beauty. Brutally torn by the madman's flailing assault she was found, still alive ... just ... but unable to talk, her beautiful blue eyes staring, staring ... in horror!' The guide looked with satisfaction around the gathered audience, pleased with himself until he noticed Newton's disdainful expression. He turned back to the more receptive faces. 'She did not last the night. So is it her poor spirit that still lingers in the darkened attic bedroom, weeping quietly, trapped forever on this earth?'

'Oh *puullease*,' muttered Newton, a little too audibly.

'Dad, shut up,' hissed Gabby.

'Sorry, did you have a question?' the guide frostily barked at Newton.

'No, don't mind me, please go on. What happened next?' Newton said, smiling apologetically and sarcastically in equal measure.

'Er, well that was it really,' the guide continued hesitantly.

'Didn't they find the wrongdoer that murdered the poor darlin?' asked a fifty-something from South Carolina.

'No madam, they did not,' flourished the guide with renewed emphasis. 'The beast was never caught. We'll never know why he perpetrated the heinous crime, my friends. The spirits that haunt this very pub have taken their secrets with them to the other side.'

'I thought the ghosts were still here?' said Newton.

'Well yes, yes they are, I just said so.' The guide was looking and sounding annoyed, the lights of the pub catching the greasy frown on his forehead.

'Well has anyone asked them who did it?' said Newton. He felt a small boot pressing down on his right foot.

'Ha my friend, you raise an interesting point. Maybe they should arrange a séance and ask that very question!'

'Hell yes,' replied Newton. 'If this place is as haunted as you're suggesting then surely we can pretty much guarantee a reply. Why don't we help clear up the whole story? I'm guessing you believe in séances?'

'Er yes, quite so. Anyway, if you will be so kind, we'll continue apace with our journey through the spiritual underbelly of London.' And with a little less confidence than he started with, the guide scampered away with his cane held aloft.

'Dad, what is wrong with you?' barked Gabby as they rushed on down the darkened streets behind the guide. 'You said you wouldn't ... you bloody said!'

'Sorry, sorry,' whispered Newton, who was not really sorry at all. In fact, he was starting to enjoy himself.

The small party weaved on through the backstreets. Occasionally, they were in almost total darkness, only the faint glow of distant offices illuminating the ancient, rugged walls of Roman Londinium. These once-impressive barricades were now strangely toy-like beneath the glass and steel of banking headquarters and cranes. At other times, the group would burst out of an alley alongside a bright busy pub where smokers spilled chaotically onto the street, piles of cigarette butts beneath their feet.

'Gather round, please, gather round,' called the guide as they stumbled up to a church. It loomed blitzed and weathered above them, its old walls crowned with gargoyles and scarred by shrapnel. The group edged into the churchyard, the more superstitious desperate to avoid treading on the graves between the headstones around them, the slabs at crazy angles like the teeth of a Somali pirate. 'Before you is the old church of St Barnabas, once one of some 100 parish churches in what was then a much smaller City of London. You will note the many gravestones that have been placed against the wall. Some of these were blown over by German bombs during the blitz, but many were moved at an earlier date. I want you to cast your minds back, if you dare, to this particularly dark time in London's past.'

'Oh, here we go again,' muttered Newton. He was treated to narrowed eyes by a woman in her sixties in a shiny pac-a-mac.

'I refer of course to the Black Death!' the guide declared.

'Oh I've heard of that!' said the Canadian woman, pulling her animal-print fleece tight around her so that the timber wolf on its back became boss-eyed. 'Isn't that a disease?'

'Yes madam, it most certainly is,' confirmed the guide theatrically, and he let the beastly subject congeal in the air for a moment for effect. 'A disease so vile and hideous that it lay waste to this and many other cities!' Imagining himself on the History Channel, he trotted out some patter from a Wikipedia entry he'd learnt nearly off by heart earlier in the season. 'The year is 1348. London is a bustling centre of commerce and the busiest port in Europe. But this year it is more than fine silks and wine that are landed on the city's teeming wharfs, for with the ships come rats, and with those rats come fleas, and with those fleas come ...'

'The *Yersinia pestis* bacterium?' suggested Newton provocatively.

'The what?' said the guide wearily.

'It's the plague bacterium. *Yersinia pestis*,' said Newton smugly.

'Well I er ... I knew that,' bluffed the guide.

'Ignore my dad,' Gabby suddenly announced to the crowd. 'He thinks he's being clever.'

'Yeah,' said a thick-spectacled student from Pasadena, 'what's yer problem dude?'

'Just trying to be helpful,' shrugged Newton, keen to do the opposite. The guide hesitated awkwardly before continuing.

'Well, er ... with the fleas came the ... um ... bacteria ... which we call the plague, or the Black Death. London was prosperous but very, very dirty and its dark narrow streets, devoid of proper sanitation, were alive with filth. Down these streets stalked the pestilence, with no respect for wealth or status, piety or honour – it killed all it encountered.'

'Woaah. No it didn't,' said Newton.

'Yes it did!' replied the guide with indignation. 'It wasn't called the Black Death for nothing!'

'Actually, it was called the Black Death because it covered its victims in nasty black acne. But in fact it only killed 30 to 60 per cent of the population,' said Newton.

'Well, that's pretty bad I'd have said,' the guide retorted, and the group staged a ripple of approval.

'Yes, but you said "everyone" was killed, and that's not factually correct.'

'I don't think you'd like to die of the black plague, young man!' said the Canadian woman.

'It's the Black Death, not the black plague. Anyway, what's this got to do with ghosts – I thought you were going to show us some ghosts?'

'Well they were all buried here, under here!' the guide blurted. He was used to a suggestible audience and warm applause, not some smart-arse undermining his street theatre with pedantic backchat. He began to look hunted.

'So that means there are ghosts here does it?' said Newton, enjoying what was now looking slightly like overkill.

'Yes, lots of them, moaning ghosts.'

'Moaning you say,' replied Newton. 'And just what are they moaning about?'

'Well they were buried alive!' said the guide indignantly.

'I thought they were all dead?' Newton persisted, despite an unspoken wall of disapproval.

'Some were nearly dead, dying ... you know,' the guide blurted. 'They did it to save time!'

'Well even I'd moan about that,' said Newton, unstoppable. 'I'd complain rather strongly. In fact ...'

'Why don't you just shut up?!' Gabby suddenly shouted. Then, in pure frustration, she let out a long, alarming scream which seemed to vibrate the very ground beneath her. Everyone, Newton included, stopped and looked at the young Goth. 'I hate you I hate you! Why do you have to ruin everything!'

'Gabby ...' Newton was cut short as she jumped furiously up and down on the spot, screaming her young lungs out amongst the gravestones, the shrill yelps of frustration echoing off the masonry.

'You think you are sooo smart, well you aint! You're a sad lame old fart!' Her black eyeliner was running freely down her pale cheeks. With one last burst of wild fury, she screamed as if she was going to explode before suddenly turning on her boots and storming away into the night. All eyes turned back to Newton, who awkwardly stood still for a second returning the angry stares.

'Ah! Now I know who you are,' the guide suddenly announced, his memory jogged by the tension. 'Bubbles! Bubbles! You were on TV!'

But Newton was already running after his daughter in a panic. He had visions of Gabby sitting amongst needle-wielding pimps in an alleyway near King's Cross and he ran helter-skelter through the narrow alleyways and courtyards. After a brief but frantic search, he finally caught sight of her in the distance, a blob of black angst on the steps beneath some bland civic sculpture. Cautiously, he walked up and sat down gently beside her, half expecting her to bound away like Spring-heeled Jack.

'Sorry Gabby. I really shouldn't have done that.' He put his hand on her shoulder but she instantly pulled away.

'You're an arsehole.'

'Yup, you're right. I am an arsehole.'

'And you're a dickwad.'

'I'm most certainly one of those,' confessed Newton.

'You said you wouldn't act up! But you did! You're a liar!' Gabby wasn't shouting now but Newton felt every word hit him like pebbles.

'You just don't get it do you! It's not all about you,' Gabby sobbed.

'What is it about?' asked Newton.

'It's about me,' she said softly. 'Well sometimes it is. I hate myself, I want to die.'

'Oh come on Gabby, you can't say that.'

'Yes I can ... I just did, I can say anything I flipping bloody, stinking well want and right now I want to say I want to die.' She hissed the last line through clenched teeth, some spital mixing with the steam on her breath in the cold air.

'Woahhh OK ... fair enough. You want to die.'

'Yes I do.'

'OK,' Newton said. 'A 14-year-old girl wants to die, I can respect that ... I think.'

'Good,' said Gabby, 'because that's what I want.'

They sat in silence for a while, a passing crowd of drunken office workers scrutinising them as they made their way to a nightclub.

'I want to die too sometimes,' Newton said suddenly.

'No you don't,' Gabby snapped back.

'No I do, really, why not? Can't let you young folk have all the fun.'

'Why would you want to kill yourself, you're grown up.'

'Well that's one reason straight off.' Newton sat back and looked up at the orange clouds scudding low above the streetlights. 'Then there's the small matter of what happened with my career, my marriage, oh and hardly ever seeing you these days.'

'You don't care about me, no one does,' Gabby continued, and it made Newton bite his lip briefly with emotion.

'Oh Gabby, I care about you alright. I love you. You're my daughter, of course I love you.' It sounded so like an excuse that Newton regretted it leaving his clumsy mouth. 'If I could see you all the time then I would. Of course I would.'

'I hate living with Mum, she's such a cow.'

'That's not a nice way to talk about your mother Gabby,' said Newton, without conviction.

'Well she's just so lame. She doesn't understand me.'

'I guess she's just busy with her own stuff Gabby,' said Newton. 'Look, I'm sorry about tonight, about everything. I shouldn't have done it ... the poor guy, he didn't deserve that.'

'Why don't you believe in anything?' asked Gabby after they'd sat in silence for a while, as she played with her laces.

'I don't believe in nothing,' said Newton. 'I just don't believe in everything.'

'No one believes in everything,' said Gabby, 'that's just stupid.' Newton, sorry for his earlier evangelism, thought carefully for a second and opted not to persist.

'You must be sick of me.'

'No ... well yes ... Look at all your stuff, all that science. Doesn't it just make the world less interesting? Makes it all boring.'

'Yes I suppose it does really ... sorry,' said Newton.

'Don't just say that, you don't mean it, do you,' she grumped from inside her folded arms. 'Why can't you be more open minded?'

'I am open minded. But my mind is not so open that anything can crawl right in. Or just fall out for that matter. But look, you don't want me to go on any more do you? I'll just make you more annoyed.' Newton seriously wished for once he could finally be allowed to shut up, but his daughter had other ideas.

'Actually Dad I do.'

\*\*\*\*\*\*

They found themselves a pizza house in the heart of old Smithfield Market and as father and daughter waited for a table, Newton wondered just how diplomatic he was capable of being. Used to fighting the supernatural with gratuitous sarcasm and glee, he was thinking hard and fast for an approach that would spare them both an awkward confrontation whilst still holding the line for the age of reason.

'Go on then,' she said as they sat down at the table. 'Prove to me there is no such thing as the supernatural.'

'OK,' said Newton, wondering where on planet earth to start. Mercifully, ordering food gave him time to get his ducks in a thin wavering line and after the waitress left them, he began. 'Well, firstly it's impossible to prove a negative. I can prove this table exists; I can prove you exist, but I have no way of proving there is not a large invisible water buffalo over there by the piano. I can't see it, can't hear it and no one else can see it, but to prove it does not exist is impossible. I can only say with certainty that there is no evidence for it.'

'You say that ghosts don't exist!' said Gabby.

'Well I do, well ... what I say is that there is no evidence for ghosts, therefore the probability is that there are no ghosts.'

'There is evidence,' countered Gabby, 'loads of evidence.'

'What evidence?' said Newton.

'Ghosts have been in history since the year dot! Every culture has ghost stories.'

'Stories are not evidence,' he replied. 'And if you're relying on another person to give you a single, accurate and truthful report about a phenomenon, then you're on a sticky wicket straight away.'

'Why?'

'Because people are unreliable, Gabby. They lie, they get confused, they get scared, hell, they get drunk. People aren't like digital cameras; they can interpret things the wrong way for all sorts of reasons. The brain doesn't always give accurate signals – it can trick you. You can see things, hear things. But people mostly just lie and that probably explains 99.9999 per cent of it.'

'But why lie about a ghost anyway?' said Gabby. 'What can you gain? There's no point to it.'

'There are loads of incentives to lie!' continued Newton. 'You may want to look interesting to your neighbours. You might just want attention from your peers. If Scooby Doo is to be believed, it's nearly always because you're trying to buy the old funfair below the market rate.' Gabby cast him a sarcastic smile. 'And ... it might be because you're fooling yourself and need other people to help build your delusion.' His daughter wrinkled her nose.

'Why would anyone want to do that?'

'Oh lots of reasons,' Newton replied looking for the waitress. 'It might be guilt, like in Macbeth, when he sees his victim's ghost. It could just be a need to have some drama in your life. Boredom.'

'Are you saying that we create all ghosts in our own heads then?'

'Yeah, sure.'

'Well,' Gabby countered, 'how do you explain when a whole bunch of people see the same ghost at the same time?'

'A whole bunch?' said Newton. 'Well, it sounds more convincing, of course, but it's not enough to just have the word of two people, or four people, or even four hundred people. There could be, and probably *is* a reason why they are all mistaken, deluded or lying. No matter how many people see the ghost, or rather say they have, it will mean absolutely nothing unless the phenomena is genuinely recorded, duplicated and tested. That's how all the big discoveries are made and verified. It applied to electricity, magnetism and a host of other observable phenomena – why should the supernatural be any different? It's the absence of any meaningful data that indicates it's a delusion. A delusion at best, mind you, at worst it's just downright fraud. Nope, to call it real, you have to have proof.'

'What could possibly make for proof though? What would it take for you to be convinced?' asked Gabby.

'Well, OK. To really prove something like that, you'd need to have an experiment where, say, three independent viewers with no connection to each other were able to see the same ghostly phenomena from differing positions. If they then gave identical responses, identical descriptions, and you could rule out any optical effect or hoax, then maybe, just maybe, you'd be on to something.'

'OK Dad, but that's not likely though is it, I mean ghosts don't work to order.'

'Well why not? If they are derived from people, then why shouldn't they cooperate like people? If you can have live scientists then why not dead ones, keen to show us what the "other side" is actually like? Why hasn't Einstein popped up at the Royal Society and said – look it's me ... ich bin ein phantasm!'

'Maybe they don't want to be seen; have you thought about that?' said Gabby.

'Of course,' Newton replied, sipping an expensive but poor bottled lager. 'But then you've got to ask why. And you have to ask why they seem happy to show themselves to the owners of hotels, pubs and stately homes with poor balance sheets.'

'Oh you are sooooooo cynical,' announced Gabby, slurping noisily on her coke. 'You think everyone is a liar.'

'Not everyone, maybe, but most.'

'Well, how do you explain that all cultures have ghosts, even way back when they didn't even know about each other?'

'Simple wish fulfilment. It's common to all human beings – we don't like death so we invent concepts to make it more palatable. The big chief dies, the tribe goes downhill and everyone longs for him to be back. So with a bit of self-delusion he *does* come back. It's a scenario that's as likely with an Aztec as it is with a Viking.'

'Hold on, what about nasty scary ghosts then? No one wants them do they? Explain those away.'

'It's just fear,' said Newton, 'stuff you can't explain, places you don't want to go, bad luck. Blame it all on something other than yourselves. Blame it on that bad chief who hit you with bamboo all the time and stole your goats. He's dead ... or has he come back? Deadly gas from a swamp? That will be the dead warriors!' Gabby sat back, folded her arms and pursed her lips for a second, thinking.

'OK then. How do you explain that most ghost sightings seem to follow a pattern?'

'Such as?'

'Walking through walls, moving objects, apparitions sitting on beds.'

'Ah, I'm glad you brought up the walking through walls thing. That's a particular favourite.' He theatrically adjusted himself in his chair and cracked his fingers as if about to start on a plate of langoustines. 'Firstly, traditions make traditions. If one person says they see an apparition walk through a wall and it gets a good response from the locals, well, then it's a tempting metaphor that others want to pick up and run with. Give it five hundred years and it's pretty much obligatory if you want to weave a ghostly yarn. But wait! Let me ask you this, why would a ghost walk through a wall anyway?'

'Because there didn't used to be a wall there,' said Gabby, as if it was obvious.

'OK but then why just the wall, and why not the floor? It doesn't make any sense – if you could walk through walls without feeling any electromagnetic force, you'd be like astronomical dark matter – you'd just fall through the floor. You wouldn't fall through the floor if you didn't have any mass though. In that case, you'd zip around at the speed of light and never hang around long enough to haunt anyone. Simple laws of nature,' Newton said. 'Anyhow, what I find most amazing about ghosts, if they exist, is that there aren't more of them.'

'What do you mean?' Gabby frowned. 'I thought one would have been too many for you.'

'Well think about it, if you go to a hospital, or a battlefield, why

106

are they not just crawling with ghosts? You'd think that in a place as awful and full of suffering as a battlefield or a death camp, you'd be pretty much certain to see the damn things. But you don't, do you? All you get are the romantic wraiths of jilted lovers who've drowned themselves by watermills or famous dead people, celebrity ghosts who turn up conveniently in National Trust properties when crazy people go there to make television programmes.'

'OK, I see your point,' said Gabby. 'But then you're assuming that the afterlife works the same way as here.'

'True,' said Newton. 'And er ... why the hell not?'

'What about electricity, though, or something like that? I mean we saw it and we experienced it since forever in history and stuff, but we couldn't explain it. Maybe it's like that? Just because *you* don't understand something, doesn't mean it's not real.'

'Maybe, but that's what science is all about. You try to explain things you can see. Things you can measure. Electricity and gravity are odd things if you think about it, but we can measure them. Eventually, after a lot of hard graft, we get to explain them, well not entirely, but we get farther and farther down the road. Gravity is still a tad vague actually,' he added, absent-mindedly.

'Well, why not try and explain ghosts then?' said Gabby.

'I'd love to darling, but no experiment has actually demonstrated that there is even a genuine phenomenon in the first place. Not one. Well not a serious one. Plenty of fun stories, sure, but nothing you can measure or quantify in the cold light of day. Or should I say the dead of night?' Newton affected a macabre *Hammer House of Horror* expression, which was returned instantly by Gabby's narrowed eyes.

'Whatever,' said Gabby. 'Oh I know ... what about that stuff they do on TV? Like on that show you used to go on, *Ghost Show.*'

'Oh that bloody thing. Are you thinking of all that so-called scientific gear those guys flash about?'

'Yeah. The stuff that shows temperature drops. What's that thing?'

'A thermometer,' said Newton impassively.

'Yeah that, and then there's the other thing, the magnetism what's-it.'

'EMF meters?' snorted Newton, and Gabby nodded enthusiastically. 'That old chestnut! Electromagnetic fields are just a bit of gobbledygook that impress people who don't know any better.

Why would ghosts create electromagnetic fields that are any different from the radiation a living person emits? They look impressive and seem scientific to a gullible audience, but trust me, they are no more scientific than a tinfoil hat.'

'Well you can't just brush away something like those voice recordings.'

'Oh EVPs, good-old electronic voice phenomena. They're always good for a laugh.' Newton theatrically brushed the comment away with a flick of his hand.

'What's so funny about them?' asked Gabby.

'Well, why are they always so vague? Whenever you have them on these TV shows, there are always subtitles to tell you what to hear and it's nearly always something like 'Get out of here!' or 'Die you whore!' Without the prompt, what you'd actually hear is something more like 'Smoke my grapes'. Or 'Is it time for some more gravel'. People hear what they are told to hear or want to hear; either that or they spend a few more pointless hours back home in their bedrooms, creating silly little hoaxes while mum heats up the TV dinner.'

'Come on,' insisted Gabby, 'that can't explain all of them.'

'Why not? Think about it. If a spirit really wanted to say something of importance, why not really clearly get that message across? You can't shut living people up for God's sake, so why are the dead so bloody reserved? Nah, if they wanted to say something then they would.'

'Maybe they can't?'

'OK. But, why should it be hard? Living human beings go to huge efforts to communicate – we have radio, print, emails, semaphore, smoke signals, gossip, graffiti, post-it notes, whispering, shouting. Why should a dead person, in spirit form, be so content with sending garbled messages via Dictaphones, Ouija boards and mediums?'

'Maybe they aren't allowed to? Maybe it's forbidden,' she said, shrugging.

'Forbidden by who,' laughed Newton, 'God?'

'Sure, God.'

'Well he can't be all-powerful then, can he, because he still lets the odd one through if you believe the TV shows – there's one on *Most Haunted* every week.' Newton savoured his own observation. 'OK, let's turn this round, let me ask you something. Why do *you* believe in ghosts.'

Gabby looked from side to side for inspiration then settled for a shrug. 'I dunno, I just like them. There are just so many stories. They can't all be lies or illusions.'

'Well have *you* seen any ghosts?' he asked.

'Dunno, I think I might have done, when I was little. At the old house.'

'OK then, describe it to me,' said Newton.

'I can't, you'll laugh.'

'Honest, I won't.'

'OK, just a vague shape. A woman, in my room,' Gabby said eventually. 'She was just kind of there, then she went. Sort of a shadow.'

'Clothes?'

'Well sort of olden-days stuff.'

'Describe.'

'Black, long dress. She had a bun I think.'

'Time of day?'

'Night time, I woke up,' said Gabby, trying to decide herself whether it had actually happened or not.

'A dream.'

'No it wasn't!' she protested.

'Probably was.'

'I was wide awake!'

'You may have thought you were awake, but you were probably half asleep. It's known as a hypnopompic state.'

'I know what I saw,' she said angrily.

'OK, sorry' said Newton. 'Look, all I'm saying is that it could easily have been something that seemed real, but wasn't.'

'How do you know what happened, you weren't there.'

'It's all to do with probability.'

'That's what *you* say. OK then, well what would you think if you actually saw a ghost yourself?'

'Well that's not going to happen is it?'

'No really, imagine it. Hypothetic, or whatever you call it. You are sitting here, eating your pizza and out of that window you see a ghost. What would you think?'

'How would I know it was a ghost?'

'I dunno, old clothes?'

'Fancy dress.'

'OK then, it's someone you know. Someone ... dead.'

Newton mulled this for a second then looked idly out towards the late-night crowds passing through the streets outside. A distant figure triggered some recognition, his size and stature not unlike his old mentor, the sadly late Dr Sixsmith. 'He'll do,' thought Newton. 'Do I see this person clearly or do I just see them far away, say like that guy over there in the distance?'

'Which guy?' asked Gabby, craning her head to look out through the glass. 'I can't see who you mean.'

'OK not that one then, what about this guy here?' He singled out a tall, jug-eared chap in black with a priestly dog collar who was scrutinising the restaurant. As Newton unsubtly pointed him out, the man realised he was being observed and he began edging awkwardly behind a kiosk.

'Yeah, that vicar. But what if you saw someone you actually know, that close, but you knew for certain that they were dead?'

'Well I'd say I was having a hallucination.'

'Well what if it wasn't.'

'But it would be,' said Newton. 'It couldn't possibly be real.'

'Oh for gawd's sake. What would have to happen to make it real for you?' Gabby asked, flustered.

'You'd have to see it too, I guess.'

'OK then, what if I saw it too?'

'We'd both be hallucinating.'

'Oh you are soooo annoying.' Gabby balled her fists up in frustration.

'Sorry,' he winced apologetically.

'How could we possibly both have the *same* hallucination?'

'Suggestion,' said Newton.

'Suggestion? How would that work?'

'We could both be reacting to the same stimuli, something that creates the same delusion in us both.' Gabby shook her head doubtfully.

'That doesn't happen,' she said.

'Oh yes it does,' said Newton. 'I could give you hundreds of examples. Mass hysteria where crowds see the same impossible things. Mostly they're religious, of course, but there are also things like the Angel of Mons during the First World War. There you have hundreds of soldiers all swearing blind they saw angels protecting them from the attacking Germans. You also regularly have people interpreting lights and balloons as UFOs, sometimes in huge numbers. The planet

Venus is a good example. Because it can often be very, very bright, it can look really artificial. As a result, it gets interpreted as a flying saucer all the time. Needless to say, along the way it picks up all sorts of embellishments, from aliens waving out of portholes to the odd anal probe. But all the time it was still just plain-old planet Venus.'

'So you're also saying that we see what we want to see?'

'I am,' said Newton, laying down his cutlery.

'Oh come on, why would anyone in their right mind actually want to see a headless horseman?'

'Good question,' said Newton, as he gestured for the bill. 'And that's another good example of why ghosts make no sense whatsoever.'

'Which is?' asked Gabby reluctantly, beginning to wane.

'Well, why does the horse haunt in unison with the horseman? Surely the horse has an entirely different set of agendas for haunting. What if the horse wanted to haunt its old paddock? Would the horseman have to join in? And, for that matter, if you get ghost horses, why are there not ghost animals everywhere? Ghost cod, dinosaurs, bacteria, wasps. And what about plants? Help, I'm being possessed by a courgette!' Gabby let the joke pass.

'Maybe it's the human connection that makes it happen?'

'Oh come on! Why should human beings be so special? Why not ghost rabbits, parrots and gerbils?'

'Maybe there are, but you just can't see them.'

'You couldn't miss a *Diplodocus* though, could you, a ten-tonne ghost dinosaur? And what about whales? Anyway, here's another one for you – clothes.'

'Clothes? What are you talking about?' said Gabby.

'Please explain to me why ghosts aren't naked?' asked Newton smugly.

'Naked ...? Why would they be naked?' said Gabby, laughing.

'OK,' Newton elaborated, 'why should they be *dressed*? I mean right now you're wearing that hooded top – if you were to suddenly choke to death on that garlic bread, would you wear that same top forever in the afterlife?'

'Maybe over time we kind of impregnate our clothes with our spirit in some way?'

'Following that hypothesis, what would happen if you'd just put on a brand-new pair of jeans then walked out into Oxford Street feeling so cool that you failed to spot a bus, which then pancaked you all over the road? Would you then haunt the world in everything but your trousers? And what about your old clothes at home? Would they haunt the world all on their own?'

'Yeah, OK, fair enough,' Gabby conceded wearily, as her chin came to rest on her folded arms.

'I could go on,' said Newton.

'I bet you could,' said Gabby, letting out a massive teenage yawn that threatened to sever her head in two.

'Come on, Gabby, I'm keeping you up late. Your mother is going to make me into a ghost if I don't get you to bed. And if I don't get you home for tomorrow lunchtime, I'll be doomed to wander the earth for eternity with no head.'

Cold rain was falling as they left the pizza house and they were glad to get into the car, even if the heater was ineffectual and the wipers smeared rather than wiped. As they pulled away, Newton caught sight of the old guy resembling Sixsmith, wandering side by side with the vicar he had pointed out earlier. They both turned to watch the Citroën as it rattled past. Newton thought about the people he'd lost and left behind him, and he felt a brief twinge of regret.

'Poor old Alex,' thought Newton, and he sighed sadly to himself as they drove on in silence, the darkness behind them swallowing up the figures in the rear-view mirror.

CHAPTER 12

# A SCIENTIFIC METHOD

Back at home after the ghost walk, father and daughter laughed together into the early hours, Newton regaling her with some of the celebrity tales he'd amassed while he'd been in the ascendant. It was outright fun, and Newton felt he was regaining something important he had lost – something he'd had stolen from him. When Gabby eventually yawned herself unconscious at 2am, he draped a sleeping bag over her and took his laptop to bed.

After sending a few emails, he took a deep breath before he took a nervous look at his bank account. What he found made him sit up in bed with a mix of surprise, alarm and unbridled joy.

There was £5,000 in his account.

He logged off and then back on again, but it was still there. He checked all the usual payments – Rowena's savage maintenance handouts, utility bills. They'd all gone out. Nope, there was no doubt about it – someone, God knows who, had made a deposit. There was no obvious clue and Newton, though delighted at the extra funds, was in something of a quandary. If he chased down the source of the payment, then he'd probably have to pay it back. Right now, that was simply beyond the laws of physics. Too tired to pursue the matter, he resolved to leave the money alone for a few days and wait to see if it was recalled.

Yawning, he was mulling this over when he finally drifted away into sleep.

Abruptly, the light was streaming through the window in unison with the 10am chime of the clock tower. Disorientated, fumbling for his glasses, he looked at the dead screen of the battery-drained laptop and then to the clock, threatening him unfocused from the side table. He hoped the fuzzy numerals on the clock were wrong. They weren't.

'Gabby ... Gabby! Wake up!' shrieked Newton, sensing his ex-wife's kinetic rage readying itself in distant Cambridge. Had he a normal car, Newton lamented, he could have made it easily, but the Citroën's tugboat inefficiency and constant mechanical eccentricity made being late a certainty even if Newton had access to a wormhole.

'Gabby, quick! I'm a dead man!' His daughter pulled the sleeping bag over her head.

'Go away!' she groaned.

'We gotta go!' Newton said breathlessly, flinching in anticipation of the tongue-whipping to come. He whisked the sleeping bag away from his dozing daughter and was lucky to avoid a well-aimed boot. Unsubtly, he threw Gabby her jacket and hooded top.

She clumsily prised herself up, wobbling like an inflatable, and stumbled towards the kitchen. 'Cooooooorrrrrffeeeeeeee ...' she moaned.

'No time!' yelled Newton, steering her back towards the door. He urged her down the steep stairs to the street and then urgently over to the old Citroën. He heaved his daughter into the back seat where, with eyes drooping, she instantly curled up and went back to sleep. Newton jumped behind the wheel, kissed the key in desperation and rammed it into the ignition. 'Please,' he muttered, praying to whatever law of physics was going to make the car start first go, and then, with eyes closed, he turned the key.

Normally the old car would have coughed and groaned itself to life. But today, as he fearfully turned the key in the ignition, there was a different sound altogether. It started at his feet, a clean, electrical whine – something he'd never heard before. It grew in intensity, louder and louder, until the teenager on the back seat had clamped her hands over her ears and Newton winced as the sound became quite unbearable. Then, with a terrifying deep growl, the engine burst into the most alarming roar. It was like a Merlin engine coming alive on a Spitfire and Newton, expecting the worst, closed his eyes, waiting for immolation. But it didn't happen that way. As the roar settled into a healthy throb, he tentatively opened first one eye and then the other. Not only was the car not in flames, it was actually sounding OK, maybe even rather good. In fact, it sounded bloody amazing.

Hesitantly, Newton tapped the accelerator and the car obligingly whirred like a thoroughbred. He hit it again, a little harder, and the interior filled with the most wonderful engine sound he'd ever heard. It was as if the sweetest song of every sports car ever made had been taken and blended expertly together. Newton glanced up into the mirror to see Gabby sitting bolt upright, looking baffled. Excited as he was by this strange development, he had to make a choice – A, abandon the car to prevent them both from being burnt to death, or B, risk an unpleasant reaction from his ex-wife when he failed to deliver his daughter on time.

He released the handbrake and edged out into the traffic.

Normally the old DS would struggle up to Muswell Hill like a canal boat up a set of locks. Now it was all that Newton could do to prevent the car from flying over the roofs of the cars in front. The smallest pressure on the pedal set it throbbing like an Atlas rocket; Newton and Gabby rocked back and forth as he bounced his feet frantically from accelerator to brake. The choked roads did little to help and it was only when they dropped down onto the north circular that Newton could stop worrying about collisions. With the dual carriageway clearer ahead of them, Newton put his foot down. The car surged violently ahead and they both let out a loud involuntary 'WOOOAAAHHHHHHHH!' as the Citroën stood on its tail and charged.

'Bloooodddyyyyy HELLLLLL!' yelled Newton, fighting with the wheel, the Citroën weaving through the traffic like a shark through a shoal of tuna. They breezed past a terrifying blur of lorries, busses and vans with just inches to spare.

The Citroën triggered fifteen speed cameras in as many minutes, the flashes catching Newton's wide eyes in the mirror. He couldn't know it, but each one of them, against statistical probability, had failed to record an image of either the car or its number plate and they sped on unchecked to the east.

With the complex turn-off for the M11 fast approaching, Newton's knuckles whitened. He was bearing down on the lover's knot of feeder roads and underpasses like an asteroid on a dinosaur. But, as they tore into the junction, Newton found the car suddenly responding more humanely. Sedately, it throttled back and they turned a graceful, controlled curve off the ring road towards Cambridge.

Being a Sunday morning, the motorway was quiet, allowing Newton briefly to gather his wits. 'You OK back there Gabbs?' he shouted, looking into the mirror. Gabby was obviously very OK, thank you. She had a huge smile on her face; her hoodie was down behind her and she'd wound down the window.

'Random!' she yelled, 'totally random! Dad! When did you get the car upgraded?'

'I didn't!' Newton screamed.

'What do you mean you didn't?' she shouted back. 'You so totally have – it's utterly pimped!'

'No, I swear I didn't,' he insisted, dodging a horsebox that left him with a vivid snapshot of a wild-eyed pony.

'You so have!'

Newton didn't restate his defence, concentrating instead on the slalom of lorries, cars and vans. 'Ohhh sheeeeeet!' he said through clenched teeth, trying to slacken on the accelerator. Instead of easing off, it barrelled yet faster towards obstructions, forcing Newton to throw the car from side to side as a cacophony of horns blared like a yachting regatta. Then mercifully they broke through to a clear stretch and like a cruise missile, they roared past Stansted airport.

'Dad, I take it all back, you are so cooooool!' exhaulted Gabby from the back seat, as they careered up to Rowena's deadline and overtook it. With the suburbs of the old university town rolling towards them, the car regained its composure. Once again, Newton felt more in control and the Citroën eased off to keep pace with the Sunday traffic bumbling off to long-drawn-out Sunday lunches and family arguments. By the time they reached Rowena's, the car had oddly returned to its old self completely.

'That was amaaaaaaaaazing!' said Gabby, giving him an unheard-of peck on his unshaven face. 'Don't bother coming in, she'll only be foul. Thanks Dad, that was fun.' With that she hopped out briskly and ran up to the door. As always, Rowena appeared at the door with a face like bad pickles; sensing something positive between her ex-husband and her daughter, she looked from one to the other with ill-concealed suspicion and resentment.

But then, thought Newton, she always looked like that.

\*\*\*\*\*\*

Half thinking he'd imagined the whole thing, Newton eased the Citroën into a petrol station. He pulled up away from the pumps and opened the hood. The engine was simply immaculate. The old fingerprints, dust, filth and oil were all gone, and there was no trace of the small bits of Christmas tree he'd picked up coming off the road in Epping Forest last year. The components were all exactly where they had always been, the solenoids, the plugs, the fan, the radiator – nothing had moved, they were now just very, very clean.

And there was more. As he got back in the car and rolled it to the pumps, he glanced at the fuel gauge, fully expecting to see it down near zero. But the tank was full, 100 per cent full. Newton sat silently at the wheel for a good ten minutes, trying to make sense of things. But, despite his finest reductionist thinking, he got nowhere.

******

Dr Newton Barlow liked to trust his mind. Like most people of a scientific bent, he tried to keep things rational and strictly under control. Observation, exploration and explanation; that was Newton's way. The odd behaviour of the car had been one thing, but the next event was altogether in a different league.

As he drove back into Crouch End, something caught his eye in the rear-view mirror. A shimmering image of the late Dr Alex Sixsmith was forming on the back seat. Newton shook his head to clear the vision. Annoyingly, it refused to oblige. It was still there, forming like a photograph in developing fluid. To make matters worse, it was now waving.

As hallucinations go, it was certainly vivid. It was unmistakeably Dr Sixsmith; there was his jovial round face, the striped shirt and the distinctive half-moon spectacles resting high on his balding head. All the gestures were spot on, the cheeky grin, that occasional knowing wink. Although the vision was starkly silent, it seemed to be trying to mouth something at him. 'Oh boy,' Newton said to himself, parking. Fighting back, he switched off the engine and screwing his eyes up tight, he took long, deep breaths to control his heart rate. When he felt ready, he cautiously looked in the mirror again, first with one eye and then the other. Sixsmith, or rather the hallucination of Sixsmith, had finally, thankfully, gone.

Rather than go straight to his house, Newton bolted to the nearest pub and downed two stiff whiskies. Was he really coming to bits? If he was, then it wasn't surprising. Hadn't he passed both ways through the mangle these last years? But although he accepted his mind might have misfired enough to generate the image of Sixsmith, the weirdness with the car was hardly an illusion – Gabby had been there too.

The money in the bank was another awkward abnormality he couldn't get his head around. Sure, he hadn't been on top of things recently, but then no matter how bonkers or feckless people get, he mused, they never fail to notice money. Was someone placing funds in his account deliberately or accidentally? He ran through the possibilities. Maybe someone was trying to have some cruel fun with him, a bit of entertainment, or possibly something far worse, like reality TV. Hadn't those harpies tried to lure him into jungles and Big Brother houses before? That must be the answer. They'd rigged up the hallucination too – of course, some kind of projection – clever. Newton ordered a third whisky. 'Hold on!' he thought. 'How would they have known to choose Alex Sixsmith of all people?' No, that didn't fit – picking his old mentor was just too personal, too private. No TV researcher, however keen, was going to put that one together. You'd have to be an intelligence agency to be that complex, thought Newton, and for a few seconds his paranoia dabbled with some ill-formed reasons why MI5 might be interested in him. He looked at his glass. It shook slightly, making the ice cubes dance. Then he glanced up at the barman who was looking back, clearly sensing that something odd was in the air. Newton smiled unconvincingly and downed the whisky. 'Perhaps I've been drugged,' he thought. But when? Magic mushrooms on the pizza last night? Nope. Gabby had the same, that didn't work either. 'Stress,' he said out loud. 'It has to be stress.'

'You OK mate?' asked the barman.

'Er … yes, thanks,' said Newton and he knocked back the rest of his drink. 'Need to get myself together,' he thought as he hurried past the shops. 'Tidy the flat, do my paperwork. Normal stuff.' Back home, he rushed up the stairs, ready to attack the apartment, but as the door opened, he stopped dead. The flat – usually a heap of divorcee chaos – was tidy. Not just a bit tidy, it was very, very tidy. Newton checked the number on the door thinking he'd entered the downstairs flat by accident.

He hadn't.

Newton edged warily into the immaculate lounge, walking in a straight line where previously he'd had to weave like a motorbike in traffic. There was no stale laundry; Newton's clothes were washed, ironed and folded neatly, airing pleasantly on top of a chest of drawers in the bedroom. The kitchen was barely recognisable. Cutlery, plates and tea towels had been put away, all with the mindboggling care and attention he'd associated with his long-dead grandmother. The flat even *smelt* clean, a crisp alpine breeze mixed with what Newton thought might be baking bread. He was not mistaken; a fresh loaf sat beside the breadbin broadcasting wonderful welcoming smells. It was not like his flat at all.

Once again, Newton's mind started oscillating. Baked bread, a classic house seller's trick, what did that mean? Oh no, Rowena! She was planning to sell his flat to get yet more child support. That had to be it! He had a short sharp vision of wandering the streets with nothing but a carrier bag. But no, it couldn't be that. That was just sheer paranoia. Not even Rowena, despite her trademark spite and talent for appropriation, would take Newton's last piece of security without at least discussing it first. Besides, thought Newton, she'd have enjoyed telling him. No, it had to be something else.

'Viv!' he blurted to the empty flat. 'Of course!' He'd just given her a spare key; she must have done it as a surprise. What else could it be? This hypothesis, as convenient as it may have been, gave him instant mixed feelings. Although it was an act of kindness, it still felt like an abuse of sorts, no matter how well intentioned. True, he'd let himself go a fair bit, well a lot frankly, but all the same, it was his place to pick himself up and dust himself down. If he gave into this kind of thing there was no knowing where it would end. No matter how awkward it may be, he'd have to put her straight. He took out his phone, took a deep breath and dialled.

'Newton, sweetie ... hi!' said a sleepy sounding Viv. 'You're back. How was it?'

'Odd,' said Newton briskly, wanting to get to the uncomfortable point. 'Look er ... Viv, about the flat.'

'The flat,' said Viv yawning, 'what, your place or mine?'

'Well mine, of course,' said Newton sternly. 'Look, it's very kind and everything but I think we need to ...'

'Sorry, you've lost me ... what's very kind?'

'The flat, you've done a great job on it, but I'm not sure I'm really comfortable ...'

'Great job? What on earth are you talking about?' said Viv.

'You, tidying my flat.'

'I did what?' said Viv, incredulity plain in her rising voice. 'Are you mad? Do I strike you as the sort of woman that breaks into people's flats to tidy them up? Have you seen *my* place? It's a bloody midden.'

'Are you saying that you *didn't* tidy my flat?'

'I'm telling you I didn't tidy your flat ... sorry I'm lost here matey. What are you going on about?' She sounded a bit rankled, and Newton felt caught by a need both to explain and pacify.

'Well, I got home here, opened the door and well, the flat is immaculate. It's perfect.'

'That's good, isn't it?'

'No it isn't, because I didn't do it, and you are the only other person with a key so I thought you must have done it. Are you seriously telling me you didn't?'

'How many times Newton, I'm telling you I have not been anywhere near your flat! I've been here all weekend. Who else has a key?'

'Like I said, it's just you and me.'

'Anything out of place?' Newton quickly scanned the flat; the TV and computer were present and correct.

'Nothing, in fact, well, actually there is something ...' he said, as he spotted a vase of flowers on the dining table. 'Flowers, and er ... fresh bread.'

'Say whaaaaat?' said Viv. 'Hang on Newton, think about this, are you sure you didn't do it yourself and then just forget?'

'Oh I'm going mad, that's it!' he snapped. 'I hate housework – trust me, if I'd tidied this flat I'd remember every bloody awful second. And I never buy flowers. Never!' All the same, now she'd said it, it was beginning to look like the only logical explanation. What was that old Sherlock Holmes thing? When you have eliminated everything impossible, then whatever remains, however improbable, must be the truth. Follow that little line, worried Newton, and it's time for the happy pills.

'I'm coming over,' said Viv decisively.

'No don't, it's OK, look ...' but the phone clicked off as Viv ran for the door. Newton, seriously frustrated by events, fell back mentally exhausted into an armchair, his galloping mind threatening to fly to pieces like a cheap spin dryer. Desperate to steady his nerves he began to take long, deep breaths. Utterly worn out and completely drained, his eyes drooped, sagged and then closed as he drifted into a fitful sleep

Sometime later he was woken, brought back to life by a sudden, unexpected chill. Drifting back into consciousness, Newton could feel the temperature in the room dipping and he folded his arms around himself as he began to shiver.

'Sorry Newton,' came a voice behind him. 'You must be finding all this a tad annoying.'

Newton froze.

There was no mistaking that it was a voice, and there was no mistaking whose. Glued in place, his eyes darted from side to side, his hands locked solid to the arms of the chair.

'I'm not expecting you to get this straight away, old boy. That wouldn't be like you at all. Take your time, please.' The voice was perfect, such an uncanny match for Sixsmith that it quite unnerved Newton, who was sweating despite the chill. 'To be honest, I was so surprised by the whole thing myself that it took me weeks to get it all together in my head. I mean, it's just so bloody unlikely.'

'This is not happening! This is not happening! This is not happening!' said Newton, slapping his face. 'Come on, snap out of it!'

'That's exactly what I said,' said Dr Sixsmith's voice. 'All quite natural of course. Really, I don't want to unhinge you. But I urgently need you to recognise that this is really happening.'

'But it's not,' said Newton defiantly.

'I assure you that it *is*, old chap,' said the persistent aberration. 'And, it's bloody hard work manifesting myself like this, so don't waste it. The least you can do is turn around and dismiss my existence to my face.'

'Good idea!' thought Newton, 'I'll turn around and you'll be gone.' He began to lean around the side of the chair.

'That's it! Chop-chop!' said Sixsmith's vision. 'Nothing to be scared of. I'm not a bloody poltergeist,' he laughed. 'Promise I won't heave anything about, especially now the flat's finally been cleaned.' Newton could clearly see the image of Dr Sixsmith sitting at the table. From top to toe, it was a perfect reconstruction of his dead friend, elbows on the table top, its semi-transparent fingers idly playing with the flowers in the vase.

'You're a hallucination!' declared Newton as he rose from his seat.

'No I'm not,' it said curtly.

'Yes you are!' said Newton. 'Dammit why did I reply? You don't exist.'

'Yes I do,' it said. 'Look, I'm waving at you.'

'I'm having some kind of a breakdown, that's it, has to be.'

'That I won't argue with,' said the apparition, grinning.

Newton crept up to the vision who, clearly amused by Newton's determination to dismiss him, aped his narrowed eyes and returned his baffled expression. Tentatively, Newton extended his index finger to touch the shimmering form.

'Go on, feel free to have a good poke, I'm not shy,' laughed the apparition. Newton jabbed his finger into the sliver of light defining Sixsmith's forehead. There was a slight electrical sensation, like the tingle from a cattle fence, and as he moved his finger around in a circular motion, the light swirled around it in a disrupted trail, like froth in a recently stirred coffee. 'Great, isn't it?' said the hallucination. 'Bloody hard work though, can't keep it up all day sadly. We'll have to keep things brief.'

'Amazing,' said Newton to himself hopefully, 'the power of the human mind!'

'Yeah, whatever,' said the image of Dr Sixsmith. 'Look, I guess we've got to work through all this denial to get you used to things, but it would help me a lot if you'd just drop the voice of reason and get on board. We've got bit of a deadline.'

'That's the last drink I'll ever have,' said Newton.

'Yes I should steer clear of the spirits if I was you!' laughed the hallucination.

'Not real, not real, not real!' Newton chanted, head in his hands. He opened his fingers. It was still there. 'Arrggghhhh ... go away damn you!'

'Blimey you're stubborn Newton! I said you would be though. I told them you'd have to be worn down over months, but would they listen?'

Newton circled the apparition, checking the angles and looking for hidden projectors.

'OK "ghost",' said Newton, changing tack. 'It's bloody clever, I give you that. You've got Sixsmith down to a tee. The mannerisms, the banter; it's him alright. But if you really were the ghost of Alex Sixsmith, which you are most definitely not, you'd be able to tell me this. What colour was the cricket bat we played with in the back garden?'

'Yellow,' said the vision. Newton clenched his fists.

'You could have guessed that one or found an old picture.'

'Granted,' it agreed. 'Try another.'

'OK, Sixsmith was a scientist, so you should be able to answer some proper scientific questions ... without hesitation.'

'I should, and I can,' said the vision gleefully. 'Fire away!'

'Tell me the name of the heaviest fundamental particle in nature.'

'Easy, it's the top quark. Heavy old thing, more than 170 times as massive as a proton. Discovered at Fermilab near Chicago – 1995 I think it was?'

'Doesn't mean much, you could be a science graduate.'

'Well I was a science graduate, a long, long time ago, admittedly.' The apparition began to play with the flowers again. It grew frustrated and tried unsuccessfully to swat the whole vase away. 'Damn it this is hard – you're meant to be able to start moving stuff around within a month or so, but I'm buggered if I can do it. Look, I'm barely ruffling them. I say, Newton old boy, any chance I can use your place to practice? It can cause all sorts of mayhem out there in the big wide world when you start shifting objects about.'

'I'm sorry? Oh sure, ghost away as much as you like, just don't leave the toilet seat up.'

'Funny you should mention that!' it laughed. 'Up there ... there is no toilet! Can't say I miss it. Some do, oddly, but not me. Oh, and you never have to change your underwear, that's the other great thing.'

'Look, let's keep on topic shall we,' said Newton, exasperated. 'I know that you can't be a ghost, that's impossible. So ... I'm going to prove it.'

'Oh you are, are you?' The ghost removed his glasses and looked up at Newton. 'You know, you could save us both a lot of time if you just accept what you're seeing. I know it's hard; it will probably make you feel like a bit of a hypocrite, but there's not much I can do about that. But, you are simply the best man for the job, we've all agreed that. So we just have to work you round as best as we can in the time available.'

'Yeah, yeah,' said Newton, waving the apparition away. 'All very mysterious I'm sure. OK, let me think ... has to be something personal or something specific to your career. Go on, tell me something personal, something only Sixsmith and I knew.'

'Something *really* personal?'

'Yes,' said Newton. 'If you are what you claim to be then you'll have to know something. Something unique.'

'OK, well, how about the fact that you were late for my death?' Newton went still. The spirit's comment was bang on the factual button, and painfully so.

'Whaaat? Hang on a second, how can you know that?' Newton

gasped. 'No ... wait a minute!' he said, trying to regain his composure. 'The sister! Sixsmith's sister could have told you! Oh good try.'

'Good point,' said the hallucination. 'OK let's see,' he continued, removing his glasses and chewing one end of the frame. 'It's harder than I thought. I can't talk about the car journey today, even though I was there. They've done a great job on the old banger haven't they? No I can't use that because you'll quite naturally assume that both events are part of the same hoax, ditto the bank accounts. Hope the extra cash is helping by the way.'

'The car? The money? That was you as well? What the hell! Who are you people? Why are you doing this to me?' Newton looked angry, his calm 'just in case I'm on camera' stance failing him utterly.

'Oh, just trying to help things settle down for you,' the manifestation said, mildly reproachful. 'You can't honestly say you don't need a bit of a leg up. And you won't be much use to us with a knackered car, empty bank accounts and a flat straight out of *Withnail and I*. Oh, and on the subject of the flat. Don't forget to say thanks to your grandmother. I say, that woman can really clean, impressive! So, any more questions?'

'Bugger the questions!' protested Newton, pointing his finger back through the vision's head to where its brain should be. 'Look, I don't know what your game is, but I'll tell you this much, it's not funny.'

'Sorry, it must feel a little invasive,' the vision said, trying unsuccessfully to rest its hand on Newton's shoulder. 'It's just there's no easy way of doing this – honestly, I've been through it from one end to the other. I'm just glad I was never confronted with an apparition when I was alive! I think I was the only person on earth more sceptical than you.'

'If you think I'm going to get taken in by this,' said Newton angrily, 'you're wrong. I haven't worked out how the bloody projection is done, but I will! I'm guessing it's something like those high-definition holographic things.'

'Newton, Newton,' said the supposed projection wearily. 'Just supposing such a technology existed, one that was this good, you have to ask yourself: why are *you* being used for its first demonstration? A bit of a waste, don't you think? They'd probably roll it out at a huge pop concert. And why a vision of me in particular – in the privacy of your flat? Why on earth would anyone want to do that?'

'Publicity, obviously!' Newton snorted. You fool a big rational physicist, film him being taken in like some sap and away you go! Even better, choose a disgraced sceptical scientist and it's way, way better. You can have a right laugh like that. I'm thinking Piltdown Man here.' Newton started checking the windows and walls again.

'Maybe, but why go to the trouble of creating a projection of a fat sixty-something old buffer with spectacles when you could have had an alien, a zombie or a headless coachman? I'm a pretty tedious illusion if you ask me. I wasn't exactly a head-turner when I was alive, why would I be one as a ghost?'

Newton was highly vexed now. He let out a long growl of frustration. 'Look you bastard. OK, so I have no idea how or why it's being done – but, if you think you can make me go mad, well then you are 100 per cent wrong! And what's more ...' He was about to really tear into the vision when he was cut short by the doorbell. Both he and the hallucination froze.

'That'll be your lady friend,' said the vision.

'Damn it,' said Newton, 'she can't see you here. Turn yourself off!'

'Turn myself off?' replied the image. 'I'm not a PlayStation!'

'She can't see you! She mustn't!'

'Oh, she won't,' the vision declared. 'I get to decide who sees me. Very neat little feature!' Newton shhh'd the hallucination. It mockingly made a zipping motion across its mouth.

'Hello?' Newton asked the intercom, trying to sound composed.

'Hi Newton, it's me.'

'Viv ... hi, come up.' As he buzzed open the main door, Newton turned to shoo the vision away.

'OK, OK ... I'm going,' it said, beginning its journey back towards invisibility. 'Oh by the way ... about Viv, she's lovely.'

'What?' Newton replied. 'Yes she is, but what of it?'

'Nice legs!' said the vision, now barely visible against the blinds.

'Nice *legs*?' said Newton, outraged. 'Have you people been spying on us together? In bed?' But the hallucination, projection, whatever it was, had completely vanished leaving Newton alone. There was no sign of anything weird, real *or* imagined, and so with Viv knocking insistently, he belatedly opened the door.

'You OK sweetheart?' she said, looking into Newton's wild eyes.

## CHAPTER 13

# A SUITABLE BOY

After the awkwardness of the whole Northumberland business, Chris Baxter struggled to regain his reputation. Just why he'd been in northern England was never really established. It was one of several questions that had baffled health professionals, police and his employers, not to mention poor Christopher Baxter himself.

In an attempt to unravel events, Baxter had consented to hypnosis at the local psychiatric unit, but his confused stories of earwigs, full English breakfasts and the last Snow Patrol album did little to clear anything up. Inevitably, his delighted colleagues muttered, none too silently, about nervous breakdowns and burn-outs. Long jealous of his stunning sales successes, they gleefully seized the opportunity to finally unseat the great Christopher Baxter from his place at the big table.

But Baxter was no quitter. Oh no. He'd refused the medication the quacks had offered, said a big NO to counselling and defiantly, heroically, hitched himself back on the horse. No one, nothing, was going to stop Chris Baxter.

He was fired the same week.

At first, still brimming with Dale Carnegie over-confidence and homespun affirmation, Baxter was optimistic that he could use the sudden downturn in his fortunes to his advantage. After all, he told himself, bad luck can make you reassess yourself and help you move on to better things. Well not this time. The credit crunch plus his now-soiled references decided otherwise; he was firmly prevented from replacing like with like and his Olympic-sized ego was kicked like a child's football over the playground wall. For the first time in years, he fretted about his finances and, horror of horrors, he even considered selling the Lexus, his lovely wonderful Baxter wagon. This awful concept drove him half mad with panic, for all the world like a desperate father fighting to save his child's life. So Baxter began searching for work beyond London's western fringes. Eventually, this one-man diaspora led Baxter to a job vacancy at an obscure property developers – McCauley Bros – way out west in Dorset.

He'd had a brief telephone interview a few days earlier with one Miss Dryer. That had been bizarre in itself. Firstly, with a strangely seductive tone, she wanted to know if he had a working knowledge of Latin. 'Oh, enough to get by on holiday,' Baxter bluffed.

'Do you regularly visit a dentist?' she continued, her voice deepening as she spoke. He could heartily reply in the affirmative; after all, physical appearances were everything to Christopher Baxter and his perfect teeth were a shade whiter than that of a head cheerleader. Baxter's insincere smile could probably be seen from space. Oddly, the remaining questions all seemed to be mere padding and they barely touched upon Baxter's considerable qualifications or sales experience, but with the clock ticking on both his flat and the Lexus, he decided to overlook the peculiar introduction and drop in salary in favour of a desperate leap of faith.

So now, here was Christopher Baxter driving across Dorset's blasted heathlands on a cold and misty Monday morning, faint outlines of straggly ponies watching from the gorse and heather as he sped by towards his early appointment. To boost his now-threadbare confidence, life-affirming anthems were thumping out from the Lexus and away across the scrub.

The McCauley headquarters at Hadlow Grange came as something of a shock to Baxter. The gates were so Gothic and imposing that he wondered initially if he'd accidently arrived at a cemetery. The ornate ironwork towered high above the Lexus in agonised Victorian swirls, the blackened metal twisting around itself, with evil-looking hooks and vicious points, hinting at a desire to prevent both access and exit in equal measure. To each side of the imposing entrance, a long perimeter wall stretched away, topped with razor wire and thorny growth, an unsightly barrier draped liberally with old carrier bags, dew-covered cobwebs and grey wool from the dirty sheep in the nearby fields. Baxter got out of the car and discovered an intercom on the gatepost, half drowned in ivy and thorns. He cautiously parted the leaves and pressed the button.

'Hadlow Grange, can I help you?' a haughty squawking voice answered.

Hello, it's er, Christopher Baxter.'

'Who?'

'Christopher Baxter. I'm here for an induction.' There was an awkward pause.

'Who are you seeing?' demanded the voice, as Chris began to wonder if he'd got the right address. He checked the headed letter.

'I'm here to see Mr McCauley.'

'Which one?' came the voice.

'Um, I was just told to ask for Mr McCauley.' There was another pause followed by a series of electrical pops and clicks.

'Come in then,' said the voice. The conversation was terminated with a burst of whistling feedback so loud that Baxter recoiled from the intercom in alarm, snagging the cuff of his favourite suit on a wicked-looking bramble.

'Bollocks!' he cursed, as the gates creaked jerkily open. Baxter jumped back into the car and rolled forward onto the gravel as the gates closed behind him. As he crawled up the driveway, the building remained resolutely hidden behind rampant foliage until finally, Hadlow Grange revealed itself. It was a classic Victorian country house with a profusion of turrets and attic windows, smothered in dark ivy. In the gravel car park, three identical black Land Rovers sat side by side beneath a vast old yew tree with massive gnarled branches.

Baxter was thinking how it could have made a good hotel or a country club, until suddenly he noticed that there was another more monstrous building looming massive behind the Grange. This was something a lot less leisure industry. Why he hadn't seen it immediately, he was unsure; perhaps it was the early-morning mist or its pallid bulk of gull-grey Purbeck stone, blending seamlessly into the overcast. There was no softening ivy on this behemoth. It was just an endless parade of small barred windows and guttering, and it could have been easily mistaken for a high-security prison, had it not been for the bizarre flourishes of some demented Victorian architect. There were cathedral-like pimples here, gargoyles there. There were buttresses and towers with tiny sinister windows, elaborate mock-Tudor chimneys and a paranoid array of lightning conductors. Its windows were all boarded up and clearly had been so for some time, hinting at a protracted vacancy.

Chris Baxter looked past the huge building into its neglected gardens, a mess of broken gazebos and summerhouses, invading gorse and rhododendrons. The whole scene, probably once a triumph of philanthropic attention to detail, gave him such a feeling of hopelessness that he seriously thought about turning on his heels and leaving. An eddy of fetid air forced its way past his collar and into his

Armani vest.

'Christopher Baxter?' came a husky female voice. He turned quickly to see an austere, pouting woman in tweed and sensible shoes. She could have been anything from 30 to 60 years old, Chris couldn't tell; with her lack of modern flair she would have looked perfectly at home in a wartime public library. She took a deep breath that made her restrained breast heave noticeably as she scrutinised him with dilating pupils from behind her horn-rimmed spectacles.

'Yes,' replied Chris, forcing a smile. 'I'm here for the induction. Are you Miss Dryer? We spoke on the phone.'

'Please, do call me Wendy. Let's not be ... formal with each other,' she sighed. 'Now, if you'll follow me.' Baxter followed, and as she led the way, he looked furtively from her tweed pencil skirt down to her legs as she strutted purposefully towards the entrance, her thick tan tights and sensible footwear triggering a not entirely unwelcome memory of female prison dramas. She held the door open leaving barely enough space for Baxter to pass, forcing him to brush intimately past her into the reception.

'Take a seat ... Christopher,' said Miss Dryer.

'Welcome to McCauley Brothers – Estate Agents and Developers' said a sign next to a sickly, dust-covered rubber plant. Baxter shuffled through some magazines; none of them was less than ten years old and they had nothing at all to do with property. There was a copy of *Handguns and Assault Weapons*, and an aged *National Geographic* with a cover feature on Aztec death rituals. Beneath them were several copies of *History Today*, all with clippings about the plague, wars and famines cut out. Baxter looked up to the small reception hatch. Miss Dryer was scrutinising him a little too personally as she snipped away at something historical with her scissors.

After ten minutes, she suddenly reappeared at his side. 'Follow me please Christopher,' she said, the words released half as speech and half as a slow, erotic exhalation.

'Err right, yes ... of course,' he said, collecting his things and following her down the badly chipped oak-panelled corridor. Baxter had never seen such an odd building; he was used to clean sterile business parks and affordable office 'solutions'. Hadlow Grange offered no solutions to a visitor at all – he couldn't fathom the purpose of any of the rooms off the haphazard corridors, which reeked of dry-rot and cheap disinfectant. 'What is that place?' Baxter asked as they passed a window looking onto the monstrous building next door, leering out of the misty shrubs.

'It was a mental institution,' Miss Dryer said, without turning. 'Of course, you'd have to call it something else now I expect. But a nuthouse is a nuthouse.' She stopped walking briefly and looked seriously into his eyes. 'And I should know.' She didn't elaborate, nor, on reflection, did Chris want her to.

'Right, yeah,' Baxter said uneasily. They walked on in silence. She showed him into a wood-panelled boardroom, once again forcing Baxter to brush uncomfortably close to her as he entered. The smell of cheap make-up and coal-tar soap caught in his nostrils, her lined skin visibly cracking beneath thick foundation. Reluctantly, Miss Dryer then closed the door behind her with an abrupt slam, leaving Baxter alone.

Propped on an easel there was a large map of Britain with flags, post-it notes and press cuttings. 'Rare heathland redevelopment causes anger,' one said. 'Unique Victorian cemetery purchased by controversial developers,' said another. The little flags marked battlefields, wildlife reserves and parkland while the clippings told of mostly abortive campaigns aimed to block the McCauleys from achieving their objectives. Bland sketches depicted one of the new developments, rank upon rank of uninspired houses, the architect merely Photoshopping the same dull visual eighteen times in a bid to get the job off his desk. 'McCauley Brothers, estate agents and developers of distinction, cordially invite you to explore this unique and very special new development,' declared the heading. 'Welcome to Juggin's Lump.'

Baxter was suddenly aware of a shadow beside him.

'Do you like history, Mr Baxter?' came the weedy voice of Ascot McCauley. Baxter turned to address his future employer.

'Very much!' he lied. With practised assertiveness, he thrust his hand forward. 'Christopher Baxter.'

'So I gather,' said McCauley weakly, reluctantly shaking his hand as if it was a sock. 'You found us easily I trust?'

'Oh yes,' said Baxter awkwardly as Ascot McCauley fixed him hard in the eye, inspecting his features. 'The old sat nav, you know?'

'You have an old sat nav?' asked Ascot, his eyebrow rising.

'Oh no, it's quite new, err I just meant ...' Baxter backed slightly away. Suddenly, he became aware of another person in the room.

When he turned to look, confusingly it was also Ascot McCauley, now behind him. Baxter, befuddled, wondered how he could possibly move so fast. He was still more baffled when McCauley was once again in front of him when he turned back.

'Can we get you anything, a coffee perhaps? I can get Miss Dryer to make you one,' Ascot said, affecting a reassuring smile.

'Er no ... thanks.'

'Dear Wendy. She's such a treasure, she's been with us ... well, forever really – she came with the building.'

'Right,' said Baxter, trying to equate the word 'treasure' with the peculiar woman who'd just shown him to the boardroom. He was mulling this over when another man appeared from behind him. 'Epsom, this is Mr Baxter,' said Ascot, introducing his identical brother. Baxter quickly looked from one McCauley to the other, astonished by their similarity. From head to toe, in face and in dress, there were no differences – nothing but the letters on their silk handkerchiefs poking neatly out from their blazer pockets and their initialled signet rings.

'A pleasure,' said Epsom McCauley, bending over Baxter like a heron at a water feature, so disquieting him that he nearly missed the new brother's thin hand as it uncurled towards him in welcome. Baxter cautiously shook the moist bony hand; it limply held his own for an uncomfortable second before slipping damply away.

'Twins?' he said involuntarily.

'Triplets,' corrected a voice from the doorway, and in walked yet another brother, no less identical than his siblings. If anything, this one was more similar than the other two.

'This is Plumpton, my other brother,' said Ascot McCauley. With that, the three brothers closed together in a row. Baxter, now thoroughly unnerved, smiled in embarrassment. He looked from one brother to another, unable to think of anything suitable to say.

'Triplets, yes, of course,' he uttered clumsily.

'Please, come and sit down,' said Epsom, and they urged Baxter ahead of them to a table in front of a case of antiques containing African masks, Nazi memorabilia and medieval carvings. Baxter sat down, one of the McCauleys taking the seat to his left, another to the right and one directly opposite. He returned their mostly blank expressions with a bad grin. 'Thank you for coming down at such short notice, Mr Baxter,' said the McCauley on the left, looking down at his notes.

'Not a problem,' Baxter replied, 'thank you for inviting me.' He tried to loosen his collar.

'So ... how much do you know about our business, Mr Baxter?' said the right-hand brother.

'Oh not much, I confess,' said Baxter awkwardly. 'I mean ... not having a website is sort of ...'

'Unusual?' said the front brother, cutting Baxter short.

'Quite,' said the brother on his left. The four-way conversation was making Baxter flick his eyes about like a soldier scanning for snipers. 'We are a very discreet business, Mr Baxter. Very discreet indeed,' said the front McCauley. 'We can't have just anyone knowing all about us, can we? McCauley developments deal with a great many sensitive projects. We have to be very discreet.' The brothers all narrowed their eyes towards Christopher. 'Are *you* discreet, Mr Baxter?'

'Oh yes,' said Baxter, shifting in his seat. 'Very discreet, very trustworthy.'

'Good,' murmured the brothers in synchrony. Baxter looked at the A and the M on the front brother's handkerchief, and felt safe to assume that this was Ascot.

'It says here, Mr Baxter, that you have a working knowledge of Latin, is that correct?'

'Er ... well not that much – a smattering,' lied Baxter.

'It's not important,' said the right brother, suppressing a smile, and all three brothers nodded at each other knowingly.

'It's not?' said Baxter, confused again.

The right brother ignored the question. 'Dental condition good?' he asked.

'Er yes ... got to look after your teeth,' said Baxter. A worry line wrinkled across his forehead. 'Can I ask why you ...'

'Publicity is so important, Mr Baxter, don't you agree?' said Ascot McCauley. 'It's so very important to look right ... on television.'

'Television?' Baxter asked. 'Really, what me?'

'Certainly,' Ascot continued. 'We find ourselves frequently dealing with the media in our line of work.'

'Ohh!' said Christopher Baxter, his reservations dissolving in barely repressed vanity. 'Cool.'

'Your health, Mr Baxter? It's good I trust?' said the McCauley on the right.

'Oh yes, indeed,' said Baxter.

'Blood pressure?'

'Normal.'

'Diet?'

'How do you mean?' Baxter asked.

'You eat well?'

'I look after myself, you know, five a day and all that.'

'Five what?' asked Ascot McCauley.

'You know, fruit,' said Baxter.

'You eat five fruit every day?' asked Ascot. The brothers looked at each other and back to Baxter.

'You know, fruit, vegetables, recommended daily doses – vitamins and minerals and that stuff.'

'Ah, I see,' said Ascot, making notes. Then he put down his pen and leaned forward.

'Religion?' he asked, his voice suddenly quieter and more serious. Baxter fumbled with the awkward question in his mind, searching for a sound-bite.

'Well, I'm quite a spiritual person,' he hedged, his eyes looking to the sky through the ceiling for divine intervention. 'But I'm not really linked to any one faith.'

'Excellent!' said all three brothers together. Baxter was left wondering which part of the cliché had pleased them so much.

'You see,' said Ascot McCauley, 'in our work, we have to deal with a wide range of faiths. It would not be becoming to appear to be affiliated with any one religion in particular.' His brothers nodded.

'Gotcha,' said Baxter, not actually having a clue what Ascot was talking about.

'Now we appreciate that you have come a long way to be with us today,' said Ascot. 'You must be keen to get to your room and unpack your things before starting.'

'My room?' asked Baxter, confused. 'But I was planning to find a hotel in Langton Hadlow, up the road.'

'Oh good lord no,' said Ascot. 'The hotels in the village have all been closed down and there's nothing else for miles.'

'Really,' said Baxter. 'Are you sure?'

'Very,' said Ascot knowingly. 'I am absolutely certain of it. Anyway, why pay for a hotel when we have more than adequate accommodation here at the Grange? We won't hear of it.'

'Well, if you're sure ...' Baxter said reluctantly. Fan as he was of corporate hospitality, he was quite certain that his room, if it was anything like the rest of the building, would be no Holiday Inn.

'Absolutely Mr Baxter,' said Ascot McCauley. 'You will find our hospitality to be of a very high standard. The meals here are created by our very own chef and all the vegetables are fresh from our kitchen garden. We are self-sufficient in almost every department, in fact, and it helps us to keep our distance from the outside world. But first, before Wendy shows you up to your room, I wondered if you would indulge my brothers and me with something of a screen test.'

'Screen test?' asked Baxter, baffled once again.

'I believe that's the technical term,' Ascot continued. 'Yes, we'd love to see you reading something for us, just like at a press conference.'

'Press conference?' asked Baxter excitedly.

'Of course! Just like on television,' said Ascot. 'You'll be wonderful I'm sure, what with your health and your perfect teeth. But that's all in the future. For now, we would so like to see you in action, reading from a little something we have prepared.'

Baxter nodded enthusiastically, encouraged by the thought of a public stage for his newly rediscovered self-respect. 'If you'll follow us then, Mr Baxter,' Ascot continued, and with that he crossed to the far side of the room. He approached a section of the oak panelling and pulled back part of the wall to reveal a low arched doorway.

Ascot gestured to Baxter to come forward. Cautiously, he shuffled through the arch into a small mock-Gothic chapel bereft of windows. Long satin and velvet drapes hung from the walls. Pews were lined up to face an old brass lectern, fashioned into an ornate eagle with outstretched wings. Upon its broad back lay a single open volume, bathed in the light of two solitary candles.

'What a cool room,' Baxter said as brightly as he could, even though the whole thing was frankly creeping him out. The far wall was a mass of glass cabinets similar to the one in the boardroom, their contents a dark jumble of antiques and curios that Baxter could see dancing in the flickering light. Every object, without exception, was ugly and unsettling; they were either badly made or portrayed subjects so unpleasant that Baxter felt mild nausea just looking at them. 'Antiques?' he said, grimly.

'Indeed Mr Baxter, how observant of you to notice them,' said one of the brothers behind him. 'We are something of collectors you see.'

'What, like the *Antiques Roadshow*?' said Chris.

'Yes,' said another voice behind him. 'Just like the *Antiques Roadshow*.'

'I'd like to show you what to read,' said Ascot. He led Chris forward to the lectern as the two other brothers took their places on the front pew. Close up to the cabinets now, Baxter could see their contents with hideous clarity. Primitive ivory eyes peered out at him and withered leather fingers with gold and silver adornments pointed from cushions of dark, blood-red velvet. And in the centre, a hooded, carved figure caught Baxter's anxious darting eyes, gilt roman numerals on a box at its base. He began to feel the same disquiet that he had felt after the unpleasant Northumberland incident and started to wish he'd grabbed the heartburn tablets from the glove compartment.

With his hand on Baxter's shoulder, Ascot pointed to the page of aged text before them. The calligraphic script was fully legible to Baxter, even though he couldn't understand a word. 'Latin,' he observed correctly. 'What does it say?'

'Oh I shouldn't worry about that!' said Ascot, laughing the issue away. 'It's just a test piece, something about folk traditions I expect. You'll note that we've put your name in it from time to time, where the blanks were. That's to make it a bit more ... "user friendly". Please, start when you feel ready. Oh, and try to ignore the illustrations if you can.'

'Illustrations?' Baxter could see them now, foul sketches of devils, fires and long precessions of sad-looking people with pointy hats. 'Er, right,' he gullibly continued, missing all the danger signs. 'I'll just read this then?'

'Yes, perfect!' said Ascot, clapping his hands together as he joined his brothers on the pew.

Baxter knew he was good at 'one-to-one sales interfacing', but he'd never really done much public speaking, especially in Latin. Yet his instinct for self-promotion was strong. 'You can do this Chris,' he thought to himself.

'Action!' shouted Ascot McCauley theatrically. Baxter took a breath.

'Er ... Ego autem sum quasi vas inane,' he began awkwardly, stuttering along the lines of meaningless prose like a small child.

'Ego donavit corpus meum ad dominum meum in exercitu magno Cardinalis Balthazar De La Senza,' he continued, quickly becoming surprisingly fluent despite his vaguely cockney tone. 'Tempore domini Inquisitoris magni voluntatis esse, aequo animo et scissa animam meam a fundamentis et suspensi in abyssum quasi stercora, nihil prorsus in aeternum damnatus egisse,' he went on, oblivious to something stirring in the small box behind him. Wisps of purple drifted from it like steam from a cooling kettle. 'Ego Christophorus Baxtere accipe usitata res est, uti et magnis La Senza caput meum corium et nervorum et magnifici primum genus dentium,' Baxter continued, strangely enjoying himself.

Far away in another place, the bound and trapped Cardinal La Senza had begun to whisper the words in unison beneath the folds of his hooded cloak. Oblivious, Baxter was flying now, quite unaware of the sinister coaching he was receiving. 'O magnum La Senza, cum venerit, et ad hoc bonum esse propter tempus, quia ego miser!' Baxter read on. A coiling snake-like tendril of purple had fingered its way through the lock of the cabinet and was creeping menacingly towards its target. It advanced up Baxter's legs, body and neck until finally, it crept imperceptibly into his ears. 'Ego Christophorus Baxtere immolare volens alumnam cerebrum meum et animam, ut vos mos postulo ut enable uariat possessione tua ...'

Pleased beyond measure by what he had fondled and explored, La Senza went still. Content for now, he drew back his sensing vines and they fell away from Baxter, unnoticed. His jailors had seen nothing.

La Senza now had the chance he'd been craving for centuries, so many lifetimes of plotting and scheming. He knew nothing of the young man he had inspected so intimately – frankly, he didn't care. It was the body, oh his body, so young and fit; teeth clean like white mice, no trace of Popery, no hint of Lutheran, Baptist, Jew, Muslim or Buddhist within his empty soul, nothing to restrain or inhibit the Inquisitor's foul purposes. La Senza knew that his escape was mere days away. Immobile, he marshalled dark reserves for the events to come.

'Nunc me vacua est anima mea praeparata et redditur supersunt, La Senza venit, et possident me! Sincere vestrum, Christopher Baxter,' finished Chris, with a flourish.

'Bravo Mr Baxter,' said Ascot McCauley, standing as he clapped enthusiastically. 'Bravo!'

'How was I?' said Baxter, grinning like a fool.

'Marvellous! I'm sure my brothers will join me in saying how suitable you have proven to be Mr Baxter, most suitable indeed.' As Ascot spoke, his eyes caught a faint flicker of purple snaking away from Baxter and back through the keyhole of the glass cabinet behind him.

'Really? Thanks!' said Baxter, naively thinking ahead to a glittering future.

'Christopher, I'd like to welcome you to McCauleys, estate agents and developers,' said Ascot, as his two brothers stood and nodded vigorously in agreement.

'Thank you!' said Baxter earnestly. 'I promise I'll put my body and soul into it.'

'Oh yes,' said Ascot McCauley. 'I'm quite certain you will.'

CHAPTER 14

# AN INCONVENIENT TRUTH

In the past, massage would have been strictly off the Barlow radar, lumped in with homeopathy, tarot and feng shui and far too new-age to contemplate. Not now. Newton was up for anything that could get the monkey off his back and he surrendered to Viv's hands without a trace of scepticism. Newton, she had pointed out, was as lumpy and wound up as an old alarm clock and she relished slapping him onto the bed and removing three years of knots from his back with her bare hands. What a contrast, thought Newton, to his ex-wife, who'd been far more interested in inserting stress than removing it.

Tonight, following the day's strangeness, Viv had been on a mission to calm Newton down. Despite his protestations, she'd boiled him in the bath then flattened him down upon his crisp clean bed and set to work with a purpose.

'You've had a lot on,' she said, attacking his rigid scapula. 'It's not surprising, what with one thing and another.'

'Snnngggggg,' said Newton, trying to nod without dribbling.

'You must have had a bit of an episode, you know, one of those out-of-body things.'

'Noooo,' he said, nearly coherently. 'The car, the money, it's all real.' She placed her elbow in the small of his back. 'Yowwwwwwww!' said Newton, trying to express the inexpressible.

'You're welcome,' said Viv, twanging him like a harp.

Newton had made up his mind to tell her about everything except Sixsmith. That would make him sound like a nut, no matter how understanding she was.

'Why would anyone want to soup up your car, tidy your flat and put money in your account?' she asked. 'And more to the point, why would you mind? I mean if that were me I'd say ... bring it on!'

'Blut it's not normal is it, I mlean, there has to be slome klind of mlotive.'

'What about Havotech? Maybe they're feeling guilty and they're trying to make up for things,' suggested Viv, chasing a knot around

Newton's shoulder blade like a gerbil under a rug.

'It did occlur to me,' burbled Newton. 'But then that suggests a clertain level of altruism, gluilt or atlonement that I can't say flits the bleed.'

'Well forget it for now sweetie – I'm sure it will all be clear in the morning.'

'Yeah, I am a blit knalckered,' said Newton.

'Exactly,' said Viv. She forced down hard onto his neck and shoulders; he crunched like a cheese cracker. Newton's eyes sagged and drooped, and as the tension lifted, he found himself drifting pleasantly away from the day's weirdness.

At least, he did until he realised that the toy cars on the mantelpiece were moving.

The movement was so subtle, little taps forward, like the smallest of nudges from a single finger. But as his eyes widened, he could see the blue Citroën 2CV that Gabby had given him for Christmas begin a careful and deliberate trip along the shelf, from one end to the other.

'Blimey,' said Viv, 'you've tightened right back up again! We'll have to work a bit harder!' With that she leant hard down on his right shoulder resulting in a spectacular crack.

'Argghhhhhnnnn!' shouted Newton, biting the pillow.

'Oh don't be a baby,' said Viv. 'Better out than in!'

Nearly all the cars were moving now, until one, pushed too hard perhaps, shot off the mantelpiece and looked like it was going to crash noisily onto the floor. But just before impact, the car stopped dead in mid-air. A striped-shirted arm, disembodied in the air just inches from Newton's face, caught the toy.

'Howzatt!' said the voice of Alex Sixsmith triumphantly. 'I think I might be getting the hang of this!'

'Did you hear that!' asked Newton, hoping she hadn't.

'Hear what,' said Viv and Sixsmith simultaneously.

'Oh you were talking to your girlie, sorry,' said Alex.

'Hear what Newton darling?' said Viv. 'Are you getting a bit weird on me again?'

'You didn't just hear a voice?'

'A voice? Nope, only yours,' she laughed.

'I wouldn't worry,' said Sixsmith. 'I told you, I can decide who hears me, or sees me. Pity I couldn't do that while I was alive. It would have got me through a lot of dismal cocktail parties.'

139

'I'm not listening,' whispered Newton at the arm, as it played with James Bond's Aston Martin.

'I didn't say anything sweetie,' said Viv, applying her knuckles.

'It takes an awful lot of energy to move things though,' said Sixsmith. 'I'm just moving these around for practise. Opening a window, pushing someone off a bar stool – that's beyond me at the moment. I'll get there though.'

'Oh you're a hard man to calm down,' said Viv sternly. She shoved him back into the bed linen.

'Ouch!' said Alex. 'I felt that! A nice girl, your Vivienne. Much nicer than that awful woman you married, what was her name?'

'Wowena,' said Newton from deep within the pillow.

'Ah yes, that's it!' said Alex.

'What about her?' said Viv. 'She on your case again? I blame her for all this. Bet she'd love it if you lost your marbles.'

'I'm not losing my marbles!' protested Newton, not at all convincing himself.

'If you say so,' she replied.

'Not going to tell her about me, eh?' said Alex, examining a pre-war Bugatti racer. 'Probably best. Maybe later – see how it pans out. I can manifest to her if it helps?'

'No!' protested Newton.

'OK, OK!' said Viv. 'Sheesh, just trying to help.'

'Sorry! I didn't mean to ...' Newton backtracked. 'You're being great, Viv, it's just I'm keen to find a rational explanation for things. You know what I'm like.'

'I do!' laughed Alex.

'Sure,' said Viv. 'But not everything is as cut and dried as all that, is it?'

'Yes it is!' Newton replied. 'Or rather, it should be.'

'Emphasis on the word "should",' said Sixsmith. 'I tell you, if you thought the whole quantum thing was weird, you should see what it's like this side of the divide. Bizarre! I mean, it would never have occurred to me that antimatter would be so ...'

But as he started elaborating, Viv began talking again, rendering Sixsmith's scientific titbit inaudible. 'Do you really think that everything can be explained?' she said. 'Seems unlikely to me.'

'What did you just say? Say that again,' Newton whispered urgently.

'I said, do you really think that everything can be explained ...'

'Not you, you!' Newton blurted.

'Actually I shouldn't tell you stuff like that. It's really bad form apparently, can cause all sorts of problems.'

'What do you mean, not me? For God's sake Newton, will you settle down.' Viv delivered a potent mix of pleasure and pain with her elbow.

'Ow!'

'Ow indeed,' laughed Sixsmith. 'She's good, I'd keep that one if I was you. Look, I can't stay, I've got some meetings. They'll want to know how you're coming along.' The hallucination began fading again. 'Byeeeeee!' came a comical mock-horror laugh that faded theatrically from the room, still audible only to Newton.

'Oh boy,' he sighed, 'oh boy.' Newton, mentally and physically wrung out like an old dishcloth, and with Viv still working away upon him, faded away into a deep though troubled sleep.

******

Viv dashed off early leaving Newton to have his breakfast alone. The fresh bread, he had to admit, was wonderful, so he made himself some buttery toast before throwing on his leather jacket and heading to work. The bus he caught was badly steamed up, and Newton had to wipe the window repeatedly to see the passing houses and shops.

Any thought that the events of yesterday were isolated were soon dispelled en route. There were three separate sightings of Sixsmith – once in the doorway of a bar, again at a bus stop and then finally, on a bus going in the opposite direction gesturing frantically. Each time the apparition was grinning inanely, clearly enjoying itself. Whatever it was, it irritated Newton enormously. His mind bubbled all day, but deep down he was still confident it was something he could rationalise. Diet, poisoning, stress – it could be any one of those. What it couldn't be, absolutely 100 per cent could not be, was a ghost. At his desk in the office, he tried to work a few times but got nowhere useful and was still aimlessly rotating his mouse when the first text arrived.

*Morning Newton, hope you don't mind me following you to work. Not familiar with the geography! Best, Alex*

Newton, far from amused, texted back.

*Don't know who U R or why U R doing this, but it won't work. N*

*Oh come on N, look at the evidence, it's stacking up. Sooner or later, you're going to have to admit it's a real thing. A*

*A real what? N*

*Do I have to spell it out? A*

*Yes, N*

*G–h–o–s–t ... ghost. Yours, the late Alex Sixsmith*

*Pull the other one, it's got funeral bells on it. N*

*Please Newton, we don't have much time. Let's talk tonight. A*

Newton ignored the last text completely and tried for the rest of the day to prove his diet was lacking in zinc or some other key mineral, or that he was having an aneurism. Deadlines came and went. Denise, nice as she was, eventually ambushed him by the photocopier.

'Newton, look, I really need to see you get stuck in here. We're not a big outfit and we have to work hard just to stand still. Why are you dragging your feet?'

'Oh sorry Denise,' said Newton distractedly. 'I'll get the article finished this afternoon, promise.'

He did get it done, though it was hardly going to win him any awards. As soon as the clock hit 5.30 he was away. Denise shouted something after him, but Newton was too preoccupied to digest it. His mental health was on the line; he was fending off an assault on his peace of mind and it was all-consuming.

Back in Crouch End, he elected to head for the bar again, hoping to work things out over a pint. The barman passed him his lager while regarding him closely with scrutinising eyes. Newton sat down and began scribbling furiously in his black notebook.

He carefully listed the phenomena that had been plaguing him, from the souped-up Citroën through to the vision of Sixsmith, as well as emails and texts he was now receiving on an hourly basis. Alongside these, he listed feasible explanations, defiantly excluding anything supernatural, paranormal or just plain weird. There simply had to be a rational explanation; he'd just missed it so far, that had to be the case. He drew lines, he made lists, but still the answer eluded him and he was just on the verge of leaving when the barman arrived by his side with a plate of food.

'Hunter's chicken,' the barman mumbled.

'Hunter's what?' Newton replied, his eyes narrowed. 'I didn't order that.'

'No, but your mate did.'

'What mate?'

'The guy who was sitting with you, the bald bloke.'

'Bald bloke? But I'm on my own!' Newton said firmly.

'You might be now, but you weren't,' insisted the barman. 'The guy with the glasses ordered it.'

'When was this?'

'Just after you came in. Look mate, I've not got time for this, he bought it for you, so why don't you just eat it?' He plonked the plate down in front of Newton and huffed off to the bar. Newton looked around the pub, but there wasn't anyone of Sixsmith's description in the place. At that moment, Newton's mobile chirped and he found yet another text purporting to be from Sixsmith.

'Tuck in Newton, me old lad! Soon as you've finished, come back to the flat and we can have another quick séance.'

'Oh for fuck's sake,' shouted Newton. He left the food steaming on the table and dashed home in something of a rage.

'You should have eaten your dinner Newton, I paid good money for that!' said the ghost of Alex Sixsmith, relaxed upon the sofa as if he owned the place. 'What on earth is a hunter's chicken anyway? I mean, if he were any good as a hunter he'd kill something impressive, like a moose. But a *chicken*? How hard is it to hunt and kill a chicken?'

'What are you doing here?' screamed Newton. 'And how did you pull that stunt in the pub?'

'That? Oh, that's the old selective visibility thing. I'm getting quite good at it. Takes practise, but you get there in the end.'

'Why are you doing this to me! Haven't I suffered enough already?' yelled Newton. He went to grab Alex by what should have been his lapels, but instead of a rough physical encounter, he plunged fruitlessly into the cushions. 'Why, why, why?!'

'Newton, my dear boy,' said Sixsmith, because it really was Alex Sixsmith. 'I know this is hard for you, what with your history, and the laws of physics and everything. But I don't know how else to tell you this. I really am a ghost. I'm a spirit, a phantom, whatever you want to call it. But that's exactly what I am.'

'You can't be!' railed Newton, his head in his hands. 'It's impossible, it's irrational! I'm imagining it, that's it. It has to be that!'

'Nope, I'm afraid not,' said the ghost, as kindly as he could. 'I'd love to leave you in blissful ignorance, but I can't. You need to just open your mind a bit and see the evidence.'

'Evidence!' shouted Newton. 'What evidence?'

'OK,' said Sixsmith. 'Firstly you can see me, here in front of you. You've looked for projectors and other gadgetry and found nothing. You can see me from every angle and I'm the same. There is no projection system on earth that can do what you see now.'

'Then it's in my head!' said Newton.

'No, Newton, it's not. Look, I've made this as easy for you as I can. The barman – he saw me, so it's clearly not just you.'

'I don't understand, I don't understand,' said an increasingly worn-down Dr Newton Barlow.

'I know you don't, and that's hardly surprising. It's a mind-blowing situation. Trust me, it took me two weeks to get my head around it and I had some of the greatest minds of the last two millennia trying to explain it to me.'

'But it's impossible, what you are saying, what you are … it's just impossible!'

'Well, yes and no,' said Sixsmith. 'Thing is, we think we science bods know everything, and with good reason, considering how much time and energy we put into digging out the truth. But we can only understand what we can observe or predict. There seems to be a whole lot more to things than we could ever have imagined.'

'Like what? What are you saying?'

'I'm saying that when you die, there are a few things that pop up you weren't expecting,' said Sixsmith. 'Some I can tell you, some I can't, sadly.'

'But if you exist,' said Newton, 'well, that turns physics on its head!'

'But that's just it Newton you see. It wasn't really upright in the first place. I mean, we try – people like you and me or your dad – oh, he says hi by the way ...'

'Whaaaa ...' said Newton.

'Oops, did it again. Mustn't tell you too much!'

'But I don't understand,' said Newton sitting wearily, now resembling an end-of-season inflatable beach chair. 'The car, the money, the flat – that's not a typical haunting is it? I mean ... what's it all *for*?'

'Sorry Newton, I don't like rushing you, but before we go on, we have to have an understanding.'

'We do?'

'Yes. We need to agree that I exist. I know it's hard, I know it's weird. I realise you will doubt your own mind, and I know you'll probably feel a bit isolated from the rational world that you've made for yourself. But I need you Newton. In fact, a lot of very nice people, most of whom are dead, they need you too.'

'Who are these people? What are you talking about?'

'Newton I mean it. We have to agree that I'm real. For Pete's sake trust your own eyes and give in to the evidence.'

Newton looked hard at the phantom again. Despite all the critical reasoning in his vast arsenal, there was now no point in denying it was Sixsmith anymore. He was no projection; he was no hallucination. From the top of his glossy bald patch to the tips of his Oxford brogues it couldn't have been anyone else. Struggling with the evidence of his own eyes and a lamentable inability to convincingly deny what he was experiencing, Newton looked at the floor between his pointy shoes like a confessional schoolboy. His mind lurched from side to side like a bear in a canoe, the implications rocking his sense of reality from its once-secure foundations.

'Oh bugger,' sighed Newton. 'You're real, aren't you.'

'Yes Newton,' replied Alex in a gentle, fatherly way. 'I'm afraid I am.'

## CHAPTER 15

# TO DIE FOR

'Well,' said Dr Alex Sixsmith, taking a long deep breath he didn't actually need. 'I suppose you want to know what happened when I died? Of course you do. Well, this is my story.' When he was satisfied that Newton was fully receptive, he began.

'I knew that I was ill. And, by ill, I mean really ill. So, being practical, I'd pretty much resigned myself to the whole process of dying. Having been a black belt in pragmatism for most of my adult life, I decided that I might as well kind of roll with the whole thing and see where it took me. Importantly, I didn't have a wife or kids, so I felt I could shuffle happily off the old mortal coil, eyes wide open, without leaving too much turmoil behind me. Well, apart from my sister and your good self of course!'

'Please go on ...' said Newton.

'Well,' Sixsmith continued, 'with objectivity as my battle standard, I decided I wouldn't do the whole drug thing. Sure I was in pain, to put it mildly, but I thought – let's treat the whole thing as one last exercise in the scientific method and see where it goes, my "final experiment" as it were. If I was going to do that I needed a good, clear head, so I said no to the morphine, Valium and whatever else was hiding in the little pot. My sister was very sweet, of course – brought me grapes, the odd magazine, made me as comfortable as it is feasible to make someone with rampant terminal cancer. So, as prepared as I could be, I just lay back and waited to see what would happen.'

'Spoken like a true scientist!' said Newton. 'What happened next?'

'Well, then Jen told me that you were on your way to see me. That buggered up my little experiment straight off. Naturally I wanted to see you, but I mean, can you literally hang on for someone? You know, delay your own death? Hang on for something important? Now I can answer that one with near certainty. You can't. Visiting time was from 3pm till 8pm, but by 10am I was already half-way to the angels, and feeling like death. Well, feeling quite close to it to be accurate. Annoyingly, my mind was slipping away too – I could barely focus and I was beginning to regret turning down the happy pills. I knew exactly what it was though, no question. Death was upon me. But with no one nearby to express this to, I just stared at the clock and tried to concentrate on staying alive till you came through the door. Well, that was the hardest 45 minutes of my life, especially, of course, as they were my last. You simply can't delay the moment with will power; the old body just seems to say "bugger that!" And so, abruptly, about ten minutes before you were due, wallop! It all went blank.'

'So, you knew that you were dead at this point then?' asked Newton, his eyes narrowing.

'Well, to be objective about it,' continued Sixsmith, 'yes and no. I mean the first thing you experience is this total blankness, like you've been knocked out with a huge dose of horse pills. The pain and the discomfort just drift away so you think "great!" And then, after that comes ... well ... nothing.'

'Nothing?'

'Well I'd describe it as a white blank, as if you've been buried in pure white snow. Not much you can do but lie there, like an idiot, wondering what to do next. And that's the thing, I was still thinking, that's the odd bit. But a sort of distant kind of thinking, like hearing your own thoughts through thick blankets. Oh and I could hear, clearly, I could hear the old heart monitor flat-lining – important bit of evidence that. I was as dead as a bloody doornail! I'd croaked and no mistake. Next thing I know I start downloading.'

'Downloading?' asked Newton, taken aback by the sudden technology reference. 'What do you mean?'

'Well, you'd know it better as "having your life flash by in front of your eyes". You know the old cliché, when drowning people get flashbacks, all that malarkey. Well there I was, stone dead, and off it went, everything I'd ever done – good, bad, ugly, but mostly just plain boring, it came flooding back. School, university, girlfriends; a very odd experience. Most vivid I must say, especially the girlfriends! It seemed to take a long time, but it was only a matter of seconds, of course. It's all quite normal, you know. Your physical state conks out and you need to sort of upload or download, depends on your point of view, but essentially you have to be kind of emailed up to the other place – bit like an FTP. Peculiar analogy I know, but it really is just like that.'

'But upload to what?' asked Newton, looking baffled.

'I dunno, the other place. You travel from one world to another, like another dimension. Funny, the so-called *real world* seems real enough when you're in it, but trust me, once you leave it, you can see just how tenuous it really is. I mean physical things only "feel" solid. It's the same up there. Soon as you arrive you think, gosh, I'm not sure I really thought things through. Makes my career seem a bit pointless in some ways. But, hey, I digress – we can discuss the physics later.'

'I bloody hope so,' said Newton. 'But go on.'

'Well,' continued the late Dr Sixsmith, 'I'm lying there and I start to feel lighter, you know, the more my, well let's call it soul, downloaded to the other side. I seemed to weigh less and less until after a few minutes, I felt myself lifting off the bed. Uh oh, I thought, another bloody cliché, I'm going to have an "out-of-body experience"! But that's *exactly* what happened! I rose up from the bed, slowly, like a magician's assistant and then, cautiously, I tried opening my eyes and found myself looking into a strange white light. It was so intense, but with vague spots and dots. Anyway, it took me a while to work out what it was, you know. Bright light, dead wasps – it was the ceiling light. I was a tad disappointed by that so I turned over, rotating very smoothly, until hey presto, there I was, looking down at my own dead body. They were all gathered about me; the doctors, a couple of rather tasty young nurses and my sister. By now they'd pulled the curtains around and it all looked a tad sombre.'

'Yes, OK ... but how did you actually feel?' asked Newton.

'Well absolutely fascinated, of course,' Sixsmith continued. 'I mean it's not every day you do something like that. I was just bobbing around up there like a balloon, taking it all in. But I thought, well I can't just arse about up here wasting time, let's do some science – let's test what I can and can't do. So I thought I'd have a go at flying about a bit.'

'You could fly?'

'Yes – you only have to think about it and off you go like the bloody snowman. Weeeeeeee!' Alex extended his arms like an aeroplane. 'Well, I found the walls a bit of a problem straight off. They were hard one minute and then offering no resistance the next. Interestingly, I discovered that hitting a National Health Service corridor wall at 30 miles per hour could still hurt – I made a right bloody noise but nobody, not a soul, reacted to it. That was interesting. It seems that passing through solid matter takes a while to set in. So I tried to be more cautious and despite ending up in a linen cupboard and a drinks machine, by trial and error, I was eventually able to master flying well enough to dodge people in the corridors. It was about then that I spotted you coming in through reception. Typically late hahaha!'

'I wasn't that late,' said Newton defensively.

'Just joking, old boy. Of course I didn't mind. But picture me there! In you stroll, all serious, and I think, wayhey! Here's a chance to have a bit of fun. So ... I whizz down and land right in front of you like Superman, hands on my hips. Well OK, you paused, I managed to make you do that at least, but then you just ambled right through me without batting a bloody eyelid. Well thank you! I wasn't going to accept that lying down, so I shot back past you and had another go. Same thing again. Typical, I thought – never could get your attention!'

'I didn't notice anything,' said Newton, looking vaguely hurt. 'I mean I thought you were still alive at this time, remember!'

'Only teasing, Newton old boy. You weren't to know,' said Sixsmith reassuringly. 'Anyway, at that moment you bumped into my sister. So I watched that, your big emotional reaction, quite moving really.' Newton blushed. 'Don't worry Newton my lad, I was rather touched. But it was very frustrating because I really, really, wanted to say or do something, and of course, I couldn't. So I just bobbed about wondering what to do next.'

'So what did you do?'

'Well, I thought, I can't stay here. Watching other people grieving over you – that's like the vainest thing ever. It's the sort of thing an actor would do. It's why they discourage the dead from going to their own funerals. It either makes people have a completely overblown view of their importance or they come back muttering under their breath about what a bunch of shits their family and friends are. That wasn't for me, so I thought, let's go walkies. So I tested the front doors to see if I could go through them, which by this time I could, easily. Then I went whizzing off.'

'Where did you go?' asked Newton.

'Well exactly, where *do* you go? Take a train, follow the roads? I was strangely worried about getting lost. Haha! I needn't have worried – I only had to think of somewhere and I'd start hurtling off at a real lick in that direction. The speeds Newton, you wouldn't believe! I was really barrelling along! Especially odd because at that stage I hadn't worked out that it's best to go over houses rather than through them. Luckily, by now the whole "going through things" business had settled down, so when I hurtled through a retirement home at 500 plus miles per hour, I wasn't breaking the china. It was bloody peculiar, but at least it wasn't dangerous. After a while I'd really got into the swing of things and I could either jump directly to a given spot, or I could go somewhere at a kind of cruise speed. At one stage I saw this jet, a fast military job. This guy was way, way off from me and clearly going flat out. But I caught up with him effortlessly, what a bloody ride! I found I could just stand on the wing as we roared through the clouds – amazing, incredible, just plain bonkers!'

'Hold on, that's not possible, what about wind resistance?' asked Newton, struggling to make sense of the physics.

'Wind? Hardly anything. If I had any hair left it might have been blowing about maybe, but no, no air pressure, nothing!'

'Like you say,' said Newton looking doubtful, 'bonkers.'

'Anyhow,' continued Sixsmith uninhibited by Newton's incredulity, 'the pilot must have noticed something because he kept casting a glance back every so often and shaking his head.'

'You think he could see you?'

'No,' said Sixsmith, 'but I think he could *sense* me, somehow. At any rate I started to feel I was intruding on his working day, so I just sort of jumped off the wing and watched him whizz off. And that's when I saw the other bloke.'

'I'm sorry?'

'Yeah, another guy was there in the clouds,' said Sixsmith. 'He'd been watching me and was having a right old laugh at my expense. I was going to say something, but before I could, he waved nonchalantly and shot off like a firework and I lost sight of him in the clouds. And then, gradually, I started to see a lot of other people; first one, distantly whizzing along close to the ground, another at high altitude. It's like when you look for minnows in a mill pond – suddenly they seemed to be everywhere! No matter where I looked, I could see them zipping about like swallows. So I thought, let's try some formation flying. But no. Just as soon as I was getting anywhere near them, either I'd slow down or they'd shoot ahead. Pretty frustrating! So I thought, and not for the first time, sod other people! The question was, could I go farther than I already had?'

'Farther?'

'Yes, you know, space. Boldly go and all that.'

'You went into *space*?' said Newton, gobsmacked.

'You bet yer sweet scientific arse I went into space,' said Sixsmith, beaming like a child just down off a roller coaster. 'I just pointed myself up, and wham, off like a sodding rocket. Amazing, simply amazing! I went right through the atmosphere like it wasn't there, and then, there I was dodging space junk. The speeds were incredible, breathtaking! My scientist's mind, as you can probably imagine, was racing. I mean Newton, all the big questions I could finally answer, a one-man space probe! So I started heading into deeper space – where no man had gone before, well at least not a living one.'

'And?'

'Newton, what can I say? Incredible. The planets close up are even better than you'd think, such colours. Such extremes ... the geology alone is to die for – literally!'

'So tell me!' urged Newton, sensing he was on the edge of something big.

'Ah, now there's the rub Newton,' Sixsmith backtracked. 'You're going to have to get used to this I'm afraid.'

'Get used to what?'

'Well the thing is, all the things I saw, the amazing, incredible science, the spectacular discoveries ...'

'Yes?'

'Well the thing is ...' He paused knowing how badly it would rest with Newton. 'The thing is ... I *can't* tell you.'

'Whaaaatt?' blurted Newton, frustrated beyond measure.

'I'm not allowed to. Not a sausage, sorry. It's the way of things old boy. Sorry but there it is. Makes perfect sense I'm afraid. Think of it like an advanced alien civilisation visiting the earth. Would it be right to pass on things that were just too sophisticated? Very dangerous.'

'But I'm a scientist – I need to know! You can trust me.'

'I can't actually, it's too risky. We've just got to let humanity bumble along alone. Let the living find things out at their own natural speed. Things I saw on Europa and Titan, for instance, I couldn't risk that getting out ahead of time, would really bugger things up.'

'Whooah! Back up there professor. What did you see on Europa?'

'There you go,' said Alex slapping his forehead. 'I've got to be more careful! Nough said!'

'Alex!' begged Newton.

'Really Newton, there are strict protocols we have to adhere to. We

151

can't risk another alchemy.'

'Alchemy?'

'Sure, the alchemists were that close to working out the connection between crocodiles and gold – all it takes is a casual word in the wrong ear and wham, meltdown. Luckily they were mostly charlatans, but it does go to show what can happen if things start leaking out.'

'Crocodiles? Gold? OK, I'll let that little nugget go for now,' said Newton reluctantly. 'Go on with the story ... you were in space.'

'Ah, yes. Well, I was whizzing around, taking in all the sights when I thought, hold on! Just how far can I go? So I put my foot down on the pedal and headed off to a nearby star, Vega I think it was. A bluish-white one. Well, I must have got half way there when I suddenly started decelerating. Eventually I just stopped, right out there in deep space. Talk about a feeling of isolation – it was the emptiest, most unexciting place I'd ever been to outside the West Midlands. Then, subtly at first, I found myself turning back. An odd feeling, just like someone else was driving. I went barrelling back past Neptune, Saturn, Jupiter and then finally, the earth again. Gutted! Well, there I am back in the clouds. There's these folk again, whizzing around in a flock like starlings. Soon I'm part of this flock. We're all kind of in a big whirlpool. In fact, if anything it resembled a planetary system forming around a new star.'

'How so?' asked Newton.

'Well, all these people were drifting in towards this single point, like gas and dust in a newborn solar system. Men, women, children; all races and creeds just zooming around in this bloody great spiral. There we were, all twisting into the centre when suddenly ... bang! The centre exploded in a monumental burst of white light. Pow! You could hardly look at it directly. It was just so bright. It just bleached out everything. And then, before I could even think about it, I was sucked straight in.'

'What happened next?'

'I found myself standing in this gigantic empty room.'

'A *room?*'

'Yes, a room, a huge room, like an enormous aircraft hangar. I stood there alone for a second but gradually other people appeared alongside me. Eventually we formed into a huge long line, basically a queue. Well an infinite number of queues in fact.'

'You were queuing?'

'Well yes, and that was when all the fun stopped,' said Alex, looking forlorn at the memory. 'One minute I'm charging magnificently around the universe, and the next moment I'm queuing to go through airport security.'

'Really?' asked Newton, more confused and incredulous than ever.

'Yup, that's the only word for it. Long bloody queue, absolutely crawling along. I was there for days! Interminable. Anyway, just as I was about to go la-la, I rolled up to this gloss-white booth with a guy in it. And he was a right case this chap, all gold hair and white flying robes, looking all important with his rubber stamp and his iPad. Well I say iPad, a tablet, it kind of worked the same way – snow-white things, marble effect. He was tapping away. Asking questions.'

'What? Have you been good or evil, that kind of stuff? I'm guessing these are ... er ... angels?' asked Newton, not quite believing what he was saying out loud.

'Nooooo, that would be too funny. No, they're mostly ancient Greeks, hence the classical robes. Sandal-mad, most of them. They've been working there a long time. First come first served, and all that.'

'Working? They have *jobs*?'

'Sure. Not for money though I must add – it's all about boredom, it's really, really boring up there. If they weren't all dead already, they'd probably kill themselves.'

'Heaven is boring?' asked Newton, oddly disappointed by something he didn't believe in.

'You'd better believe it, though this is Purgatory Newton, not heaven. Big distinction. Anyway, this classical guy asks me about how I died. Where was I from? Languages I could speak? Office skills, that kind of thing. A huge great list of questions, and then eventually, up comes the barrier and you go in for your strip search.'

'Er ... hello ...'

'I'm not kidding, they have to make sure you've not sneaked anything naughty in,' said Sixsmith.

'Like what?'

'Mobile phones, laptops, camcorders, digital cameras.'

'You can sneak in electronics?!' Newton was shaking his head.

'Well sort of, I mean if you're really wedded to something like that, which of course we all are now, you can bring the damn things with you as phantoms. It's a real headache, actually, because there's a risk that sooner or later some buffoon is going to start broadcasting stuff from up there that we shouldn't see down here. They go to huge efforts to make sure you don't have any recording equipment or online facilities.'

'But you emailed me. How did you do that?'

'We're not luddites, we have a few terminals where we can tap into mortal communications. Which is very useful, frankly, because of ... well I'll come to that.'

'So you weren't judged on your life and all that?'

'Nah, that's a myth, all that stuff. The guilt and retribution is all self-administered when you have your life played back during the download. That's enough to sort some people out for good, though the really bad eggs are another issue. No, you just go into this series of seminars and they teach you how everything works. To be honest, I found it a bit tedious.'

'Why is it so dull?'

'Well, the presentations are awful for a start, and it's mind-numbingly bureaucratic.'

'It is?'

'Hell yes. Sorry, bad choice of words! But yes it's bureaucratic, it's all rules and regulations and the colour, white ... everything is bloody white! Half of the new arrivals get snow blindness. And there's so much paperwork. You're forever filling out forms about this that or the other, endless. I can see why they have to do it – peace is never exciting and thrills mean danger – but all the same, it drives you so nuts you start wandering round desperate to entertain yourself. So with eternity to kill, what do you do? My first thought was to hunt down some of the really famous historic people I'd always wanted to meet – say hi. Well that turned out a bit odd, I can tell you.'

'Why?'

'Well I thought, who shall I see first, and my mind went blank, such a big choice. But after a while I thought, I know, Nelson! I'll find Lord Nelson!'

'You met Lord Nelson?!'

'Sure,' said Alex smugly. 'So, here's this hugely well-known historical figure sitting on a bench, a white bench of course, looking as bored as it's possible for a man to look. I sidled up to him and I said "hello, you're Lord Nelson". "Yes," he says without looking up, "so I bloody well am." He looked really annoyed, and I can see why now.

I came out with such an inane series of questions, every one of them a cliché of gargantuan proportions. How did it feel to win the battle of the Nile? What do you think of Nelson's column? All that kind of crap. He was actually quite nice about it, considering, and once he'd stopped swearing at me in this rich Regency maritime vernacular, he put me straight about a few things.'

'Such as?'

'Well you simply can't ask someone like that a question they haven't heard a million times before, so it can get bloody annoying for them. It's even worse for the ancients. Poor old Caesar, Agamemnon and that bunch – those guys have been driven half mad by the new arrivals for millennia.'

'I can imagine, especially with the numbers constantly swelling. It must be wall-to-wall up there.'

'Ah well, the thing is you see, it's *not*, and this is where it gets really interesting. Most of the new arrivals are your average man and woman, part of that huge mass of humanity that just come and go unnoticed both here and there. They're heading for whatever it is that happens *after* Purgatory. Bless them, they are so nondescript and un-newsworthy that they are quickly and utterly forgotten, the lucky blighters. With no one remembering them beyond the odd photo in the family album, they can fade happily away to the other place – they can rest in peace.'

'The *other* place? Is that heaven?'

'Would love to tell you, but in all honesty, we don't know any more about that than you do. All we're sure of is that you can't get the hell out of Purgatory until people stop talking about you, here on earth. That seems to be the substance of it. And bear in mind, Purgatory is so boring that it's, well ...'

'Purgatory?'

'Yep, it's absolutely tedious. So what you really want is to get out of there and get some decent eternal sleep. But, if you've made the mistake of making yourself famous, infamous or leaving some other form of historical legacy, you've really shot yourself in the foot. Every time you crop up in the national consciousness, there goes your chance of getting away from an eternity of mindless boredom. I wonder just how keen people would be to make themselves famous if they knew the truth. I've seen celebrities banging their heads on the white walls after a month or two.'

'So it's better to live a quiet life then?'

'Oh completely. God, if you could see the state Lawrence of Arabia has got himself into. And Alexander the Great – well, he's a lot of things these days and "great" certainly isn't one of them. Nothing gets you down as much as boredom, Newton, and Purgatory has that in spades.'

'Isn't it something that the Bible goes on about? Or, Dante's *Inferno*? That has Purgatory in it. If we aren't meant to know these things, then how does it leak out like that?'

'You're quite right; it *has* leaked out over the millennia. That's because when all this got started and civilisation was being test driven, a few bad mistakes were made. Secrecy wasn't as tight as it is now. Back in those days you'd tell some guy – and Dante's a good example – then as soon as you turned your back he'd use what he'd learned to gain power, start a religion or write a simply divine comedy.'

'Ah, so they did tell people the truth?'

'Well they had to, there are a lot of loose ends that need tying up, you know, when people die.'

'Loose ends?'

'Yes, you see, just like the mobile phones and the cameras, there are things that are kind of stuck between the two realities, awkward things, and they have to be "cleaned up". I'll give you an example. There are relics, accidental and deliberate, that get left behind here on earth. These have the effect of keeping specific individuals in a vivid state up there in Purgatory. Some of them are useful people – good souls who help things tick over in a controlled though admittedly boring state. These people are not especially famous, so they have to do things to keep their memory alive.'

'Such as?' asked Newton.

'Well they create relics. They hide things in antiques, buy up their personal possessions, and clean headstones. There's a bit of cheating, you know – they make an artist more famous than he ought to be just so people talk about them a lot. Edvard Munch, for instance. Those awful miserable things he did, they should have been forgotten a long time ago, but it turns out he's great at double-entry book-keeping so they had to cheat a bit and keep him in the public eye.'

'That's not fair on the art world is it?'

'Well, since when was the art world *fair*? Have you seen Tracey Emin's stuff?'

'Good point.'

'Now the other side of the coin is that there are bad people, nasty, evil mean-spirited, err, spirits. You'd think people would want to avoid thinking about them as much as possible but, in fact, sadly, the opposite is true. Half of what is on the History Channel is about Hitler or some other historical scumbag. Every time they run *History's Top Ten Evil Men*, they all start swanning around again causing trouble.'

'Can't you stop them?'

'Well yes, thankfully, there's a kind of prison, they keep the worst ones in there.'

'Prison? How can you detain somebody who can whizz through walls?'

'It's not easy. I don't understand the science and I certainly don't understand all the chanting and other mumbo jumbo required – all I know is that they've got these bastards all tied up in ectoplasm.'

'So what happens if they get out?'

'Bad stuff. Invariably, they're hell bent on getting back to earth and causing mayhem. Possessions, poltergeists, arson, reality television, anywhere they can cause trouble, they will. You've got to keep a close eye on them. And of course, they're not moving on up there so long as people down here insist on finding evil fascinating.'

'But how are you defining evil?'

'That's a complex one. Other people can explain that better than me. Suffice to say, evil is a major headache for the people that run the place, the council so to speak. Without those chaps and the solid bureaucratic effort they put in, the earth would be awash with all manner of nasties.'

'So are these cells filled with people like ... er ... I mean, is Hitler there?'

'Oh hell yes, he's not what he was though. After the war he kind of lost his puff a bit and he doesn't do much beyond muttering. Goebbels and Himmler are much worse.'

'Any other big names?'

'Jack the Ripper, lots of serial murderers.'

'Jack the Ripper. Does that mean you know who he was?'

'I do now. Sorry, can't tell you though.'

'Dammit! Protocol?'

'Sorry, yes. Not everyone is well known though – evil isn't always front-page news, quite often it's hidden in the small ads. The evil deeds hang on whether they're famous or not. Either way, they have to be sealed off and removed, one relic or memory at a time.'

'You can do that, how?'

'Well you have to root the stuff out. Once you have it you can "dispose" of it.'

'And that gets rid of them?'

'With the older villains it does. They might be on a bit of papyrus here, a wall carving there. That's not such a problem. With the Nazis it's just not on, they're bloody everywhere, all over the historical record like flies. Films, memorabilia, fetish parties ... everywhere. All you can do is truss the buggers up and hope for the best. But for the older scumbags, well that's where we need the odd mortal agent here on terra firma who can root the stuff out for us.'

'Interesting,' said Newton, who by now was worrying that he would believe anything. 'Ludicrous but interesting. OK, so let me summarise ...' Newton thought for a painful mind-flipping second while he gathered his frazzled wits. 'If I'm to believe everything you've told me, the following is true:

(1) When you die you can fly?'

'Yessum.'

'(2) When you die, you eventually end up at something akin to a flight check-in and queue for three days to have an intimate body search?'

'Sadly ... yes.'

'(3) The afterlife is very white and very boring?'

'Dull as ditchwater, yes.'

'(4) Famous people are forced by their own fame to stay in Purgatory longer?'

'Correct.'

'And ... this I particularly like, they hate it.'

'They do, they loathe it ... well, not Marcel Proust, oddly he seems to thrive on it.'

'(5) Evil people are kept in cells to stop them returning to earth as ghosts?'

'Essentially, yes ...'

'(6) When you're forgotten, you just fade away?'

'So I gather.'

'(7) Purgatory employs living people to do small jobs for them on earth to help keep things under control?'

'Yes that's about it – I have to say you are a lot better at explaining it than I was, very succinct.'

Newton closed his eyes and leant back, sighing. 'You've got to be fucking mad if you think I'm going to buy all that.'

'Oh not again, Newton, I thought we were past this.'

'Oh I'm convinced you're a ghost. But the rest of it ... that's just mad!'

'Newton! Dammit, I'm telling you the truth!'

'Yeah right! I'm sorry, it's all too unlikely.'

'Well of course it is!' exclaimed Alex.

'Look, if I take all this onboard then it makes my whole life a complete farce!'

'You can't blame *me* for that!'

'But you're telling me that all these nut jobs I've been debunking all this years, all the mediums and ghost hunters, they were *right*?'

'Actually, no, no I'm not. You can rest easy there. Most of the loons are definitely loons – liars, dreamers and fantasists. They mostly made it all up. In that respect, you were on the button. It's just that you didn't realise there was something else going on. Something real. The real mediums work in the shadows – unseen.'

'Oh boy, my head hurts.' Newton sat glumly for a moment, trying to sort everything into a natural and pragmatic shape, which he couldn't. 'Hold on a moment Alex, why are you telling me all this? Surely that's the last thing you should be doing?'

'Well look, that's the thing. When I rolled up in Purgatory, I was sent to this office where this robed chap starts asking me all about science. He tells me all about the problems they've been having working with the living, going way back. When they first started to need a presence here on earth, they just weren't sure how to go about it; after all, at that time everyone was three sheets to the wind on myth and magic mushrooms. They tried to recruit the odd bloke as an agent and that started up all sorts of weird stuff. He'd start wearing feathers on his head, go mad or jump into a volcano. Later, they managed to get a bit better because people were getting smarter – the Greeks were pretty good, the Romans less so. Apparently, the Dark Ages were a bloody nightmare. You could fill a peasant's breeches just by saying hello to them in those days, and once the Middle Ages proper had started, it was all witches this and heretics that. With the

Enlightenment, you get a whole set of new problems.'

'How so,' said Newton.

'Well, questioning people like Newton or Halley – give them an inch and they'll want to go the full nautical mile. Do that and you create a monster, from sedan chairs to the Space Shuttle in ten years, very dangerous.'

'Ah, so there *is* science up there then?'

'Sure, in a way, but not in a way you'd recognise. It's all a lot more instinctive. Proper science with experiments, peer review, university research – all that's impossible, everything is so unfocused. The emphasis is on all these powers that everyone seems to possess by default. Up there, we can see everything in a way that you can't when you're alive. You can sort of see into things like atoms, molecules, particles. There's no equivalent to CERN up there, if that's what you mean. You don't need all the equipment because you *are* the equipment.'

'OK, so how come there's a danger of knowledge leaking out to us mere mortals then?'

'Well, it's all to do with knowing what's possible. We can't afford to give anyone any ideas. It would end in tears. Weapons research would be on it like a shot. You can't let the living anywhere near that. You see, a lot of the stuff I thought I understood, I didn't really. Well … I do now.'

'Such as?' said Newton, chancing his arm.

'Dimensions, quantum theory, string theory. Some right, some wrong.

'Which are wrong?'

'Aha. There you go again. Nice try. But Newton, really, I can't tell you. What I can say is that having seen under the bonnet, so to speak, I can now understand so many, many things.'

'*All* things? You mean a theory of … *everything*?'

'Oh good lord no! There's always more out there, some of the new phenomena I've seen, well … you couldn't make it up. Even a third-rate science fiction writer out of his nut on LSD couldn't contrive the *real* nature of matter. And anyway, up there we've no way of testing or analysing this stuff I've seen – well not yet anyway. No, there's no theory of everything in the end, Newton, just more "everythings" to look for.'

'I don't know whether I find that frustrating or comforting,' said Newton. 'I mean, it does kind of underline the idea that we've all been spending our lives chasing shadows.'

'Oh sure, but they're *important* shadows. One day I suspect the two worlds will connect, mainly because of the effort people like you and I have put in. But for now, I'm afraid they have to remain separate.'

'Oh boy,' said Newton, wearily. 'I don't know what to make of all this.'

'Yup, that was my thought initially. We just aren't wired up to take it in easily. Even old-fashioned mediums take years to settle in.'

'Mediums? I just can't believe that mediums are real,' said Newton incredulous. 'I spent most of my adult life knocking those people down.'

'And rightly so,' confirmed Sixsmith. 'In reality, a good medium wouldn't do TV, séances or anything like that. They'd work discreetly doing the odd job that was requested and then blend back in with normal life. Sadly, a lot of the time they find out the truth and take advantage – or worse. We've had people starting religions, robbing people blind, fraud. Quite a large number just go stark raving mad, they can't deal with it rationally at all.'

'I'm not surprised to be honest.'

'With the age of reason, the plan in Purgatory was to avoid the rational and use all manner of crazies to do the work. So they recruited fortune tellers, religious separatists, hermits, witches. Well, needless to say, that was a big mistake; they all ended up dunked, burnt or beheaded. All the same, they kept doing it, so worried were they about a bridge between rational analysis and the afterlife.' Sixsmith then paused in his story and looked at Newton. 'Until now.'

'Uh oh,' said Newton, 'I think I know where this is going. You want *me* to be one, don't you?'

'Be one what?'

'A medium.'

'Err ... well frankly, yes.'

'Are you serious?! After all I've been through, all I've said on the subject, and you want *me* to be a bloody medium?'

'Oh go on.'

'No, that's N O. No.'

'Wait ... Newton, let me explain. It's a great deal.'

'You have to be joking, Alex. How can I be a medium? The whole idea is ludicrous.'

'You're thinking of the old-style medium, this is the new version. Medium 2.1! It's pragmatic, it's scientific, you'd love it!'

'Scientific my arse! After everything you've been telling me, you expect me to buy that? No Alex. I won't do it.'

'You'd make a great medium. You'd be practical, pragmatic, grounded and logical.'

'Bugger off, I won't do it.'

'Oh go on.'

'No.'

'How about if I explain the staff benefits?'

'The whaaat? Now you're just taking the piss.'

'No really! It's a proper paying job. You get holidays – loads of holidays – and there'll be a lot of travel.'

'Oh come on, you just suggested I become a medium, now you're making it sound like a position in middle management. Anyway, I've already got a job.'

'Oh yes, I noticed that,' Sixsmith muttered dismissively.

'What's wrong with it? I had to start somewhere.'

'Well, it's hardly stimulating compared to what you can and did do!'

'We all know what happened there, and by the way Alex, dead or not dead, why don't you just say it?'

'Say what?'

'I told you so. About Havotech.'

'Oh yes, good point,' said Alex, 'I told you so.'

'Yes,' said Newton flatly, 'but you really did though, didn't you? Sorry Alex, you were right. I was a pompous arrogant little tit. I should have listened.' Newton was so far from his comfort zone he could no longer see it, even with binoculars.

'Well listen to me now. Newton, seriously, this is an interesting job I'm offering you. Unique. Well not *unique*, I suppose, there are a few other people helping us.'

'How many?'

'Not sure, couple of hundred.'

'Worldwide?'

'Oh no, that's just in the UK.'

'Well I'm not going to be one of them Alex. Sorry. You'll have to ask someone else.'

'Newton, I'm begging you to reconsider. This is the chance of a lifetime. The work is fascinating, the pay is good, the hours are flexible and you get to meet lots of interesting people, most of whom,

162

admittedly, are dead.'

'Sorry Alex, I can't, I just can't. Maybe it's a pride thing. But I just can't. I'd be an unhappy medium.'

'Look,' said Sixsmith softly, 'I understand, I really do. I'd be exactly the same in your place.'

'Well you're *not* in my place Alex. I'm sorry. I can't do it.'

'But why not at least have a think about it. Give it a few days?'

'OK,' said Newton reluctantly. 'I'll think about it. But don't hold your breath. I won't change my mind.'

'Thanks,' said Sixsmith, transparency beginning to return to his outline. 'Look I've got to go now, I'm puffed out. Have a good think. You know how to reach me.'

'I do?'

'Sure,' said Alex, 'just whistle and I'll come to you my lad.'

CHAPTER 16

# HOSPITALITY

Chris Baxter, salesman, sat immaculate on the lumpy old bed and breathed out a long frustrated sigh. He'd been living and working at Hadlow Grange with the McCauleys for an entire week, yet nothing had actually happened. Sure, they'd showed him a few local developments – Juggin's Lump and the Cemetery Estate up by Blandford – but they'd hardly made use of his sales acumen and there had been no further mention of the whole television thing. Also, he wasn't at all happy about the conditions in the Hadlow Grange residential suite, as Ascot had called it. He'd put a suit on every morning, just to fly his own flag, but the absence of any real business environment was starting to make him feel a bit of an idiot. He looked around the distasteful little attic room with its damp patches and peeling paper. There was a framed jigsaw of Constable's The Hay Wain on the wall; several pieces had fallen down behind the ill-fitted glass, including the bits showing the dog and the cartwheel.

Baxter's first proper meeting with the McCauleys had also been something of a disappointment. It didn't really seem to go anywhere at all, though the brothers had at least explained something about the company strategy.

'We specialise in the more *controversial* sites,' Ascot had told him. 'We buy up prisons, graveyards, sites of special scientific interest, beauty spots, nature reserves, public spaces … it's a bit of a calling frankly. We then turn these locations into cheap affordable housing or industrial units.' Ascot showed Chris the big map of Britain, his bony finger seeking out sites amongst the flags and post-its. 'Of course, you can see that there are so many places simply begging to be developed! I mean, look here.' He pointed up at Scotland. 'Oh, if we only had the freedom to break free of restrictions and petty bureaucracy! Culloden Moor – we could put five hundred new residences on that little beauty, no problem. And as for Glencoe, well! The views are magnificent, the setting breathtaking – perfect for a leisure resort.'

'Great!' said Chris Baxter, hoping for a cut of the action. He'd never heard of either the battle or the massacre, but he wouldn't have been interested anyway.

'People are so sentimental, don't you think Mr Baxter?' Chris nodded back obligingly. 'But progress, my dear boy, that's the thing.' Ascot's finger drifted south. 'Look here, a massive plague pit in Northampton. A historic tythe barn in Cirencester, circa 1250, but with perfect access to the M4 and ample parking – but oh no, listed!' he snarled with frustration. 'And here, a petting zoo, smack bang in the centre of Wolverhampton, the perfect site for a Toys R Us or a B&Q. You know, Mr Baxter, it breaks my heart.' Ascot attempted a sincere expression, like a hyena begging for scraps at a safari park. 'I have a *big* heart,' he continued, 'and it breaks that heart to see prime unexploited real estate left to rot for what is laughingly called "the nation". After all, what is a nation if it is *not* a large-scale housing development? When you can have a brand-new house with a built-in garage and picture windows, why would you prefer to wander around the site of some dreary massacre or battle?'

'Absolutely,' said Chris.

Later, when the day was over, the McCauleys invited Chris and Miss Dryer for dinner in the Grange's old dining room, the food served by the impossibly old chef, a wizened gentleman with chronic shakes. The cook had been travelling backwards and forwards from the walled kitchen garden via a service tunnel all morning, sacks of spuds and winter vegetables slung over his bowed shoulder in a netted shopping bag. The resulting meal, when it finally made it to the table, was foul. Even the water was watery. The unidentifiable meat had been boiled until it was grey, the cabbage until it was transparent, and the potato hovered uneasily between mash and soup. They ate in silence, their knives scratching uncomfortably on the chipped china, setting Baxter's wonderfully intact teeth on edge. As if that wasn't enough, he became convinced that Miss Dryer, pouting like an elderly Monroe, had winked continuously at him during the main course. By desert, a bowl of prunes in custard, he was certain something was up when her stockinged foot began playing with his right leg under the table. He danced his feet from side to side to avoid the unwelcome attention until a big grandfather clock mercifully clanged 9pm, giving Baxter the chance to make his excuses and a quick exit to his ugly damp attic room.

'I'll give it a few weeks,' thought Chris, as he tried to get comfortable beneath the blanched covers. 'I'll get a flat nearby if I have to.' As always, he repeated his nightly prayers to Dale Carnegie until, finally, he began to drift away into an itchy sleep. He was on the verge of a wonderful dream about international business travel when he heard a distinct creak in the corridor outside and his eyes flipped wide open.

He could think of no reason for anyone to be there. His room was up more rickety small staircases than Chris had ever seen before, each one smaller than the last. Up in the attic, there were only a few store cupboards and empty offices, and no one else had a bedroom there. He was relieved he'd locked the door. As he turned his head towards the sound, he noticed the hall light shining through a sizable gap below the door and distinct shadows cast by two small feet hesitating outside.

'Hello?' he said quietly, swallowing, half wanting no reply.

'Hello Mr Baxter, are you in there?' came Miss Dryer's voice with a worrying, homeopathic trace of kitten in it.

'Err hello, Miss Dryer, yes ...' said Chris, pulling the damp covers up to his chin. She left a long pause.

'Is there anything I can get you, Christopher?' she said in an artificially low register.

'No, I'm fine thank you,' said Chris.

The door handle rotated, but the lock held.

'It can get very lonely out here on the heath,' said Miss Dryer. 'A woman can get ... ideas.'

'Ideas?' said Chris.

'Oh yes,' came the deep-breathing voice through the door. 'I shall have to watch myself. I wouldn't want to lose my virtue.' The handle was pulled a little harder, a trace of frustration in the rotation of the doorknob.

'Well it's a bit late,' said Chris, directing a long ostentatious yawn towards the door. 'I should be getting to sleep, busy day and all that.'

'My room is on the second floor,' said Miss Dryer, ignoring Chris's evasion. 'I never lock it, you know, never!'

'You don't?' stuttered Baxter.

'Oh no, there might be a fire.'

'Well quite.'

'I might need to go and get some water ...' she continued, pausing for effect, 'in my nightclothes.'

'Right ... of course,' said Baxter. 'Well if you don't mind, I'd best get off to sleep now.'

There was a long pause followed by a brief but frantic turning of the door handle. 'So it's goodnight then?'

'Goodnight Miss Dryer,' said Chris firmly. Finally, to his great relief, he heard reluctant footsteps descending the narrow staircase. He lay still for a while, looking at the ceiling, trying to get things in perspective.

'You've still got it,' he said to himself and turned off the light.

CHAPTER 17

# AN UNHAPPY MEDIUM

How did ghosts work? What particles did they use? Where was this Purgatory, and was it made of solid matter? Or for that matter, did it matter? Did anything matter? Dr Newton Barlow's mind was full of questions and no satisfactory answers whatsoever. His old life with its certainties, nice comfy laws of physics and everyday common sense lay winded on the canvas. None of it made sense, not even slightly. He sighed heavily yet again and looked at his monitor. He was trying desperately to make himself complete an article about ten-dimensional space-time for Living Physics, but now, devoid of all his old reference points, he felt that he might as well have been typing an alphabetic list of famous clowns.

Physics, he thought bitterly, had disobeyed the laws of physics.

Perhaps, deep down, he'd kept alive a hope that somehow, against the odds, he'd regain his old position in academia, somehow escaping the mushroom cloud of doubt that had tainted his reputation. Now, he felt surer than ever that this could never happen. How could he hope to unlearn the bizarre truths bubbling through the once-watertight lid of his own personal universe? He couldn't even try to explore these weird revelations using hard science. Not only was there no hard science anymore, he couldn't possibly explain to his fellow physicists where these revelations were coming from. All that was over and he knew it, so sitting there in the magazine's office, struggling to describe multidimensional spaces in the light of recent events – it was about as futile as a degree in Klingon.

At least things had improved with his daughter. Halfway through the interminable morning, Gabby sent him a grounding text, and he'd reassured her he'd be taking her out again soon and pressed send. But that didn't alleviate the ennui for long, so sighing, he turned back to struggle half-heartedly with the article, feeling increasingly like an atheist editing a parish magazine. He found himself aimlessly moving the mouse around in circles while he pondered the endless implications. In a last bid to shake himself out of the rut, he rang Viv, who was at home celebrating the fact she'd been rejected for

168

another job.

'Hello fruitcake!' she teased. 'Whassup?'

'I'm leaving crumbs everywhere thanks,' sighed Newton, desperately wanting to share the unsharable.

'Any new phenomena you'd like to tell me about?' said Viv, munching on toast.

'Oh just the usual,' said Newton wearily. 'It's fun going mad. I've never had such clean laundry.'

'I usually associated madness with soiled clothing,' replied Viv. 'You should count yourself lucky. Anyway, when are you going to take me for a spin in this weird car of yours then?'

'How about the weekend? I've promised to take Gabby out.'

'Woahhh!' said Viv. 'Is it meet-the-kids time already?'

'Well, it's just that we seem to be getting on well for a change, and it might be a good time to get it over with.'

'Get it over with?' Viv said, slightly annoyed. 'Well seeing as you put it so nicely.'

'Sorry, that sounded bad. I mean, if you don't want to ...'

'No it's fine,' Viv said reassuringly. 'It's one of these classic awkward things you have to do I guess. Just hope she likes me.'

'She will! Of course she will. OK look, let's say I give you a ring on Friday to arrange things.'

'OK,' said Viv doubtfully, 'love you.' She rang off a trifle more abruptly than normal, leaving Newton sitting there even more despondent than before. Utterly distracted, he ground once again to a halt.

Lunchtime passed in a blur of half-eaten sandwiches and a sly pint of lager in a nearby pub. Newton returned reluctantly to his desk to find a post-it note from Denise slap-bang in the centre of his monitor.

'See me,' it ordered.

'Sorry Newton,' she offered apologetically as he entered her office, 'this just isn't working out.'

'Err no,' said Newton. 'Bit of a bad week. Sorry.'

'Bit of a bad month,' she corrected. 'Look Newton, I'd love to help you but I can't. The stuff you've been doing – it's all over the place.'

'It is? I hadn't noticed.'

'Well that's just the problem. I can't cover for you Newton – the other staff are getting really peeved. Look at this!' she said, pointing at a subbed printout covered in corrections. 'You've even stopped using spell-check, there are two s's in pointless.'

'I knew that.'

'And everything's late. I can't protect you, it's not fair on the others.' He looked out through the glass at the other staff. As one, they quickly looked away and pretended to work.

'Err no, sorry,' he said, shuffling awkwardly from foot to foot. 'So you're letting me go? Don't I get a warning?'

'I sent you two, Newton, and they're still unopened on your desk.'

'*Those*? I thought they were pay slips.'

'No.'

'Oh right. Well fair enough then, I guess.'

'Look, maybe you need to do something completely different – get away, clear your head.' Denise tried again to look kindly. 'Have a word with Viv, she seems good for you. Ask her what she thinks. I'm sure you can get some amazing offers if you think things through.'

'Funny you should say that ...' started Newton, before changing his mind. 'I'm sorry, look I mean thanks for helping me and I'm sorry I couldn't hold it together. Things are a tad ... complex.'

'I do understand, really.'

'I doubt you do actually,' thought Newton as he pecked her gratefully on the cheek. And once again, yet another bridge had been burnt, this one while he was standing on it. He cleared his desk of not very much at all, and with his thoughts pressing down on him like a fallen bookcase, he wandered out onto the street and straight into a pub.

Five pints later, Newton was wandering aimlessly around north London feeling a mix of euphoria, pointlessness and self-destructive nihilism that only comes from draught lager and/or a sudden unexpected familiarity with the afterlife. He eventually found himself up on Hampstead Heath, the huge sprawling survivor of woodland that had once surrounded London when it was still unpleasantly small and yet to burn down. He grumpily wandered, hands deep in his jacket pockets, along the footpaths between the old trees.

Eventually he found himself at Highgate. From the High Street he looked towards the crowded roads of Archway and Holloway to the south, getting a clear if wind-chilling view of the spectacular dome of St Paul's in the old heart of London some five miles away.

Then, backtracking towards home, he headed into a leafier corner of the village until he began to notice overgrown gravestones and mausoleums appearing behind old railings at the northern outskirts of Highgate Cemetery. They looked so clichéd in their topsy-turvy ivy-clad disarray, so *Hammer House of Horror*, that Newton snorted a derisive harrumph, as if their spooky Gothic pretensions were mocking him. He pondered the bizarre appeal of the cemetery, where the Victorian obsession with death, immortality and classical funeral architecture faced a counter-attack by ivy, weeds and trees. The result was half film set, half nature reserve.

Reaching the ludicrous Gothic entrance to the western cemetery, Newton crossed the road and ducked into the eastern section, newer but no less peculiar, which was open to the public without a guide. He paced the avenues of mausoleums, half expecting to see stereotypical ghosts popping out from behind graves and running around, heads tucked below their arms, ridiculing his scientific method as pointless pedantry. He kicked the gravel. As his mood blackened, he was rewarded with a sudden glorious downpour, the cold rain coming down in great icy sheets, making the distant tourists belt manically for cover. Caught out in the open and hardly in the right clothes for a soaking, Newton dashed for the nearest shelter, a red marble mausoleum with a small covered entrance. Shivering, he watched the rain crash down upon the gravestones.

'You'd better come in,' shouted Dr Sixsmith from behind the cast-iron doors. Startled, Newton looked in through the small barred window. The ghost of Alex Sixsmith was inside, sitting on a coffin, playing with his spectacles.

'Oh no, not you again,' said Newton.

'Push the door, it's open,' said Sixsmith.

Newton looked around to make sure no one could see him then leant hard against the heavy old door. Creaking and resistant after two hundred years of rusting, it gradually yielded and Newton reluctantly stepped inside.

'No, don't sit down,' said Sixsmith standing, 'we shan't be staying.' And with that a small hatch opened to reveal a stone staircase.

'Oh very Gothic,' Newton muttered. 'I hope you don't think I'm going down there, I'm claustrophobic.'

'Are you?' said Sixsmith, laughing. 'Well, can't be helped, there's someone you need to meet.' He gestured to the steps. 'Please, after you.'

Newton pulled his keys out, switched on his small Maglite and began to descend the stairs.

\*\*\*\*\*\*

Two learned men, one dead and one in a right bloody mood, made their way along the musty tunnel.

'You'd never know all this was here, would you?' said Sixsmith. 'It was all about avoiding being buried alive, you see.'

'Eh?' said Newton. 'Why, what is this?'

'Escape route. If they'd woken up in the coffins, they could nip out, sharpish like, and dash home to ruin the wake.'

'Where does it go?'

'Pops out in a pub. Sensible move I reckon. By the way, sorry to hear about the job,' said Sixsmith, trotting ahead.

'Yup, thanks for that,' said Newton, brushing away some cobwebs. 'I couldn't have lost it without you.'

'Now, now,' said Sixsmith. 'It was probably for the best.'

'How can it possibly be for the best?' replied Newton curtly. 'I've lost my job and my income, in no small part because I've been contacted by the kingdom of the dead. That will look good on my CV.'

'Ah,' said Alex, 'does leave you free to do something new, though, doesn't it?'

'Oh I get it – that's what this is about? Well just because I'm technically destitute doesn't mean I'll do any job. Actually, I was thinking of something in mine clearance. Outdoor work, you know.'

'You'll say yes, though?'

'Are you serious?'

'Very, and you'd be mad to say no,' said Sixsmith. 'Especially in your somewhat complex situation.'

'Yes well, thanks for that. Anyhow, how can I work for the afterlife? I mean, how will it affect my tax?'

'Haha, very good,' chortled Alex. 'Actually, we worked all of that out. You'll seem perfectly normal from the outside – no one will notice anything out of the ordinary.'

'Apart from the headless horsemen and the ectoplasm,' said Newton derisively, dodging a huge arachnid.

'Oh there'd be none of that!' said Alex reassuringly. 'Anyway, it's not my place to explain the job to you. It's better that I let the personnel department handle that.'

'Personnel department? Oh come on, you have to be joshing me!'

'No really, I told you it was bureaucratic. I'll let them explain it.' With that, they emerged into an underground chamber with frescos flaking from the walls. In recesses, Victorian coffins were crumbling to dust. In one corner of the chamber, invisible at first in the gloom, stood a figure. He was wearing long robes and at first, Newton mistook him for a statue. But then the figure turned, and Newton's small torch began to light up his golden hair and earnest face in the blackness.

'Newton, I'd like to introduce you to the head of personnel,' said Sixsmith, chuckling slightly.

'Really? What, *really*?!' said Newton sceptically.

'Yes really!' protested the being, his camp tones mingling with a faint Greek accent. 'And what's so amusing about that? At least I've got a job.'

'Sorry, no offence intended,' said Newton.

'Anyway, call me Eryximachos. It's better to be informal at interviews I think.'

'Your name is *what*?' said Newton, with no intention of attempting to repeat it.

'Eryxima ... Oh hell, call me Eric if makes it easier,' said the Greek, huffing. 'You are Dr Barlow are you not?'

'Err yes, that's me,' said Newton, folding his arms defensively. 'And you said an interview, but I haven't said I want the job yet.'

'Dr Sixsmith,' said Eric with some agitation, 'I was under the impression that Dr Barlow was ready and available for the position. This is most inappropriate, most inappropriate indeed! Protocol has to be followed you know.'

'Oh don't sweat it Eric,' said Sixsmith, waving the issue away. 'He'll come around, he just lost his job.'

'I could get another!' protested Newton.

'Of course you could my dear boy, of course you could,' Sixsmith continued. 'But, you probably won't, well not quickly at any rate.'

'Am I to understand that you don't want this job Dr Barlow?' added Eric disappointedly.

'Me ... a job as a spiritual conduit? Well, who could possibly say no?' said Newton snidely. 'I mean, it's everyone's dream, isn't it?'

'Is he being sarcastic Dr Sixsmith? Sarcasm really wasn't an ancient Greek thing – I find it hard to spot,' said Eric, perplexed.

'Yes, he's being sarcastic,' said Alex, wearily. 'Newton look, it's pretty straightforward; it's a normal job for all intents and purposes. Proper employment, taxed at source, health benefits, pension. All that.'

'Normal? Are you *sure?*'

'Most certainly,' said Eric. 'My department is very careful to ensure employees receive excellent benefits. We run a happy ship.'

'What's the salary then?' asked Newton.

'Oh really, this is most irregular,' said Eric in a queenie huff. 'I should be asking the questions, not you.'

'I'm sorry. Do go on,' said Newton, suppressing a grin.

'Well, I should ask some of my usual questions for a start,' said Eric officiously.

'OK. Fire away.'

'Well, where do you see yourself in five years' time?'

'What? Are you serious?' said Newton, and he laughed so hard he had to rest his hands on his knees. 'Oh priceless!'

'He's laughing at me, Dr Sixsmith,' said Eric.

'Sorry,' said Newton, suddenly feeling pity for the poor man. 'Please, Eric, please go on.'

'Thank you,' said Eric cautiously. After holding his eyes sternly on Newton's sceptical face for a couple of seconds, he consulted his tablet again. 'Dr Barlow,' he continued warily, 'what would you say was your biggest failing?'

'Well,' said Newton after some thought, 'if you had asked me that a few years ago, I'd probably have said that I was a bit of a perfectionist. Now though, I'd have to say it's that I see dead people.' He affected a look of bewilderment to frame his sarcasm.

'Oh really, this isn't funny Dr Barlow,' huffed Eric. 'This is a matter of life and death! Your flippancy is really not helping – not helping at all!'

'Eric, why don't you just explain the job to Dr Barlow – that might speed things up a bit,' said Sixsmith, trying to smooth things over.

'Yes please,' said Newton, obstructively. 'I'm listening.'

'Well, it's like this,' said Eric. 'You have your ... err ... good, and then ... well, you have your evil. Good is good, and evil is essentially bad. We need help clearing up the evil.'

'And how the bloody hell do I do that?'

'I was getting to that! You see, evil leaves traces here on earth, it hangs around like a stain, like a kind of poison, a pollution. It lurks in relics, paintings, the popular consciousness, songs even. The living hold the dead back, sometimes for good reasons, sometimes for bad. Mostly for bad, sadly, now I think about it. But it all needs cleaning up you see. Filing away and putting straight, that's what we do. Though we, the dead up in ... I suppose you'd call it ...'

'Purgatory?' said Newton.

'If you must,' said Eric. 'We the dead can do a certain amount but, in this modern world it's getting harder and harder to be discreet. There's all this stuff lying about you see, all over the place, and we just can't keep track of it anymore. Not just that, but my generation ... well to be honest, we just can't keep up with the software. Even Pythagoras was flagging by the time we got to Windows 7.'

'You need IT support, not a physicist.'

'Oh no Dr Barlow! We need you a great deal. You have such practical skills, logic, objectivity! Frankly, we've had enough of the traditional mediums. Dr Sixsmith here was adamant that you'd make a superb alternative. You came highly recommended.'

'This is all your doing, is it Alex?' said Newton, raising an eyebrow.

'Certainly,' said Sixsmith, 'because I think you'd really love it. It'll be a hoot! Plus, of course, you need the money.'

'Well, I can't argue with that, so what is the salary?'

'Well, what do you want?' asked Eric, as if it didn't really matter.

'What do I *want*?' asked Newton, standing back upright from his slouch. 'Are you serious? Do I look like a banker!'

'Newton, go on, name a figure,' said Sixsmith.

'OK, I'll make a stab,' said Newton. 'How about 100k, plus a bonus?'

'Certainly Dr Barlow,' said Eric. 'That's not a problem.'

'Hello? Are you saying yes to that? Should I have said 200k?'

'Well you could have done,' said Eric, rolling his eyes. 'But you didn't. What is your actual figure please?' He prepared to make an entry on his tablet.

'300k,' said Newton, now strangely interested in the venture.

'Are you mocking me Dr Barlow?' said Eric, folding his arms defensively. 'I don't have all day you know.'

'350k?' said Newton mischievously. 'Most of it will go in maintenance anyway.'

'Don't take the piss,' said Sixsmith, sighing. 'Eric here is seriously trying to offer you a salary. But bear in mind, money attracts attention and any sizable salary will need justification.'

'It's hard to think of any of this that doesn't,' said Newton wryly.

'Really, people will ask questions,' Sixsmith said. 'Eric, I suspect Dr Barlow here is more interested in the nature of the employment than the financial package.'

'Quite right!' said Newton cockily. 'In fact, I've never really been interested in money, though I've found the absence of it absolutely riveting.'

'Shall we say £100,000 per annum, Dr Barlow, while you are on your probationary period?' said Eric.

'Probation?'

'It is protocol,' said Eric as if it was all perfectly normal.

'100k is fine,' said Newton eventually, after yet again shaking his head in disbelief. 'How do I explain it anyway then?' asked Newton. 'I mean, who do I tell what?'

'Ah, well, that's the clever bit,' said Alex. 'We've had a good long think about that and we've drawn up a dossier for you. It's over there on top of that coffin.' He pointed across the gloomy chamber to a manila envelope amongst the bones and dust.

'What's this then? A training manual?' said Newton.

'In a manner of thinking, yes,' said Eric. 'It's a job description – it explains what we need you to do and outlines your cover story.'

'Which is?' asked Newton impatiently.

'We thought antiques,' said Sixsmith.

'Antiques? But I don't know anything about antiques,' protested Newton.

'Well not just any old antiques,' Alex continued. 'Scientific instruments, that kind of thing.'

'OK, fair enough,' said Newton shrugging. 'And where's my employer? Is there an office I have to go to?'

'You will find all that in the package,' said Sixsmith. 'It's a small shop in Greenwich market, very specialist. A handy arrangement, I thought, since it's just round the corner from where your new squeeze Viv lives. The proprietor of the shop will be your main point of contact.'

'The correct term is line manager, Dr Sixsmith,' stressed Eric, trying to maintain his professional air. 'He'll also send you your wages, unless you want it paid via the information superhighway of course.'

'Yes please,' said Newton, incredulous.

'So you're saying yes then?' said Sixsmith, smiling broadly.

'Not sure I've got any choice,' said Newton, still determined to at least sound reluctant. 'Nothing to lose so I guess that must be a ... blimey I'm saying it ... yes!'

'Excellent! Excellent!' clapped Eric. 'Everyone will be so very pleased! Welcome on board, Dr Barlow!' With that he offered his hand to Newton who tried to shake it, but of course, failed.

'You're making a good choice, old boy,' said Sixsmith. 'Really, it will be fun. A blast!'

'Fun eh? I've heard of that,' said Newton. 'So what happens next?'

'Well, there will be the regulation induction of course,' said Eric. 'We'll have to fill you in on all the protocols, regulations and the basic organisation ethos. Oh, and then there's health and safety.'

Newton shook his head in disbelief yet again. As he looked ahead into the unknown, he felt a hysterical vertigo in all of his internal organs at the same time.

'OK,' he said eventually, 'where do I sign?'

## CHAPTER 18

# INDUCTION

Newton Barlow passed the National Maritime Museum and dropped down towards the Thames. He bought himself a coffee and a bacon roll and sat watching the river, killing time before he was due at the antique shop. He'd left Viv blissfully unaware of his appointment and snuck out quietly so he could avoid awkward explanations, leaving her burbling in her sleep, hugging the pillow like a toy koala.

He opened his dossier and read the terms of his employment again.

'Protocol 1. Do not involve family members in any project or case,' it stated firmly. 'Protocol 2. It is forbidden to use any information gained whilst in the employment of said party to make profit or exert power within the human realm ... Protocol 15. There is no dress code, but funereal visits are to be accorded respect according to local traditions and etiquette.'

I'm going to have to buy a suit, thought Newton. He looked at his pointy black shoes and sighed. Not really funeral-friendly either. He rolled the dossier up and slipped it back into his jacket then finished his breakfast, blowing on his cold hands as the wind whipped up from the river. He walked back past the Cutty Sark, its rigging singing in the freshening breeze, and entered the old market.

Greenwich market sits within an intricate network of tiny old streets; if a town-planning officer suggested it nowadays, even as a joke, he would be made to clear his desk. Small shops lean in towards each other, muscling forward into the meagre available space, barely leaving room for the huge mass of tourists and shoppers that descend on the place every weekend. Mid-week though, after the visitors have gone, it's often nothing but a sea of stacked tables and it's once again possible to stroll about freely. The antique shop was in a narrow side alley, and even though it was small and unassuming, Newton was surprised that he'd never noticed it before. He looked up at the sign: 'M. R. Jameson Antiques. Specialist in brass scientific instrumentation and astronomical collectables.' Looking through the window between the metal shutters, he could see a sea of brass glinting in the meagre light.

Eventually, the proprietor rolled up, Newton guessing correctly who he was when he was still some distance away. He was probably in his fifties, and seemed to have been using some kind of manly hair product to keep his pointed beard and swept-back hair as dark and mysterious as possible, giving him an air of Omar Sharif playing a magician. Beneath his wine-red corduroy jacket, he had an equally Shiraz-coloured polo neck, around which hung a large brass pendant. As he drew near he raised a suspicious eyebrow and looked straight into Newton's eyes as he lifted a key up to the padlocks.

'Are you Dr Barlow?' he asked coldly.

'Yes, yes I am,' replied Newton, smiling weakly. 'I'm here for the ...'

'I know what you're here for. It would help if you introduced the necessary discretion from the outset. As a man of science, it shouldn't be beyond you to notice that this is a public space.'

'Oh right, yeah, sorry,' said Newton, mildly stung by the rebuke. 'I'll be more careful in future.'

The shop owner relentlessly worked his way through the bolts and padlocks until after some time the shutters rolled noisily up. 'You'd better come in.' Brusquely he entered with Newton following. There was instantly an overpowering smell of Brasso, and Newton was thankful for the fresh cold air they'd brought in with them. The shop owner switched on strip lights that flickered erratically before finally lighting up a glittering interior of telescopes, astrolabes, globes, microscopes and cases containing complicated objects that Newton, despite his advanced scientific knowledge, had trouble identifying.

'Wow, great shop,' said Newton, genuinely impressed. 'Very cool.'

'Cool, is it?' said the shopkeeper grumpily.

'Err ...' said Newton, 'well maybe not cool, but these instruments are amazing. I'd always fancied a brass telescope, like this one,' he said, reaching out.

'Don't touch that!' barked the owner, rushing forward to deflect Newton's curious fingers. 'That's worth £20,000. We've been polishing that bastard for months. Last thing we want is your greasy fingerprints all over it.'

'Sorry,' said Newton, suitably chastised.

'If I can trouble you to sit down out of the way for a few minutes

I might have a chance to get things prepared, then perhaps we can start your induction.' The doorbell chirruped as a sickly looking lad awkwardly shuffled in through the door.

'Mornin' Muster Jameson,' he muttered sullenly, conspicuously reluctant to meet Newton's gaze.

'Hello. I'm Newton.' The lad did not return the greeting and simply bustled away into the shop's interior.

'Morning Trevor,' said the owner. 'Be a good lad and put the kettle on please – I'm sure Dr Barlow here would like a hot drink.' Trevor grunted away to the small kitchen as the proprietor busied himself preparing the shop for what was unlikely to be a busy day.

'So are you *the* Mr Jameson?' asked Newton.

'Yes,' he replied indifferently. 'The shop was my father's, his father founded it before him.'

'These things sell well? They must be valuable ...'

'Oh sure, when they sell they can be very good for us. After all, every bloody fool self-made man in Canary Wharf wants a brass telescope for the top office. What a pathetic cliché.'

'Yes, I suppose they do,' said Newton, looking at a price tag dangling from an astrolabe.

'I just wish I liked them myself, Dr Barlow. Actually I hate old things. I'd rather have a shop selling smart-phones or surfboards, but no, I'm stuck with this.' The assistant arrived with a tray of tea and biscuits. 'Good boy, Trevor, take them up to the training room, will you, and then you can start polishing again.'

'Pol.....ish,' said Trevor, his eyes glazed and focusing on two different objects at the same time.

'Yes, polish. Oh and keep an eye on the shop properly today please, we lost another sextant yesterday.'

'Yus,' said Trevor, narrowing eyes at the door like a cat.

'OK I'm finished here. If you'd follow me please,' said Jameson, heading through a parade of telescopes and up some narrow stairs to a small room with rows of seminar chairs, and an overhead projector. 'Sit down, Dr Barlow, I'll put the heater on and we can get started. Personally, I don't find low temperatures conducive to clear thinking.'

'No,' said Newton, 'I suppose you're right.' He sat in a seat at the front feeling somewhat foolish, being the only person in the room apart from his inductor.

'I take it you've brought your information pack, yes?'

said Jameson.

'Yes, I have it here.'

'Be aware please, Dr Barlow, that the things you hear today are not, I repeat NOT, to be discussed with anyone except your colleagues, spirit guides and other team members. You haven't told anyone about this so far, I trust?'

'No, not at all,' said Newton.

'Girlfriend?'

'Nope, she'd think I was mad.'

'Quite,' said Jameson knowingly. 'It's very important that you observe the protocols. If the true nature of the afterlife became common knowledge, well ... normal life, such as it is, would become impossible.' He switched on the overhead projector. 'Normally, we would have inducted several people together,' he said, indicating the empty chairs. 'Since the new directive, however, we've put that on hold. As I gather you have been informed already, traditional spiritualists and mediums have been proving very troublesome. True, they're only too willing to take on board the idea of contact from the other side, but they have a tendency to be somewhat, how shall I put it?'

'Flaky?' suggested Newton.

'Flaky, yes. Also fraudulent, crazy and mentally unstable. We've had people using the connections they made via the afterlife for personal gain, which is totally unacceptable, of course. A fair number have just dropped stone dead.'

'Shock?'

'Yes, total and complete shock. Ironic with professional mediums, don't you think? They're happy enough to pretend these things are true but you should see how they react when a real ghost turns up. Hysterical. The nuthouses are full of those. Well if they survived the madness stage, they then had to be willing to make themselves available to us and be capable of keeping a secret. And if they passed all those barriers ... well, the next problem was that mostly, they just weren't any good.'

'They weren't?'

'No, they had the skills set of a circus performer, that's if we were lucky – not even slightly up to speed in an office sense. Many of them were so anti-technology that they refused to use computers, dressed like wizards and couldn't do any task for us that didn't involve divining rods. So ...' Jameson continued, 'this new directive has come after some considerable rethinking. Some of the greatest minds in history have pondered long and hard about these issues and this is why we have decided to start recruiting the people who are least likely to believe in us. That's right. Scientists. It's a radical departure, as you can imagine, and you, Dr Barlow, are the first of the new intake.'

'Ah, I see where you're coming from. Surely, though, there's a risk that you'll give too much away to scientists isn't there? I mean, they're inquiring, probing people – I could really do something with the small amount I've got wind of already.'

'You could indeed, Dr Barlow, but you won't. You're something of a godsend for us because you have two unique qualities that serve our purposes admirably. Firstly,' Jameson took a deep breath, 'you are a full-blown analytical scientist with the ability to make clear and incisive judgements based upon purely observable phenomena, then to make rational decisions based on those without resorting to traditional belief systems, emotional considerations and mindless superstition.'

'True,' said Newton, proudly. 'What's the second quality?'

'Well,' said Jameson, 'you are an utterly discredited fraud, and no one with any sense would believe anything you said.'

'Oh,' said Newton meekly, 'thanks a lot.'

'Nothing personal, Dr Barlow, but I'm sure that you'll see why, compared to many other scientific professionals, you have qualities that are perfect for us. You have a ready-made cover story that keeps you off the main scientific radar and you are available for full-time employment. You're still young enough to get out there in the field where you'll be of most use and you have good communication skills, which can be helpful. I gather from Dr Sixsmith, however, that you have a liking for sarcasm. You should know right now that I'm not a great fan of such a style of humour, so I would ask you kindly to refrain from inflicting it on me.'

'Err ... OK, if you say so,' said Newton, for whom sarcasm was as familiar and as natural a trait as yawning.

'Yes I do say so. Now, with that issue understood, it's time to start my presentation.' With that, Jameson placed a transparency on the overhead projector. On the screen above, a single word was projected in big bold red letters.

EVIL

'So Dr Barlow, what can you tell me about ... "evil"?'

'Evil?' Newton hesitated. As a scientist, he was used to objective concepts and far from comfortable around moralistic issues. 'Well, it's a bad thing?' he offered.

'A bad thing?' said Jameson slowly. 'That's it, is it? A bad thing?'

'Well, it's certainly not a good thing, is it?'

'Well, I suppose it could be reduced to such a simplistic level. But, Dr Barlow, evil is indeed a real issue and from the point of view of our friends in Purgatory, it's something of a bloody nuisance. It leaves a moralistically unsightly stain all over the place, induces others to duplicate its characteristics and it has a nasty tendency to stop everybody having a nice time. It will play a big part in your day-to-day work, so listen up. Right then, your responsibilities can be roughly divided into three sections.' He replaced the word 'evil' with a new transparency.

(1)   To help eradicate the manifestation of evil upon the earth

(2)   To preserve the manifestation of good upon the earth

(3)   To prevent the transfer of evil from Purgatory back to the earth

Jameson paused for a second and paced thoughtfully before continuing. 'So, Dr Barlow, let us first look at point number one. Eradicate the manifestation of evil upon the earth. So what do we mean by this? Well, evil, Dr Barlow, just like good, is kept alive by memories. In Purgatory, the good and the evil both exist side by side, sustained by the memory that each has left on earth during the extent of their mortal lifetimes. This memory exists in everyday objects, human remains and history. It can be found lurking in art, in deed and in tradition. As there is no way to switch this process off or prevent it occurring, there is much that is helping to sustain evil in Purgatory where quite frankly, it's a pain in the arse. A good example is the Nazis.'

'I was going to ask about the Nazis,' said Newton.

'Of course you were!' snorted Jameson derisively. 'Everyone *always* asks about the Nazis. They really are the Rolls-Royce of evil aren't they? People have such a morbid fascination with them, and that's exactly why they won't just fade away and be forgotten. The afterlife is crawling with the mean-spirited little buggers, goose-stepping around like they own the place. We can get rid of a certain number of the minor Nazis, the second in commands and the third Oberleutnants – so far so good, after all there were so many of them that even the most die-hard neo-Nazis can't keep reviving interest in them all. So thankfully, they've got the numbers down. The big guys though, well, it's like the Nuremburg rallies every day up there, I gather. All the big bad names. All wanting to come back and get stuck in all over again – you can see the problem.'

'Can they come back? How?' asked Newton. 'Hauntings? Possession?'

'Well possession can be a bit of a problem, though to be fair, it's a bit old-school. The evil spirits who like that most are the ones from periods up to the 17th century, max. Modern villains tend to prefer planting ideas all over the place for new earthly villains to pick up – idea transference, that kind of thing.'

'They can transfer ideas?'

'Sure. Via dreams is the preferred option. You know the sort of thing – you go to bed at peace with the world and then next day you wake up in a foul mood hating altruism. Ayn Rand was doing that a lot recently, until we caught her. But it's important to define "evil" properly first in order to fully understand the concept. You see, evil is in everyone to some extent. Sadly, it's actually a very mundane feature. People always make the mistake of turning the likes of Hitler, Vlad the Impaler or Ivan the Terrible into full-blown almost supernatural monsters, beasts or demons. But that's all far too grandiose – hell, it even helps them to some extent. In reality, evil is just an exaggeration of common human traits like mean-spiritedness, selfishness or jealousy. You can find the roots of evil in a school playground, a team-building exercise or a wine and cheese party, just as much as you can find it on a battlefield, in a torture chamber or a prisoner-of-war camp. In people we define as evil, these basic traits are just turned all the way up to the maximum setting, so high that the said individual has trouble acting in anything like a normal manner. You could almost feel sorry for them if they weren't so horrible. Hitler, for example, he may have laid waste to a continent and caused a global conflagration that sucked in some 56 million souls, but deep down, he was primarily an arsehole.'

'I'm sorry?'

'An arsehole, a creep,' said Jameson. 'Other words could

be dickhead, twat, cretin, scumbag ...' He took a breath. 'Punk, sonofabitch ...'

'OK OK! I get the picture!' said Newton, taken aback by the abrupt change in language. 'So are you saying that all you have to do to be classed as evil, is to be ... an arsehole?'

'Technically yes, though modern psychiatry likes to burden us with a million ways of saying the same thing. Narcissistic personality disorders, psychopaths, crazy mixed-up kids to name but three. Essentially, the big thing to watch out for is uptight control freaks with no sense of humour who can't empathise with, forgive or understand the rest of us poor saps.'

'I think I may have met a few of those. I may even have married one.'

'Quite possibly, Dr Barlow. They are simply everywhere.'

'Fascinating,' said Newton. 'That's a bit of a blow to the concept of something like say ... the devil.'

'Well quite. Human beings just can't stop putting the bad guys on a pedestal, I'm afraid, and that merely encourages them. It gives them an even bigger complex than they had in the first place. Look what it did for bin Laden. And, once they're dead, they're often so obsessed with status and revenge that they will do all they can to come back and give their detractors a good kicking. Very annoying.'

'You said we can clear them away though – how?'

'As I said, it's all about memory. We have to keep an eye out for traces that can be wiped from the collective memory. Here's an example. Imagine you have a bad guy who left a number of portraits of himself about the place. Well, we find them, discreetly dispose of them and then, hey presto, no more bad guy. He just fades from his little corner of Purgatory and that's that. Job done. But it's a lot harder with one of the big hitters like Idi Amin or Vlad the Impaler because the memory of those toss-pots is spread all over the historical record, like sand on a beach towel. They just have to be trussed up and left to sulk for eternity.'

'So are all these bad guys the famous ones then?'

'No, not by any means, Dr Barlow. Remember, normal average people are being evil all the time. Some of the really bad ones have yet to carry out their evil potential. Right now, the most evil person on earth is a human resources manager in Wisconsin, a ghastly woman of such hideous malignancy that she makes Stalin look like a children's entertainer.'

'I'm confused!' said Newton. 'If you know this woman's so evil, why don't you stop her? Stop her before she gets out of hand? Nip them in the bud? I mean, why didn't they stop Hitler, Pol Pot, Simon Cowell?'

'Protocol, Dr Barlow, protocol. Think about it. How would it look? Innocent-looking babies getting snuffed out all the time? You'd scare the living daylights out of everyone.'

'But you could have if you wanted to?'

'We could, but we're not allowed.'

'Not allowed? Not allowed by who?'

'Ah, that's where we drift onto forbidden territories, Dr Barlow. As you have been told, there are some things we are entitled to tell you and some we most certainly are not.'

'But you know?'

'I know more than most. I have a very high level of security clearance for a live human being, yet I know but a fraction of what I suspect may be the case. I must be content with that.'

'What do you suspect?'

'Now *that*, Dr Barlow, is not going to work. Desist. I can assure you that I shall not be drawn upon the matter any further. It is not professional so that is an end to it.'

'But surely ...'

'An end, Dr Barlow, an end!' said Jameson, staring fiercely at Newton. 'It is better that we concentrate on the points above. So, we shall return to the matter at hand. You, Dr Barlow, will be going after the relics and memory of what can be described as secondary evils. These are typically your lesser-known personalities who have to some extent already been eradicated from the historical record. However they are still "vivid", so to speak, and that means they have left behind them certain objects, relics, that enable their malignancy to continue on the other side. So we'll look for these in museums, antique shops, car boot sales and on eBay.' Jameson sipped his tea. 'Now, that brings us to the second part of your job Dr Barlow, namely to preserve the manifestation of good upon the earth.'

'OK,' said Newton. 'What's that all about?'

'Well, as we have noted, the living have a morbid fascination for evil, often at the expense of the good. The Nazis we have discussed, but what about the never-ending passion people seem to have for serial murderers? Or gangsters, warlords and terrorists? Bastards, people can't get enough of them. But let's say that you've had a life of total benign charm. What if you've lived a life that has helped humanity in innumerable ways? Quite frankly, you'll be lucky if they're still talking about you by the end of the wake.' Jameson sighed. 'It's a sad fact that humanity focuses on the bad guys, and the good guys, as the saying goes, they always finish last.'

'So I've noticed.'

'But, not always,' Jameson continued. 'Some people have invented stuff that keeps their memory fresh forever just because they have their name attached to something benign, something good that stays alive forever in the public consciousness. Thomas Crapper, for instance – no one is going to let him rest in peace, he's always getting his cord yanked. But Crapper is an exception, sadly. Many very good people are getting overlooked and we need to strike a balance down here if evil is not to triumph – up there. Keeping the good guys alive and well in the afterlife, Dr Barlow, will be one of your primary tasks.'

'OK, so how do we do it then?'

'You'll have to help us dig out preservable relics for these benign individuals. You will be directed to their location and you'll have to find a way to ship them back to somewhere safe, somewhere we can keep them out of harm's way, but sufficiently in the public eye that they can be remembered. Your friend Sixsmith, for instance, he'll need to be sorted out soon if he's to continue in his current position.'

'So how do we preserve these good guys?'

'Well, if there's a portrait, say, then we'll try and make sure it's on display somewhere prominent. The National Portrait Gallery is a good example. We've snuck a few very dull but able people in there to keep them going. Anything to keep the ball in the air will do; Dr Sixsmith has some distinctive spectacles, for instance.'

'OK. What if there's no relic though, then what?'

'It's rare for there to be nothing. We all leave a pile of rubbish behind us throughout our lifetimes. It's unlikely you can get rid of everything, unless, as in the case of the evil, you are really going out of your way. Which we do, of course.'

'So is it only physical manifestations of an individual's life, or do you include electronic media?'

'Oh good lord no!' Jameson laughed. 'Doesn't matter how much you tweet or blog – no one is ever going to remember that in five hundred years. It's gone in seconds. Same with reality TV appearances. Here today, gone tomorrow! If you want to be utterly forgotten in this world and the next, enter the Big Brother house.'

'OK,' said Newton, looking far from sure.

'We really don't expect you to get it all at once, Dr Barlow. You've no choice but to learn on the job.'

'Well that's reassuring,' said Newton, who hadn't heard anything reassuring for some time. 'So what about part three of the job?'

'Ah yes,' said Jameson. 'Preventing the transfer of evil from Purgatory back to the earth. That's the really exciting part. Evil, Dr Barlow, it likes to find a way. It creeps, it slithers and it flows. It tries every path it can until it causes mischief, so we have to block it. But trust me, evil wants nothing more than to bridge the gap between the living and the dead. Consider the living who court the twisted expertise of some of Purgatory's most malignant inhabitants – people who'll stop at nothing to restore or create dynasties of pure, mind-rotting unpleasantness. And of course there are monsters up there,' he stabbed his finger upwards for emphasis, 'just itching to regain purchase upon the earth so they can once again propagate their sick dogmas, pollute all that is good and noble, and plunge the earth back into new dark ages filled with fear and loathing. Our job, Dr Barlow, is to block all these avenues using every weapon at our disposal.'

'No pressure then?' said Newton, wondering what he'd got himself into. 'When do I start?'

'Well, firstly we'll get you some simple auction work. I've made an account available to you so that money will not be an issue. There's an auction in Tunbridge Wells on Wednesday – some ivory-handled duelling pistols we need to purchase and then dispose of. Nasty little things. The "ivory" is actually human bone; the owner rather fancied himself as a bit of a cannibal. Caused a bit of a stir in Budapest during the 1760s, killing and eating the daughters of aristocrats. Bit of a charmer I gather, but then so many of these foul people are.' Jameson handed Newton a slip of paper. 'Here's the account details. You'll have a bank card and authorisation sent in the post to your Crouch End flat. It will be there waiting for you when you get home. I'll be at the first event, and others from the organisation will be nearby keeping an eye on things,' said Jameson, as he switched off the projector and tidied away his notes. 'I'll leave you to read and digest the sections in your info-pack dealing with holiday entitlement and pensions. Likewise, health and safety considerations.'

'OK, is that it then?'

'Wait ...' said Jameson, 'there's something else. Has anyone mentioned how sensitive you are?'

'Sensitive?' asked Newton baffled. 'What like, tearful? Fond of puppies?'

'No, I mean *sensitive*,' continued Jameson impatiently. 'Sensitive to spirits. You might start seeing things.'

'Things! What things?'

'Dead things, people ... murder scenes, you might see things.'

'Are you saying ghosts?'

'Yes I'm afraid so.'

'What, like in *The Sixth Sense*? Oh, great.'

'It's all quite normal, well sort of. Parts of your brain – bits you weren't aware of before – well, they've been switched on, activated.'

'I wish you'd told me that before,' said Newton.

'Oh it's nothing,' Jameson replied, glossing it over.

'Nothing?' said Newton, looking dubious, 'are you *sure*?'

'Initially it'll be a bit sporadic,' said Jameson. 'It can depend on all sorts of issues – tiredness, alcohol, blood pressure, hunger. It will come and go, so be prepared. In time, you'll be able to control it, use it even.'

'But until then, there'll be corpses everywhere? Oh great,' said Newton.

'Oh I shouldn't worry,' said Jameson. 'We've all been through it. Seems a big deal at first but in time you'll just take it in your stride. Even enjoy it. Now if you don't mind Dr Barlow, I need to get back to my normal work. I have to post a 17th-century brass telescope to a rich but clueless gentleman in Las Vegas. We'll have to leave it there.'

He showed Newton back out through the shop. 'I will see you on Wednesday morning in Tunbridge Wells Dr Barlow. Be at the auction house at 10am sharp. Good day.'

Newton stepped back out onto the small narrow passageway and hesitated for a long second, unsure of which way to go. Part of him wanted to rush back to Viv's and tell her everything, just to get it off his chest. But another stronger instinct made him keep his council and he set off to Crouch End, his mind whirring. But this time it was less with worry and more with a sense of intrigue and excitement.

Despite the fact that it made no sense, contradicted everything he stood for and was, essentially, impossible, he was rather looking forward to it.

## CHAPTER 19

# THE TWO CROWNS

Running the cover story past Viv proved much harder than Newton expected. Used to the pursuit of truth, he found the absurdity of the antique story almost impossible to make convincing, especially the monstrous salary. Nonetheless, Viv had been pleased for him. It was clear that they could at last make some plans for the future that did not involve rivers of wishful thinking.

On the way down to Tunbridge Wells, Newton's old Citroën was once again on form. In the crisp morning light, Newton streaked round the London orbital like a meteorite, arriving early enough to take a leisurely stroll down the famous old Pantiles, a Georgian colonnade with wonderfully eclectic architecture and more than its fair share of nutty shops. A few brave souls sipped coffee alfresco in the weak winter sunlight, wearing sunglasses and fielding ski jackets to ward off the pronounced nip from a crisp frost still hiding in the shadows. Newton burnt up half an hour in one of these cafes before making his way to the auction house.

A crowd of collectors and bargain hunters had already gathered ahead of Newton's arrival, and he had to weave through them like a waiter at a wedding reception before he finally found Jameson perusing the forthcoming lots.

'Nice drive down, Dr Barlow?' he said over his spectacles.

'Not bad thanks,' replied Newton. 'So where are these infamous pistols?'

'Over there,' Jameson discreetly indicated with his programme. Newton followed his gaze.

'What, those?' he said loudly, pointing with his finger, until Jameson knocked it down. On the other side of the room, two men noticed the interaction and exchanged knowing glances.

'Don't point them out you idiot!' said Jameson. 'You've half given the game away. That's Thomas Sherman and his son; they've got one of those ghastly black museums. You can bet they'll be after the pistols. Now, thanks to you, they know we want them too. Great. That's going to make our job harder.' Newton looked over to the thin weedy father and his fat sweaty son, who both returned his glance with obvious bad intent.

'Sorry,' said Newton. 'My bad. Can't say I like the look of them. Black museum, you say? What's that, murder collectables?'

'That's about the size of it,' said Jameson. 'They buy and sell the stuff, it can end up anywhere in the world. Then it's a nightmare tracking it down. I was worried they'd be here.'

'Can't we just outbid them?'

'We can try. They're not our only problem, however,' Jameson added, looking over to his right. 'Do you see that guy over there, flat cap, sheepskin coat?'

'Yes,' said Newton, 'who's that then?'

'That's Herbert Corbin. He's been buying up our target relics for a while. We don't know why yet, but we will in time. Might have to burgle the bastard.'

'Burgle? Is *that* what we do?!' said Newton, alarmed.

'Oh it's all in a good cause,' said Jameson, 'and keep your voice down will you.'

'Sorry,' whispered Newton. 'But isn't that criminal?'

'Maybe,' Jameson replied indifferently. 'But what's worse? A bit of smash and grab from a crazy man with a love for death and pain, or the preservation of the earth in the face of an infestation of dead murderers? Take your pick, Dr Barlow, take your pick.'

'I get your point, but I hope you don't think I'm up for any of that kind of thing!'

'Oh don't trouble yourself. We leave that kind of thing to the professionals. You are hardly cat burglar material.'

'No I'm not,' replied Newton, suddenly wondering why being judged useless as a criminal made him feel oddly slighted. 'So when does the auction start?'

'Be about 30 minutes,' said Jameson, looking at his watch. 'Let's have a look to see what else is here. Might be something we weren't expecting. Any indications yet? Any sightings?'

'Sightings? You mean of ghosts? Spirits? No, not yet, apart from Alex.'

'Well keep your eyes open, there's a lot of nasty-looking stuff in here. Who knows what it's witnessed.'

'I'll bear that in mind!' said Newton, with some foreboding. They walked through the crowds and idly perused the accumulated lots.

There were pots and paintings, tired furniture and the odd stuffed animal. As they passed a large mirrored wardrobe, Newton caught Jameson making subtle eye contact with a non-descript gentleman in a macintosh, leaning against a wall and apparently reading a catalogue. They nodded with a barely perceivable acknowledgment.

'Who is that?' asked Newton. 'Another buyer?'

'Backup, Dr Barlow, backup. Just in case things get sticky.'

'Sticky?! What? Violent-sticky?'

'Oh good lord no!' said Jameson. 'That's highly unlikely. Sometimes there's a bit of an altercation, but it's purely verbal on the whole. Some people want these horrible things at any price and they can get a bit shirty. Anyway, we'd best take our seats – the auction will be starting shortly.' He motioned to a pair of seats near the back and they sat down, Jameson busying himself with the catalogue while Newton's eyes glanced around the cluttered auction room. After Jameson's comments, frankly, there wasn't anyone in the room who didn't look dodgy.

'Do you think you could look any less conspicuous Dr Barlow,' said Jameson, without looking up. 'This isn't *The Bourne Ultimatum*. Try and look natural will you.'

'Right ...' said Newton, suitably chastised.

The auction began. Jameson and Newton endured a run of very dull watercolours, Welsh dressers and vases before finally, the pistols made their appearance.

'Lot fifteen,' announced the auctioneer. 'A pair of antique duelling pistols with ivory inlaid handles, inscribed upon the box to one Baron László Norbert von Kovordányi. The handles are also inscribed with several female names, most illegible but they include Fuzsina and Katalin. Lovers I expect. Bidding starts at 1,500 pounds. What do I hear?' The auctioneer peered over his spectacles at the seemingly disinterested punters until he caught a nod from Herbert Corbin, a few rows in front of Newton and Jameson. '1,500 in the room ... 1,600?' The elder Sherman waved his catalogue. '1,600 in the room, 1,700?' Jameson raised his finger discreetly. '1,700 there, 1,700 in the room.' Corbin nodded. '1,800, I see 1,800.'

'We'll keep it up, I don't think either of them can go the distance,' whispered Jameson, and he raised his finger again.

'1,900 in the room,' announced the auctioneer, and Corbin turned to look for his rival amongst the seated crowd. Catching sight of Jameson, he smiled insincerely and turned back to the auctioneer with a raised catalogue once again. '2,000 in the room!' The bidding war continued until Corbin, frustrated, offered £3,000. But Jameson was a millisecond behind him and took it higher once again. '3,100 now, 3,100 in the room.' Corbin was now shaking his head; he'd clearly hit his ceiling. The auctioneer moved to wrap up the sale. 'So, 3,100, we have 3,100 in the room, 3,100, going, going ...' But suddenly he stopped, craning his neck to see someone at the back of the audience. '3,200, 3,200 there from the gentleman who has just joined us.' The entire room turned and looked back towards the rear of the hall to see a stick-thin figure standing like a well-dressed undertaker behind them.

'Oh shit!' said Jameson.

'Who's that?' asked Newton.

'Trouble,' said Jameson, raising his finger again.

'3,300 in the room.'

'One of the McCauleys,' whispered Jameson, shifting uncomfortably in his seat. Ascot McCauley nodded to the auctioneer.

'3,400,' said the auctioneer, '3,400 in the room.'

'McCauley? Who's that?' asked Newton.

'Big money, small conscience, I'll tell you later,' said Jameson, raising his hand yet again.

'3,500 in the room.'

As Ascot McCauley trumped every offer, he grinned to himself in a manner that made Newton vaguely nauseous. The crowd was clearly enjoying the renewed battle, especially the Shermans, who looked at Jameson with distinct 'now you know what it's like' expressions on their sweaty faces. Jameson signalled back to the auctioneer forcibly, all pretence at subtlety lost in the heat of combat. 'We have 4,100, that's 4,100 in the room.' Ascot, cool as a cucumber, nodded like a Roman Emperor presiding at the Colosseum. '4,200,' said the auctioneer. 'Lots of interest in this set of ivory-handled pistols today!' he enthused. Jameson and Ascot came back with another wave of bids. '4,500! 4,500 in the room ladies and gentleman.' Ascot nodded again, slightly less sure now, and he adjusted his already-perfect tie in an effort to calm his nerves.

'Come on you bastard, back off,' whispered Jameson earnestly. 'He must be near his limit; he always sets himself a limit.'

'But he's rich, isn't he?'

'Absolutely loaded,' said Jameson. 'But he's tight with it – hates spending above the odds.'

'What about us?' asked Newton. 'Do we have a limit?'

'Of course not, we have limitless funds. But we can't make that obvious – people will start asking questions. Have to go through the motions.' With that, Jameson raised his hand once again and an excited murmur rippled around the room.

'4,700 in the room!' Ascot threw an acidic 'how dare you' expression at them and nodded with a tense flick that looked for all the world like a head butt. '4,800 in the room!' Jameson raised his hand once again. Ascot McCauley looked flushed, his smug expression lost to pent-up aggression. He rubbed his thin hands together and narrowed his eyes, then once again twitched his head at the auctioneer, a sneer of defiance growing on his top lip like a duelling scar. '5,000 there, we have 5,000.'

Finally, Jameson raised the stakes to £5,100. There was a gasp from the audience and all eyes flipped back to McCauley, whose eyebrows were wrought by frustration into a perfect waveform, his left eye owl-wide and his right one as small as a microchip. The seconds ticked tortuously by.

'Hummmppphh!' blurted Ascot McCauley, and in disgust and humiliation he turned smartly on his heels and left the hall, his brogues clacking like skittles on the wooden floor. In the charged silence, the door slammed shut like a whipcrack. As one, the crowd turned back to the auctioneer.

'5,100, that's 5,100. Do I have any more offers? 5,150, anyone for 5,150? Any final offers?' There were none. '5,100 going once, going twice ... sold to the gentleman near the back.' And with that he smacked down the hammer.

'Nice,' said Newton.

'Quite,' said Jameson, putting on his gloves with a small sly grin. 'Always a pleasure to outbid a McCauley. He won't like that.'

'Collectors?'

'Of a sort. He's got a company that does property development. You've probably heard of them. You know that battlefields business in Dorset a while back, the one with all the protests?'

'Oh yeah, I saw that ... what was it called?' said Newton.

'Juggin's Lump, typical McCauley project; battlefields, graveyards, all the grim stuff. They describe themselves as sensitive developers. Well, whatever they are, it isn't sensitive.'

'He did look a tad sinister,' said Newton. 'The other people that were bidding against us seemed pretty unsavoury too. Is it big then, all this evil relic thing? I mean, do they know what *we* know?'

'I strongly doubt it. Probably just that nauseating fascination for the macabre again. Either way, we can't let them have these objects – far too dangerous,' said Jameson, standing. 'Come on, let's go get our prize and then I'll give you the address for the disposal.'

'Disposal? What's that all about?' asked Newton, as they walked to the cashier.

'Well, we can't have these things just hanging around; we have to cut them off from the linked spirit in Purgatory. And frankly, the sooner the better. Anyway, no point in me explaining it – you can see it for yourself when you get there.' He handed Newton a business card:

Thomson and Adams
Specialised Product Disposal
Unit 14, Deptford Arches
London SE8

'OK, so I take them there, do I?'

'Yes,' said Jameson, slipping the case into his bland holdall. 'And I'd go there straight away, if I were you. Personally, I hate having these things around me – nasty histories have nasty smells and you can only spend so much time in a gas mask.

As they walked outside into the sunshine, Jameson turned to Newton and held out the bag. 'Here you are. I need to get going. If there's any problem, give me a ring. We'll discuss your next job later. Good day.' With that, he walked off back towards the station leaving Newton alone.

Despite Jameson's recommended urgency, Newton chose instead to take his time, walking in the sunshine until finally, hunger led him to a couple of picturesque old pubs. He chose The Two Crowns, the larger of the two, partly for its roaring fire, but also as there was a sign outside claiming it to be 'the most haunted pub in Tunbridge wells'. 'Why not?' he thought, 'it can be research.' Inside, it was mortuary quiet. Alone at the bar, perched on a stool, a man of indeterminate age sat hunched over his second pint of the morning. As Newton entered, he nodded a greeting.

'Awww-right?'

'Hi yeah, great thanks,' replied Newton. 'You?'

'Yeah, not too bad mate. Nice and warm 'ere next to the hearth.'

'Nice fire.'

'Yeah, real 'eat off a fire like that, nuffin like a proper fire.' With that, the pub regular downed his pint and lent down to grab a fresh log, which he expertly propped on the embers. The barman had by now come down the stairs behind the bar and with the practised indifference beloved of British bar staff, the kind that simply horrifies American tourists, he sighed with weariness and looked Newton in the eyes.

'Yeah?' he said, more of a challenge than a request.

'Pint of ... err ... what's a good local ale?' asked Newton.

'They got plenty of ale,' said the guy on the stool. 'None of it's any good though.'

'Fuck off Pete,' said the barman politely. 'We've got Abbot ... Old Speckled Hen?'

'Speckled Hen,' said Newton, 'that'll do.'

'We've also got Goblin Balls, Old Lizzard, Uncle Chutney's Wind Wizard, Gut, Hang Bats and Devil's Haircut.'

'Piss,' said the regular. 'They all taste of piss.'

'Fuck off Pete.'

'Speckled Hen is fine,' said Newton. 'You serving food?'

'They do food, they just don't do *service*,' said Pete.

'Fuck off Pete,' said the barman casually. 'Menu there,' he said, nodding at a stained printout. 'No chips, fryer's broken.'

'Fryer's always fucking broken,' said Pete.

'Once again, why don't you fuck off, Pete.'

Newton cursorily scanned the menu and opted for something safe.

'Ploughman's please,' he said, handing the menu back.

'Cheese or ham?'

'Cheese please.'

'Cheddar, Stilton or Stinking Bishop?'

'Stinking Bishop?' asked Newton. 'Sounds interesting.'

'It only *sounds* interesting,' said Pete.

'Fuck off Pete.'

'You fuck off,' said Pete back to the barman. 'Fuck off twice.' He winked at Newton. 'My pint seems to have run out,' he said, staring down into his nearly empty glass as though this was an enigma beyond all human experience.

'OK, a pint for my friend here,' said Newton, 'and I'll have the cheddar ploughman's'.

'Pint of Abbot,' said Pete. 'Nuts would be lovely.'

'OK, nuts too,' said Newton.

'Fanks mate,' said Pete, and he raised up the dregs off his last pint in a cheers of gratitude. Shaking his head, the barman pulled the pints and took Newton's money. 'Have a seat and I'll bring it over.'

Newton chose a table where the sunlight poured through the window onto an old table, then sitting, he idly watched the comings and goings. A young man arrived and jumped onto the seat next to Pete.

'Awwww-right Pete?' he said with a raised thumb.

'Yeah Scott mate, I'm aww-right.'

'Cool,' said the young man, and he began to dig in his wallet. The barman reappeared.

'Uh-oh, here's Scott,' he said affectionately.

'Allo mate,' said Scott, raising his thumb positively once again.

'OK Scott, what you got?' said the barman.

'Mmm' said Scott, rubbing his chin. 'I reckon it's gonna have to be pint of Hang Bats mate.'

'A fine choice,' said the barman, 'I can see that you are a man of fine tastes.'

'I am,' said Scott. 'Can I have some peanuts?'

'Indeed you may sir,' said the barman. 'I'll have a word with chef.' Scott raised his thumb.

In time, the bell rang and Newton's food was delivered to his table. Despite the somewhat casual presentation, it was a reasonable meal, good even. Newton, sated, washed it down with his pint until, sitting back, he looked down once more at the holdall. He realised then that he hadn't even seen the pistols properly, despite the fact that now, for all intents and purposes, he owned them. Throwing caution to the wind, he reached into the bag, pulled out the case and placed it carefully onto the table in front of him. Looking around to make sure he wasn't being watched, he slowly lifted the lid.

Inside, the two small, aged pistols rested in a tired velvet insert, a silver nameplate nestling next to the ivory stocks, scratched in a spidery copperplate.

'Baron László Norbert von Kovordányi,' read Newton. He cautiously reached out a finger, and despite an instinctive dislike of guns, lifted one of the pistols up by its handle.

Almost at once he felt a strange coldness in his brain. It was something he'd never felt before, and it heralded the firing of dormant neurons, a release of fantastically rare hormones and some strange biological processes, occurring for the very first time deep within his normally sensible grey matter. With it came a sudden flash of images: darkened chambers, sudden violent fluttering silks and lace. There was also a vile, cackling male laugh and a weeping female voice – a frail voice pleading, pleading. Then blood. Lots of blood.

This sudden rush of unexpected imagery shocked Newton so much that he dropped the pistol as if it was a hot brazier; it clattered noisily to the pub floor. The sudden severed contact mercifully stopped the grim presentation dead. Newton, back to his senses, looked around in alarm. While the old bar had been almost deserted a minute ago, he could make out traces of human forms flitting silently about in the motes of dust. In period dress, visible only in the lightest of outlines, they were all around him, sitting at chairs, drinking, passing through blocked-up doors and standing at the bar like regular drinkers. Stunned by these apparitions, Newton now knew exactly what this so-called 'sensitivity' actually meant. He sat fixated at the eerie phenomena, not knowing whether to be scared or fascinated. But it wasn't long-lived, for even as Newton watched, the effect was already beginning to fade. It had obviously been triggered by his direct contact with the duelling pistol. That was clear enough, so, looking down at the gun on the floor, he opted to take precautions, gingerly lifting the gun back into its box with a napkin before firmly closing the lid.

'Dr Newton Barlow, isn't it?' said Ascot McCauley, suddenly leaning over him like a scaffold. Newton, startled, grabbed the case tightly.

'Err yes. That's right. You were at the auction.'

'Yes,' he said with a slimy menace. 'Yes I was. May I introduce myself? My name is Ascot McCauley.'

'McCauley,' said Newton, 'so I gather.'

'You will forgive my familiarity with your name, Dr Barlow. But I recognised you from your television days, oh, and that later "fraud" business. Bubbles wasn't it? How very unfortunate for you.'

'So nice to meet a fan,' said Newton defensively. Ascot McCauley looked down at the bag. His fingers fidgeted against each other with a mix of desire, lust and hunger. Then he fixed Newton with a resentful, jealous eye.

'You drove a hard bargain today.'

'Well, you know, that's an auction for you,' said Newton, smiling awkwardly.

'Quite,' said Ascot McCauley. 'But you see, Dr Barlow, unfortunately, I have a problem. The pistols you see – I *want* them.' The sickly smile abruptly fell from Ascot McCauley's face like a fried egg from a non-stick frying pan.

'Well then you should have bid higher,' said Newton.

'Oh I don't think flashing around one's money in a public space like that is very seemly, do you? No, I think these things should be settled in a more gentlemanly way. The pistols, how much do you know of their history?'

'I know some.'

'Baron László Norbert von Kovordányi – quite a character, you know. He had a taste for beautiful women and fine food.'

'Did he?' said Newton, feigning disinterest. 'Did he really?'

'Yes he did, Dr Barlow. Sadly, though, he had trouble telling them apart. A sort of Baroque Hannibal Lecter, if you will. Those pistols there – he didn't use those on the girls, oh no. He duelled for fun, for money. But he believed that consuming the blood and flesh of aristocratic virgins brought him luck, and power.'

'Well that's nice. So did they?' asked Newton, looking past Ascot for an exit.

'For a while, maybe. He certainly killed a great many of his rivals with those guns. But of course, it didn't last, well, how could it? They caught him with one of the girls. Pretty grisly, I gather. It was the talk of Budapest for a while. They called him a vampire, a demon. Maybe he was.'

'And that's why *you* want them? Nice,' said Newton, pulling a face.

'Oh I'd love to lay my ... hands ... on ... them. Touch ... them. My brothers and I have a large collection of such ... how to put it ...'

'Crap?'

Ascot narrowed his eyes to demonstrate his inherent lack of humour. 'I was going to say, dark ephemera.'

'Well, you must be very *disappointed* then,' said Newton, slipping the box back into the bag. 'Anyway, if you don't mind, I'll be off.' As he stood up, Ascot's hand suddenly descended with surprising force, pushing down on Newton's shoulder until he was pinned back onto his chair.

'Hey! Get off me, arsehole!' Newton yelled.

'Give them to me.'

'No.'

'How much do you want?' hissed Ascot.

'Not selling,' said Newton. 'Take your fucking hand off me.'

'Don't make me use force, Dr Barlow, I really don't want to have to hurt you.' Ascot McCauley then tightened his talons into Newton's clavicle, making a stab of unbelievable pain shoot up his neck like an electric shock, leaving him unable to move, let alone retaliate.

'Argghh,' yelped Newton. 'What are you doing you weird bastard?!'

'Give them to me now! Do yourself a favour!'

'Oi!' came a voice behind Ascot McCauley, who turned around surprised, but maintained his grip on the subjugated Newton, who was wincing and paralysed. 'Leave my pal alone,' said Pete.

'Mind your own business,' said McCauley, infuriated by the interruption. Turning to face the threat he was obliged to then release Newton, who immediately grabbed the holdall and backed fast away from the table nursing his pain-stabbed shoulder.

'I don't like you,' said Pete, smiling.

'This is private business!' said McCauley, taking in the now-apparent bulk of the regular. A full six feet tall in his steel toe caps, his giant fists, toned by a life of casual labouring and professional bar fighting, had balled up, ready.

'That there is my mate, and this is my boozer, so therefore, most assuredly, it is *my* business,' Pete said with meaningful deliberation. 'Sling it, ya toss-pot.'

'Don't talk to me like that!' said Ascot McCauley. 'I'm a property developer!'

'You're not a property developer,' said Pete, 'you're a knob.'

The barman and Scott had appeared at Pete's side now, and Ascot was conspicuously outnumbered. Even the landlady had appeared, her publican's nose for trouble bringing her down from the upstairs rooms.

'What's happenin' here?' she asked.

'This guy is starting a fight,' said Scott.

'Oh is he now?' said the landlady. 'Well we'll see about that won't we? I think you'd better leave sir.'

200

At this moment, Ascot McCauley's muscle-bound driver chose to make an appearance, and seeing how the numbers were starting to stack up, he began to drag his infuriated employer away towards the door just as yet another customer appeared, blocking the exit in his work overalls.

'Pint of Guinness!' he said to the now-empty bar before noticing the direction of the collective gaze. 'Ello, something tasty kicking off?'

'Allo Bill,' said Pete. 'Arsehole 'ere was just leaving, weren't you mate?'

'Yes, and it's time to go if you don't want to say hello to the police,' said the landlady, rolling up her sleeves. Ascot looked around him; things were most certainly not going in his favour. It was not something he was used to.

'You people need to learn some respect,' snarled Ascot, as he and the hired muscle edged towards Bill at the doorway.

'Well I'm so very glad I popped in,' said Bill, taking off his coat and hanging it on a beer pump. 'I could do with some exercise.' He adopted a somewhat theatrical threat posture, his fists before him all Marquess of Queensberry.

'Call off your little friends Barlow, we're leaving,' hissed Ascot defiantly, and he and his driver quickly bustled past Bill and out to the shiny black Land Rover parked outside. As they climbed in, Ascot turned back. 'By the way, I know what you do, Barlow. I know everything. I just hope you know what you are up against. Trust me, we will resume this conversation another time.' The black door then slammed shut and the Land Rover screeched away in an ostentatious squeal of rubber.

'I didnae remember to tell him he was barred!' laughed the landlady, as they all watched from the doorway. When the blue smoke cleared, they returned to the bar.

\*\*\*\*\*\*

Newton had some pleasurable difficulty extracting himself from The Two Crowns via several rounds, all of which he found himself happy to finance. They were a pleasant crowd and they waved Newton off as he finally left to begin the journey back to London. The early darkness of a winter evening was upon him as he finally parked up.

'Deptford Arches, Unit 14' read a badly painted sign on the

rusted corrugated iron entrance. He knocked at the secure door, noticing a strong smell of burning and something uncomfortably reeking of incense.

'You're late,' came a voice, as the door was unlocked. 'We were expecting you three hours ago.' A nondescript man with brown overalls and greased back hair held the door open to allow Newton into the enclosed space of the unit. Inside, what looked like a furnace was burning brightly, casting the overhanging arch with a deep orange light. By its side stood an ageing industrial grinding machine and a tall serious-looking chap who may or may not have been a priest.

'Yes, sorry about that,' Newton lied hopefully. 'The traffic was bad.' He hoped that the ale wasn't too noticeable on his breath.

'Been here sitting on our arses for three hours, haven't we padre?' the man said to the priest. 'It's not time we're here to burn, mate.'

'Well said,' replied the priest. 'You have the items Dr Barlow?'

'I do,' said Newton. He handed the case containing the pistols to the man in the overalls.

'Nasty,' he said as he ran his hands over the guns, his eyes closed, sensing. 'Very nasty.' He closed the box with a snap. 'Padre, you wanna get started? I'll get the flames up.' He walked purposefully over to the furnace and with metal tongs opened the thick doors wide. A shock of intense heat scorched the room, making Newton retreat. Adjusting controls on the side of the furnace, the man focused the gas into clean blue jets, and with deliberation, placed the pistols, still in their case, onto a wheeled trolley, moving it closer to the furnace doors in readiness. Beside him, the priest had spread out what appeared to be a small altar. On a purple velvet blanket, he had laid out a mix of religious and other objects, a melange of creeds and chemistries, all piled together with no obvious pattern or doctrine.

'Wanna kick off, padre?' said the man in the overalls. With this signal, the priest began a low murmuring, his head bowed in concentrated contemplation as the furnace operator began to slide the box forward. Deep into the intense destroying flames it went, until finally the evil pistols and their box were utterly engulfed.

In Purgatory, the sinister cackling soul of Baron László Norbert von Kovordányi was hanging restrained inside his bonds like a vampire bat in a fishing net. Mad as a pewter spoon, and as malicious and self-interested as a hookworm, the one-time cannibal smiled to himself in a last moment of beastly ignorance. The moment was short. The wooden case, blown away by the furnace operator's gas jets, sizzled and spat into smoke and charcoal as it burnt briskly away, and the murderer's final earthly relics began to ignite in the intense fires. His pompous, dandy face was suddenly a picture of astonished shock and horror. His laced-cuffed arms tensed and writhed in the restraints as his weedy frame panicked and flailed in a pointless futile jig. Like a puppet in a washing machine, he wriggled and tensed as the flames began to clean and wipe him finally from the earth. And as his foul memory left the earth-bound record, so his tormentors also erased him finally and totally from Purgatory. His clumsily made-up features were now shrieking in terror, just as his terrified victims had shrieked while he had laughed and teased them in their dying moments. In his wheezy little voice, he begged, he pleaded, he squealed – but the councillors and administrators floating around him only watched impassively as he finally began to dissipate into the plasma around him. Relentlessly, he drifted into an utter and complete nothingness, the flames of the furnace and the grinding of the machine destroying his last reliquary, pounding it into an inert and meaningless dust.

He was gone.

Newton sensed much, if not all, of this. It came to him in a distant echo, a vague sense of the events glimpsed with a feeling not unlike déjà vu or the half-remembered bad behaviour of a stag night – faint inexplicable pictures drifting on the edge of observation. He was fascinated and for once, too dumbstruck to ask any meaningful questions. Their work at an end, the priest and the furnace operator led the quiet, thoughtful Dr Barlow to the door.

Mildly stunned and overwhelmed by the events of the day, he drove home.

## CHAPTER 20

# ASTROLOGY

Newton Barlow woke up with Ascot McCauley's talon marks still red and painful on his shoulder. In the shower, he let the hot water linger on the injury while he stood lost in thought, mulling over the bizarre first day at work.

Once dressed, he phoned the telescope shop.

'Well, I did tell you to go straight to the Arches,' countered Jameson reproachfully. 'You have to be very careful with people like that. These collector bods can be a tad obsessive.'

'He was a bit more than that,' replied Newton, wincing as he tried to settle his collarbone back into position. 'If the locals hadn't waded in ... well, I'd be a bar snack by now.'

'Oh the McCauleys are all puff, don't let it bother you.'

'Maybe,' continued Newton. 'But something he said worried me – McCauley said he knew what we're doing. Could he?'

'Did he now,' answered Jameson thoughtfully. 'That's interesting.'

'Just *interesting*? That could be serious couldn't it?'

'Oh I shouldn't worry,' said Jameson, brushing it away. 'He might have suspicions but I doubt he can really know anything we need to be concerned about.'

'Anyway,' said Newton, getting to the point, 'yesterday, was that a typical day? I mean it was all very interesting and everything, but I can't say it really used my skills. How does a fully qualified physicist particularly help you with that?'

'Oh that was just a warm-up,' said Jameson. 'Just to get you in the zone, so to speak. As it happens I've been drawing up a few proper jobs for you. There's one in particular you will enjoy – you can start today if you want. Perfect job for an academic.'

'What's that then?' asked Newton, intrigued.

'Let me see,' said Jameson, ruffling some papers. 'Ah yes, here it is. Case 225/7A, Flavian LeClarard.'

'Who's he?' asked Newton.

'An astrologer, 17th century. Mean-spirited little charlatan. Nowadays, he'd be called a mere conman, but back then his mumbo jumbo was no joke, no joke at all.'

'OK, go on.'

'The little tosser flitted from court to court giving bogus advice. Really, really bad advice. In fact, it was downright evil. It says here that he's thought to have started five minor wars, one revolution and a famine – all in the name of the stars, of course. He's supposed to be trussed up and forgotten, but he's been getting back to earth somehow and causing mayhem.'

'What kind of mayhem?'

'Well he's been popping up at religious settlements, you know, the whacko fringe stuff, cults and so on. He goes all end-of-the-world on people, scares them senseless, then talks them into doing the old mass-suicide shindig. Nice easy target for him, you see – those culty folk have the most concentrated gullibility on this earth. We've had incidents in Brazil, Honduras, the Solomon Islands and Bishop's Stortford. Adds up to about 200 dead, all attributed to our little friend here.'

'Nasty,' said Newton. 'For fun or profit?'

'Fun, we think, it's all a bit senseless. He's just carrying on with what he liked to do when he was alive, namely using mysticism to persuade impressionable people to commit horrible acts. Turns him on, I imagine. Classic psychopath. Now here's the thing, we don't know how he's getting out of Purgatory, but there is a pattern.'

'Which is?'

'It's always on the bastard's birthday. Some kind of sick yearly outing. We can restrain him every day of the year but one; somehow he's breaking free on the same date. He must have a relic somewhere on earth, but so far none of our team has found it. The suspicion is that he's used his own considerable talent for deception to hide something, something that's helping to keep himself vivid down here. Eric the Greek has been interrogating the little sod for centuries, but all he can get out of him are riddles. But there's one thing to go on – LeClarard was a great lover of codes and ciphers, and he's hinted that he's set up one of these puzzles for our benefit. Since you have a predilection for code breaking and linguistics, you might be able to figure it out so we can finally rein the little twat in. I've emailed you a short report containing everything we currently have on our LeClarard. I suggest you get started so that we can solve this before his next birthday party.'

'Which is when?'

'19 February – two weeks.'

'Yikes – no pressure then!'

'Sorry, but you'll need to move fast.'

Newton, galvanised by the challenge, rang off, made himself a strong coffee and opened Jameson's report. Suitably prepared, he began to acquaint himself with his target.

\*\*\*\*\*\*

Flavian LeClarard was born in Geneva in 1694, the son of a travelling salesman specialising in tapestries and yo-yos. The family led a peculiar life, all the more peculiar after Flavian's alcoholic mother died in a gambling argument in Limoges. On long, interminable sales trips, his remaining parent had both educated and distracted his son with the help of mouldering books that he picked up cheap on their dreary travels. These volumes, together with the cynical lessons he took from his snake-oil father, marked the boy for life. Spared the usual religious indoctrination of the seminaries and church schools, the young Flavian instead developed a passion for maths and magic. One tome in particular had fired the young lad's imagination. It was an astrological guide that was near dripping with mildew, its rank pages sodden with the damp of the ages.

On one long sea voyage, Flavian, utterly engrossed, read it cover to cover. As the storms lashed and the sun beat down, the boy had soaked up more and more from the old book until in time, he had become confident in its contents to such a degree that he felt ready for a practical demonstration.

One day, an illiterate old sailor, seeing the boy reading, had asked young Flavian to read it out loud as entertainment. On long voyages the sailor had grown bored and listless, and unable to read himself, was in need of erudition. Sensing the possibilities, this was something that Flavian, already a nasty piece of work, was only too willing to do. Had it been the Bible or a simple storybook, well, then perhaps things would have been all so different. But this was the poor sailor's first taste of applied superstition and he became very upset, badly troubled by the boy's many clumsy predictions. As he listened, his old brow became twice as creased as it was already. Totally hexed, for two days the sailor sulked and moped around the grubby merchantmen until finally, in a fit of deep melancholy, he threw himself from the stern.

Far from guilt-tripping the lad, the incident seemed instead to give him something of an adrenalin rush, and empowered by this sick compulsion, he spent many of the following days trying to freak out the rest of the crew. Not surprisingly, father and son were soon forcibly disembarked on the island of Corsica. It was a lucky escape. The LeClarards were but hours away from being murdered by the superstitious crew, who by this time had lost four of their number to fate-related suicide.

The LeClarards languished on the island, the father resorting to gambling and extortion to keep himself and his son in food and lodgings. Soaking up these base lessons, the boy gained a first-class education in the dubious. Armed with low cunning and his self-education in astrology and the sciences, he was fully qualified to begin his career as a mind bender.

He was to fall on these cruelly sharpened wits when in 1714, his father upset a visiting admiral during a game of backgammon and was violently dispatched with a cutlass. Flavian was now all alone in the world, a spotty twenty-year-old psychopath with nothing but a trunk full of books, two yo-yos and no moral compass.

Superstition was then, as it is now, very good business. Just as a newspaper often has an astrology column to beguile the credulous and naive, so it was then on Corsica. Flavian LeClarard hit pay dirt. The previous charlatan on the island had a glowing reputation for prediction, but he failed to see his own embarrassing fate when, with no advance warning, he'd been gored to death by a mountain goat in his bedchamber. It may have been curtains for him (and the goat) but it was a godsend for LeClarard. There was now a frustrated backlog of fee-paying gullibles, all fearful of the future and just waiting for LeClarard. The newly installed astrologer was soon positively wealthy, and thus emboldened, he began to dress the part: velvet cloaks, a pointed juvenile beard and silver-topped cane. Suitably attired, he strutted his way along the seafront at Ajaccio.

But Flavian LeClarard's youthful inexperience and overconfidence soon proved his undoing when, over-reaching himself, he amplified the animosity between two rival Corsican families into a violent blood feud. Belatedly, after much street fighting, the families realised that the young astrologer had set them one against each other, and in a rare moment of cooperation, they came together looking for revenge. The knives were out.

Flavian escaped the resulting lynch mob with seconds to spare, departing by brigantine to Marseille. He was penniless again, maybe, but he was rich in experience. Falling back on his own dark cunning, he wormed his way up to Paris, acquired a central apartment and began his comeback.

In the capital, LeClarard's skill for manipulation of the weak-minded pre-revolutionary elite became horribly refined. Soon, the Francs were just pouring in. However, though he earned accolades from his clients, he also fostered an intense jealousy from his rivals. They may have been equally cynical, but they lacked the real killer instinct that LeClarard, master of scams that he was, could rustle up with ease. What started as mere whispers of resentment grew quickly into something far darker, and as things started to get ugly, once again, the trickster found himself escaping the noose by a cat's whisker.

So began a nomadic existence. From city to city, Flavian LeClarard pushed his luck as far as it would go before escaping, just ahead of the extreme end of customer dissatisfaction.

And during these twelve years of astrological wandering, the astrologer refined his dark influence again and again until, eventually, his twisted artistry could hoodwink even the most sceptical or objective of monarchs. So, trusted by many a ruler who should have known better, LeClarard was able to act as a catalyst in the outbreak of wars and the trigger for violent assassinations and civic catastrophes, all for his own twisted amusement.

Back in his lodgings he would laugh like a filthy drain. Safe in his privacy he would share the joke with none but his young hunchbacked assistant, a ragged simpleton from whom he exacted a fierce if misguided loyalty.

As LeClarard's dubious reputation grew, so did his ghastly psychosis. He wasn't motivated by his growing wealth – now only catastrophe gave him any real sense of satisfaction. But even LeClarard knew that nothing could last forever, and as he reached the height of his cruel influence, he began to plan for his own inevitable comeuppance. Perhaps his death at the hands of an angry client had somehow always been part of the plan, like a serial murderer who wants to be caught.

Whatever the case, there were indications in Jameson's file that in 1746, Flavian LeClarard had begun to research the afterlife, cryptology and engineering. He must have been planning a venture outside of his normal activities, but it was unclear what. Maybe this project, whatever it was, was not complete upon his death in 1752, in an execution that was frankly well overdue.

Chancing his arm, LeClarard had recently caused a costly war between Franconia and Saxony, but this time he was seemingly reluctant to bolt. In chains, he was brought before a tribunal and made to explain himself. He put up a good defence – some said it was brilliant – but with the livid representatives of both warring factions sitting in front of him, their knives all sharpened and pointy, it was never going to wash. After a short and lively hearing, Flavian LeClarard was taken out to a gibbet and hanged in front of an enthusiastic local audience. As was the fashion at the time, his corpse was locked in a cage and strung up as food for the crows and kites, and while his forlorn assistant watched this supercharged decomposition from the ground below, LeClarard faded, peck-by-gruesome-peck, from the historical record.

Except – he didn't. Not entirely. Somehow, he was getting back for day trips and the chaps in Purgatory were at their wits end trying to find out how. Apparently, he'd just go walkies and then, clearly having enjoyed himself enormously, return to his confinement, a huge smirk playing on his malevolent face. Stubbornly, he refused to play ball with Eric the Greek and his questioners. Enjoying the game, he'd bait the Purgatorians with riddles and rhymes until Eric, possibly the worst interrogator in human history, was close to tears – that much was clear from the transcripts.

Reading the report, Newton noted that certain cryptic phrases popped up regularly, such little snippets as 'hidden in the spheres' or 'betwix the stars'. It was obvious the astrologer was enjoying flirting around the edges of some disguised revelation. Needless to say, it didn't help that Eric was so emotional; the interrogation transcripts made for toe-curling reading. Newton wondered why, given that Purgatory was full of investigative geniuses like Arthur Conan Doyle, Carl Sagan and Alan Turing, the council had opted for the weepy Eric to crack the cases.

Newton then spent a frustrating hour or so surfing the net without finding any useful leads until, eventually, he stumbled upon a brief reference to LeClarard in a report from 1756. This indicated that he had finally settled at a fixed address by the time of his trial and there it was – a central building in downtown Heidelberg. What's more, it was now a publically accessible museum.

Newton booked a flight to Germany.

## CHAPTER 21

# THREE LADIES

Viv finally rolled up, characteristically late and windswept, at 7pm. Enthusiastically in love, she and Newton treated themselves to a vast, almost biblical curry, but it left both of them unable to do much when the lights went out except gasp like freshly caught fish.

With the first meeting between Viv and Gabby bearing down on them like a train, the evening shot past like a lunchtime, and morning found them fuzzy-headed and silent, stumbling bleary-eyed out to the car. Viv, despite her obvious anxiety, was so taken back by the performance of the mighty Citroën that she managed to forget the whole thing until they were coming off the slip road into Cambridge. As the moment got closer, she became distressingly unlike her usual casual self, causing Newton to nurse an awful guilt for putting someone so laid-back in a position that was, if anything, bolt upright.

Newton kept the car as quiet as he could as they nosed up to Rowena's house, but even then it was hard to hide the noisy beast, and faces began peering out from the neighbouring windows. Leaving a pale and subdued Viv in the car, he walked up to the door, took a deep breath and pressed the bell. It felt horribly like detonating an explosive vest. Rowena, who possessed a bitch's instinct for other people's awkwardness, looked straight past Newton to the Citroën and fixed Viv with a hunter's eye. Viv, with nowhere to hide, squirmed like a Taliban at the end of a laser designator and slid downwards in the passenger seat.

'Is that ... her?' Rowena asked, with a barely concealed cocktail of malice and pity.

'That ... err well yes ... that's Viv,' Newton mumbled to his shoes, and he found himself pulling one of the expressions that had made Mr Bean so popular. Rowena, aware that public conventions, fair play and common human decency were blocking her instinctive urge to eviscerate them both with a scythe, merely raised a patronising though perfectly made up eyebrow and called up to their daughter.

'You'll be back ... when?' asked Rowena, as Gabby shuffled past them and out to the pavement.

211

'Is six OK?' offered Newton, shrugging.

'Six? Well I suppose so. No later though, she's got school in the morning.'

'Do you have to talk about me like I'm not here?' huffed Gabby, exaggerating her natural angst.

'She's being very difficult,' said Rowena, ignoring the substance of Gabby's comment utterly. 'Perhaps you and your new girlfriend will have more luck communicating with her than I do.' With that, she closed the door smartly in Newton's face.

'Well, bye then,' said Newton to the doorknocker. He turned to his daughter. 'Hope you don't mind meeting Viv today – she's very nice, you'll really like her.'

'And if I don't ... what then?' said Gabby, sneering.

'Err well, oh I'm sure you will,' said Newton, fully aware that Rowena was probably watching and waiting for a good view of Viv from the window as they both climbed into the car. Like drug mules passing through customs, they set off slowly past the house and away.

'Hi, I'm Viv,' said Viv abruptly, opting for a buoyant 'who cares' approach. Gabby, determined to make them both pay for every inch of familiarity, opted for the 'who gives a shit' approach and grunted a minimal 'hi' in return.

'You must be Gabby. Newton's told me so much about you.' Gabby, Newton could sense, was in a quandary. She was deeply uncomfortable, but since the previous ghost-walking weekend had left her considerably more at ease with her father, she didn't want to be difficult. Then again, in typical teenage daughter style, she also didn't know how to be that nice and relaxed either. So the three of them were silent for a while as the air chilled, defrosted, chilled, super-chilled and then eventually, thankfully, defrosted once again. This time the freeze melted a tad more permanently.

'Dad says you live in Greenwich – that sounds fun,' said Gabby unexpectedly. Newton and Viv exchanged an expression of surprise and relief.

'Yeah, that's right,' said Viv. 'Have you ever been down there?'

'My friend said it's cool – she says the market is wicked.'

'The market's great. You must come down and see it some time. Would you like that?' said Viv, desperate to build a bridge.

'Maybe,' said Gabby, who then left another silence, less awkward than before but still a silence none the less. 'Where are we going?' she said, after a few long minutes.

'Oh I don't know,' said Newton. 'Just thought we'd get out there and nose around a bit. Get some lunch, you know.'

'Can we go to a pub?' said Gabby.

'Sure, let's see if we can find one we all like,' said Newton.

'Actually there's one I've been told is really good,' said Gabby, leaning forward into the space between the two front seats. 'It's called The Fensman, somewhere off the main road to Huntington. It's meant to be the oldest pub in the country. Can we go there?'

'Of course we can,' said Newton. He and Viv smiled discreetly to each other, the pressure lifting enough to give them the freedom to relax, if only a little. 'There's a road map under my seat – do you wanna see if you can find it? We're coming up to the Huntington road now.'

'Cool,' said Gabby, 'does that mean you can go fast again?'

'Oh ... I don't know ...'

'Oh go on, Newton,' said Viv, 'let's do it!' She looked back conspiratorially to Gabby, who let down her guard and returned a grin.

'OK,' said Newton, with exaggerated nonchalance, 'if that's what you want.' As soon as the way was clear, he put his foot down. The old car hesitated for a second, almost as if it was unsure whether it had permission to let rip, but then, with a glorious throaty roar, the engine once again unleashed its alter ego. The three of them let out loud, involuntary yelps as, somewhere between fear and delight, they hammered up the dual carriageway, halfway to the land speed record. Viv was holding onto the upholstery for dear life, while Gabby was pinned back on the rear seat where she was giggling.

'This is just soooooooooooo coool!'

'Wow!' mouthed Viv above the engine. 'Just ... wow!' Nearing the motorway exit, Newton slowed down and they took a more moderate pace towards the pub.

Many pubs claim to be old, even the new ones, but The Fensman was old, *really* old. Records state that it was serving alcoholic brews back in the Dark Ages. It had been refurbished once or twice since then and now, finally, also served food. Newton left Viv and Gabby chatting awkwardly at a table while he went to the bar to order lunch.

As he approached the crowded bar, he was obliged to step out of the way of a rushing barmaid, and as he did so, he inadvertently placed his foot on a rectangular slab of stone. The slab was sitting plumb in the middle of the pub's polished wooden floorboards. He stood there for a second or two, his right foot on what he was about to find out was a grave. Once again, there was that odd sensation deep in his brain and a weird coldness, seeping over him like chilled treacle. As the hair prickled at the nape of his neck, he cast his eyes quickly around the bar. Eventually, in a space between the regulars and the tourists, he saw her – a pale young girl, her only clothing a simple off-white dress of coarsely woven linen, the edges ragged and torn. The girl returned Newton's stunned gaze with impossibly huge, tear-filled eyes, her tiny hands clinging in desperation to a straggly bouquet of dead wild flowers. Newton swallowed. He knew in a heartbeat that she was a ghost and he stared back at her sad face with incredulity. Then, looking down again at the stone slab beneath him, he finally made the connection. The poor girl, it was her grave. With something of a hop, he jumped back from the stone, an odd sense of intrusion and disrespect washing over him. In doing so, Newton also jogged a passing drinker who, elbowed unexpectedly in his ribcage, spilled a sizable amount of his ale. He responded with a well-seasoned curse. With the connection broken, the girl abruptly vanished, and Newton, seconds from a bar fight, rushed quickly to apologise.

'Sorry, oh God sorry, please ... let me buy you a new pint.'

'No problem mate,' said the man, who clearly thought it *was* a problem, possibly of epic proportions, but to Newton's relief he opted to merely walk away slinging 'arsehole' glances back at Newton as he sat down with his sullen family.

Keen to experiment, Newton placed his pointy black shoe back on the stone. Sure enough, the poor girl was there again. He was astonished. So were Gabby and Viv, watching Newton from their table as he placed his foot on and off the slab in some peculiar new variant of the hokey cokey. Finally, Newton realised they were watching him and grinning awkwardly, he slinked off to the bar to belatedly order the food.

Returning to the table, he sat quietly, happy to take a back seat as the two girls chatted pleasantly away about the pub and life in general. Content that things were working out better than he had dared to imagine, his thoughts drifted off again to the afterlife, his enquiring mind once again trying to match physics with the paranormal and failing miserably.

'Newton ...' Viv said nudging him. 'NEWTON!'

'Sorry ... what was that?' said Newton, snapping out of his train of thought.

'Gabby was just telling us about the history of this pub, weren't you Gabby.'

'Yeah Dad, it's dead interesting,' said Gabby.

'Dead is the right word,' continued Viv. 'Apparently it's haunted by a young girl.'

'I know,' said Newton before he could stop himself.

'You know?' said Viv, surprised. 'I thought you weren't into that stuff.'

'Oh I'm not,' said Newton evasively, 'anyway ... go on.'

'Gabby, tell your dad the story.'

'Well, there was this girl see, it was in the real olden times. She loved this woodcutter or something. He didn't love her though, what a jerk! Anyway, he told her to bog off so she killed herself, hung herself from a tree. Broken heart.'

'Isn't that sad Newton, don't you think?'

'What? Oh yeah, it is,' said Newton. 'Poor kid. No wonder she's hanging around.'

'They didn't bury her in the churchyard,' continued Gabby, 'because in those days suicide was illegal, so they buried her here.'

'It's a bit weird to bury someone in a pub, isn't it?' said Newton, looking back at the slab.

'Wasn't part of the pub at the time I guess ... it is now though. Cool story, eh?' said Viv.

'So it's haunted then?' said Newton, half trying to look like his old anti-paranormal self, but gathering information while he did it.

'Yes, actually it is,' said Gabby, defiantly. 'Loads of people see her – there's a thing on the wall about it, by the toilets.'

'Is there?' said Newton, feigning mild interest. 'Fun story, doubt there's anything in it though.'

'Well you would say that,' said Gabby, as a barmaid arrived and placed three sizable plates before them. 'Well, Viv thinks it's cool.'

'I do,' said Viv. 'And I also think this is a rather splendid dinner – a four-roast-potato job!'

'Great!' said Newton, who tucked into his lunch in silence as he watched the two women in his life, at least the two nice ones, finally together. Gabby and Viv were chatting like old friends, and another knot on the rope of stress Newton had carried around these past years gently unravelled.

CHAPTER 22

# SMOKE AND MIRRORS

Monday found Newton landing at Frankfurt. He took a cab to Heidelberg, checked into his hotel, grabbed a light lunch and then headed purposefully over to LeClarard's last known address in the old town. He asked a museum official at the front desk if he could look around, and got a cheerful nod in reply.

Sure enough, just as Newton had expected, there was a noticeable astrological theme to the decor. LeClarard had clearly indulged himself around the old place – there were tapestries, sculptures and paintings, all featuring zodiacal symbols and the planets. A stern notice proclaimed a prohibition on photography, so Newton fell back on his faithful old leather notebook, taking notes about the arcane decoration.

Straight away, like any good cryptologist, he was looking around the ornate room for patterns. Newton had always had a certain love for riddles and codes, though often he found the examples in popular books and computer games so laughably easy that he would become angry and impatient with them at an almost indecent speed. However, during the lifetime of LeClarard, cryptology had become an increasingly sophisticated and multilayered art and any puzzle he had left was unlikely to be simple. Still, a cipher had to be capable of translation or it simply wouldn't have been a cipher at all – there had to be a chink in it somewhere. It seemed clear to Newton that such a vain personality, with an endless appetite for his own self-aggrandisement, would be driven to place some of these clues in plain sight. There would be no sport in total concealment.

Newton walked through the ornate rooms several times until finally, he was drawn to a single wall. It was distinctive mainly because it was so bland – merely an expanse of drab period wallpaper with a few run-of-the-mill oil paintings. There was none of the exotica present in the rest of the collection. The longer Newton scrutinised it, the surer he became that something had been replaced, defaced or obliterated at some point in the past. But what?

Seeing no clues, Newton strolled back towards the entrance and collared the man at the front desk.

'Excuse me, I wondered if you can help me?' he asked.

'Of course,' replied the attendant in near-faultless English. 'How may I help?'

'The astrology rooms up at the top.'

'Ah ya. They are magnificent are they not?'

'Yes, spectacular,' said Newton. 'And that's just it you see. There's one wall up there that seems different in style. What's the story there?'

'Do you mean the wall at the far end of the building? Ah, you are most observant, sir, ya, it was redecorated, I think in the 1920s. Apparently, there was nothing much there before anyway, except a list of meaningless letters.'

'Do you know what it said?'

'No ... but if you wait a second, I think I may be able to give you a picture of the original wall.'

'Can you?' said Newton enthusiastically. 'That would be very helpful.'

'Helpful?' asked the attendant, suddenly suspicious of Newton's angle.

'Sorry ... interesting, I mean, fascinating,' said Newton quickly. The official bustled away into a small office and soon emerged waving a photocopy.

'Here we are. This is an engraving that was made shortly after the astrologer had the place decorated. It was quite sensational at the time of course.' He handed the image to Newton.

It was not a perfect copy, but then it didn't need to be. The errant wall was there in all its glory, its decoration being admired by several finely attired wig-bearing dandies, one of whom was almost certainly LeClarard himself. Newton was optimistic that he now had the lead he was looking for – there on the wall were two lines of huge letters.

JLZGCVQUHT

MDCXCIV

'That's great!' said Newton enthusiastically. 'May I keep this?'

'Of course, sir. Please.'

Newton thanked the attendant and strolled thoughtfully out onto the street. After finding a cafe, he sat down, ordered a strong coffee and read the letters on the photocopy again.

'How are you getting on then?' said Sixsmith, abruptly interrupting Newton's concentration from the chair opposite.

'Alex!' said Newton, glancing quickly around to see if anyone was within earshot. 'Not here, we're in public!'

'I know, naughty, but I promised Jameson and Eric I'd keep an eye on you. Check your luggage, you'll find my specs – can't get too far from the old relics, I'm told. So I thought I'd get you to cart me onto the plane. Any developments?'

'I'm not talking to an empty chair Alex. Heidelberg is pretty but I don't want to stay in its Baroque nuthouse just yet.'

'Oh there's a good trick for that,' said Alex.

'There is? Do tell.'

'Pretend to make a call. Who's to know that you're not actually talking to anyone on the old dog and bone.'

'Clever,' said Newton, who had been expecting something slightly more paranormal. He pretended to dial and put the phone to his ear.

'Well?' said Alex, looking at the menu. 'Oh look, paprika cream schnitzel, you should try that, delicious! I had that in Nuremberg.'

'I'm not hungry thanks,' said Newton impatiently. 'You wanted to know what's up so far?'

'I do.'

'Well I think I might have got the code.'

'Really? That was fast, what does it say?'

'I said I've got it, I didn't say I'd cracked it.'

'Gotcha,' said Alex, flipping the menu over, something seen only by Newton and a small boy on a nearby table whose eyes widened into saucers as the stollen fell from his mouth.

'Nice selection of pastries.'

'Careful Alex, you're meant to be off the radar remember, enough of the telekinesis already.'

'Yes, sorry. Old habits die hard. No bratwurst in Purgatory, as you can imagine – or samosas, pizza, crispy duck or Cornish pasties for that matter. Oh lordy I miss Cornish pasties I can't tell you ... Sorry, you were saying, the code ...'

'Yes, here it is.' Newton discreetly turned the photocopy round until Alex could see it clearly.

'Well the bottom line looks like a year in Roman numerals.'

'Yup, my thoughts entirely,' said Newton into the phone. 'And it's a bit of an obvious one as it happens.'

'It is?'

'Yup, it's 1694, the year LeClarard was born.' Alex thought briefly, mulling the letters.

'Do we know the exact date of his birth?'

'Yes, it was 19 February 1694. But the top line is the hard bit – that's not a Roman number. Even if we crack the top line, then there's the small issue of what we do with the code once it's cracked. I'm pretty certain it's not the number of a locker at Heidelberg station.'

'Any ideas?'

'Not sure. I'm wondering about all these gizmos he was building leading up to his execution. Must be valuable things, curios and all that. I think I'll take a return trip to his old house, see what they can tell us. Wanna stay here and have some cake while I find out?'

'Oh you bastard,' said Sixsmith, only too aware that he couldn't. 'What kind of sadist are you?'

'Oh you have no idea,' said Newton, throwing some coins onto the table.

Back at LeClarard's old house, the attendant was topping up the postcard stand as Newton reappeared.

'Ah Mein Herr, we are not used to many visitors, especially the same one twice!'

'Yes sorry,' said Newton. 'Quick question about the astrologer that lived here.'

'LeClarard?'

'That's the chap. Did he leave any instruments here after his execution?'

'Ah yes, and a sore point frankly,' said the attendant. 'Telescopes, globes and things ... we would like all that here, of course, it would add so much an increase in visitors I am thinking. Yes I think so.'

'So where are they now?'

'The story is that he bequeathed his instruments to the city as an act of atonement for his crimes, so now they're at the Kurpfälzisches.'

'Sorry, I'm new here, is that a museum?'

'Ya – all the town's finest art is there, it's on Hauptstrasse, four streets away. You cannot be missing it.'

'Wonderful. I can't thank you enough!' exclaimed Newton, and he positively flew out the old doors and back to the cafe. Alex was having fun with the dumbstruck child on the next table when

Newton returned. He was moving a salt cellar around on the table like a Dalek whenever the boy's parents were looking the other way, leaving the poor boy gesturing wildly and no doubt initiating years of child therapy as he did so.

'What did I tell you?' said Newton, but his conversation with the empty chair only made matters worse so, wasting no time, he subtly urged Alex away towards the museum.

******

The Kurpfälzisches turned out to be an imposing Baroque structure in a building called the Palais Morass. Its façade was a dramatic rust and white confection, but Newton was not there for the architecture, and leaving Sixsmith bobbing outside like a party balloon, he dashed through the grand entrance.

Newton, excited as he was, was trying hard not to attract too much attention, so casually he sauntered through the galleries past the archaeology, fine art and ceramics until finally he entered a room packed from end to end with brass instruments. There were telescopes, ornate globes, sextants and astrological calculators. Most of them were from LeClarard's bequest.

'This will be the place then,' said Alex suddenly into Newton's ear.

'Jessuuusss Alex, don't do that.'

'Sorry old boy, but I think I'd better let you know that the place is going to close in half an hour.'

'So, what's the rush? We can always come back tomorrow.'

'It's closed tomorrow.'

'Brilliant, how am I ...' At that point, a couple strolled quietly through the room and out the other side before Newton could continue. 'How am I supposed to solve this thing in only 30 minutes?'

'26 minutes,' corrected Alex helpfully.

Newton quickened his pace as he searched anxiously around the ornate instruments in glass cases, until one caught the corner of his eye. It was a large brass orrery, a clockwork mechanism designed to calculate and display the movements of the planets around the sun. Inscribed on its base – the Roman numeral MDCXCIV, the year of LeClarard's birth.

Newton's mind was racing when a distinguished-looking man

suddenly appeared from a nearby doorway. 'Mein Herr? Did you require something please?' Alex vanished. The museum official took his glasses from his grey-bearded face and cleaned them with a handkerchief before replacing them. 'You are aware that the museum will be closing shortly?'

'Yes, so I gather,' said Newton. 'What a pity, I have come such a long way to see these exhibits. Do you work here?'

'Yes Mein Herr,' he said defensively, 'I am the curator.'

'Ah excellent,' said Newton. 'Do I have time to ask you a few quick questions?' The curator looked at his watch and sighed.

'Ya, I suppose so. You have come from England no?'

'Yes, London. I'm very interested in these things you see. I'm in that line of business.' Newton handed the curator his card.

'Dr Barlow. You are familiar then I think with these instruments. They are beautiful but we find them most peculiar. Many people are not even sure what some of them were for. Maybe you can enlighten me – my only speciality is the modern art. What about this, for instance.' He pointed to a round brass clock-like device, about the size of a dinner plate, with curious inscriptions.

'Ah yes,' said Newton helpfully. 'That's an astrolabe, although an unusually complicated one. They were used for working out the positions of the sun and stars in the sky – surprisingly accurate for their time.'

'And this, we have had no luck with this at all.' The curator pointed to a device with rings interlocked at different angles.

'Well, that's another clever one,' says Newton. 'It's a kind of pocket sundial that can tell the time anywhere in the world. Used a lot during the 18th century.'

'Goodness, you really *do* know about these things doctor. I feel glad that you have come.' The curator's demeanour softened noticeably.

'And what about this? We thought it is for tracking comets as they are moving between the stars?'

'Ah, no,' said Newton gently, 'that's a clockwork potato peeler. See, the potato is placed here and the blades rotate in a clockwise motion. Hey presto, ready to roast. Sorry.'

'You need not be sorry, Dr Barlow. I am just glad that it has been spotted before we made further fools of ourselves. I am most grateful however for the information about the other instruments. I shall label them accordingly. You have helped me, of course I will be helping *you* now. Is there something particular you wish to see?'

Newton pointed to LeClarard's orrery. 'That's a fine orrery – is it working?'

'Oh ya,' said the curator. 'It is clockwork and it is kept wound up by someone here. Not sure who but it is not only working, I'm told it is correctly calibrated to the movement of the planets.'

'Is it now?' said Newton thoughtfully. 'Would you mind if I had a look at it? I'd very much like to see it up close, without the glass.'

'Oooooh. It is most irregular Herr doctor. I am not sure I can ...'

'I've come a very long way to see these things,' Newton pressed, 'and as something of a historian it would be lovely to get that proper "close-up" experience.'

'Well ...' said the curator, wavering nervously. Then, with theatrical eagerness on Newton's face urging him on, he fumbled with his keys and the glass doors swung open.

'Beautiful,' said Newton leaning in. 'It's a remarkable piece.' He looked over to Sixsmith, who had reappeared to his right, and gestured none too subtly with his eyes.

'What?' said Sixsmith, missing the signals spectacularly. Newton persisted. As he made a big show of investigating the large brass ball of the sun, he twitched his head towards the door in frustration.

'Ah right ... OK! Gotcha,' said Sixsmith belatedly, and he shot off between the cases and away towards the offices leaving Newton with the curator babbling beside him.

'Of course, the museum business is not what it was, Dr Barlow,' he said. 'The federal government here in Germany is not really interested in the antiquities I am thinking. Even so there is much interference in our work.'

'Really?' said Newton absent mindedly, as he scribbled frantically in his notebook. 'Do go on.'

'No, I think the budgets will soon be cut.'

'You don't say.' Newton was champing at the bit. He was convinced that the orrery held LeClarard's relic, and all he needed was a moment alone with the damn thing so he could prove it.

'No. I could have been earning of the good monies in business I am sure. But my passion was for history, always the history. My father said I was foolish but I followed my heart ... why I ...' At that point, just before Newton would have happily zapped him with a taser, there was a spectacular crash from a distant room. Like a meerkat reacting to the roar of an approaching lion, the curator stood bolt upright, startled.

'Mein Gott, was ist das!' he blurted. 'Herr doctor, excuse me please!' And with that he dashed away leaving Newton finally alone with LeClarard's clockwork enigma. Alex reappeared beside him.

'Don't worry, he'll be a while, I knocked over a coffee percolator. Right bloody mess.' As confirmation, there was a distant bout of tutting and fretting that echoed past them in the now-empty museum. 'So what's what then Newton, old boy?'

'OK, the riddle is about time and ... the orrery is basically a clock, right? The key is to put in the right date, and we can do that by moving the alignments of the planets to the date in question,' said Newton.

'Right,' replied Alex. 'So are we setting it for his birthday?'

'I'm guessing, let's try that first.' Newton wound the planets around using a small brass handle in the base. The mechanism, beautifully engineered, moved with oiled grace until finally it reached 19 February 1694. 'And ... voila!' said Newton with a flourish.

'Or not ...' said Sixsmith after an unsatisfying silence.

'Dammit,' said Newton. 'I should have known he'd make it harder than that. OK let's think.'

'Oh yes, let's!' said Sixsmith. 'Er ... think about what?'

'The first line of the code,' said Newton distractedly. 'Maybe it's a Vigenère cipher, very popular when laughing boy was around.'

'A what?'

'Vigenère code. It's a code that shifts letters along the alphabet – so maybe C represents A, D means B, for instance. But a Vigenère code is more complicated because each letter is shifted by a different amount depending on the sequence of letters in a separate keyword. So LeClarard's code, JLZGCVQUHT – that could only be decoded if you know the keyword.'

'Which is?'

'I've no idea. But we've got to start guessing right now.' Newton leant back out of the case and grabbed his phone.

'What are you doing?' asked Sixsmith.

'Well back in the day you had to have a deciphering chart, but an app on my phone can do it, no worries. We still need the keyword, though, and we're going to have to guess it. Can you keep an eye on the curator? I can't have him stumbling back in on me.'

'Gotcha,' said Alex, and he flitted silently away towards the back offices.

Newton started to try possible keywords on a Vigenère decoding app. First he tried the vain man's name, 'LeClarard', and came up with the useless answer 'YHXVCEQDEI'. 'Dammit!' said Newton. 'OK sunshine, let's try your first name.' He punched in 'Flavian', but once again the answer came back as gibberish.

In Purgatory, the astrologer slowly opened his eyes. He was only too aware that his puzzle was under attack, but cunning little weasel that he was, he was still confident that he was one embarrassingly obvious step ahead of Newton. A broad grin spread across his thin lips. The game was on.

Newton, frustrated, paused. 'Bugger bugger ... come on ... think.' He cast his eyes around the room for inspiration but found none. 'Globe, geography ... could be Corsica.' Newton punched in the name of the island. Once again the deciphered text was pure drivel. 'Wait, he wouldn't have called it Corsica, it would have been Corse. Of course!' Newton confidently punched the word in and hey presto ... more gobbledygook.

LeClarard's smile became broader still and sickeningly smug.

Sixsmith abruptly appeared beside Newton. 'Get a bloody move on, the curator's nearly finished cleaning up.'

'I'm doing my frigging best, thank you very much,' said Newton angrily, as Sixsmith faded away again.

He was grinding his teeth, prepared to try anything. Then it came to him – maybe LeClarard had made the keyword blindingly obvious. He punched in the lower line of the inscription, MDCXCIV.

'XIXJANVIER' came the answer.

LeClarard stopped smiling.

'Gotcha!' said Newton. '19 January 1694'. Wasting no time, he rotated the planets on the orrery to match the date, a month ahead of LeClarard's birthday, and was rewarded with a loud clunk.

'No!' shrieked LeClarard. 'NOOOOO!'

The sun, a three-inch brass sphere at the centre of the instrument, split apart across its equator. A wisp of sickly purple light seeped out from inside like steam from a kettle.

'Bingo,' said Newton. He leant carefully forward across the fragile brass solar system and lifted the top half of the sun upwards, then retrieved the object inside.

'Quick!' said Sixsmith from behind him, 'he's coming back!'

Looking into the palm of his hand, Newton was confused by what he saw. For all the world it could have been a dog snack. But it wasn't. To his horror, he suddenly realised he was holding the preserved leathery shell-like ear of Flavian LeClarard. A golden hoop earring pierced its foul lobe and Newton saw several nasty little hairs poking out from the ear hole; it looked uncomfortably like a pork scratching. Gingerly he stuffed the withered ear into his jacket pocket trying not to gag, then quickly returned the orrery clock back to its original time and tried to appear unflustered as the curator reappeared.

'Ah Herr curator,' said Newton, 'you're back.'

'Ya Dr Barlow,' said the curator. 'I am so sorry to have been delayed. It was a most annoying technical failure of the coffee percolator. So typical you know. Our budgets are very low you see. If it was one of the government ministries I am quite sure that it would have been of superior manufacturer, but not for us the Miele or the AEG. No. It was cracked very badly and poured all over the carpets. What a mess! Mein Gott what a mess.' He sighed. 'Such is the lot today of a modern museum professional,' he went on. 'You know, Dr Barlow, the government is quite indifferent to the way that ...' Newton cut him short.

'Sorry. You must forgive me but I have a plane to catch. Thank you so much for your assistance.'

'Oh,' said the curator, somewhat crestfallen. 'Do you have everything you came for?' He scuttled after Newton, who was hurrying away towards the exit.

'Oh yes,' said Newton smiling, 'I certainly do. Thank you so much.' He emerged onto the busy street and patted his pocket smugly.

Cockily pleased with himself, Newton virtually skipped all the way back to the hotel. Safe in his room, he carefully took LeClarard's mummified ear from his pocket, placed it in a small plastic bag and hid it amongst his toiletries. He headed for the airport and by six o'clock he was back in London at the Deptford disposal site.

LeClarard's ear burnt brightly, if only briefly, in the furnace. Then, thankfully, it was gone. In Purgatory, his cell fell silent. A small religious community in the jungles of Guatemala was spared the deaths LeClarard had been so looking forward to arranging, and now they could live in peace. Until the day, that is, when they would kill themselves all on their own without any outside assistance.

Needless to say, Jameson and Eric the Greek were delighted. What had been puzzling and perplexing the Purgatorial council for some thirty years, well, Newton had solved it with stylish academic panache in the space of a mere afternoon. Newton's probationary period was officially over – time for new assignments.

On a roll, he went on to locate and secure the last mortal remains of one Tobias Conroy, a nondescript accountant who died in 1768. His polite presence on earth had been drab and uneventful, but in Purgatory he was revered as a tireless mover and shaker. Newton placed his bones in a safe deposit box in Mayfair just in time to prevent him being mashed up in a road-widening scheme.

Next, he uncovered the hidden relics of a colonial sadist in a junk shop in Welwyn Garden City, his timely disposal preventing the embarrassing haunting of a lap-dancing club in Ashford. Newton solved puzzles, broke codes and outbid his rivals at auction. Alex's relic, the half-moon spectacles he'd been so wedded to, were also placed safely in a museum case at the Wellcome Trust in London. Newton travelled all over Europe and the Home Counties, righting wrongs, burying monsters, and saving the nondescript but useful. In the process, he made himself something of a star. With a new job, the trick is to make yourself indispensable and already, judging by his astonishing success rate, Newton was certainly that.

Fantastical months passed. Income poured in and Newton's new relationship with Viv grew into a permanent and content fixture; he was once again a very happy boy. On top of all that, despite all Rowena's increasingly petty efforts to derail it, his relationship with his daughter was blossoming. His new life was bizarre, maybe, but it was full of complexity, intrigue and a sense of purpose, and although he couldn't tell anyone about it, Newton Barlow was having the time of his life.

CHAPTER 23

# THE FAITHFUL

In the grounds of an old French manor house, the Bonetaker sat immobile and massive amongst the frosted shrubs, steaming gently like a compost heap. Wisps of vapour rose from his mildewed mass as he sat, stock still, watching the brightly lit windows.

He sighed wearily to himself as he pondered his next move, bitterly cold but unmoved by the frigid air. He was not a complex spirit, this Bonetaker. But as he followed his relentless pathways across Europe, he felt an acute sadness that would be a hard burden for anyone, let alone one so utterly alone, to carry. He was not only the last of his kind, he was the last of the most rejected amongst his own, cast away so far back in his primitive memory that the bitter details were lost to him. Only the lingering sting of that hurtful departure remained upon him, heavy and perpetual as only a really great pain can be. His Neanderthal tribe, low-brow in more senses than one, had once lived all over Europe, weathering ice storms and a savage natural world, the population reaching all the corners of the once-virgin land. Despite their historical notoriety for brutishness, these thick-set peoples had actually been surprisingly sophisticated, making jewellery, decorating themselves in vivid colours and using cunning new hunting techniques to harvest the plentiful game that covered the continent. Mammoth, bison and deer had been their quarry. Gifted as the highest manifestation of an evolutionary tree, they had made the most of their golden time.

Everything is relative, of course, especially relatives, and once the all-new smarter-than-thou *Homo sapiens* began showing up, the Neanderthals regressed from state-of-the-art humanoid brain box to dumb-ass throwback within geological seconds, just as today a brand new smart-phone can become as impressive as a breeze block in the time it takes to open the packaging. And so it was that the Bonetaker's people were thrown firmly onto the back of their huge hairy feet. They were inexorably marginalised into the tougher landscapes where the game was rare, the firewood was non-existent and the berries gave you diarrhoea. In the swamps, mountains and moorlands, their

228

besieged populations grew so small that inevitably, as their social lives shrivelled, they began to inbreed. As the top-of-the-range *Homo sapiens sapiens* (so good they named them twice) multiplied in fertile plains and valleys, the Neanderthals struggled to maintain a gene pool deep enough to reach their hairy knees.

Birth defects and mutations were rife. Dwarfism, gigantism, humped backs and webbed feet proliferated, and the small desperate communities cruelly banished those with such freakish novelties into the wilderness before settling down to a night of hairy lovemaking with the family.

And when these poor souls were banished, they were banished for good. Ideally, to die.

Giant as he was, the Bonetaker was mutated in another more complex sense. Not only did he fail to succumb to the elements in the deep dark forests, he lived to a ripe old age – one might even say over-ripe. For this outcast, all 25 stone of him, had a highly unusual gift.

The Bonetaker could not die.

No matter what the elements or the landscape threw at him – disease, blizzards and droughts – he lived on. Year after endless year, decade on decade and millennium upon crawling millennium, time passed taking the gentle giant with it. He'd outlived his heartless parents and his cruel, mocking siblings by a hundred thousand lifetimes, wandering heavy hearted through the landscape, headed who knows where.

Such longevity, married as it was to such utter rejection, is no gift at all. It is hard to imagine such loneliness. The Bonetaker had hidden from primitive villages in the Stone Age, the Iron Age and the Bronze Age, watching silently from the tree line as the humans raised their young, farmed, and ate together. Huge tears avalanched down his monstrous filthy cheeks.

Inevitably, he spawned a thousand folk tales, spun and exaggerated by liars and attention seekers, none of them accurate or kind. As he moved around Europe, one step ahead of the last manhunt, he would inspire a tale of goblins here, trolls there and Almases out on the Steppes. Always he would be portrayed as a monster, a terrifying supernatural killer of livestock and a ravisher of virgins. It was of course, utter nonsense. In reality the Bonetaker, despite his rugged bad looks and Gothic nightmarishness, was a committed vegetarian who only reluctantly killed in self-defence. Sadly though, this was an outcome he was forced to resort to all too often. Hunted by dogs, burnt from his forest refuges and driven high up into freezing mountain passes by swarms of vengeful, ignorant humans, he learnt to avoid the judgmental, superstitious peoples who now ruled the earth. Alone and despairing, he waited for a death that never, ever, came.

When his salvation did eventually come, it came from an unexpected direction, one humid summer night in the Black Forest of Germany, somewhere in the middle of the middle bit of the middle of the Middle Ages.

The Bonetaker had been sitting, forlorn and immense in the treeline above a walled city, watching, as he so often did, the more blessed lives unfolding beneath him. Lonely as ever, he was primitively mulling over how unfair life was, when he became aware, gradually, that he was not alone. Instinctively, he adopted a defensive posture to the white-robed man who now floated before him. But this strange human male was quite unlike those who had been tormenting him most of his unhappy life. This one was bright and smiling, exuding an unfamiliar kindness, glowing and benign, albeit with the unmistakable whiff of a petty bureaucrat.

'Please, do not be alarmed,' said Eric the Greek, oddly making himself understood to the Neanderthal, for whom illiteracy, on every level, was a defining feature. The soft words echoed in his heart and head with a beautiful clarity, and the Bonetaker, unused to communication from any source, was stopped in his massive tracks.

Goodwill was a total stranger to this poor outcast, as mysterious as love and as precious as gold. The warmth and kindness washed over him like a healing balm, soothing the pain and rejection he had carried for so long.

The glowing being told him of the earth, of heaven and of hell, the meaning of nature and magic and then, already intoxicated by contact, the Bonetaker and his new friend were joined by others. They clothed and fed the giant, and taught him a rudimentary language, training him to be their agent on earth. For the first time, a sense of purpose and meaning found lodging within the Neanderthal and he embraced it as fully as his small but perfectly formed soul could bear without exploding like a firecracker.

They filled his sloping forehead with strange and powerful new compulsions. More than happy to oblige his kind benefactors, the Bonetaker was soon travelling the length and breadth of Europe. He set forth in search of foul relics, trinkets and individuals, targets his patrons needed eliminated to rid Purgatory of its most evil souls.

And once he had located them – he destroyed them utterly.

But in time, his guardians drifted on. Gradually, they stopped coming at all, leaving the Bonetaker alone again in the dark forests. His big heart would have burst if it could have done. Yet, imprinted as he had been by these odd mystical beings, he remained compelled by their programming to seek out evil and all its traces upon the face of the earth. So, for centuries, he had wandered alone and unbidden, sniffing the winds for the traces of the malignancy that they had made his perpetual quarry.

It was just such a compulsion that had now led him here, across the narrow sea from England to Normandy. Steaming in the frost, the giant sniffed the air, focusing his odd senses on the manor house, feeling to pinpoint the precise location of the creeping evil that was arousing him. From the neglected shrubs, he impassively watched the tall windows, some partially unshuttered to reveal frantic activity inside. Outside on the gravel, men were dragging full jerry cans out from two BMWs.

The Bonetaker edged forward. He weaved silently through the vegetation, seeking to gain a better view through one of the tall windows. He saw a large roaring fire, heaped with files and documents that kept the flames leaping high in the hearth. Men in combat fatigues busied themselves packing suitcases and hold-alls, periodically checking their automatic weapons and ammunition pouches. But there was another man in the room that the Bonetaker could not clearly see – a grey-haired man, hidden from the Bonetaker in a high-backed chair. A young bearded man cradling a submachine gun walked up to the chair and addressed the mystery figure.

'Father, we are nearly ready, you'll have to move soon.' A dark-suited arm extended, cradling a carving of Cardinal La Senza in his left hand as if it was a brandy glass. The Bonetaker's nostrils flared.

'Wait!' said the old man, raising his other arm to solicit a pause in the frantic preparation. 'Have your men face the windows, slowly and carefully.'

'But father ...'

'Do it now Gunter,' he said, softly. 'Do it now. We have a visitor.' Gunter turned alarmed towards the windows. He motioned to his men. Obediently, the black-clad gunmen took up station at the windows, their automatics held up in preparation. Ostentatiously, they cocked their weapons.

'What is it father? What have you sensed?' The old man stood slowly and deliberately.

'There is someone outside, no, not someone, *something*.' He pulled on his leather gloves finger by finger. 'It is watching us.'

'Something? What do you mean?' asked Gunter.

'What the hell mun? Enough riddles,' said one of the gunmen, backing behind an ornate 17th-century chair.

'I was expecting this,' said the old man, putting on his pale raincoat with agonising slowness. 'Maybe not so soon, but it is not wholly unexpected. Gunter, are the cars packed and ready?'

'Ya father, we await your command.'

Seemingly unruffled, Gunter's father placed a small homberg hat on his head and wrapped a scarf around his neck. 'Have your men back away from the windows,' he said, looking around the room at the gathered henchmen, a mixed bunch of wannabe Special Forces, Serbian war criminals and Russian pay-as-you-go thugs. But Gunter Van Loop and his father were in a different league altogether, hardened believers interested in more than mere money. The Van Loops were cold and utterly ruthless. They harboured a multi-generational memory of a despicable master who bound them to kill, scheme and plot, ready to re-establish his brutal leadership on an unsuspecting earth. Father to son for generations, they had waited.

The men were grouped now in a black semicircle facing the windows and the brooding darkness beyond. They looked at each other apprehensively, then back towards the old man.

'What is it?' said one of the men anxiously. 'What da fuck are we looking for?'

'Hold yourselves, gentlemen,' said the old man, cradling the figurine of La Senza in his liver-spotted hands. 'He will be here soon enough.'

'Don't you ever get bored of being enigmatic?' asked one of the more grounded hard men, sarcastically.

'Mind your tongue!' spat Gunter. 'Show my father respect!'

As Van Loop's men stared hard into the dark shadows of the garden, the Bonetaker, unseen, stealthily crept across the lawn between the pools of light.

'He is near,' said the old man, his eyes closed to increase his senses.

'You'd best get ready.' The guns all raised a notch higher.

As if on cue, the Bonetaker triggered a security sensor. Abruptly his huge form stood bathed in the harsh blue light of floodlights, massive, terrifying and wholly unexpected.

'Holy fff ...!' said one of the men involuntarily as the shock of the Bonetaker's size became apparent. Instinctively, they pulled their triggers.

The dimly lit room was suddenly vivid with muzzle flashes. Rounds tore through the glass towards the Bonetaker, splinters of wood from the shutters and tatters of ripped curtains erupting outwards as he reared up in the naked light. He roared in a loud primal agony as the slugs found their mark – painful maybe, but a very long way from fatal. Instinctively he rolled to the side and out of the line of fire before repositioning himself and lunging headlong through the last intact window. There was an explosion of glass and printed fabric. His spectacular arrival took the gunmen so by surprise that their fingers left the triggers. There was the Bonetaker, in all his horrifying fairy-tale splendour, crouching amongst the broken glass on the Persian carpet. Shocked and stunned into immobility, they stood glued to the spot as he picked up his vast bulk, glass tinkling to the floor. He rose up to his eight-foot height, his head knocking away the chandelier.

'What the fuck is thaaaat?' said one of the men.

'Father, father, what is it?' said Gunter, backing slowly away as he recharged the magazine on his machine gun.

'Isn't he magnificent,' said the old man, strangely unfazed, as the Bonetaker sniffed the air for his unpleasant quarry. 'He's a troll, a giant – history has many names for him.' To Gunter's amazement, his father calmly walked towards the Bonetaker and stared into his bloodshot eyes. 'Tell your men to lower their guns,' he said.

'What? Father, are you mad?'

'Lower your guns I say. They will not help us, I doubt they can kill him anyway. He is here for something, and we can guess what, can't we big fellow?' He held up the wooden figure of La Senza. 'Is this what you have come for?' The Bonetaker's eyes widened in programmed recognition, the relic reeking of vile intent and accumulated malice. 'Yes, my old friend, this is what you have been seeking is it not? It has drawn you here from so far away.'

The monster, its senses working overtime, bellowed, the old man's thin grey hair flip-flopping in the foul draft. The Bonetaker began to lift his gigantic filthy hand up to grab the relic. But Van Loop moved it away from the Bonetaker's grasp, soliciting a loud grunt of aggravation. With his other hand, he indicated the door.

'Gentlemen, the cars,' he said calmly over the Bonetaker's panting growls. 'I will follow.'

'Father?'

'*Now* Gunter!' he said sternly, and he raised the carving high until it was nearly level with the Bonetaker's bloodshot eyes. The huge head began gradually to bare its yellowed teeth, huge canines emerging at each side like daggers. He growled like a wild dog; the men needed no more urging.

'Go go go!' yelled Gunter Van Loop, and the henchmen, with their guns trained on the monster dwarfing the old man before them, backed out from the room one by one, then dashed to the vehicles in the driveway. But the Bonetaker's eyes never left the figure held up by Van Loop senior; oozing cruelty and terror, it crouched defiantly upon its box.

Taunting the giant, Van Loop waved the relic from side to side. The Bonetaker obediently swayed with the movement, clearly hypnotised by its pungent stimuli. Outside, the cars were revving urgently, steam rising in thick clouds from their exhausts. A horn sounded.

Catching the Bonetaker by surprise, Van Loop slung the reliquary violently across the room. It thudded hard upon the threadbare carpet and rolled away under the furniture. The Bonetaker roared in frustration. He lunged after the relic as Van Loop limped quickly in the opposite direction, pausing only to kick over a jerry can. It spilled its contents towards the raging fireplace and as the old man hobbled as fast as he could towards the front door, he heard the gratifying 'whumpf' as the fuel ignited. Instantly, the room was ablaze. The Bonetaker, however, was too busy tearing the room to pieces to notice, sofas, chairs and tables flying about him as he scrambled to find the remains of Cardinal La Senza.

Van Loop staggered to the cars as the flames behind him mushroomed. Gunter bundled him into the rear of the BMW before jumping into the passenger seat. Even as the car doors were slamming, the Bonetaker finally located the box. Without hesitation, he slammed it violently against the stone fireplace. As it fragmented, the deception was clear. Inside, where there should have been one of the Inquisitor's five fingers, there was nothing. Van Loop had foreseen this moment. He had taken the age-blackened finger bones and their attendant ruby ring from the box, transferring them to his large anonymous necklace for safety.

'Drive!' he screamed. The two vehicles spun their wheels in the gravel, just in time to avoid the enraged Bonetaker as he thrust himself through a large flaming window and lunged out towards them.

'Go, go, go!' screamed Gunter, above the roaring engines. Behind them, the Bonetaker reared up and steadied himself, then began his pursuit.

At first it was nothing but a slow ambling run. But then he began to gather pace, his gait changing every few seconds as if he were a truck climbing steadily up through the gears on a motorway. In under a minute, he was pounding along like a rhino after a poacher.

Charging away down the high-hedged lanes, the Van Loops felt confident they'd evaded the bizarre threat, and they eased off to play it safe on the narrow, icy back roads. It was a mistake. The Bonetaker was now clocking up more than forty miles per hour, his massive feet pummelling him towards the vehicles.

He was closing in fast, suddenly rearing into view in their mirrors on a straight stretch, lit in all his glory by the moonlight, smouldering embers streaming behind him like smoke from a funnel.

'My God Gunter, it's following!' came a scream from the back. 'How is that possible? What is that thing?'

'We'll worry about the details later,' yelled Gunter, as the driver slammed his foot back onto the accelerator, throwing the vehicle savagely around a corner. 'Müller, make contact with the Antonov – tell them to be ready.'

The man fumbled with his radio handset as the car bounced along the icy tarmac. 'Canary, Canary, come in, this is Pussycat, start the fucking engine for Christ's sake, we are coming now!'

Behind them, the Bonetaker was virtually on top of the second car, taking wide swipes with his monstrous hands at the rear bumper. Their automatics cocked and ready, the occupants positioned themselves for a clear field of fire as both they and the Bonetaker rushed headlong along the narrow lane. Briefly, the Bonetaker came charging into view, clear for a second as they barrelled over a crossroads. Instantly, his huge form was greeted with a volley of automatic fire. He bellowed in pain, but did not slacken his pursuit in the slightest. Instead, he smashed through a gate and off across a small field that hugged a sudden tight bend. Crossing the field, he shaved away a few vital seconds, just enough to demolish the remaining distance to the second vehicle. In the car, the terrified gunmen craned their necks desperately in and out of the windows, alarmed by the Bonetaker's sudden disappearance. They looked everywhere except ahead.

Seemingly out of nowhere, the Bonetaker tore directly into the side of the crowded car, sending it lurching into a banked hedgerow. It slewed sickeningly to a halt, damaged far beyond any help from the extended warranty. It lay there hissing and fizzing for a few seconds before finally a bent door creaked open. The Bonetaker stood stock still, panting and steaming like a small shunting engine, sniffing the oily, smoking car wreck for any trace of the La Senza relic. But he found none. He raised his head in annoyance and looked down the lane, watching the receding lights of Van Loop's lead vehicle. Certain that the relic was inside it, he once again began to pound down the lane.

Ahead of him, Gunter was trying frantically to contact the rear vehicle. 'Dammit, dammit! They've gone! You, give me that bag!'

'My God! He's back again!' came a terrified shout. Gunter wound down the window to see the Bonetaker tearing down the road towards them like an armoured car. They were approaching a small village, its warm lights shimmering erratically through the leafless trees. From the holdall he grabbed a small cylinder.

'What are you doing?' asked his father.

'Meeting force with force Popa,' said Gunter, and he leant back out of the window to sling a grenade into the road. His timing was perfect; the grenade exploded just as the Bonetaker drew level, the thunderclap slinging him abruptly to the side so that he found himself unintentionally tearing like a bulldozer through a hedge into a small market garden. His speed unchecked, he smacked through a row of greenhouses in an eruption of glass and last year's vegetable matter. It did nothing to slacken his momentum. Pounding forward, he pulled away the dead vines and aluminium framing, then lurched back violently onto the lane. Mere feet apart, they thundered into the village.

The dark car bounced off buildings as it careered frantically down the small high street, wing mirrors lazily cart-wheeling in its wake.

The Bonetaker was close behind them, leaping over parked cars and a traffic island to close the gap. With chaos erupting in their wake, they burst out of the hamlet and back into the dark lanes leading to the airstrip.

The Bonetaker was closing fast. Gunter fumbled manically in the bag and retrieved another grenade; he allowed it to cook for a few seconds before slinging it viciously from the window. The heat and blast shook the rear of the car as much as it shook the Bonetaker, the rear wheels leaping upwards, causing the driver to fight for control. Blinded by the sudden flash and the searing shrapnel, the Bonetaker tore away into a plantation of young fir trees, the thrashing branches adding to his disorientation and forcing him to raise his filthy sleeves in front of his face. It was just enough to allow the car to charge out of danger and it screeched hard off the road, smashing through a closed gate onto the moonlit airstrip. An aircraft was running its engines in the freezing air.

They screeched up to the old Russian Antonov biplane, and skidded to halt in a cloud of ice and steam. Even before the car stopped, Gunter was out. He dragged his father towards the revving aircraft. Behind them, they could see the small plantation rustling as the Bonetaker, infuriated, fought his way through.

The old man was pushed unceremoniously up the small access ladder. Gunter threw the bags in behind his father then looked warily back at the threat tearing towards them through the plantation like a lawnmower.

'You,' Gunter motioned to one of the men. 'Hold him off.' With that he urged his last three gunmen into the impatiently roaring Antonov.

'What?' said the man in disbelief. 'Why me?' But there was no time left to debate the matter. Even as Gunter closed the door and the pilot slammed the throttle forward, the Bonetaker, in a very bad mood indeed, erupted from the trees. The solitary gunman began firing at the Neanderthal now pounding towards him across the frosted grass. Alarmingly, his constant gunfire had no obvious result, so he primed his launcher and began to pump grenades at the looming giant. But the Bonetaker wasn't interested in the mercenary. He charged past him like a train through a station, the explosions erupting around him in lurid flashes of flame and frozen soil.

The escaping Antonov was accelerating frantically across the treacherous icy grass, yet the gap between it and the Bonetaker's relentless bulk was narrowing by the second. Gunter had opened a small side window and looking back into the chilled slipstream, he could see the mayhem exploding around the Bonetaker, just yards from the fragile tail assembly. Desperate, Gunter locked onto a last grenade amongst the socks and aftershave. Wasting no time, he primed the device, waited three seconds then let it go.

The sudden flash and crack of the stun grenade hit the Bonetaker with agonising shock. Its million-candle brightness seared his ancient bloodshot eyes shut, rendering them useless. Simultaneously, his eardrums suffered a blast so loud that his head rang like a cathedral bell. Robbed of every sense but smell, he lost his footing and tumbled over and away from the fleeing aircraft. With its engine screaming, the Antonov slipped, slid and then finally leapt from the frosted grass, barely clearing the perimeter fence. Struggling for altitude, it clattered away across the low trees like a huge insect.

The lone gunman ceased fire and he stood still, his assault weapon smoking blue in the moonlight. Emboldened, he swaggered slowly up to the immobilised Bonetaker as he rocked backwards and forwards upon the grass strip, hands clasped over his ringing ears and eyes still sealed shut by the grenade's flash. Disorientated and thoroughly disappointed in himself, the Bonetaker let out a long, low moan. Recharging his automatic with a fresh clip, the gunman walked forward to deliver the coup-de-grace.

'Hey you,' he mocked. 'Not such a big boy now, eh? Gunter got you gud and pruper.' He raised his gun execution-style to the head of the kneeling giant. 'OK boy. Time to go.'

With one clean swipe the Bonetaker's huge arm shot out.

The Antonov hedge-hopped noisily away to the north and was gone, the still of the cold night disturbed only now by the piteous screams of the gunman, drifting away across the grass on the frozen air.

## CHAPTER 24

# PROMOTION

The massive branch had fallen directly through the roof of Baxter's Lexus like a fist through a cereal box. Glass from the windows hung limply on their plastic edging like empty pockets hanging out of trousers, while the savaged engine bled oil onto the gravel.

Christopher Baxter wasn't going anywhere.

He'd hoped to spend Saturday speeding away from the surreal atmosphere of Hadlow Grange up the M3, making London by midday in time to preen himself, stop the persistent itching and chase down some old pals for a night out in the West End. Not now. As he looked at the punctured glory of the Baxter wagon, he had to fight hard to stop his bottom lip wobbling.

'I'm so terribly sorry,' said Ascot McCauley, resting his hand on Baxter's shoulder. 'What rotten bad luck. We'll have to have someone from Dorchester come and look at it on Monday.'

'But I was going to go to London,' whimpered Baxter.

'Oh dear, were you? How unfortunate,' said Ascot. 'Now you'll be stuck here for the weekend. I'm so dreadfully sorry.'

'What am I going to do *here* all weekend?' Baxter said glumly.

'Oh, I'm sure there will be something for you to do. Do you like walking? We are not very far from the coast here, not far at all. And the heaths are nearly all free from unexploded ordnance now. All I ask is that you please avoid the old asylum – the building is sadly in a state of some disrepair, it's a little dangerous. I tell you what, Miss Dryer is at a loose end at the weekends. Maybe you could entertain each other in some way?'

Baxter looked back at the Grange. Miss Dryer was at a high window, brushing her greying hair slowly and methodically in her dressing gown, her crazy eyes fixed on Baxter.

'Oh I'm sure I can keep busy,' lied Baxter, feeling uneasy at record levels. 'How did the branch come down like that? Isn't that a new cut?'

'Yes and no,' said Ascot. 'We had the tree surgeons in last month, I suspect it's something to do with that.'

'Just brilliant,' said Baxter. 'Do you think I can get it paid for? You know, compensation?'

'Oh I'm not sure about that,' said Ascot. 'It's an act of God is it not?' With that he turned smartly on his heels and set off to the house leaving Baxter fuming by the wreck.

'But, but ... I mean, it's on your property ...' he shouted after Ascot, but he was rewarded only with a dismissive flick of his employer's cufflinks. 'Bollocks, bollocks, bollocks!' said Baxter, frustrated and angry. He'd half intended not to return from London; he could maybe take his chances again on the job market and put the McCauleys and their considerable weirdness behind him. He stomped past reception and up to his room, where he sat white-knuckled on the faded bedcover, seething.

By mid-day he was too hungry to avoid the lamentable dining room. Again, he had to tolerate the old chef's grey and lifeless casserole, its dumplings looking for all the world like washed-up polystyrene on an industrial coastline. All through dinner, the doddering old cook could be seen through the serving hatch, dropping in and out of a service tunnel then re-appearing in the grounds beside the walled kitchen garden before abruptly returning to the kitchen with a sack of filthy vegetables, slung over his shoulder in a string bag.

Miss Dryer was watching Baxter again as she picked bird-like at her rhubarb crumble. She winked directly into his evasive eyes.

'So what will you be doing with your Saturday then, Christopher?' she announced when the room cleared. 'It seems we are both at something of a loss. Perhaps we could take a stroll in the old vegetable garden? We could get to know each other a little better.'

'Sorry, I've got something on,' said Baxter.

'Have you, have you really,' she replied, her eyes narrowed suspiciously. 'Perhaps I should approach you again, when you've got *nothing* on.'

'Yes ... I mean no,' said Baxter, flummoxed. 'It's just that I was hoping to catch up with a few things.'

'Which are?'

'A bit of research. A bath maybe.'

'A nice ... warm ... bath?' said Miss Dryer, dragging out the words.

'Uh yes,' said Baxter. He wolfed down his glutinous pudding and dashed quickly out of the dining room before Miss Dryer could untangle herself from her desert and follow him. Then, with no other options, he climbed wearily back to his room. After trying unsuccessfully to gain a meaningful signal on his iPhone, his restlessness grew to epic proportions. He found himself climbing onto the rickety bedroom chair to peer out of the skylight at the grounds beyond. His sudden appearance at the glass frightened away a gang of rooks; they chuckled and cackled in alarm before wheeling chaotically away in the sharp wind.

Off to his right, the mass of the old asylum loomed like a scuttled warship beneath the low clouds, its sinister bulk drawing Baxter's gaze like a magnet. He looked up and down the endless ranks of shuttered and barred windows until his eyes snagged unexpectedly on the rear top corner. At the summit of a precipitous metal fire escape, an open door was swinging forlornly in the gusts of winter wind. Baxter was hardly the most curious of individuals yet despite his employer's warning, he was compelled by boredom and ennui to take a closer look. He'd made his mind up that McCauley Bros was not going to work for him and that therefore, there was nothing to lose from a little poking about.

So he left his tiny attic room and returned to what had recently been his car. After much resistance, the buckled boot eased open enough for him to reach in and retrieve a torch.

Outside the big building there was a sea of detritus, something that old hospitals shed like middle-aged men shed hair. There was wood, shards of broken glass and countless old mattresses mouldering in puddles of anonymous stagnant fluids. The fire escape that led to the open door was corroded like the handrails on the Titanic, and as Baxter walked up the steps, the rust crunched underfoot like coarse sand before whipping away in the frequent gusts. Keen to avoid getting it on his hands, Chris tried not to touch the handrail, but vertigo set in, forcing him to grab it frantically like a mother's hand. With the fire escape noticeably shifting under his weight, he eventually came level with the swinging door and entered the empty building.

Glass and nails cracked on the linoleum beneath him as he entered a long corridor. There was a faint tang of antiseptic. The natural light behind him flashed on and off as the door, caught by the wind, swung on its hinges. He had only gone some ten feet into the corridor when the wind outside finally found enough strength to heave the old fire door firmly shut, the loud crash leaving Baxter suddenly in total darkness. Immediately he fumbled with the torch and its blessed

241

beam led him back to the door. He pushed it hard. Now it felt like it had been welded shut, and even with his full weight behind it, the door simply wouldn't budge. Unsettled, he shone the torch down the long corridor hoping to see another exit. He swallowed hard. The beam, for all its advertised strength, hit nothing in the distance, only an endlessly receding line of heavy cell-like doors fading into the inky blackness. Unnerved, Baxter opted to try the jammed door one more time. Nothing. Reluctantly, he began to edge forward past the endless horrible doorways and into the guts of the asylum.

Mercifully, most of the doors were locked shut, but occasionally they were ajar. His torch beam caught old metal beds with filthy sheets in chaotic arrangements, hinting at a sudden forced departure. On the walls there were posters, childish drawings and confused scribbles. In one cell, a repetitive hand had scribbled the same words again and again in a meticulous copperplate script. 'Naughty girl' it said, again and again and again, a desperate confused mantra. Baxter shivered, the cold damp atmosphere reaching deep beneath his tailored Italian shirt. A mood of dark despair oozed out from the cells as he nervously advanced. After what seemed like an eternity, he came to a T-junction. Instead of an exit, he just met two more corridors, each another endless line of cells fading away into the gloom. He took a chance on a left turn and eventually, after another twenty or so rooms, he stumbled upon a staircase. Peering over the wooden banisters, he shone the torch down to the floors beneath.

Suddenly, there was a crack of glass. Startled, he turned to point the flashlight behind him. 'Who's there?!' he called. A distant muttering washed down the corridor, so faint that he wasn't even certain he had heard it at all. Subtle as it was, it was more than sufficient to make Baxter hasten down the staircase. As he descended, he heard it again. But it was clearer now. It sounded like a female voice, a whispered repeating phrase. But, equally, thought Baxter to reassure himself, it could have been the jackdaws or the rooks cackling, deadened by the boarded windows. Badly rattled, he descended. At each landing, he shone the torch around him to reveal the same dispiriting view – endless cells, broken glass and oppressive damp. A persistent drip from the top of the stairs caught in the beam as it passed, before splashing far below him.

Reaching the second floor, just as he thought he might be close to finding a way out, he heard more movement on the staircase directly above him. Baxter leant over the banister to shine the torch back up the stairwell. This time, the beam caught an undeniable movement on the banister above. There was a young female hand and the sleeve of a dressing gown. Baxter's perfectly groomed hair prickled as the air around him began to freeze.

'H ... h hello, hello?' he stuttered, panicking. The sound was there again. It was clearly, most definitely, not the crows.

'I'm a naughty girl, naughty girl, naughty girl ...' It came drifting down the stairs in a hideous cascade. 'Naughty girl, naughty girl ...' it lamented. Chris Baxter's eyes widened so far he began to resemble a character in a manga comic. Led by his terrified legs, he fled down the stairs at alarming speed, tripping and skidding over the cracking glass and damp, ragged lino. To his utter dismay, the stairs did not drop straight down to the ground floor at all. Instead, he was forced to move along yet another nightmarish corridor of cells, most of which had open doors. Tracking the walls with the torch, Baxter could see that some of the doors seemed to be actually in the process of opening. Bewildered, he almost cut back, but there was that sound again, nearer now. 'Naughty girl, naughty girl ...' As he swung the torch frantically behind him, he was horrified to see the figure of the girl near the bottom of the staircase, the beam partially cutting though through her as if she wasn't there. But she *was* there, and more to the point, she was getting nearer, her jaw mouthing 'naughty girl, naughty girl'.

Gibbering with terror, Baxter bolted down the corridor, the ghost girl at his back. But now, as he passed the countless cells, there were ghastly new sounds – male voices, weeping, cackles from the left and screams from the right. Baxter fled on, not daring to look into any of the foul interiors. But thankfully, the end of the corridor was in sight, its twin fire doors slightly ajar as he barrelled towards them. With the cacophony of lost souls at his back, he burst through the doors and skidded to a halt.

Baxter was at the head of a grand staircase. The darkness and lack of detail ahead of the beam made him hesitate for a second and he stood breathless and pale, looking down the semi-derelict steps. The sensitivity within him was horribly strong. Uncomprehending, he had allowed the McCauleys to switch on receptors and senses that Baxter didn't even know he had. In this most awful of environments, he was being treated to a spectacular demonstration. Just how unpleasant this 'gift' could be, he was about to discover.

A creak on the floorboards behind him made him freeze. Slowly, Baxter turned. Ahead in the beam, mere inches from his own horrified face, was a hideous new apparition. A terrifying nurse, austerely clothed and horribly disfigured, was staring directly at him. Her cheeks and forehead were gashed and scratched, the long wounds appearing as if they had been gouged by desperate fingernails drawn hard down her face. The horrific vision peered malevolently into Baxter's eyes. Involuntarily, he let out a piteous whimpering cry. It stuck at the back of his throat like a cocktail stick, and without thinking of the health and safety implications, he lurched backwards into space.

Baxter bounced chaotically down the grand staircase like a plastic football, tumbling painfully, first in the accidental strobe of the flash light and then, when it finally shattered and died, in horrifying darkness. He thumped heavily onto the hard floor and rolled to a halt. His eyes flashed with stars and he lay there confused for a second or two, unsure where he was. Finally, he pushed himself up and took a fearful look back towards the staircase. A skylight far above him was casting down its pitiful light, just enough for him to see the stairs. It was a small blessing, because now he could also see the apparition of the ghostly nurse again, inexorably descending the steps. He bit into his hand and let out a squawking whimper before attempting to hobble away. Desperate, he began casting around for an escape route while from high above, the pitiable girl repeated her sad refrain over and over. Behind Baxter loomed the asylum's huge main doors, and seeing a brief chink of light, he staggered over and grabbed their large, ornate handles. He began pulling frantically, shaking them pointlessly and screaming for help.

'Oh God! Help, help me! Someone ... please!' The ghostly nurse was merely one flight of steps away, so he abandoned his efforts and ran into one of the large adjacent rooms. He limped past countless old tables and piles of scattered chairs. Terrified out of his meagre wits, he stumbled and fell. 'No, please no!' he screamed. 'Leave me alone!'

He forced himself up and ran on through room after room, the building still echoing with sobs and screams from its horrible past, mingling now with the wheeze of Baxter's hyperventilation. He was working his way further and further into the dark heart of the asylum, drawn on by a distant light in the gloom ahead. He dashed towards it, begging for salvation. The ghostly nurse, even though she never seemed to be actually running, was always just one room behind. On and on she came, unstoppable.

Finally, he was upon the source of light – a small utility room. Boarding had come free from the window and a watery light revealed austere ancient washing machines and dirty shattered basins. In raw panic, Baxter climbed up onto one of the washers to pull and yank at the tiny window above in a manic frenzy. Looking back, he saw the nurse drift into view again in the corridor. Baxter was shedding tears.

Provoked finally into life-preserving action, he jumped down, grabbed an old wooden stool, and with a strength born of mortal dread, propelled it through the window. There was a crash of glass. The phantom nurse was no more than an arm's length from Baxter; he leapt back up onto the washing machine and away through the ragged hole like a paratrooper.

Tumbling through the cold air, he screwed up his eyes in anticipation of a hard landing.

Baxter was lucky, at first, for instead of falling hard on the concrete of the basement yard, he landed on something soft. Whatever it was, it had mercifully stopped him from breaking a limb, or worse, and he rolled comfortably until he smacked his head hard on a wooden box and was momentarily stunned. Mildly blinded by the sudden daylight and the brief concussion, he watched rooks wheeling above him for a pleasant second.

But it wasn't pleasant for long.

Turning his head to the side, he was greeted point-blank by a skull. Leathery skin was falling away from its mildewed features, and it stared back at him resentfully. Baxter screamed. Pushing himself backwards, he fell into a huge lead-lined coffin, a grey-haired, lace-clad cadaver cracking beneath him like stale biscuits. He screamed again and tried to stand. Christopher Baxter was perched awkwardly upon a huge mound of cemetery spoil liberally mixed with the sad armies of Juggin's Lump. Bodies and coffins lay all around him in total disarray. Bony arms, wrapped in rags, rusted chain mail and armour, and a whole legion of Ötzi the Iceman lookalikes crowded around Baxter, leaning horribly towards him, animated by his own frantic struggle. He screamed a lot louder this time. In raw panic he stumbled through the damp nightmare towards the basement wall.

'Argghh, argghh, no!' he yelled, as the bodies seemed almost to reach out for him, his own weight flipping the cadavers into a grotesque contemporary dance class. 'Argghh, no, no, NO!'

Suddenly, two rubbery hands hooked themselves under Baxter's armpits. Crying like a baby, he was hoisted unceremoniously upwards and thrown away from the body pit and into the rear garden like a landed fish. Winded, he lay stunned, unmentionably vile ooze covering his second-favourite suit like jam on a muffin.

Utterly traumatised, he squinted up at a silhouette above him. In waterproof boots, apron and gloves, a McCauley was staring down, the normally slimy smile replaced with a scowl of disapproval.

'Ascot, is that you?' stuttered Baxter. The McCauley did not answer. He removed his large rubber gloves with a slow deliberation and then threw them angrily at the prostrate figure of Christopher Baxter, squirming frantically for purchase in the unmentionable slime he'd brought up with him from the pit. The McCauley retrieved a mobile phone from a pocket of his rubber apron and dialled.

'It's Plumpton,' he said. 'I've found him. He's at the back of the asylum and he's found the dump ... Yes, *that* dump. I did warn you ... Well in that case you'd better come and get him then, hadn't you.' He rang off then turned his icy glance back down at Baxter. 'Oh Christopher,' he said softly, but with a new menace lurking in his voice. 'You have been a bad boy.'

Baxter looked frantically around him. To one side, a pile of corpses had been sorted and catalogued. Beside them, neatly arranged on a rubber sheet, there was a collection of jewellery and other precious objects – swords, brooches, rings, and even the lead from Victorian coffins.

'Wh..wh ... what, what are you doing?' stammered Baxter as he struggled to take the ghastly concept on board. 'Why are all these bodies here?'

'Oh Christopher, really,' said Plumpton, his left eye twitching. 'You don't really think we'd all these little trinkets go to waste, do you? We are big on recycling at McCauleys. We recycle everything. Every battlefield we acquire, every graveyard. Precious stones, lead, brass, gold, silver. To most people it's just horror and distress. But to us, Christopher, it's a business opportunity.'

Baxter looked frantically towards the Grange. The other brothers were running towards him with determination bringing some thickset men with them that he hadn't seen before. Belatedly, Baxter began to join at least some of the dots. He was in trouble; that was obvious enough. But exactly what sort of trouble, he was having difficulty deciding.

He tried to clamber to his feet amidst the goo, but failed miserably, skidding, slipping and sliding helplessly upon the rubberised sheet. The two other McCauleys and their hired muscle arrived. He stared up at them, cowering and stark-eyed.

'What do you want?' he yelled in alarm. 'I'll g..g give you whatever you want!'

'We already have what we want,' said Ascot McCauley matter-of-factly, as he directed the two heavies to heave Baxter off the ground.

'No, don't! Leave me alone!'

'Clean him up, and lock him up,' said Ascot. 'He'll need to be presentable.'

'I told you we shouldn't have waited,' said Plumpton crossly to his brothers. 'He could have hurt himself in there! And then where would we have been? But would you listen?'

The hired men began to drag Baxter unceremoniously back towards the Grange. Bickering, the McCauley brothers followed closely behind.

'Careful, careful!' said Epsom. 'He's hurt enough already. Our guest won't be pleased if he's bruised.'

'Pleased? Pleased? Who won't be pleased?' demanded Baxter. But he wasn't answered or acknowledged, and the men relentlessly dragged him onwards until Epsom McCauley's phone suddenly chimed with an inappropriately pleasant ringtone and they stopped. Epsom pointed at the skyline.

'Our guests ... are arriving,' he announced.

Almost on cue, the large antiquated biplane burst over the tree line. Noisily, it passed low above them, so low that they could see its faded markings.

'Excellent, excellent!' yelled Ascot above the noise. 'We can make our final preparations. To the house!' And as the plane dipped to land on the heath behind the asylum, they continued on, Baxter wriggling pathetically like a child in the grip of the hired hands.

He was dragged howling up the staircase and into a communal shower, where he was forcibly stripped of his second-favourite suit and his underwear before being hosed down with freezing water.

'Nice and clean, gentlemen,' Ascot commanded, a faint smile playing on his features. 'I don't want a trace of filth on that body when our distinguished visitor arrives. Do you hear me?'

After drying poor Baxter with towels as soft as sandpaper, they threw him whimpering into his room and handcuffed him to the bedstead. The muscle left, leaving Ascot standing alone at the foot of Baxter's bed.

'You know I envy you Christopher, really I do,' Ascot said, walking around to look directly into Baxter's terrified eyes. 'You are going to have such an adventure; you really are. You are going to be *somebody* at last. That's what you've always wanted, isn't it Christopher, you nauseating little worm?'

'Whaa ... wha ... what do you mean? What are you going to do to me?'

'Oh there's no need for you to trouble yourself with all that. Better to let someone else do all the thinking for you from now on.' Laughing, Ascot McCauley left the room, gently closing the door behind him.

A key turned heavily in the lock.

CHAPTER 25

# NINE TENTHS

In all honesty, Chris Baxter wasn't sure whether it was worse to be cleaned regularly by Miss Dryer or to lie there in his own filth. Today, she'd spent a lot more time cleaning him than normal, that's if you could call that kind of thing normal. Baxter correctly sensed that there was something up besides Miss Dryer's warped libido.

She had sung softly to herself while she prepared him. Baxter concentrated on the darkening skylight like a patient in a dentist chair determinedly reading an oral hygiene poster during root-canal surgery. Thankfully, the McCauleys came in from time to time to supervise her work, preventing her from expressing herself a little too freely with his restrained body. The triplets had watched the preparations with some satisfaction, indifferent to his rising panic and pathetic pleading. But the dreadful moment, whatever it was to be, was approaching and there was nothing Baxter could do about it.

A fruit drink was fed to him as darkness finally claimed the skylight. He was almost relieved when the dreamy sedative it contained began to infiltrate his knife-edge state of mind. The room began to warp and twist gently, and as soon as he was burbling softly like a baby, they untied him. The elderly Van Loop had joined them, the book from the chapel beneath his arm like a motoring atlas. He spread it upon the rickety dresser and after consulting its aged pages, he began to cover Baxter in cryptic scribbles using an Estée Lauder eyeliner pencil. Drugged like a happy hippy, Baxter was quite mellow, and equally content with the silk bathrobe that they slipped on above his loincloth. A blur of images whizzed past Baxter's eyes as they lifted him down the staircase. Faces he'd not seen before were watching him intently as he was taken past their black-clad ranks like a new baby at a royal court. They entered the chapel.

There was a lot of muttering. Whispers of Latin and ancient Aramaic hissed around the dribbling, grinning Baxter. Finally, he was placed like a showroom dummy into an ornate armchair and carefully secured.

'We will need music,' said Van Loop senior. 'You can't have a

249

gathering like this without suitable music.'

'I'm sorting that,' said Plumpton. 'What do you fancy? I've got Enya, Simple Minds, the *Chariots of Fire* soundtrack ...'

'Are you mad?' barked Ascot. 'You can't summon the dead with Simple Minds. There must be something better than that. How about Enigma? That had a load of chanting in it ... do we have that?'

'Only on cassette,' said Plumpton grumpily.

'I've got a cassette player in my room,' said Miss Dryer, helpfully.

'We can't have Enigma, that's dreadful!' said Gunter. 'It's far too upbeat – it's chill-out music.'

'Well, what do you suggest then?' said Plumpton, crestfallen.

'Here, my iPod,' Gunter threw the player to Plumpton, 'just press play.' Plumpton reluctantly plugged it into the speakers.

Finally, with preparations near complete and the guests assembled just outside the door, the Van Loops and the McCauleys gathered around the inanely burbling Baxter. Having vaguely registered the musical debate, he was singing 'Don't You Forget About Me' like a train-station drunk, a blob of drool dripping down his freshly shaven chin.

'Did we have to drug him?' asked Plumpton, wiping the slobberings away with a sheet of kitchen towel.

'Oh yes,' said Van Loop. 'He would resist otherwise, and there would be bruising.'

'Well, I suppose you're right,' said Ascot. 'But, doesn't that mean the possessor will end up drugged as well?'

'Oh I shouldn't worry,' said Van Loop. 'It's a short-lived sedative. He will be fully back to normal soon. Well ... normal-*ish*!' They all laughed and cackled, Baxter joining in pathetically, a bubble of saliva appearing briefly in his maw before popping. 'I must say he is a most perfect subject – my congratulations to you!' continued Van Loop. 'He is fit and healthy, and from what I have seen, his mind is as blank as an A4 jotter.'

'Utterly empty,' said Ascot. 'Totally self-obsessed – doesn't believe in anything but his own advancement. Quite ghastly, yet perfect for our requirements.'

'Wunderbar,' said Van Loop. 'The smallest trace of idealism, conscience or empathy and it might not take. The Cardinal, may the spirits preserve him, is not partial to anything of that nature. Mr Baxter here is just ideal.'

Baxter looked up and smiled gormlessly as Van Loop senior solemnly began to put on his silken robes. The lights were dimmed as Van Loop carried the book to the lectern. Many guests filed silently in and with the last of the gathering seated, Gunter closed the doors. The excited whispers petered out like escaping air. As the final candles were lit, Van Loop, his mad eyes animated with anticipation, bid them silent.

'Friends, believers, loyal trusted companions ... you join us here on a momentous evening. It was more than five hundred years ago, the great Cardinal, the Grand Inquisitor himself, was taken from us!' There was a ripple of angry muttering. 'He, who should have risen to take all of Europe from the Church – he who should have taken all the earthly realms from the heathens, the infidels, the non-believers – he was taken. Those fools and cowards were not strong enough, my friends. They were afeared of our great leader, as well they should have been, for he, *he* was the judge, the jury and the executioner. It was his destiny to have power over all the earth, and let me tell you this, my friends – he still will! He will!' There was a gasp. 'Yes my friends, despite the greatest attempts by the weak-minded fools that history deems to label "good" ...' He sneered the word as if he was describing a fungal skin infection. 'The attempts to silence, shackle and control our leader have utterly failed. For tonight, here before you, in this very place, you shall witness his return!'

'The great one ...' gasped the crowd in unison. 'Blessed be his nastiness! Return him to us!'

'Friends, friends,' said Van Loop, bidding them quiet with open palms. 'Calm yourselves please, I beseech you, for in this great endeavour we must be resolute. I must ask you to peruse the info packs beneath your seats. This is an ancient procedure and there is much at stake. Be vile of thought and quite horrible in your imaginations. The great one will be here soon, and in this visitation he will require much from you. You will be his foot soldiers, his arms and his legs, his willing executioners, ready to carry out his dreadful will. Doubtless he will have some truly horrible activities planned for you in the weeks ahead, so, as we look ahead to the future, I urge you to turn away from weak conscience and pity. Blacken your hearts in a new mercilessness. Even now, our guards and gunmen are patrolling the grounds to ensure that we will not be disturbed. After tonight they will serve as our shock troops as we head out into this land of Engerland to begin our fateful adventure. I must say that they are without doubt some of the vilest henchmen that an evil plot could desire.' There was polite applause and Gunter, who was in charge of all things paramilitary, took the bow.

'I also urge you to make your acquaintances with our hosts, the McCauley family. They have kindly allowed us to use their facilities for this ritual and it is they who will provide you with refreshments later in the day room. Though not strictly members of the great La Senza cult, they are nonetheless to be considered our equals during this process. We have agreed a mutual exchange of benefits, and frankly, without their unique skill base, it is unlikely that we would be here today.' The brothers McCauley nodded appreciatively.

'It was they who secured the book,' Van Loop continued, as he held the old volume up to the awed audience. 'And it was they who helped us find the second relic. Sadly, as you know, we never did find the fifth box. Doubtless history has swallowed it, but it is of no significance now.' Van Loop looked over to Baxter who was shaking his head in confusion. The sedative was wearing off.

'Ah good!' said Van Loop. 'Our donor is beginning to come round – we shall soon be able to begin our incantations! This, mein friends, is one Christopher Baxter. His name is not significant, though, for he shall not be Christopher Baxter much longer. All that matters is that his mind is empty and his teeth are perfect. Both of these he possesses, may it please our Grand Inquisitor!'

'Please him! Please him!' chanted the audience enthusiastically.

'Plooose hem?!' said Baxter, shaking his head as if trying to clear a blockage. 'Pleash who?' The audience giggled at his intoxicated panic.

'Now, now, Mr Baxter,' said Van Loop cracking his fingers. 'It is better to just relax and allow the event to unfold. You have the privilege of possession. You should be proud.'

'Plossession? What the ...!' said Baxter as the words sank in. 'Whaaaaaa!'

'Miss Dryer, I fear we shall need the gag,' said Van Loop. 'I think he's going to be a screamer and I can't incant properly with that kind of distraction going on. Could you, please?' Miss Dryer stepped forward and whispered into Baxter's ear.

'Don't fight it my love ... give in, it's the only way.' Chris's protestations were swallowed up in the fabric of Miss Dryer's gag as his fearful mumblings were smothered.

'That's better,' said Van Loop, and he motioned to Epsom to begin the proceedings. Dutifully, Epsom pressed play and the opening refrain from David Byrne and Brian Eno's *The Jezebel Spirit* menaced out from the speakers. The masterly blend of native rhythms and a radio exorcism could not have been more perfect, or ironic. Despite their seeming conservatism, the audience began to sway to the beat. The three McCauleys stepped respectfully forward, each holding in their thin hands a small sealed box with a carving of the Grand Inquisitor himself and the Roman numerals I, III and IV. They placed them on the floor in a triangle and Van Loop, chalk in hand, then dragged the line of a circle around poor Baxter. The hapless salesman was fully in control of his senses now, his wild eyes flitting left and right like windscreen wipers. Box II had been destroyed by the Bonetaker in France, but Van Loop took the bone it had contained within the pendant around his neck and went to drape it over Baxter's head. Mystified to its significance, he tried to resist, moving his head violently from side to side until Gunter grabbed him and forcibly stilled the frantic movements. The relic slipped over Baxter's skull.

'Muff, floofm, murrffff,' he screamed, the sound deadened by the gag.

The thumping beat of *The Jezebel Spirit* was rising. The cloaked and silk-gloved believers were twitching and dancing in cabalistic movements, somewhere between a gospel service, *Rosemary's Baby* and *The Night Garden*.

'Oh La Senza!' began Van Loop, coming back to the book on the lectern. 'Feel the pulling of our cheap desires! Come back, oh Lord, and judge us again, we worthless devotees who have waited for you these long centuries.'

'Judge us! Judge us!' parroted the gathering.

'Oh Grand Inquisitor, by the power of the circle beneath this putrid mortal, this worthless human shell, feel the time that is yours!'

In Purgatory, La Senza, who had been much quieter than usual, suddenly opened his eyes beneath his red silken hood. The bridge between the two worlds had cracked – tiny fissures, just enough to alert the Grand Inquisitor to the fact that his liberation had finally arrived. His face broke into a smug, sinister grin and his eyes widened. Nearby, his jailor slept, blissfully unaware of the threat.

At Baxter's feet, the boxes began to emit the vaguest purple glow.

Van Loop put his hand to his neck and pulled out an ancient rusted key and held it up to the audience. There were gasps. He nodded smugly; the plan, so long held by the vile sect, was sliding inexorably towards its hideous climax. Dutifully, the gathering squealed and shrieked in ecstasy, writhing orgasmically to the music.

Van Loop turned to the wide-eyed Baxter then knelt beside him. One by one, he unlocked the boxes. They released thin snake-like wisps of violet plasma, which burst out like angry cobras then hesitated, swaying, as they sensed the room. Baxter was looking down, uncomprehending fear gripping him deep within his heaving breast and rising in dizzying intensity. The tendrils began weaving towards him. The music was building in its pulsing native frenzy, the relentless, hypnotic beat infecting each menacing strand until they too pulsed to the diabolic rhythm.

'La Senza mortuis, audi nos tue fraternitatis! Mortem, mortem! O La Senza. Christophorus Baxter, est tibi! Ut auferam ex corpore et tuis! Christophorus Baxter, exi!'

In his cell, the purple glowing orb around the Inquisitor was expanding, his malevolent life force pulsing out of him in preparation for his departure. His attendant tendrils flew away into a spiralling vortex within which the suspended figure of the Inquisitor – his head now high and defiant – stared in evil intent at his jailor. Belatedly the guard was finally beginning to stir. Seeing La Senza pulsating before him, the jailor gasped, panicked and then slammed his hand against the alarm.

'There is none but La Senza, the dark one with nice teeth!' bellowed Van Loop.

'The great one, the terrible one. The one that's really quite nasty!'

In Eric the Greek's office, the dull morning paperwork had seemed endless. When the alarm blared, it was almost a relief. Jumping to his sandalled feet, he ran down to the control centre to find a small group of agitated bureaucrats pointing excitedly at the monitors. Eric quickly ran his eyes along the names. Berin, he was OK, likewise the Ripper. There was nothing going on with any of the Nazis and thankfully Ivan the Terrible was still bound up like a late present. When his eyes came to rest upon the name next to the flashing lamp, however, Eric pushed most of his hand into his mouth. Cardinal La Senza. The most vile, the most awful and the most unpleasant spirit in a place where mean spirits were as common as lice at a primary school.

'Oh no ...' said Eric. 'Oh please no, not him.'

Without even thinking, he threw the biggest alarm that Purgatory possessed – a shattering blast of horns like a whole army of brass sections attacking Jericho. Sixsmith, who had been deep in conversation with the Marx Brothers, made his apologies and flew off to find Eric. All around him, benign spirits were flying chaotically about like parrots in a burning aviary.

'What's happening?' shouted Sixsmith as a Greek zoomed past.

'It's a breakout, one of the really bad ones!' he shouted, not even bothering to look back.

Eric, meanwhile, had joined the onlookers at the edge of La Senza's confinement. In alarm, they watched the final stage of La Senza's escape, the purple vortex too violent and powerful to approach. Unsure of how to proceed, they chattered like scared pensioners. To one side, a small group of counter-incantors were hysterically trying to bang out something contradictory on their lutes and lyres. Out of their league, they were soon overwhelmed. La Senza's swirling tendrils snapped their instrument strings and then hurled the hapless minstrels back against the walls.

'Eric!' shouted Sixsmith, fighting his way through to join his associate. 'What the bloody hell is happening?'

'Ah Dr Sixsmith, it is terrible!' shouted Eric above the gale-like noise.

'Why, who the hell is that?'

'It's the bad one, the really bad one ... it is La Senza. The Inquisitor! You must believe me, we are in big deepy do-do. The fate of the mortal world is at stake!'

Christopher Baxter, meanwhile, was in a heap of do-do all of his very own. The whips around him had grown into animated snakes, not so much cobra as anaconda, and the amulet at his neck had released a further purple vine that was entering his nostrils.

'Murppphhh!!!!!' he screamed into the gag. 'Snorble!'

Poor Baxter, poor innocent Christopher Baxter. Uncomprehending, he struggled, trapped within the writhing purple constrictors, the diabolic snakes assessing and preparing his sacrificial body. Van Loop was ready to make his final, fateful incantation.

'Now we greet you, our horrible prince, La Senza! LA SENZA!'

255

The gathering, whipped into a frantic ritualistic dance by the thundering climax, chanted hysterically.

'LA SENZA! LA SENZA LA SENZA!!'

There was a bang.

There in the chapel, as in Purgatory, there was a rumbling crack as the separated dimensions containing the living and the dead fused. Matter touched antimatter, negative and positive charges came together; good met evil and even yin head-butted yang. A thousand strange opposites attracted and there was a truly awful pop. La Senza, laughing manically in Purgatory, brightened into a blur of purple and a sickly yellowy white. Then, suddenly, he was gone.

Baxter felt the tendrils enter him in one ghastly rush. At first, the foul sensation was merely physical, albeit several thousand times worse than an appointment with a blind back-street dentist. But then, as if that wasn't pain enough, he felt the same fingers of purple push past the merely material and enter his soul. He stiffened and twitched like a stunned cow.

In an indescribable mix of pain and horror, the soul of Christopher Baxter was heaved brutally aside. And in its place came the savage and endlessly overbearing soul of Cardinal Balthazar De La Senza. What had once been a rather successful salesman from Middlesex flopped forward and was horribly still.

Epsom McCauley turned off the music.

Cautiously the Van Loops, Miss Dryer and the triplets approached the lightly smoking figure. Only the restraining ropes were preventing the inert body slumping to the floor.

There was a pause. 'I don't think it worked,' said Ascot McCauley, raising a single eyebrow. 'I think you just killed him.' They peered at the seemingly lifeless form, purple vapours still rising up like steam from a hot bath.

'Wait!' said Gunter Van Loop, suddenly. 'Look!'

What had once been the body belonging to Christopher Baxter was tensing. Gradually, it began to sit upright. A very slight movement, like an inflating beach toy, its ghastly slowness made it all the more alarming to behold. Instinctively, in the total silence, the Van Loops and the McCauleys began to back cautiously away as fear began to replace fanaticism. The restraining bonds were creaking loudly as the twine became horribly taut, and then ...

Crack, snap, twang!

The ropes burst, whipping back in a blur. La Senza's gathered loyalists jumped back as one in sudden shock.

Now, at last, the figure began to raise its head. It was still *sort of* Christopher Baxter, only it wasn't. The empty vessel was filled with something that twisted those once self-satisfied, gormless features into something even less palatable. The transformed eyes had a hyena's laughing indifference, an eagle's focused malice and the heartlessness of a parasitic wasp. His bowed head became level, turning slowly to each side to look with a mixture of pity and hostility at those gathered around him. The air seemed to have a static charge; as one, they felt their hair prickle. La Senza cast his darkening eyes down to his new body and flexed the manicured fingers before raising a hand and smearing it across the pronounced six-pack and pecs that Baxter had so lovingly built over the past 150 weekends. What had been Christopher Baxter looked into his palm then rolled his fist in and out of a ball. Gradually, he turned to look at Van Loop senior, who he fixed with two terrifying eyes. There was utter silence.

The newly arrived La Senza then opened his mouth for a moment before snapping it violently shut, the teeth clicking together like colliding billiard balls as Van Loop gazed on in stupefied adoration.

'What are you looking at?' said Cardinal La Senza.

## CHAPTER 26

# CARDINAL LA SENZA

Dr Newton Barlow arrived back at his flat after yet another triumph on the frontline of good versus evil. He'd used a series of algorithms to crack a Tudor code, the puzzle intended to maintain the dark souls of twin brothers with a liking for entombing Catholics, Protestants and anyone they met with freckles. A 500-year-old mystery had been laid to rest by Newton with the help of Wikipedia and an iPhone in the space of an afternoon, and consequently, he was somewhat buoyant as he parked the Citroën and ran up the stairs.

His flat was not empty.

'Ah Newton, there you are,' said Alex Sixsmith, also buoyant, floating as he was just above the sofa. 'Thank goodness you've got here.' Mr Jameson was standing with a concerned face at the fireplace and Eric the Greek was fussing about by the bookcase, anxiously nibbling his fingernails. On the armchair, the spectral figure of a 15th-century Spanish clergyman sat awkwardly, complete with Shakespearean beard and ruff. He rose slowly to his feet as Newton closed the door behind him.

'No, please, I insist, let yourselves in,' said Newton sarcastically, the unexpected home visits from the dead now starting to get a bit old.

'Sorry Newton, old boy,' said Alex. 'Hate to show up like this, all mob handed, but I'm afraid it's an emergency.'

'Emergency? Like what?' said Newton, throwing his keys onto the table with a clatter. 'I've got quite a lot on already, frankly. Got to go to Oslo to hunt for a sociopath's self-portrait next week. Then there's another Roman puzzle in Chelmsford ... and then ...'

Jameson stepped in. 'You're going to have to drop all that, Dr Barlow – we have a crisis that takes precedent over everything. There's been an escape, a really bad one, probably the worst.'

'Escape?' asked Newton. 'From where to where?'

'From Purgatory to here,' said Eric, looking pale. 'He's on the earth again! Oh dear me, oh dear me!'

'Now, now Eric,' said Sixsmith soothingly. 'Try to stay calm. Let's give Dr Barlow here the full story.'

'I'm listening,' said Newton. 'Who is it? Stalin? The Ripper?'

'You won't have heard of him, Dr Barlow,' said Jameson. 'The team in Purgatory has spent 500 years trying to remove him from the historical record so that you wouldn't have to. However, trust me, he's a bloody nightmare.'

'Name?' asked Newton, opening his notepad.

'His full name is Cardinal Balthazar De La Senza. An Inquisitor, Spanish. Early years of the Inquisition.'

'He's terrible, really terrible!' said Eric, his head in his hands. 'And we let him escape! It's all my fault.'

'Now now, Eric, please! There's no point in torturing yourself about it,' said Alex. 'There probably wasn't much you could have done – it was clearly a professional job with outside help. All that matters is that we find him.'

'And find him you must, Señor Barlow,' said the ecclesiastical Spanish spook from the armchair. His face was ashen, even for a man who had been dead since 1508; his expression was as grave as an expression can be without falling off the face and running under a table.

'Sorry, I should have introduced you,' said Alex. 'This is Chaplain Diego Hernández de Macanaz. Chaplain, Dr Newton Barlow.' They nodded respectfully to each other. 'Diego here is our specialist on Cardinal La Senza. He knew him when he was living and there is no one else alive, *or* dead, who can give us a better insight into this monster.'

'Nice to meet you Diego,' said Newton. 'So what are we dealing with here? I mean just how bad can a man be?'

'He is the very devil, Dr Barlow,' said the Chaplain. 'Not literally, of course, but that would be only marginally worse, for he is as near to the Lord of the Flies as it is possible to get without horns and red skin. He is motivated by urges and desires that would make a demon violently sick. He kills, he maims and he destroys. To La Senza, human life is as inconsequential as a gust of wind or a mote of dust. The thought of him back here amongst the living – it is chilling. He must be stopped. And stopped fast!'

'OK OK, so he's a bad boy,' said Newton, somewhat impatiently. 'But I'm going to need some background here. Is there a report?'

'I'm sorry Dr Barlow,' said Eric, wringing his hands with self-disgust. 'There simply hasn't been time. We came straight here. It's an emergency!'

'I will tell Dr Barlow the story,' said Diego. 'After all, I was there was I not? I suggest you make yourself a drink and sit down Señor, it is not a short narrative.'

'OK,' said Newton. He went to the kitchen and filled the kettle. 'So this guy got out today?'

'Yes Dr Barlow,' said Eric, close to tears. 'It was awful, he simply couldn't be stopped! He will be the ruin of us all, I tell you.'

'It's OK Eric, please,' said Alex. 'Relax if you can – we'll fill Dr Barlow in on the details.' Newton sat down on the sofa, sipped his coffee and opened his notebook.

'OK Chaplain, fire away.'

******

Balthazar De La Senza was born in 1463 in Guadalajara, Spain.

Back then, the Iberian Peninsula was still a collection of separate Kingdoms, among them Castilla, Aragón and Portugal. The south was unique in medieval Europe for the manner in which its religious groups lived in perfect harmony with each other, brought together by Moorish expansionism and the presence of a thriving Jewish community. Together with the local Christians, there was a tolerant interaction between these different faiths and cultures that brought mutual support to a country that, in many respects, was something of a backwater.

Outside of the cities, medieval Spain was dirt-poor. The landscape was barren and unforgiving, and the climate uncompromising. But the cities contained a heady mix of Arabic and Christian architecture, their mosques and churches rubbing shoulders with synagogues and culturally diverse markets.

However, it was not all love and roses. Tolerance soon took second place to resentment as bitter fighting erupted, the Spanish Catholics fighting south to regain territory from the Moors. As ground fell to the Christians, the resident Muslims and Jews decided to play things safe. They converted, quick as you like, to Christianity. It was a smart move; something nasty was brewing. There were riots against Jews in Toledo and laws began to creep in that forbade the converted Jews – the Conversos – from holding any official positions.

In the 1470s, when Catholic Isabella and her husband Ferdinand took the thrones in Castilla and Aragón, things were already unpleasant, but they were about to get a lot worse. Like all zealots, the royal couple believed their faith was the one true faith, and with this in mind they boosted the existing medieval Inquisition up to a new intensity. So began a period of religious paranoia and mindless intolerance. Terrified that the Jewish Conversos and the converted Muslims – the Moriscos – represented a form of fifth column, waiting to destroy the re-established Christian Spain, the establishment let loose a storm of crazed Inquisitors. These charming individuals scoured the land for whatever feeble evidence they could fabricate, proof that no one had converted at all. As with the denunciations under Stalin, the McCarthy witch hunts in 1950s America and season seven of Big Brother, human nature is such that ruthless opportunism will inevitably creep into these nauseating investigations. Before the change, many of the Moriscos and Conversos had thrived, building a good honest fortune from their own endeavours, inevitably inducing some jealousy amongst their more feckless neighbours. It didn't take much to switch the attention of the Inquisition onto a rival and soon, bogus denunciations were like rats in a sewer.

The self-styled investigators were hardly Sherlock Holmes in their approach. They were just as happy with a half-baked lie as they would have been with a hard-bitten fact. Many of the charges were laughable, and it would all have been just as comical as Monty Python would have us believe, had it not been for the sheer scale of what happened next.

Torture, burnings and the appropriation of goods were just a part of it. La Santa Inquisición provided a playground for the sadist, the vengeful and the petty. Religious justifications masked a wave of base mistrust, sexual predation and common bloodlust, and soon there was no person in the whole of the Iberian Peninsula who did not fear the knock at their door. When the Inquisition came to town, the only person to benefit was the one selling toilet paper. Paranoia spread like wildfire and in medieval Spain there seemed to be no one willing to step back, take a deep breath, and say: 'Hold on a sec – this is bonkers!'

In fact, there *were* some heroic stands. Some communities, perfectly happy with the multicultural nature of their towns or villages, reacted badly as the Inquisition crept nearer. For instance, in 1484 in Aragón, there were rational people who decided to stand up for themselves in the face of institutional intolerance.

In the small regional town of Teruel, the arrival of a new Inquisitor didn't go down too well. In fact, they didn't even bother to put on a welcome party for the nasty little man. News of resistance to the Inquisition in Castilla had recently reached them and here, far from the cities, they felt bold enough to treat the Inquisition with the contempt it deserved. The town boasted a substantial population of both Conversos and Moriscos, all quite happy with the benefits their tolerance and understanding gave them. The idea of outsiders coming in and messing things up went down like a lead balloon. The Inquisitor met a wall of mistrust, defiance and official obstruction.

Used to inducing fear-inspired toadiness in all he encountered, the Inquisitor had come to expect five-star treatment from those he was about to oppress. However, he instead found himself bundled into a nearby monastery, where he was prevented from preaching his hateful nonsense to the locals. Spitting holy blood, he threatened all and sundry with excommunication until, thanks to the mean-spirited double-dealing of an opportunistic local, he was equipped with an armed militia. Thus emboldened, he swanned back into town and arrested everyone.

An auto de fe was soon arranged and the first burnings began. An auto de fe was a nasty invention if ever there was one. In a mix of pantomime and ritualised murder, suspects were interrogated with a clownish amateurism. It inevitably resulted in conviction, the due process being about as just as a school bully on the hunt for lunchboxes. Those that the Inquisitors could get their hands on were tried and burnt. Those who had read the runes and fled were burnt in effigy, a bizarre act of madness where a representation of the culprit would be tied to a post and burnt because the real thing had sensibly bolted. To the addled mind of the Spanish clergy, all this seemed quite normal, sensible even.

Sitting behind the Inquisitor was a priest merely 20 years old – Balthazar De La Senza.

Balthazar's father had been a close ally to the ruling Mendoza family and had thrived under their patronage, giving the family not unsubstantial wealth and influence. Balthazar's eldest brother had followed their father into the military at a high rank while the second son had been assigned to the office of a senior diplomat. Both young men were soon enjoying adventures around the kingdom and beyond.

Not the young Balthazar. His father used the young boy as a mere bargaining chip in his dealings with the Church, and to win approval with Cardinal Pedro González de Mendoza, the father heaved the reluctant young boy into the priesthood.

He wasn't happy.

The young La Senza had dreamed of conquest, power and warfare, not prayer and contemplation. He was already a nasty piece of work who dreamt of sacking towns and pillaging victims. So much so that his caustic personality may well have been the driving force behind his father's decision. After all, wasn't it Balthazar who had been caught drowning kittens at the water mill? Wasn't it Balthazar who had saturated the dovecot with burning oil? It was Balthazar who had ruined every Christmas and feast day, upset the neighbours and generally been a ghastly foretaste of *We Need to Talk about Kevin* whenever the mood took him.

However, when he was exiled to the priesthood, La Senza was pleasantly surprised to find that far from blocking him from warfare, intrigue and power, it actually did the opposite. He met an environment laced with hypocrisy and corruption, and using his own natural talents for backstabbing self-advancement, he soon won patronage from his seniors. In no time, La Senza became deeply involved in a sinister world of power struggles and persecution, and he enjoyed every foul minute. In 1485, fatefully, he was sent to Teruel to assist with the first autos de fe.

It was to be the beginning of a love affair with fear, terror and intolerance that would last as long as his brutish, malevolent life ... and beyond.

The poor convicted penitents were taken out before the seated officials of the court, and even though they'd already suffered torture by the rack and the wheel, they were then subjected to huge lengthy trials in which they were dressed in all kinds of humiliating costumes, their garish tabards and clownish hats intended to make them feel utterly subjugated. Bored into listlessness, they sat for hours under the beating sun and the haranguing judges. Then, to the delight of the mob, they were burnt. Those who confessed were granted mercy, this sadly only extending so far as a kindly garrotting before the flames kicked in. Defiance could result in other charming derivatives such as slow cooking inside purpose-built metal statues or boiling in vats of oil.

If you were creative, psychotic and a dab hand with a box of matches, this was your time in the sun.

Balthazar De La Senza loved it.

His dedicated enthusiasm in Teruel was duly noted by the Inquisitorial management. With blood and smoke still fresh in his nostrils, he was sent to work with one Pedro de Arbués, a favourite of Tomás de Torquemada, the most infamous of the Spanish Inquisitors and a thoroughly nasty piece of work in his own right. Pedro welcomed the enthusiastic young priest into his hit squad and together they set out to impose authority on Aragón, a region with a serious attitude problem as far as the Church was concerned. Recalcitrant locals were to be confronted, judged and burnt. Resistance was futile.

Arbués gathered his team of torturers and zealots then set out in force for the capital of the region, the old city of Zaragoza.

Fear gripped the population. They watched through shuttered windows as Arbués and La Senza trotted their horses into the town centre and made camp. Soon the newcomers began to preach and edict away like there was no tomorrow. A happy, tolerant atmosphere that had persisted for centuries began to implode and soon the locals, especially the poor Conversos and Moriscos, began to whisper about a fight-back.

Arbués may have been as intolerant and as unforgiving as a cholera outbreak, but he was no fool, and he sensed the trouble stirring downtown. Assassination in the air, he decided to back up his defensive prayers with a steel helmet and chain mail – just in case the Lord wasn't on side. On the night of 14th September 1486, as La Senza watched from the cathedral shadows where he was heroically hiding, the Grand Inquisitor was ambushed at prayer. His armoured hat and underwear offered little protection as the assassins punctured his body with their blades. Bleeding like a stuck pig, he was taken back to his lodgings where he lingered painfully for a few hours before dying.

La Senza sensed an opportunity and felt a thrill of excitement course through his body like a spicy paella, for even as the Grand Inquisitor lay dying, the first fires were being lit.

The Inquisitorial reaction was instant and savage. There was no shortage of jealous enemies ready to shop their Converso neighbours and soon the culprits, anyone who might have been a culprit, and anyone who even looked *slightly* culprity in certain light conditions were dragged before the Inquisition and subjected to a barbaric reckoning. There were hangings, drawings and quarterings, and, of course, burnings. At a series of fourteen grand autos de fe, some forty two Conversos were put to the flame and another fourteen were burnt in effigy, their targets having wisely thrown everything they could grab onto the back of the family donkey then headed for the hills. Under the orders of Torquemada himself, these grand autos were something new altogether, a mix of show business, revenge and Catholic kitsch. For the hapless Conversos and Moriscos, the epic show trials must have been mind-bendingly scary. The last serious attempt to resist this growing nightmare had merely increased its tyranny exponentially. Torquemada's power was now near absolute.

Others vied for a piece of the action; many a priest, cleric and confessor joined this new wave of misery and terror in search of a good time. Across the length and breadth of Spain the Inquisition grew, its nightmarish logic burning its way into the pages of history. And right in the middle of the firestorm – still a novice in many ways, but every inch the perfect Inquisitor – was Balthazar De La Senza.

Still only a mere Monseñor when his boss was murdered in Zaragoza, La Senza rushed to his masters brimming with Inquisitorial righteousness. Just as he calculated, he was propelled by his proximity to the frontline onwards and up the greasy ecclesiastical pole until by 1487, he was handed a Cardinal's robes and assigned enough autonomy to begin a wave of Inquisitorial visits all of his own.

The newly promoted Cardinal La Senza descended like bad news upon a range of small towns and villages in northeast Spain. Now he could act on his own sick impulses, and he threw himself into the role with the kind of vigour only a really first-grade bastard can muster. In one village, he burnt everyone taller than five foot two, despite the fact that they were neither Conversos, Moriscos or guilty of anything worse than poor dental hygiene. In another town he held an auto de fe for some five weeks; it was so protracted and stressful that some of the locals succumbed to hypertension before La Senza had finished haranguing them, and the bodies had to be reluctantly torched without the satisfaction of any decent suffering.

Cardinal La Senza loved gizmos. He employed a team of technologists who travelled with him, and under his patronage they developed a whole range of nasty new ways to make people tell you whatever you wanted to hear. They boiled, they scooped. They stretched people out on racks until they looked like harvest spiders. They trapped suspects inside iron boxes and dry-roasted them until they shrank to the size of children.

La Senza laughed long and hard.

Dealing with small towns far from the city, Cardinal La Senza was able to act with near impunity. But eventually, the sadism and pointless nature of the new boy's methods began to raise eyebrows within the Inquisition itself. Chaplain Diego Hernández de Macanaz witnessed La Senza's abuses first hand. Horrified, he tore back to headquarters to report what he had seen. There was a mixed response to his story. The real zealots thought the imposition of mindless fear, no matter how severe, could only be a good thing, perfect for culturing a cowering obedience amongst the population. But others, mindful of the potential fallout for the Inquisition's mandate, found such obvious applied psychosis alarming. Eventually, a cadre of slightly less nasty Inquisitors was chosen to sort the awkward matter out.

It would not be easy. Torquemada had taken a personal interest in the meteoric rise of La Senza, and to bring down this maverick could be seen as an attack upon the great Inquisitor himself. A challenge to the authority of such a man could, and usually would, result in a one-way trip to the iron maiden. The campaign would have to be subtle. Gradually, reports were gathered and Chaplain Diego was given the task of building the case.

But La Senza was not about to be stopped – in fact, he was now on a roll. Not content with mere hamlets and villages, he took a crack at a few recalcitrant towns along the edge of the Pyrenees before pushing up to the Atlantic coast near San Sebastián.

For the locals, the arrival of La Senza and his entourage was like some psychotic circus riding into town. Instead of clowns, Inquisitorial judges; instead of trapezes, the rack and the wheel. Their passage across the parched landscape of Aragón and the Navarre was marked by columns of rising smoke and the stench of burning human flesh.

Oh, happy days.

Fearful of treading on toes, La Senza halted his entourage short of the city of San Sebastián to consolidate, and while his followers enjoyed a little rest and recreation in Pamplona, the Cardinal retreated to a monastery to plan his next move. It was here that he picked up his fearsome acolyte, the dreadful, sadistic, though some say cruelly beautiful, Sister María de la Encarnación. As far from Julie Andrews as it is possible to imagine, Sister María inspired dread in the other nuns at her convent. Not so La Senza – the Cardinal was quite taken with her Gothic good looks, callous indifference to human suffering and total absence of morality.

It was love at first sight.

They became inseparable. Balthazar and María would watch the horrific proceedings unfold before them at the autos de fe, caressing each other with barely disguised erotic excitement, their eyes wild with sadistic arousal.

Not that it raised any eyebrows within La Senza's camp, of course. The Cardinal had been careful to recruit a fiercely loyal and immoral team around him. He rewarded them with anything they wished to appropriate from their victims, be it wine, women or material wealth. The La Senza road show, as a result, became a hugely profitable and self-contained travelling nightmare. Funded by plunder and cruelty, loyalty and fanaticism grew like fungus around him and he attracted more and more devotion from his clan as the months passed.

Above all others he trusted one. Ceferino de Lupero was a mean fanatic who saw in Cardinal La Senza a force of purifying evil, something that elevated man above the mere human into something more arcane and potent. Frequently he told the Cardinal, usually on bended knee, that there was nothing, nothing on this earth that he would not do for him. Lupero pledged the ultimate in protection in this world and the next; the Inquisitor could rely on his dark lieutenant for eternity. With his fanatical henchmen in tow, Lupero provided La Senza with a state-of-the-art private army. No one could stand up to him now. In his wake he left poverty, tears and a cultural desert.

Newton lifted his pen from the notebook.

'OK, I get it, the guy is a sadist, a creep. Nothing unusual about that though, is there? The historical record is full of this kind of thing. What's so special about this particular monster?'

'You're right,' said Jameson. 'So far he's just your regular, run-of-the-mill psychotic opportunist.'

'He's not run-of-the-mill!' wailed Eric, his head in his hands. 'Tell Dr Barlow. Tell him!'

'Tell me what?' asked Newton. His visitors shuffled uncomfortably. 'What happened next?'

'The machine Diego,' said Alex solemnly. 'You'd better tell him about the machine.'

## CHAPTER 27

# AN ILL WIND

That same year, even as La Senza and his team consolidated their grip on the north, there was a storm. A tempest of huge magnitude slammed in from the Atlantic, first making landfall in Portugal then tearing its way up through the Bay of Biscay in a vast spiral that hurled winds and waves against the coastline from Lisbon to Southampton.

Its destruction became the stuff of folklore. Church steeples toppled in a thousand hamlets; cows and sheep were said to have been lifted into the air like kites. In Gironde, ships were found as far as fifteen miles inland while a vast brass cathedral bell in Bordeaux broke free and fell on a brothel. Even allowing for the medieval tendency to exaggerate such things until the facts are meaningless, it was one hell of a storm.

In such dire weather, the worst place to be was at sea. With no early-warning system beyond seaweed, the tempest obliterated unsuspecting fishing boats, men-of-war and trading vessels by the hundred. More than a thousand women living on the Atlantic coast became widows over the course of that dreadful day. But it was the fate of one vessel in particular that was to have truly dire consequences.

Caught by vicious storms in the Bay of Biscay, a modest carrack carrying a strange group of scholars, technologists and artisans had been blown off course and torn to pieces on the coastline of Inquisitorial Spain. The bedraggled survivors lay utterly dejected in the surf together with a curious mess of flotsam and jetsam. Thanks to the prompt action of nearby militias, they were spared from being stripped, murdered and then burnt by the friendly locals, though not necessarily in that order. Quite frankly, they'd have been better off drowning.

Stories concerning the strange survivors soon began to spread out from the wreck until finally, they reached La Senza, who was resting with his entourage after a long hard season of murder, torture and perversion. La Senza, the black-leather-clad Lupero and the fearsome Sister María saddled up and rode out.

In no time they arrived at the small coastal town to see what the tide had brought in. The poor shivering survivors were in a pitiable state and had the Cardinal and his followers been capable of pity then surely they would have shown it. No, almost as a reflex action, they set about torturing the poor wretches – partly for amusement, but also because La Senza correctly suspected the cargo of the wrecked vessel could benefit his own murderous agenda.

Under the unsubtle pressure of Sister María's nipple clamps and Lupero's water boarding, the three survivors soon divulged enough to give the sinister gang the story they required. One was an Englishman, an alchemist from London, who specialised in base metals and complex powders that could blast, blind and intoxicate. A Dutchman, after a few hours with the tongs, confessed that he was a maker of machines for war and entertainment. This ingenieur was fresh from the courts of France and the Low Countries where he had been in the employ of eccentric barons and the military. Several examples of his wonderful automata were discovered in the wreckage, but they were damaged beyond operation by the disaster that had befallen their ship. Though broken and sand-blasted by the surf, they were still a wonder of gears and carving. After much incentivising with head clamps, a third survivor, a German, admitted to being a necromancer, skilled in magic that could be used to connect one with the dead for fun and profit. It was he who had foolishly brought on the voyage an extraordinary book.

Given to La Senza by a terrified fisherman, the book had been found floating off the coast in a sealed box. Which was unfortunate, because if its bizarre contents had made contact with the sea, then the water-based instructions and weird incantations it contained would have been lost forever and out of La Senza's foul clutches. As it was, for the evil, twisted mind of the Inquisitor, it was an absolute gift. Sensing its import, La Senza led the party back to the monastery to continue their interrogations, the poor foreigners slumped over the donkeys like saddlebags.

Realising just how deep in the brown stuff they really were, the three survivors bravely confessed everything. They gave a good account of their travel plans, namely to proffer their unique services to the authorities in Bordeaux. There, they had hoped to find a willing market for their peculiar skills, just as they had done with much success in Calais, Liège and Amsterdam. The brutal storm had caught them as they rounded Brittany. Driven far south by mountainous seas, they floundered on possibly the worst coastline in Europe if you were hoping for tea and sympathy. Having heard the nightmarish rumours of the Inquisition, they buckled like cheap deckchairs. Soon they were grovelling pitifully before the evil Cardinal, desperate for mercy, wailing compliments, promising favours and generally offering a small target in the hope that La Senza would spare them a hideous death. This, much to their surprise, they were granted. Realising how potentially useful they might be, La Senza whisked his captives further into the mountains and away from prying eyes. He rolled up at a remote monastery, promptly evicted the resident monks and made himself at home. The alchemist, the technologist and the necromancer were duly thrown into cells and Cardinal Balthazar De La Senza, by the light of a roaring fire, settled down to read the book.

And what a fantastically odd book it was – one vast volume, its words inscribed upon a thick vellum that looked suspiciously like it was made from pale human skin. There were instructions for the destruction or preservation of souls, incantations for making reluctant lovers passionate and spells that could cause friends to become foes and vice versa. But what really interested the coal-black, devious heart of La Senza were the full descriptions of the real nature of heaven and hell.

These were not the usual goblin-filled terror texts so popular with the impressionable medieval mind. No, these were extremely factual outlines of the true nature of Purgatory, written by a genuine authority on the subject. Now, through the twists and turns of wicked fate, they had fallen into the hands of what can only be described as the enemy.

For this necromancer, sadly, was an agent of the organisation. Recruited by Eric the Greek back in the early days, he'd been told explicitly that he should never, but NEVER, write anything down. Sadly, for personal gain or because he had a lousy memory, that is exactly what he had done. La Senza, who knew a bad thing when he saw it, understood immediately what he was holding. Excited, he showed himself into the cell where the poor necromancer hung from the wall like a barometer. Wanting to keep his prey fresh, La Senza had the necromancer taken down and he was given normal quarters, reasonable rations and a reduced torture regime. Over the next few months, under the threat of a slow agonising death, the necromancer told La Senza everything he knew about life, death and Purgatory. He told him about how the spirit could be preserved or destroyed with the use of reliquaries. Finally, after many long months of detailed interrogation, he was hung back on his wall, this time upside down, while Cardinal La Senza, now thoroughly in the know, wondered how best to use the revelations.

But this long sojourn in the mountains had not gone un-noted by the Inquisition. Diego and his team managed to locate the maverick Cardinal and they made a point of visiting him before the first snows of winter. La Senza, contrary to his natural persona, presented a cheerful reassuring air, affecting to be resting and contemplating all things biblical in preparation for a return to the day-to-day grind of Inquisitorial mayhem in the spring. But Diego was not convinced. He correctly assumed that the Inquisitor was up to something. Choosing his moment, he proffered gold pieces to one of La Senza's less fanatical entourage. With an agent deep inside the La Senza clan, the Chaplain retired to Zaragoza to deliver his report.

Of course, La Senza was contemplating nothing other than triple-distilled evil. In his dark imaginings, he plotted something so hideous, so vile and senseless that all other vile, senseless things would look pleasant and sensible by comparison. The three shipwrecked foreigners were dragged up from their damp cells and as Lupero heated a series of ambiguous metal objects upon a portable barbeque before them, La Senza gave them an offer too horrific to refuse.

'Build me something if you wish to live,' he told them. 'Build me a machine of wood, glass and metal – a machine that takes the living, as it takes the dead, and removes them utterly from this world – and the next! Make it big, make it mobile and make it strong. Give it the power to function wherever it may be and make it much afeared by all who see it, smell it or hear it. Build me this and I will spare you a fate so mind-blowingly nasty that merely telling you about it in advance would probably result in your premature demise. The choice, gentlefolk, is yours.'

What else could they do? As the first snows fell across the western Pyrenees, the three fearful foreigners began their bizarre project.

By now, La Senza was rich beyond his wildest dreams on the spoils of his ghastly enterprise, and able to acquire every item on the shopping list with ease. Couriers were dispatched far and wide in search of rare metals, the finest clock mechanisms and precision tools. The automata maker toiled long and hard into the nights, his chisel carving diabolic forms upon the machine's outward surfaces and internal fittings, while the alchemist, working from detailed descriptions within the book, mixed foul-smelling chemicals that often rendered part of the monastery uninhabitable for several days. And the necromancer, he inscribed with his own hands the horrid medieval software that would operate the behemoth. Sitting upon gigantic cartwheels, it finally shrugged off its scaffolding just as the snows began to recede up the mountain slopes. With spring now reclaiming the high pastures, the three exhausted men went to the Cardinal to inform him that the device was ready.

To this day, no one knows exactly how the machine worked or how it was operated. But we can be sure that its operation was explained to La Senza and Lupero in great detail, and that by the end of their instruction, they decided it would be somewhat remiss not to test it.

First in was the alchemist. He fought and he struggled, but tied up in a bag there was little he could do and he disappeared inside the machine to face a processing so terrible that it cannot be imagined. Diego's agent was not present in the workshops, but even so, he heard the screams and pleading through the monastery's thick walls. The alchemist's final awful seconds were heard only as a pathetic echoing rattle that ended none too soon. When all was done, mere dust puffed out from the rear of the horrible contraption, and the alchemist, who'd once been a huge fan of powders, was now one himself.

Next in was the ingenieur. The ornate beastly carvings and the diabolic cogged and barbed machinery, made with his own skilled hands, dragged him deep within the man-made tube of terror and in time, he too had gone, a mere gust of dust the sole sign of his passing. Finally, inevitably, in went the necromancer, his soul and body brutally separated and his total being shredded like crispy duck at a Chinese restaurant. Nothing physical or spiritual remained.

La Senza, of course, was delighted.

This machine would give him the ability to judge on an industrial scale, to rip through a town like a vacuum cleaner on an anthill. He could hoover up a population faster than they could confess. Now, he could judge both the living and the dead in equal measure. He could destroy the saints, kings and queens; he could wipe out any opposition on his road to total control. Those who came before and those present today, all would crumble before him into inert, helpless dust. He would rule the Church, the country, and he would rule the world.

Over the next few days, La Senza amused himself enormously by feeding all sorts of wastrels and strays into the machine. He 'processed' the poor, the rich and the elderly. He processed animals, furniture and food. He shovelled in relics from the catacombs and paintings from the walls. It was a multidimensional bloodbath, both on earth and in Purgatory, and it caused panic in both realms. This was merely a prelude. With the Inquisitorial season imminent, La Senza began to plan his activities with a new glint in his murderous eyes.

Diego's spy decided to act. Terrified he'd end up inside the monster himself, he made his excuses and disappeared into town for the day. Frantically, he wrote a horrifying report about La Senza's machine and sent it to his boss in Zaragoza.

Diego could hardly believe what he was reading. Such a terrible thing seemed impossible. Could La Senza really have such a device? And what of his growing megalomania? It was time to send in the big guns. Off went a deputation led by a high-ranking Cardinal with both Torquemada's ear and, unusually for the times, a sense of moderation.

After a month it was clear that he'd met with difficulties, writhing in both spiritual and finally material agony within La Senza's evil mechanism, cooked like braising steak. With La Senza mobilising for an assault on the Aragón heartlands, Diego decided to throw caution to the wind. He went to Torquemada.

The old Inquisitor, bad certainly, but nowhere near as bad as La Senza, listened in cold silence as the details were explained to him. Clearly this time, there was nothing that could be done to protect his one-time favourite. Discreetly, the Inquisition would have to silence this home-grown embarrassment before his sickening deeds became public. The country could turn against them, then all the fun of the autos de fe would have to end. So with his face as blank and as cold as a dead saint, Tomás de Torquemada signed the warrant. For crimes against the Church, for the use of sorcery, for the appropriation of wealth and power by dodgy means as well as the public display of lust and fornication, La Senza was to face the Inquisition himself.

With the decree safely in his hand, Chaplain Diego left the Grand Inquisitor brooding upon his throne and hurried away to arrange the details.

\*\*\*\*\*\*

Out on the road at last, La Senza and his team were in high spirits. During the winter, they had grown bored and restless, longing for a bit of savagery to lighten up the lengthening evenings. They rode high in their saddles as the circus rolled down from the foothills onto the plains below. The horrible machine, its foul design hidden under a covering of oily tarpaulins, edged slowly forward at its maximum speed of a mere two miles a day. Pulled by eight oxen, it creaked on huge wagon wheels along the rutted tracks.

Progress was slow, but after a week of heaving and pulling, the cavalcade finally approached the small town of Bolea. Operating to a plan, Lupero's men sealed all the town's exits. Despite whispered advance warnings and the tolling bells, the entire population was still bottled up in dusty houses when La Senza rolled in. The sight of the Inquisitor in his red robes, leather gloves and vestments caused a ripple of terror to course through the town like an electric shock. The Conversos, the Moriscos and just about anyone with a trace of imagination began to wail and gnash their yellowed teeth in fearful anticipation of what was to come.

We know little about what actually happened next because there were no witnesses. Not a one. Not a cat or a dog was left to tell the tale. Chaplain Diego's spy was patrolling the roads to the south and therefore did not see the slaughter himself. Suffice it to say that when Diego's men picked up the trail a week later, all they found were the ruts in the ground carved by giant wheels and great clouds of sad dust, picked up and swirled in the air by the fierce Sierra winds. They passed a wasteland of dead villages and hamlets, farms and encampments where there was nothing but dust – no people, no cattle, no horses. No birds were singing and even the cicadas seemed to crouch in mute trauma at La Senza's horrific passing.

Looking at his maps, Chaplain Diego made a decision. La Senza was obviously moving south, and they would have to cut him off. It was too late to save the villages directly in the Cardinal's path, but there was just a chance that by crossing wastelands and hills to the south they could swing around La Senza's course and reach the small market town of Sierra de Luna before the cavalcade arrived. They might even have time to prepare a reception, and so, with the devil himself behind them, they rode.

Sierra de Luna was a happy little place. No one had any idea of what was bearing down upon them along the old pilgrim route to the northeast. As Chaplain Diego rode in with his fifteen men, the locals were yawning and dozing as they always had, oblivious to the impending threat. The mere mention of La Senza brought them to their senses, however, just as if a bucket of ice-cold water had been thrown into their faces. Diego had to think fast. He quickly gathered all the able-bodied men in the town and organised something of a fighting force. He posted lookouts. Mere minutes had passed before the first signal, a glinting reflection from a sword on a distant hill, indicated that La Senza's ghastly road show was approaching.

Diego's men melted into the houses.

Stopping short of the town by some three miles, La Senza and his men began their preparations. They halted the machine and their supply train beside an orchard while the advance guard assembled. Then they moved on with the cartload of self-assembly furniture for the auto de fe, a sort of quick-build court-cum-stage with associated Inquisitorial bling. Diego and his men watched from behind the shutters as La Senza, Lupero, Sister María and their entourage rode into the town square, and although the place seemed deserted, a hundred eyes were upon them.

Cardinal La Senza dismounted, removed his gloves and looked on with satisfaction as his underlings began to assemble the auto de fe. Once the stage was ready, he sat down and sipped the wine given to him by the nun. He waved a hand, and at once, Lupero's men began to fan out in search of victims. Soon they had gathered a crowd of women and children as well as a few thin, weedy adolescents and old men who stood shaking and terrified before the Cardinal.

'Where are your men?' he asked eventually, picking at his teeth with a splinter of wood. 'Tell me?'

'Www ... we don't know,' said an old man, shaking like a fern in a strong gale.

'Don't you, don't you really?' said La Senza. 'How about we help your fellow villagers to remember for you?' With that, he signalled to Lupero, who unsheathed his sword and in one ghastly slick movement separated the old man's head from his body. The townsfolk gasped in terror and there was a rapid muttering of prayers. 'Any ideas?' continued the Inquisitor. 'Oh come on, don't be shy. I really haven't got all day, I still haven't had my lunch.'

Behind the shutters, Diego had a tough decision to make. The timing had to be spot on. He had around forty men hidden around the square, twice the number of La Senza's gang. But these local men were not trained soldiers and things could easily degenerate into a pointless bloodbath. Then again, it was only a matter of time before Lupero's men searched the buildings with a similar outcome.

It was now or never.

Chaplain Diego burst out on the auto de fe like an avenging storm, his militia beside him. They caught the majority of La Senza's bodyguards lounging lazily against the walls, laughing at the weak townsfolk with their swords sheathed. Consequently Diego and his men were able to dispatch at least half of them before there could be any real fight-back. But soon there was much flashing of steel as a full-blown skirmish erupted across the square. La Senza and Sister María hid behind the throne on their stage as below them the battle ebbed and flowed, but Diego's men won the day. Soon, Lupero's bloodied men began to scatter away or lay dying upon the cobbles. Perched above the townsfolk in their ludicrous little theatre, La Senza and the nun hissed defiantly at their tormentors like cornered rats. Lupero himself, separated from his master across the square, thought better of the fight and dashed inside a merchant's house, making his way to a rooftop where he could witness the end of his idol. La Senza could do nothing as the locals, laughing and cackling, pulled at the flimsy stage. In no time at all, it collapsed to the ground in a mess of splinters, dust and vestments, sending the Inquisitor and his fearsome acolyte tumbling. Sister María defiantly clawed at the mob as they closed in upon her lover but she inevitably paid with her life; spliced in two by a well-handled scythe, she slumped bloody to the ground and was trampled underfoot. La Senza, however, was denied a mercifully fast dispatch. He was dragged like a wild animal to the centre of the square and the mob, blood in their nostrils, cleared briefly to make a circle. At bay, the crimson Cardinal turned and snarled at his tormentors.

They began.

A hundred hands pulled and tore at the Inquisitor's arms and legs, his fingers and his hair. All began to separate like a lobster dinner. The bloody tatters flew high above the crowd and bit-by-hideous-bit, he was ripped, quite literally, to shreds.

Above on the rooftop, Lupero was in tears of frustration and anger. His great master, the evil, vile La Senza, was now nothing more than a big mess of body parts and torn red cloth. Lupero had promised the Inquisitor that he would protect him, or preserve him, and yet here he was unable to do either. Powerless, he watched the bloody display run its course. Then he was horrified to see one of the town's mangy dogs rush into the fray and re-emerge seconds later with his master's disembodied hand. The mob, knee deep in bloodlust, was oblivious to the dog as it ran away, keen to dine on La Senza's hand at its leisure. Suddenly, Lupero came to his senses and remembered his master's instructions: 'Should I ever be killed in action, you must preserve of me some reliquaries, for now I know that I cannot and must not die. Some part of my physical being must be taken, hidden and you shall await the instructions for my return.'

Galvanised, La Senza's dark lieutenant jumped from the roof into an alleyway, landing heavily, wincing in pain. Then, hobbling, he dashed after the opportunistic mutt, his bloodied and broken body hurting badly as he raced to keep the dog in view. The dog was having none of it. It dashed and weaved through the grubby back streets with a defiant purpose. Far from the shouting and yelling of the square, they broke out into a backyard and the dog, cornered in a pigsty, dropped La Senza's mangled hand with its rings and rubies before snarling back at Lupero.

Like most people, he tried the 'good doggy' approach first. But the dog had heard that one before, so as soon as Lupero tried to reach for La Senza's severed hand, the hound bit hard into his leather glove and he screamed in agony. Wasting no more time on dog whispering, he stabbed the mutt into a violent silence, grabbed the hand and stuffed it into his jacket. After a desperate search in the surrounding scrub, he found a tethered horse and struck out for the encampment.

As he tore into the camp in a cloud of dust, Lupero ordered La Senza's remaining team to move out. However, the unexpected news of their master's death, proven by the bloody hand of the Inquisitor himself, caused an immediate switch in loyalties. With the head of the snake removed from its body, base opportunism quickly surfaced and most of the men rode for the hills, unfortunately including Chaplain Diego's agent. Consequently, what happened next remains something of a mystery.

Probably, it was all that Lupero could do to keep order and ensure that La Senza's machine could be moved. He'd have wasted no time making his reduced manpower heave the behemoth back onto the road. The oxen would have been whipped into a frantic pace. Likely, Lupero left the main roads with the now-mouldering remains of La Senza still inside his jacket, then hid in the mountains as Diego's men scoured the countryside. All this was mere conjecture.

\*\*\*\*\*\*

'That is the story, Dr Barlow,' said Diego heavily. 'We never recovered the machine, never found Lupero and we never found the Inquisitor's hand. There is, however, a lead – a small one maybe, but a lead nonetheless.'

'Which is?' asked Newton.

'A woodcarver from Carcassonne, over the border in France. Swore under oath that he had done five carvings for a man called Lupero a month after La Senza died. He says he saw the hand and filled the boxes with the fingers.'

'Fingers? Is that all he said?'

'Sadly he went missing, probably murdered,' Diego sighed. 'We just don't know. But the trail went cold. We stopped him Dr Barlow, but that's *all* we did. The machine is still out there – the five boxes have clearly been activated and La Senza is back, ready to start where he left off. But this time, he knows about everything, and he'll be coming for us. He'll wipe out our relics and God knows what else.' Eric the Greek began to whimper, rocking back and forth as Diego let the idea sink in.

'It's obvious he has help,' said Jameson. 'But as to who, and why, well, we have no idea. Right now La Senza could be anywhere.'

'Blimey,' said Newton.' That's not much to go on is it? There's no codes, nothing but a search on foot, are you sure I'm your man?'

'Trust me, we've got everyone on it,' said Jameson. 'If La Senza gets that damn thing back out there then we've got a real nightmare on our hands. This guy knows how everything works, all the dead–living stuff, all the magic, all the spells, all the tricks of the trade. And he's equipped with a 500-year-old mincing machine that could wipe out every single good guy in Purgatory. Trust me, he'll be coming for us all. And if he succeeds, Dr Barlow, it will *literally* be hell on earth.'

'You're going to have to give me more chaps, any details, however small – I need them.' Newton thought for a second looking at his meagre notes. 'The boxes, tell me about the boxes – what are they like?'

'The description is poor, I'm afraid,' said Jameson. 'Something about La Senza crouching in his robes, that's about it. They only contain his fingers, so probably we can guess they're about six inches high, max. I'll have the art department send you a sketch.'

Newton's head began to whir and pop, the neurons firing and fizzing as he began testing all the combinations, looking for openings and connections within what he had been told so far. There wasn't much to go on but the challenge, well that was certainly there.

'Well, do you think you can do it?' asked Alex, strangely sullen.

'I'll have a bloody good go,' said Dr Newton Barlow, snapping his notepad shut.

CHAPTER 28

# AMONGST US

Cardinal La Senza glared out from within the body of Christopher Baxter, stray ripples of purple plasma drifting lazily off him towards the vaulted ceiling.

'My great Inquisitor!' fawned Van Loop senior, a distant descendant of La Senza's loyal medieval lieutenant Lupero. 'We have waited so long to see you return!'

'*You've* waited?!' snarled La Senza. 'What do you think I've been doing? Making tortillas?'

'My deepest apologies, my Lord. But it has taken so many generations to release you from your tormentors. How could those beasts do that to you?'

'Yes, it was a bit annoying,' hissed La Senza. He leered at the gathered followers. 'Who are these idiots?'

'Why, my great Inquisitor,' offered Van Loop, 'these are the devoted ones who have waited for you all these years. It is these people who have kept your name alive when the forces of good sought to wipe you from our memories.'

'Do you want me to thank you or something?' said La Senza, tidying his nails nonchalantly. 'Because I'm not going to.'

'Wow, he really *is* horrible!' said an admiring voice from the pews. La Senza's eyes darted toward a balding sweaty man holding two brass candelabra.

'You, what did you say?' asked the Cardinal.

'Err, I was just saying how unpleasant you are, oh great La Senza,' continued the man, oblivious to the outcome. The room froze.

'Kill him,' said La Senza, idly.

'What? Really?' said Van Loop. 'I mean *really*?'

'Yes really, I'm your master, am I not?'

'Well yes ... It's just that ...'

'Well kill him then, or I'll have someone kill you.'

'But I meant it in a good way!' said the sweaty man, frantically scanning the room for back-up. It was not forthcoming. Gunter signalled and the man was dragged away, loudly protesting his loyalty.

Abruptly, the begging was silenced.

'That's the spirit,' said La Senza. 'Now, you, Van Loop, tell me, what are my teeth like?'

'Perfect my Lord, like little white mice!'

'Excellent!' said La Senza. 'Nothing worse than lax dental hygiene. I have had people burnt for less.' La Senza glanced around as everyone made doubly sure they had closed their mouths. His gaze fell upon the McCauleys. 'Who are these three fools?' said La Senza, dismissively. 'Are they jesters? I can't stand jesters, you should know that.'

'No Cardinal, these are our hosts in this great endeavour. May I introduce the three McCauley brothers – Ascot, Epsom and Plumpton.'

'Well they look like jesters. What are you, triplets? Three jesters for the price of one.' La Senza narrowed his eyes and stared at Ascot. 'You'll be the dimwits who've arranged this little party,' he scowled. 'Out for personal gain, furnishing your own needs at the expense of others? I can respect that.'

'Oh yes,' said Ascot, wringing his hands like a funeral director. 'It is purely a business relationship, Cardinal, although I trust it shall be a matter of some mutual benefit.'

'Mmm,' said La Senza. 'Well it had better be, because a contract that does not suit Cardinal Balthazar De La Senza will almost certainly end in screaming and damp towels.' He sat back in his chair, suddenly weary, and took a deep long breath. 'But,' La Senza continued, 'I am too weakened by the ritual of possession to discuss such tawdry matters.' He waved Ascot away like a waiter.

'As you wish,' said Ascot, bowing.

'Oooh hold on,' said the Cardinal standing suddenly. 'Who is *this*? Come forward child, let me see you.' Nervously, Miss Dryer emerged from behind her employer. La Senza, his dressing gown open to reveal his loincloth, sensuously wove towards her.

'Well, tell the Cardinal your name,' said Ascot under his breath.

'I'm ... I'm Miss Dryer,' she stuttered.

'First name?' demanded La Senza, a licentious grin appearing on his lips.

'Wendy,' said Miss Dryer, and for some reason she could not understand, she curtseyed. The Cardinal unfurled his hand like an octopus until it came to rest upon her neck. He pulled Miss Dryer suddenly towards him, and as Ascot and his brothers winced at the spectacle, he French kissed her violently. Miss Dryer's eyes widened as her austere sensible bun fell down from her head. As La Senza released her, she basked in the afterglow and her chest panted and heaved like a pair of bellows as her cheeks flushed.

'Goodness!'

'You shall be my consort,' said La Senza. 'We shall have to dress you in the proper manner in due course.'

'Goodness,' said Miss Dryer again, reaching for support as her legs began wobbling.

La Senza gestured to Van Loop senior. 'My rings, in the boxes – fetch them.'

'I have them here Cardinal,' said Van Loop, offering them on the flat of his hand.

'Excellent,' said La Senza. He picked out the dark red ruby ring given to him so long ago by the fearsome Sister María de la Encarnación, its precious stone still sitting above the long-dead nun's lock of jet black hair. 'Here, I'd like you to have this.' He slipped the ring onto her finger and whispered an incantation into her uncomprehending ear. 'Tolle corpus hoc mi dulcis María. Mittendum diu perditus vester La Senza in terreno regno.' Miss Dryer, still reeling from her first proper snog, was too far gone to notice the thin purple wisps that danced over the trinket. Satisfied, La Senza pulled away.

'I'm hungry,' he said abruptly, wiping some drool from his lips. 'This body has not eaten recently. I need meat.'

'There's some finger food in the day room,' suggested Epsom.

'What? Are you cannibals? I can have you burnt for that!' said La Senza sternly. 'I don't want fingers! I want meat. Kill a deer, a pig, roast it.'

'I can get chef to rustle you up some beef sandwiches,' said Epsom apologetically.

'Whatever,' said La Senza. 'I can see you will need educating. I'm not a common parish priest, I have special tastes, desires ... needs. You will learn them. In the meantime I will see my chambers.'

'Yes Cardinal,' said Ascot McCauley stepping forward. 'We have prepared our best room for you.'

'Take me there,' he ordered, before crooking his finger at Miss

Dryer. 'You, come with me.'

'Goodness,' said Miss Dryer.

\*\*\*\*\*\*

In his flat, meanwhile, Dr Newton Barlow was growing flustered by his singular lack of progress. Swamped by unanswered questions and with a skip full of loose ends, he was struggling to get the new investigation underway.

What baffled Newton most was how such a large, slow object as La Senza's diabolic machine could have made itself so scarce in such a short space of time. Newton looked at the roads around the small town of Sierra de Luna on Google Maps, hopeful that something would jump out at him. It didn't.

To the south of the town, the parched plains gave way to an intricate series of dry riverbeds and ridges. To the northeast the land was mainly barren and open; it was hardly suitable for an off-road experience even in a modern all-terrain vehicle, never mind an eight-tonne Gothic nightmare on cartwheels. The rest was just flat open farmland.

But Lupero had to have gone somewhere.

Newton was beginning to realise the limitations of remote viewing. Amazing as Google Earth and Google Maps could be, they were no substitute for pointy shoes on the ground.

Newton Barlow was going to Spain.

\*\*\*\*\*\*

At Hadlow Grange, La Senza was laying down the law. All business arrangements having been settled with the McCauley brothers, an awkward discussion if ever there was one, the Cardinal issued his orders.

Van Loop and his men were duly briefed and all the necessary arrangements were underway. All day long, vehicles had been coming and going, and the phone lines from the office were constantly engaged.

'It is time that we did something about our attire,' La Senza suddenly announced over dinner that evening. 'This robe you have given me, it is absorbent, yes, but it is far from suitable. I will need something more befitting of my great rank.' He leant over to kiss Miss Dryer on her neck and her eyes crossed. 'Also, this woman of mine, she is not dressed in-keeping with her profession. She must have a nun's habit if she is to accompany me as my acolyte. Isn't that right my dear?' Wendy merely nodded, as she had been nodding most of the night. The ruby ring upon her finger was slowly and persistently leaking a purple light, subtly penetrating the receptionist's skin like moisturiser.

'We can take you into Bournemouth in the morning, Cardinal,' said Plumpton, refilling La Senza's sherry for the third time in half an hour. 'I'm sure we can find something suitable.'

'Is the large vehicle on its way?' asked La Senza abruptly.

'Yes Cardinal,' said Van Loop. 'The dimensions are perfect, just as you requested.'

'Protection?' asked La Senza. 'Have no doubt that they will do everything in their power to stop us.'

'Yes Cardinal,' said Van Loop. 'Gunter has arranged for a group to meet us there. We will have gunmen all the way. If they try anything we will be ready.'

'Excellent!' said La Senza, slapping Miss Dryer on her thigh. 'Excellent.'

\*\*\*\*\*\*

Viv had been preparing the flat in Greenwich all week. The thought of Gabby actually staying there was unsettling, but part of her also was looking forward to the three of them hanging out in the old market and down on the riverside.

The flat was finally near to tidy when Newton turned up, breathless. In his hand, he clutched a bundle of printouts and notes he'd picked up from Jameson. Flustered, he dropped tired onto the sofa and he let the papers fall from his grip. A sketched impression of La Senza's carved box slipped to the floor and before he could retrieve it, Viv had enthusiastically pounced.

'Interesting,' she said. 'This thing is ghastly. What is it?' Newton snatched it back as subtly as he could.

'It's a rare, er ... thing, a collector is looking for it. Or something. Not sure of the history. It's worth a lot, apparently.'

'Takes all sorts,' said Viv. 'Presumably you've looked online?'

'Good lord ... nooo!' said Newton sarcastically. 'Online you say? I'd never have thought of that!'

'OK ... be nice,' said Viv.

'Sorry. Look Viv, I need to talk to you love, something's come up,' said Newton. 'The thing is see, I've got to go to Spain – it's a really sudden thing and I can't get out of it. Can you entertain Gabby for me?' The atmosphere spoke before Viv could.

'Are you kidding me?'

'Oh God, I'm really sorry!' said Newton. 'It's a big ask, I know.'

'A big ask?' said Viv, her eyes wide and her head tilted in disbelief. 'It's only the most awkward thing I can imagine short of getting stuck in a lift with your ex-wife. It had better be bloody important!'

'It is ... really,' said Newton, frantically trying to concoct a convincing excuse. 'It's all part of my responsibilities, I can't say no. I'm still new.'

'Oi vey!' said Viv, unable to stay angry for long. Wearily she caved in. 'What do I have to do?'

'She's going to make her own way down. Can you show her the sights, take her out for lunch, shopping or something? I don't know. I'll leave you as much money as you need. You'll work it out.'

'Well it looks like I'm going to have to!' said Viv. 'When are you going?'

'In the morning, I've got to get a ferry to Dieppe first thing, driving down.'

'Why Spain? What's there?' asked Viv.

'Um ... a collector, might want to buy or sell some stuff, could be worth a million or more.'

'And you can't change the date?'

'Sorry,' lied Newton. 'I can't, really. I'll make it up to you.' He pulled an astonishingly feeble expression to emphasise how contrite he was feeling.

'Yes,' said Viv, 'yes you will.'

\*\*\*\*\*\*

Plumpton carried breakfast up to La Senza and his lover in the guest suite. They were still in bed when he entered; wide-eyed, La Senza was watching Jeremy Kyle on TV as the tray was laid on the bed in front of him.

'My God!' said the Cardinal, grabbing a piece of toast and shouting at the screen. 'She has been found guilty of fornicating with this man's best friend's uncle. Guilty! And yet, despite her proven guilt, he is failing to burn her!' Bits of toast shot out towards the TV and all over Plumpton's brogues. 'Burn her you idiot!' he screamed. 'What kind of half-arsed Inquisitor is he, this Kyle man?'

'Excuse me, Cardinal,' said Plumpton wearily, 'but I think you should know that my brother Ascot will be ready to take you into Bournemouth for your shopping trip in an hour.'

'You have horses?'

'Er no, not horses – you'll be going in the car.'

'Car?' asked La Senza. 'Oh one of those chariot things, coaches with no horses? I've been looking at those on this tele-vision. They seem to be very popular with clowns, those Top Gear people, that prince, his knave and the dwarf.'

'Well,' sighed Plumpton, 'if you want to go shopping, be in reception by 10am sharp, or you can forget all about it.'

'I'll be ready by 10.30,' replied La Senza petulantly. To make sure Plumpton knew how little he cared, he rolled over and licked Miss Dryer's neck. Plumpton sighed again and closed the door. Epsom and Ascot were waiting outside.

'Look, I'm not sure about this,' said Plumpton. 'I mean, I know he's evil and everything, but I wasn't expecting him to be such an annoying prick. If he keeps talking to me like that I'm going to shove one of those carved boxes right up his Inquisitorial arse.'

'Brother, calm yourself,' said Ascot. 'No pain, no gain. To get what we want we must learn to live with his ... er ... peculiarities.'

'Peculiarities?' asked Plumpton. 'He's had three of his own supporters murdered in the last twelve hours and he's turned our receptionist into a crack whore. Does that strike you as a good business partner?'

'I don't want to go through this again Plumpton,' said Ascot sternly. 'We all agreed that this business cannot expand without an outside partner. It's unconventional, I grant you, but then, frankly, so are we.'

'Yeah, shut up Plumpton,' said Epsom.

'I'm telling you this won't end well,' Plumpton snapped back angrily. 'You just can't trust someone like that.'

'Well as head of the family I am insisting that we continue as we are,' said Ascot.

'Head of the family? Oh puleassssseeee. You've only got 120 seconds more life experience than Epsom and 270 more than me. Oh haven't I got a lot of catching up to do if I'm going to be as smart as you two.'

'Haven't you got some cadavers to pickpocket?' said Epsom snidely.

'Oh fuck off,' shouted Plumpton, storming away to the kitchens.

\*\*\*\*\*\*

In Bournemouth, Ascot McCauley parked up in the multi-storey car park and La Senza, who'd spent most of the journey fondling Miss Dryer, stepped out onto the tarmac, stretched and yawned, then scowled at a young couple and their toddler.

'Why are these peasants so well dressed?' he asked, genuinely baffled by the quality of the shell suits and sportswear.

'Well dressed?' asked Ascot, doubtfully.

'They seem to be wearing silks of the Orient,' continued La Senza. 'And who is this Adidas to whom they have pledged their allegiance?'

Ascot huffed. 'Look, there are all sorts of shops in the streets around here, Cardinal. Here's some money. Why don't you just go and get what you need and we'll all meet back here in an hour or so?' The Cardinal snatched £300 from Ascot's narrow hand.

'I'll need three hours,' said La Senza.

'OK, *three* hours,' said Ascot. 'But don't be late, we need to get to the ferry on time.'

Miss Dryer, increasingly impregnated with the spirit from the ruby ring, grabbed La Senza's arm and purred like a wildcat. A sense of dread came over Ascot as he watched his former receptionist, drunk with sexuality, wander away arm in arm with a 15th-century Inquisitor. What on earth had the McCauley family got itself into?

\*\*\*\*\*\*

Back home, Newton was kicking himself. Leaving the artist's impression of La Senza's reliquaries at Viv's flat was proving to be a real headache. She was trying to be helpful by looking for it herself, thankfully so far without success. As a one-time picture researcher, she was keen to show her mettle, and with Gabby due to arrive there in a day or so without him, he felt he could hardly ask her to stop. Hopefully she'd soon lose interest; besides, he reasoned, what were the chances?

So, with time to kill before he could set off, he packed and repacked his bags and refreshed his Spanish. He was superb at languages, always had been, but he wondered how good he'd be in the more rural locations. He'd probably get by in a smart bar in central Seville, but he had serious doubts about cross-questioning a farmer in the boondocks.

Impatient at the best of times, and with a sense of urgency pressing down insistently from his line manager, Dr Newton Barlow paced his flat like a caged puma.

\*\*\*\*\*\*

Ascot McCauley had sat stewing in the car for more than an hour past the prescribed time, itching to give La Senza and his receptionist a piece of his mind. However, when he finally spotted them in the rear-view mirror, his chinless jaw dropped. La Senza was decked out in tawdry fancy-dress Cardinal's robes, for all the world ready for a tarts and vicars party. Meanwhile, Miss Dryer had been transformed from a drab receptionist into a naughty rubber nun, complete with stockings and suspenders. Tottering along in her stiletto heels, Ascot couldn't believe he was looking at drab old Wendy Dryer from the front desk.

'What the hell? Miss Dryer, what have you got on?' said a perplexed Ascot winding down the window.

'She is not to be called Miss Dryer any longer,' declared La Senza with a flourish. 'She is now to be known only as Sister Wendy.'

'I can't call her that, that's Miss Dryer!' said Ascot, somewhat flustered.

'You can and you will,' said La Senza sternly.

'Obey the Cardinal' said Sister Wendy breathlessly, and she began to rub her hands over the Cardinal's chest like he was a cheap glam rocker. 'I feel so different now. So liberated.'

'Can I have my change?' asked Ascot pointedly. He held out his hand.

'Change? Oh there's no change,' said La Senza, squeezing another lusty giggle out of Miss Dryer.

'You're not telling me that lot cost three hundred quid, are you?' La Senza held up a bulging pink carrier bag; 'adult shop' it declared in flowery letters. 'Oh, and we had some of those burger meal deals,' said La Senza. 'I had four McFlurries.'

'Oh boy,' said Ascot. Correctly judging that an appeal to reason was probably a waste of effort, he climbed back into the Range Rover, and with the two lovers giggling and snorting on the back seat, he angrily drove back home.

As they pulled up in front of Hadlow Grange, the hired removal van and its escort were assembling under the yew tree next to the sad wreck of Chris Baxter's Lexus. Epsom ran up to them impatiently tapping his wristwatch. Then he caught sight of Miss Dryer, now the seriously slutty Sister Wendy, climbing out of the car on her six-inch hooker heels.

'Err ... I was going to, er ...'

'Yes I know,' said Ascot wearily.

'Yes ... er ...' continued Epsom, struggling somewhat, 'the van and the car are packed, the paperwork is all sorted and we're ready to go.'

'Did you get that, Cardinal?' asked Ascot, as the Inquisitor and Sister Wendy worked their way through another messy snog.

'Oh my lord,' said Epsom. 'Has that been going on all day?'

'You have no idea,' sighed Ascot.

Eventually, after some false starts, La Senza, Sister Wendy, Ascot and Van Loop were in the Range Rover, ready to go. With Gunter leading in the truck, they headed out into the darkness and away towards Portsmouth.

******

Back in London, Newton Barlow was also pressed for time. Lagging some twelve hours behind La Senza's convoy, he threw his bags into the Citroën and pulled out into the traffic, bound for the continent.

CHAPTER 29

# SPAIN

Newton finally emerged, blinking, from the ferry's vehicle deck. He drove out into Dieppe then south through France.

Despite the instinctive fear of foreign policemen, which all Englishmen seem to have from birth, Newton decided to trust Sixsmith's assurances that he was immune to radar traps and speed cameras. So with confidence, he let rip as soon as he hit the autoroute. Back in the country of its birth, the old car seemed happier than ever. The dial nudged 100 miles an hour with ease and it purred like a tiger as it barrelled like a racing car across the countryside. Le Mans, Poitiers, Bordeaux – the towns passed in a blur.

As he drove, Newton's analytical mind was fully occupied arranging and reassembling the sparse available facts about the case, mostly without conclusion. By the time he was nearing Biarritz and the Spanish border, he'd given himself an award-winning headache.

After stopping for a coffee and two ibuprofen, he opted to give his beautiful mind a rest and popped on some music. Crossing the border near San Sebastián, he took the motorway south towards Zaragoza. After the damp, grey English winter, Newton found the landscape of the Basque country refreshing and bright.

It was dark now, but Newton arrived early enough in Sierra de Luna to get himself a cheap flea-bitten hotel room. Bereft of an evening meal, he made the best of his remaining travel snacks, sitting on his itchy bed with several bags of French crisps, car-warmed processed cheese and beer before drifting quickly into a deep sleep.

In the morning, after a shower in a bathroom that actually made him feel dirtier, Newton stumbled out, bought a detailed local map then sat down at a cafe in the Plaza Mayor, ordering the strongest coffee available.

Halfway through his breakfast, Newton was distracted by the growl of a very cheap moped. A man on an aging Vespa made two sedate laps of the square. He seemed to clock Newton, then rolled up to the small cafe and stopped. Climbing from the scooter, he unfurled spider-like in a thin black suit and clergyman's dog collar, and stretched. He removed his crash helmet revealing a balding head, buck teeth and enormous pink ears. He smiled politely to Newton before taking a seat at the next table, then ordered himself a coffee.

'Turning into quite a nice day,' he said in an obviously native English accent, after watching Newton scrutinising the map.

'Yes,' said Newton, trying to keep his usual mass of disparate thoughts in a coherent pattern.

'On holiday?' asked the priest.

'Yes, that's it,' said Newton, keen not to engage.

'Me too,' the priest said. 'Sorry, I'm interrupting you. Is there something particular you're looking for?'

'No,' said Newton warily.

'That's the spirit, see how it pans out eh? Best kind of holiday there is,' the priest said jovially. He finished his coffee then dropped some coins onto the tabletop. 'I'd best be on my way. I'm sure we'll see each other on our travels, good day!'

'Err yeah, right,' said Newton, and he turned his attention back to the map as the priest donned his helmet and scooted away in a cloud of dust and noise. After finishing his own coffee, Newton folded his map, climbed into the DS and drove out of town. Heading west, he was soon in the area where Diego had reported the last sighting of Lupero. He pulled up.

The fields hadn't yet started their spring growth and a brisk wind was cutting across the farmland, making the low pine trees sway gently as Newton walked along the single-track road. To the south, low hills ran a pale green along the horizon while in the fields around him the flat farmland was broken at regular intervals by deep channels, formed by the winter rains. Small dwarf pines and thorn bushes dotted the roadside. It was a tough landscape. Looking back towards the town, Newton could see the church tower and the roofs of some of the larger buildings poking up above the scrub. Diego's lookouts had been up in the tower, but by all accounts, they only saw the horsemen, not the machine. Lupero, being of a military bent, would have chosen a site that had good cover, and it was reasonable to assume that La Senza would have wanted the town secured before they'd rolled in with the beast itself. Consequently, it was a reasonable hypothesis that the machine had to have been farther back. Newton walked a few hundred yards to where the road bent around a rise in the ground, and as he suspected, the church tower was no longer visible. Happy with that line of enquiry, he decided to test a few of the other ideas he'd mulled over on the motorway.

The machine, drawn by eight oxen, had moved so slowly that it simply couldn't have outrun Diego's search parties. Lupero must have decided to go to ground. Newton quickly eliminated where he couldn't have gone. One small lane ended in a path through some rocks that had clearly been drilled and split in recent times, so that was out. The other routes merely led to locations that would have afforded Lupero no sanctuary whatsoever. The farmland was just far too open to enable them to escape; they'd have been very conspicuous and Diego would have had to be blind or drunk to have not seen them.

To the left, the road was nestled against the low rise – hardly a mountain at some fifteen feet or so, but steep enough that there could be no way that it could have been climbed head on. Newton strolled back down the road again and stopped in the shade of a few taller trees tucked into the bank until, frustrated by the lack of resolution, he headed back to the car. But when he put his key in the ignition, his mind snagged on a detail. 'Hold on,' he thought, and he got back out then walked purposefully back to the trees. Just as he suspected, there was a dip in the bank, the fig trees and pines making use of its protection to grow larger than the vegetation around them. Safe from the rain, the sun and decades of farming, they had grown to what was, locally at least, a respectable size.

Picking his way cautiously forward through the thorn bushes, Newton confirmed a notch in the bank. It wasn't that wide, but to Lupero it may have been just enough to enable him to drag the behemoth through the rise and into cover before Diego and his horsemen arrived. Newton broke through the shrubs to find that the other side was flat, hemmed in by a series of low banks and ditches. It made up an area around half the size of a football pitch, and all of it would have been out of sight of the road. Towards the back, Newton could see a series of low walls.

There wasn't much, just enough to imply the outline of old farm building, the walls and weathered timbers hinting at destruction by neglect rather than force. It was also plain that someone had been there – recently. Something had flattened the thin grass and there were fresh tyre tracks, enough to suggest a vehicle had pushed through the undergrowth. Searching, Newton came across a pile of discarded burger wrappers and several garish cartons that had once contained McFlurries. They were fresh; the flies and the beetles had not had time to clear them out. Newton stumbled on the receipt – they had been bought in Tudela to the west only the day before.

At the back of the ruined farmhouse, a fresh spoil heap indicated that the occupants of the vehicle hadn't just been there for a picnic. They had levered up a large stone slab, sliding it out of position to reveal a deep cellar. Footprints in the mud nearby implied several men. Newton, hardly a fan of dark underground spaces, took a deep breath, then cautiously went down the steep steps with his small Maglite shining.

A mass of cobwebs trailed from the cracked ceiling down to the damp ground, where huge spiders were dashing erratically past gouges and scratches that criss-crossed the floor. Heavy objects had recently been dragged outwards. Newton followed the marks on the ground until they stopped.

Then he found the body.

It had been there a long time. It was darkened and stained by subterranean condensation, the man's skeleton still partly clothed in the rags he had been wearing on the day Lupero appeared. Newton's scientific curiosity overwhelmed any squeamishness as he knelt down to examine the body, a simple silver crucifix still in place around the neck. As Newton handled the cross, he once again began to feel the odd sensations he had felt after the auction; his new 'sensitivity' began to kick in.

Jumbled images started to flash and surge through his mind. The old man was rushing out, oxen pulling a large tarpaulin-covered machine over a bank. Lupero's men charging forward. Then they seized the poor hermit, leather-gloved hands cupped tight over his mouth. Other wagons, filled with gold and plunder were being unloaded. Now the cruel men were busy dragging the boxes of gold down into the deep cellar until finally, as the darkness fell, the old man was brutally hurled in with the treasure and, to his horror, entombed. His pitiful cries went unanswered; there was no hope of rescue. Eventually, the rumbling above him faded as the men and their machine left, and alone in his tomb, he awaited his inevitable end.

Newton dropped the cross back onto the skeleton. 'What a bunch of bastards,' he said to the body, his outrage giving him a renewed determination to follow Lupero's trail. And although his mysterious vision was hardly something he'd want to include in a scientific paper, Dr Newton Barlow knew he had picked up the trail.

\*\*\*\*\*\*

Viv was waiting cold and awkward at the station as Gabby lolloped out from the train in her huge Dr Martens. Every inch the pale Gothic runaway, Gabby was lugging a bag that seemed twice her size.

'So this is Greenwich?' she said, with her eyes everywhere but on Viv. 'Doesn't look that special to me.'

'Oh this isn't the famous bit,' replied Viv, apologetically. 'I'll show you all that later. Let's go and drop your bag off, then we'll see what you feel like doing.'

They walked in silence until they reached Viv's flat. Once inside, Gabby sat defensively on the sofa, her arms folded, until Viv gave her a mug of tea. Thankfully, the mood began to lift.

'So where's Dad?' she asked.

'Spain, northern Spain somewhere, apparently,' said Viv. 'I don't think he wanted to go, it's to do with his new job.'

'Yeah, whatever,' said Gabby. 'So *you're* stuck with me.'

'Oh I don't feel like that Gabbs,' said Viv brightly, hoping the abbreviation wasn't crossing a line. 'I'm cool about it if you are.'

'Cool?' snorted Gabby. 'Yeah, I'm ... *cool*. It's not like we haven't met before is it?'

'Exactly,' said Viv, 'and I love showing people around Greenwich. It's a fun place.'

'What's this?' asked Gabby, holding up the artist's impression of La Senza's box.

'That? I'm not sure I want to know!' said Viv. 'It's some antique your dad's looking for. Horrible, isn't it? Actually, seeing as he wants it so bad, I thought I might have a go myself – I used to be a picture researcher you know. Would be a nice surprise for him if I could find it while he's away. Wanna help me?'

'Well I am good on the net,' offered Gabby. She looked at the foul hood and grasping evil hands. 'Wicked! Can't be many of those around. Bet we can find it. Dad's smart, but he's not that clever. Bet we can do better than him.'

'I reckon you're right,' said Viv, and they both laughed. 'First though, I owe you a guided tour of Greenwich. Help you get your bearings, and maybe we can find somewhere you want to eat later. Your dad's left us a fist full of notes – loadsamoney – so let's splash out!'

'Really, what, anything we want?' asked Gabby.

'Sure, why not?'

'OK,' said Gabby. 'It's a deal. I'll bring my laptop.'

'Sounds like a plan – let's go!' said Viv. Throwing on their coats, they barrelled enthusiastically out into Greenwich, the weekend ahead of them.

******

Back in Sierra de Luna, feeling pleased with himself, Newton climbed out of the Citroën. He went straight to the town hall. A man appeared at the front desk when Newton rang the buzzer.

'Si?' he asked, looking Newton up and down suspiciously.

'Buenos días, can you help me?' asked Newton.

'No sé,' said the man, shrugging. 'You have not told me yet what you want.' Newton walked up to a large and detailed topographic map of the district then pointed to the ruins he had just explored.

'These buildings here – can you tell me anything about them?'

'Those? Just ruins Señor, they've been ruined as long as anyone can remember.'

'Who owns them?'

'A foreigner, we've not seen him in years. A Dutchman I think he is. May I ask what is your interest please?'

'Oh, I'm thinking of moving here,' Newton lied. 'I notice no one's farming the land and the buildings haven't been renovated. Any idea why?'

'Hard to say. It's had some odd stories attached to it over the years. Not sure anyone would like to work that land even if it was offered to them for free.'

'What sort of stories?'

'Curses, ghosts,' huffed the man. 'All nonsense, of course. The people round here have always been a bit loca. It's probably something to do with the landscape. Luna by name, luna by nature! I'm a Zaragoza man myself. Not sure what I'm doing here.'

'Well, it's certainly the middle of nowhere,' said Newton. 'I gather the town has an interesting history. Something about the Inquisition?'

'How would I know. I'm just a funcionario, not a historian.'

'Right, OK. Well, thanks for your help,' said Newton. With the man's eyes locked on the back of his jacket, he opened the door and headed back to the square. Shielding his eyes from the climbing sun, he wandered away into the backstreets. Behind him, as soon as he was sure that Newton was gone, the man in the town hall lifted the receiver.

'There's been someone here,' he said. 'Yes just now, an Inglés, he's still in town. He was asking about the farm, I think he might have found something.'

\*\*\*\*\*\*

Newton wandered around the small town's dusty streets for a good half hour, looking for inspiration but coming up short. Frustrated, he began to mull the clues as he ambled on, oblivious to his surroundings while his mind whirred on like a laptop.

He was lost in these thoughts when, from nowhere, a pair of hands shot out, grabbed Newton by his lapels and with terrifying force swirled him off the bright pavement and into a dark side alley. He was caught completely off guard and tumbled arse over tit into a pile of overdue dustbins, landing hard on his backside. But instantly he was back up on his feet as the dark figure of a man headed aggressively towards him. Newton edged fearfully away. A thin watery light was seeping down between the buildings as Newton looked in alarm at the swarthy bulk of one of Van Loop's henchmen. The glint of a wicked-looking switchblade was waving from side to side just inches from his chest.

'Hello Engleeesh,' he hissed. 'You been asking questions, eh? Well, I gonna teach you a little lesson about minding your own business.'

Scared as he was, Newton was not inhibited enough to drop his trademark sarcasm.

'Where do they train people like you to talk like that?' said Newton. 'You must practise a lot.'

'Qué? You think you funny Engleeeesh? Maybe I teeeeech you some manners, eh?'

'Teach me some *manners*? Oh that's just priceless.'

'What? What do you mean?'

'Well its textbook assassin-speak, isn't it. And good for you! Why

297

don't you tell me I'm going to sleep wid-da-fishes? That's always good. Stitch me up like a kipper, why don't you.'

'Cállate!' screamed the man. 'I will keeell you!'

The man began to move towards Newton, who backed away into the dead end, his sinking feeling in no way assuaged by the satisfaction of annoying the knifeman. Newton was flat against damp bricks awaiting the fatal stab.

'Excuse me,' came a voice from behind the assassin. Surprised, the thug turned to face the thin silhouette of a man blocking the light from the road behind him. Newton instantly recognised the large ears of the vicar who he'd tried ignoring over his coffee mere hours earlier. The knifeman held up his six-inch blade.

'No te metas! Get away from me or I keeeel you also priest,' he snarled.

'Oh I don't think so sunbeam,' came the reply, and with an astonishing sweep of his thin right leg, the vicar sprung his shiny shoe upwards into the thug's jaw where it impacted with a sickening crack. Spinning round, the vicar then threw his other sensible shoe hard into the knifeman's solar plexus, where it landed like a claw hammer on a toy train.

'Argghhhhhhhh!' yelled the goon, recoiling backwards, a mass of arms, legs, fighting to keep his balance amongst the filthy dustbins. With a roar of pure rage, he launched himself back at the vicar, knife extended before him like a bayonet. However, the clergyman had correctly anticipated the move and deftly, swerving to the side, he allowed the yob's momentum to carry him into empty space before ramming his thin elbow hard into his neck. The blow sent the thug crashing like a drunk into the rubbish. Squealing with frustration, he raised himself painfully up again, desperate to equal the score. Before him, the vicar swayed gently from leg to leg, his thin hands all kung-fu in readiness.

'I have to warn you that I will almost certainly harm you substantially if you do not desist,' said the priest. But the heavy wasn't in the mood for defeat. Despite his flagging energy, he came hurling back at the clergyman.

'Hijo de putaaaaaaaaaaaaaa!'

The priest dissipated his violence with childlike ease. The knifeman's thick head was rammed, with an awful clang, directly into a water pipe. Once would have probably been enough, but as the vicar was keen to resolve the matter decisively, he treated the thug to two more impacts.

Clungggg! Cluunggggggg!

The blade dropped to the ground with a clatter as the knifeman sank slowly to his knees. He balanced there for a brief second before finally, he collapsed head first into the discarded remains of a tortilla and was still. Newton's jaw was right there on the ground beside him.

'The Reverend J. M. Bennet,' said the priest, holding out one of his lethal hands. 'You must be Dr Barlow? I'm so very pleased to meet you.'

CHAPTER 30

# EL COMBATE

Dr Newton Barlow and the Reverend J. M. Bennet sat quietly in the sun with their coffees. Only minutes earlier, Newton had witnessed the impossible – a Church of England priest with the physique of a prisoner of war battering a fifteen-stone hoodlum to a pulp in an alleyway with his bare hands.

'How did you do that?'

'What? The unarmed combat? Oh that's all part of the training,' said Bennet, wiping the blood off his fingers with a paper napkin.

'Training?' asked Newton incredulously. 'But you're a vicar. Vicars don't do that kind of thing!'

'You get warrior priests in all the other faiths don't you? Buddhists, Ninjas, why not in the Church of England?'

'But surely you're meant to do weddings, baptisms, fêtes and jumble sales.'

'Oh of course I do, most of the time,' said Bennet. 'But it can get so awfully boring. That's why I signed up for the organisation.'

'By organisation, you mean ...'

'Yes, the Purgatorians, same as you. Been in it a couple of years. Always been a big fan of the martial arts, you see, and as there was a chance for a bit of hard action, I thought I'd get stuck in. Of course, it's murder keeping things secret from the bishop and the parishioners.'

'So you were following me?'

'Sorry. I have to confess I was,' said Bennet. 'For months actually – back-up, you see, just so things don't get ugly, which of course they just did.'

'Yes, I noticed.'

'I was trying to hang back a bit – didn't want to cramp your style. But when I saw that goon grab you, well I thought, OK Reverend, show time!'

'Well I guess we may as well team up,' said Newton. 'I think I'd rather have you close, these guys are pretty dodgy. I'm many things but I'm no Ninja.'

300

'Indeed,' said the Reverend Bennet. 'I suggest you let me know where you've got to so far. Puzzles are not really my thing, I have to admit, but it's best I know what's what, just in case we need to call in back-up. Besides, there's another reason I'll need to travel with you.'

'There is?'

'Yes,' said the vicar sadly. 'Someone's stolen my moped.'

'Well that would slow you down a bit,' laughed Newton. 'OK, I'll talk you through what I've found out so far.' He spread out the map. 'Now then, I suspected that Lupero hid the device near to where they were camped. He couldn't have outrun the good guys, so he went to ground here.' He tapped the map. 'It's a ruined farmhouse. I checked it out and sure enough, someone's been there recently. Not only that, but I had one of those charming "sensitivity" moments, and that confirmed it. Lupero did indeed hide up at the farmhouse. He offloaded all the loot he couldn't carry into the cellar, sealed it, then waited till the search parties gave up. Then, under cover of darkness, he moved out. This loot has just been dug up again, so I'm guessing that these people who're helping La Senza came back for it before heading off to wherever this bloody machine is.'

'Which is where?'

'Well, that's the biggie isn't it?' said Newton. 'Lupero can't have gone far before they'd have had to hide it again, but more permanently this time.' He traced his finger up the map. 'My money's on the mountains.'

'The Pyrenees?'

'Well not the top of a peak maybe, but at least somewhere in the foothills. Not sure how many of these modern roads are old enough to have been an option for him at the time, though. Back in the day, they must have been awful, no better than the footpath to the toilets at Glastonbury. Shit.' Newton winced at his own language. 'Whoops, sorry about the swearing.'

'Oh don't mind me Dr Barlow, I can swear with the best of them,' said Bennet, smiling. 'Actually, I think I can help you there. You see, there were a few routes through these mountains in the Middle Ages, pilgrim routes. There were only two decent passes – one to the west of here, nearer the coast. Too far away. No, the only possible route would have been this one here.' Bennet pointed to a thin line on the map, wiggling like a doctor's handwriting through the peaks. 'Runs due north out of Jaca and comes out in France, here, at Oloron.'

301

'So he must have taken that then,' said Newton.

'I doubt it,' contradicted Bennet, sipping his espresso.

'Why so?'

'It would have been a very busy route, he'd have run headlong into a steady stream of pilgrims. Lupero was a killer, sure, but not even he could have killed that many travellers without leaving a conspicuous trail.'

'So he hid.'

'Must have done – but where?' said Bennet. Newton sat back and closed his eyes, visualising the events.

'OK ... he's travelling at night, that's a fair assumption. But even then he must have avoided any serious towns. You might be able to scare people into silence in your average pueblo, but anything bigger would never wash. My guess is he nabbed a local guide and took the fastest route he could find off the plains.' Newton ran his hand up the map to the wooded areas north of them. 'Here, this high ground, he could see it from here – it's a natural target. That's what I'd do.'

'Interesting,' said Father Bennet. 'I can see your thinking. Clever. It's not proof though.'

'No, it's just a hypothesis,' said Newton. 'But he must have followed the roads to some extent – look at the rivers and valleys. He couldn't get past those.'

'So, what's the next step?' said Bennet. Newton stared hard at the map.

'I guess we have to just get up there and look around, see if anything stands out. It's the only way to test the theory. Bear in mind though, Reverend – these jokers helping La Senza may well be in the area.'

'Good point,' said Bennet. 'That's why I've brought my gun.'

'You've got a *gun*?'

'Just a small Beretta. Px4 Storm, 19mm, semi-automatic.' He patted his jacket. 'Of course, I'd be happier with the old assault rifle, but I couldn't find a way to hide it on the Vespa.'

'OK ...' said Newton gingerly. 'Anyway, there's no point in us waiting around. Let's get going.'

'Right you are Dr Barlow.'

The scientist and the priest got into the Citroën, slammed the doors, and in a cloud of dust, tore out of the sleepy town square heading north for the hills.

\*\*\*\*\*\*

Like many teenagers, Gabby had a vast appetite and a skinny physique that were hard to reconcile. Viv watched her cut through another huge slice of cake, the third in twenty minutes, wolfing down the coffee gateau like a family dog. She smiled. They'd had a great day so far; Gabby had not only liked Greenwich, she was completely bonkers about it.

Her appetite finally sated, Gabby pulled out her sticker-plastered laptop and logged on.

Finding the weird box wasn't going to be easy. But Viv, in five years of frustrating picture research, had been asked to find a lot worse – such as the idiot junior editor who had once insisted that she dig out a photograph of the big bang. Viv and Gabby tried all the image libraries first, and after coming up with nothing, they browsed a few online antique catalogues. There were a few red herrings – begging Indian women in mahogany, praying nuns – but the misses were all as good as a mile. Then, quite by chance, they came across a picture on a special-interest forum, a photo of the grim and horrible item. There was no mistaking it.

'Bloody hell!' said Viv, coughing out her complimentary macaroon. 'That's it!'

'It really looks like it, doesn't it,' said Gabby. 'Look at the hands and the robes – it's identical.'

'The V on the front though, that's not the same. This sketch has an I.'

'Yeah, and what's all that tape and wire about?'

'Yes odd … you wouldn't do that to a valuable antique,' said Viv, frowning. 'I'm not sure your dad's going to be pleased when he sees the state of it. So what does it say next to the pic?' asked Viv, pouring herself a refill.

'It's someone saying he's a curator – he has this object in his museum and he says it's been causing him a few "unexpected" issues, whatever that means. He's wondering if anyone might have any idea what it is or where it came from.'

'Does it say where the museum is?'

Gabby looked again. 'Somewhere called Langton Hadlow.'

'Langton what? Where the flipping flip is that?' asked Viv. Gabby deftly flitted around Google.

'Dorset. The Purbecks.'

'The Purbecks?' said Viv, her interest piqued. 'I love it down there. We used to have family hols down that way. What's the nearest town?'

'Swanage, it's about three miles away.'

'Hey! Tell you what, we're both free tomorrow, wanna go?'

'*Really?*' said Gabby.

'Sure, it'll be a laugh! The car's just been MOT'd and we've got more cash than we know how to spend. We can be down there and back in a day – easy.'

'Honest? Do you think Dad will mind?'

'Nah! Anyway, never mind him. He's not here, is he?' said Viv, winking. 'I'll text him and let him know later, when he's finished whatever he's doing. Besides, he told us to have fun, so ... let's have some fun! Besides, I'm desperate to get out of London. I need to see some countryside or I'll explode. Then on Sunday, we can do the market before you head back up to Cambridge on Monday.'

'Sounds good to me,' enthused Gabby.

'Better give this curator guy a ring and tell him we'll be popping in. Would be a shame to arrive and find no one there.'

\*\*\*\*\*\*

Newton and the Reverend Bennet raced across the plain towards the high ground. Soon they were entering a greener landscape of hills, gullies and pines. They tried to picture La Senza's ghastly device crawling up the roads at night on its huge cartwheels. Undoubtedly, someone as unpleasantly resourceful as Lupero would have found a way. He'd have found it at the point of a sword or he'd have found it with a handful of gold coins, but he would have found it one way or another. Chasing such an ancient trail was baffling and frustrating, maybe, but its imponderables fixed Newton's attention completely. Add to this the growing concern about what these ghastly people might be up to, and there was an irresistible drama thrown in. Newton was like a dog with a big fat juicy bone.

They were driving through an increasingly steep series of gorges, with rough tracks disappearing to the sides behind rocks and bushes. Many of them would have been capable of taking the device. But if so, which one? Newton drove on up the road until they finally they reached the summit. It was no Matterhorn, but it was high enough for them to look back over the mass of ridges and gullies that spread out from the main road like the branches of a tree.

'Here,' said Bennet, handing Newton a pair of binoculars. 'See if anything stands out.' Newton walked to the edge of a small rise and looked down. There was an occasional bell tower and eagles floating in lazy circles on the thermals. Below them on the road, a large freight lorry and an attendant black SUV were crawling away to the south.

'Almost every one of these valleys has a church or something, most ruined by the looks of it,' said Bennet. 'I count fifteen side tracks in total. We've no choice but to try each bloody valley, one by one.'

'Looks like it,' said Newton, resigned. 'Pity you don't still have your moped, we could have split them between us. Oh well, we may as well get started.' He looked at the map. 'OK, I reckon we start on the left side and then come back up on the right.'

'Right oh, Dr Barlow,' said Bennet, 'sounds like plan. So, first up is this one, Valle de los Manzanos – apple trees. Then we do Valle de las Espinas. Thorns, nice.'

'OK – let's get on with it.'

Newton and Bennet drove away down the road and into the first valley. True to its branding, the valley was almost choked with apple trees. They reached some sad ruins at the end then turned around. They repeated the same futile performance eight times before finally they were back at the base of the hills and ready for a repeat performance up the right-hand side. They wound their futile way up the Valley of the Crows, the Valley of the Four Streams and the somewhat annoying Valley of the Flies, which had them rapidly winding up the windows. Now, with only three turn offs left, the whole exercise was starting to feel like a washout.

'OK,' said Newton, leaning on the wheel wearily like a tired chauffeur. 'What's next?'

'Three more,' said the Reverend. 'First the Valle de las Ortigas.'

'Ortigas? What's that in English?'

'Stinging Nettles. Then Eight Oxen, then Water.'

Newton and the Reverend looked at each other intently, eyes narrowing. The penny rolled and dropped.

'Why would you get oxen up *here*?' they said, together.

'That has to be it,' said Newton, slapping the wheel. 'Lupero and his boys would have let them go once they'd hidden the damn thing.

They'd be so intent on hiding the machine, they didn't notice the oxen had wandered off. Good news for the locals though – a fully grown ox would be like a lottery win for some poor half-starved peasant in the 1500s, never mind eight of the critters.'

'Quite, and they wouldn't have reported it either, would they,' said Bennet. 'A gift from God! They'd have kept quiet for fear the animals would be taken away again.'

'Exactly,' said Newton. 'But, the story would have stayed strong with the people that found them, a real folklore moment. Hence the name. And there are *eight* of the oxen, the number matches. Forget the other valleys,' said Newton decisively, 'let's go.'

Newton gunned the Citroën and they careered back up the narrow winding road until they reached the Valley of the Eight Oxen. Gingerly they nosed their way inside. They noticed evidence of recent intrusion from the get go. Something sizable had clearly barged its way up the simple track – something big enough to snap and break the branches hanging low from the steep banks; they lay in broken bunches on the dusty track and there were fresh treads in the thin mud.

As they neared the end of the track, Newton and Bennet came upon an ancient chapel, long abandoned, and now only a home to nesting rock doves and bats. The late afternoon sun was starting to dip beyond the narrow valley, casting the scene in deep purple and crimson.

They climbed out of the Citroën, cautiously approaching the building, Bennet keeping his hand ready on his Beretta. Where the chapel nestled into the massive overhang, a neat new hole had been punched through a long smooth wall. Rubble was strewn around, and given the intact walls to the sides, it was clear to Newton that this had once been a very neat subterfuge. To anyone passing, the wall would have seemed nothing but a blank expanse, a simple blend between the natural rock and the chapel with no hint that it had anything behind it. Lupero and his men would have worked long and hard to accomplish the job – but it had worked just as La Senza's lieutenant had intended. An ugly mess of graffiti hinted that visitors had been here many times in the past, but clearly they had all left oblivious to the chamber behind. It was to remain so, until Lupero's heirs returned to reclaim their lost property.

Walking over a mess of discarded ropes and tackle, Newton and the Reverend Bennet entered the hollow. As expected, the dimensions of the space matched everything they had been told of the machine. The hollow was dry and dusty, and the device could have been safely preserved indefinitely.

And there was a strong smell of cigarette smoke – someone had been here recently.

Very recently.

'The truck!' snapped Newton abruptly.

'Truck?'

'Yes, the white truck. We saw it from up on the ridge. It's in the bloody truck. It didn't pass us on the road, that means it *must* have come from here. Don't you see? It's in the sodding truck!'

'Bloody hell!' said Bennet. 'What are we waiting for!?'

Newton drove the Citroën crazily down the track back towards Sierra de Luna, so fast that the Reverend Bennet had trouble hanging onto the map as the air rushed in through the open passenger window.

'Looking at this, there are not many turn offs,' he shouted. 'They have to be going on all the way to Ejea de los Caballeros.'

'Gotcha,' said Newton, 'and that lorry is going to be crawling on this road, it's hardly the M4.'

'As to what we do when we catch them ...' said Bennet, pulling out his pistol and checking the magazine. Newton looked over and shook his head.

'You gonna use that?'

'Certainly, though I'd rather use it on their tyres than on any flesh and blood. Thou shall not kill and all that. Mind you, the good book doesn't say anything about winging them in the legs.'

'I'll bow to your greater knowledge,' said Newton, and with the road improving, he began to build up speed as they twisted and turned down the switchbacks.

Above them on a hilltop, another vehicle had stopped, its passengers watching with binoculars as the Citroën tore along in a cloud of pale dust.

'You are being followed, Mr Van Loop,' said one of the men into his phone. 'Two men in an old blue and white car.' Gunter, in the truck cabin, instinctively reached for his stubby machine gun and rammed in a clip.

'Roger. Contact the other teams and have them form some

road blocks.'

'Yes sir.' They jumped into their jeep and sped back down the goat track onto the road, beginning their pursuit.

Some two miles ahead of Newton and Bennet, a jeep skidded to a screeching halt as three men spilt out onto the road. Running to the steep embankments they took up their positions. Using the rocks for cover, one of the men shouldered a rocket-propelled grenade and waited. As the streamlined form of Newton's Citroën rounded the rocks below, he let the missile loose. It hissed and fizzled away in a cloud of smoke and sparks, and for a second, it looked certain to tear into the old saloon. Inside the noisy car, Newton and Bennet didn't even hear or see it coming. The first signal they were under attack came as the blast erupted in front of them in an ugly grey fountain. The Citroën barrelled through a torment of fire, stones and broken tarmac.

Astonishingly, there was nothing worse than damaged paintwork and ringing ears. But even above the Citroën's screaming engine, the staccato rip of two assault rifles was clearly audible. The tarmac rippled and danced as bullets flayed the ground around them. One of the rear passenger windows shattered into a cobweb and there were clangs and thuds in the bodywork. The vicar, his eyes steely and full of fight, wound down his window. To Newton's horror, he leant out and pointed his weapon up at the gunmen.

'Thou shall not kill!' he shouted, and he let fly a superbly aimed round that took out a gunman's knee from a range of some fifty feet. The thug crumpled, his gun spraying bullets high into the air above him as he fell. With a sinuous turn, Bennet then lay his arm across the roof and fired again. With stunning accuracy, the slug tore into the second gunman's shoulder and screaming, he jerked back like a puppet. 'Thou shall not kill again!' Bennet righteously proclaimed and then plopped back grinning into the passenger seat. With the failed roadblock behind them, they pressed on towards the distant truck.

Gunter took the excuses from the savaged roadblock with disgust and frustration. Swearing angrily, he called the second ambush. Just a mile ahead of Newton, more gunmen were heaving boulders into the road until they lay plumb centre of the tarmac. As Newton finally rounded a sharp bend into view, they began firing. Newton threw on the brakes and screeched to a halt. Frantically, he backed up. The gunmen, now out of range if not out of sight, waited behind cover for Newton's next move. As he revved his engine expectantly they steadied their weapons.

'What? Why are we stopping?' asked Bennet. 'Can't we just go round?'

'Not round,' said Newton, 'over.' He leant down to activate the old car's hydropneumatic suspension. The enlarged hydrospheres charged and the Citroën majestically lifted itself up off the ground. Like a hovercraft, up and up it rose until finally, it perched high above the tarmac like a container dock crane. The Reverend looked down at the ground from his side window.

'Streuth! That can't be normal.'

'This will probably feel a bit weird,' said Newton as he slammed his foot hard down on the accelerator.

Normally, the hydropneumatic suspension on his car only went to three settings, but whoever had been consistently pimping Newton's ride had added an extra two. At full elevation, it felt as if they were flying above the ground like one of the cars in *Blade Runner*.

Fazed as they were by the oncoming novelty, the gunmen unleashed their first volleys from a hundred yards, wildly inaccurate at that range, but intended to unnerve Newton, now hunched down behind the dashboard. It certainly didn't unnerve the Reverend Bennet. He took careful aim out of the window, his arm outstretched, trading fire.

Gunfire began impacting all around them. Neat holes appeared in the Citroën's bodywork and one of the wing mirrors cracked off its mount, flapping against the metal with repeated loud clangs. 'Do unto others what they are intending to do to you!' yelled the vicar, as one of his bullets slammed into the shoulder of a gunman, spinning him round and down. Newton wobbled the Citroën as fast as he dared up to the makeshift roadblock, deftly swerving over the top of the obstruction as if it wasn't there. Gobsmacked, the gunmen watched in disbelief as the 70's classic passed harmlessly through the kill zone like a carnival float. They pressed on.

Newton and Bennet were closing fast with their quarry. For the first time, as they took a switchback at speed, they caught sight of the truck on the road below them, a black Range Rover close behind.

'There they are!' yelled Bennet, as he reloaded his Beretta.

'It's not all good news,' said Newton, looking in the cracked rear-view mirror. 'We've got a jeep on our tail. Closing fast.' The vicar looked back.

'OK, I'll deal with them, you just keep going.' A flailing mass of arms and legs, Bennet flopped over his seat. Using Newton's battered old road map, he knocked away the shattered glass in the rear window, opening up a clear field to fire. Their pursuers were appearing and disappearing on the tight bends, closer each time. Finally, as they came onto a straight stretch, the occupants began to trade fire with the vicar. Flickering muzzle blasts reached out to the Citroën and there were yet more thunks and clangs as the bodywork took punishment. The Reverend was less profligate in his ammunition usage, however, and he took his time before sending his first round dead centre into the jeep's radiator. Shifting his aim as the rounds cracked just over their heads, he sent another bullet into its windscreen. Instantly opaque, the driver was forced to smash his thug's fist through the glass to restore a view of the winding road before replacing his bloodied hands on the wheel. Newton looked up in the mirror to see the jeep getting alarmingly close, the flashes from the automatics clearly visible.

'The tyres, shoot out their bloody tyres!' screamed Newton.

'On this road? There'd probably be an accident!'

'What ... are you mad? They're trying to kill us!'

'Oh but I mustn't kill anyone, I'm a man of God.'

'I thought you were a holy warrior? OK, tell you what. How about an eye for an eye, a tooth for a tooth ...' argued Newton urgently, 'only pre-emptively?'

'Mmm ... OK,' said Bennet, 'I suppose it *is* in self-defence.' Happy with that, he then casually aimed the Beretta, firing twice. The jeep behind them, its front tyres flapping uselessly, swerved off the road and away in a cloud of steam and vegetation as it ploughed savagely into a ravine.

Back in the passenger seat, Bennet closed his eyes and bowed his head, his hands clasped around the pistol in contemplation.

'Praying?' asked Newton respectfully.

'What?' said Bennet. 'Oh no, sorry, just trying to remember how many rounds I've got left, my maths is terrible.' Newton shook his head again as they careered on down the road towards the truck.

They could see the massive white vehicle clearly now; it was dropping in and out of the curves no more than half a mile ahead. Blood in his nostrils, Newton put his foot down.

Van Loop was furious.

'Why do we pay these bloody people!' he screamed down the phone to his son. The sudden outburst made Ascot McCauley grind his tiny teeth. Nasty as he was, the property developer had nerves as tight as catgut and the increasingly action-filled afternoon was putting him seriously on edge – even more so now that he was being handed an Uzi.

'What? I don't know how to use this.'

'Learn!' said Van Loop brusquely.

'Father, I can't do much from here unless they get close,' radioed Gunter. 'You'll have to fend them off yourself.'

'Ya son, I'll give them hell,' said his father, somewhat unconvincingly, and so Gunter made a snap decision.

'Oh dammit,' he shouted suddenly, and without giving himself time to think twice, he opened the door and climbed out of the cab. Alarmed, his driver stared at him. 'Forget me!' yelled Gunter at the driver. 'Keep driving, don't stop for anything.' Gunter slammed the door. Holding on to the bucking swerving truck he edged along the meagre handholds towards the rear, his assault rifle swinging dangerously around him.

'My God ... Gunter!' yelled Van Loop senior, as he spotted his only son hanging from the side of the truck. Several times, Gunter nearly lost his hold as the truck bounced on the uneven road surface, and then finally reaching the rear, he abruptly lost his footing. Against all the odds, his gun strap caught the door handles and he hung there briefly, swinging back and forth helplessly like a bunch of keys. After a long minute in which he came close to battering himself mad, he managed to gain purchase. Clawing his way back up, he rammed his arm in hard behind one of the uprights, planted his feet firmly upon the lower bars and after a very deep breath, opened fire.

Gunter's years as a mercenary were instantly telling. A neat series of holes appeared in the roof between Newton and the vicar, and beams of sunlight streamed down into the Citroën's dusty interior.

'Woaaahh,' said Newton with feeling.

'We've got to get in closer,' yelled Bennet, ignoring the incoming rounds. 'I can't possibly hit the tyres from this distance, especially with that bloody Chelsea tractor in the way.'

'Closer?' said Newton, adrenalin running through his system like petrol in an engine. 'OK!' He pushed down the accelerator until they were close enough to see the outline of people gazing back at them through tinted windows. Three times they tried to break past the big car; three times they were skilfully blocked. Repeatedly, the driver slammed his vehicle into their path.

Unable to fire for fear of hitting his father and his companions, Gunter waved his weapon from side to side frantically looking for the shot. Seeing the gun aimed intermittently at his head, Newton ducked the Citroën back behind the mass of the Land Rover.

Suddenly, the road straightened.

They were back out onto the flat, dry plains; the road was as straight as an arrow. To its side, beyond the tarmac, the dusty banks were flat enough for Newton to risk overtaking. He swerved suddenly to the side and surged ahead. But the guy behind the wheel of the Land Rover was having none of it. With a burst of power, he walloped through a wire fence and once again blocked the Citroën. Countering, Newton threw the wheel hard over and in this millisecond of separation, a low wall appeared between them in blur of old stone. The sudden obstruction left the Land Rover trapped off-road.

Either side of the wall they were neck and neck, the bucking Land Rover charging ahead in a hurricane of small stones and clouds of dust as Newton started to close with the truck. Predictably, the windows came down and the guns popped out.

But Newton was surprised. Instead of yet more thick-necked hired men, he was staring at a frail ninety-year-old man and the unmistakable weasely face of Ascot McCauley. At a loss, the property developer was cradling his weapon like a nervous grandmother. Newton and Ascot's eyes met. In a tiny but significant instant, they exchanged an expression of mutual loathing. Newton, now more determined than ever, turned back to the truck ahead of them and charged. Despite the enthusiastic urging of the old fascist, Ascot McCauley fired his gun at the Citroën with all the professionalism of a drugged Congolese militiaman. Within ten rounds, he'd lost the tip of his left index finger and dropped the weapon out of the window. Squealing pathetically, he fell back into the car. As he did, he was pushed away again by La Senza and Sister Wendy who, for some reason all of their own, were busy finding the whole thing wildly erotic.

Van Loop did his best to regain the militaristic bearing of his misspent youth in the Waffen SS and he let loose a clip from his machine pistol. But the bucking car and his diminished eyesight sent the stream of bullets wildly above the Citroën and into a passing flock of woodpigeons, scything them down in a cloud of blood and feathers. Gunter frantically waved his gun at his father in an attempt to stop him. But the mad old man's nostrils were flaring. He was back in Poland, Russia, Biafra, Columbia, the Balkans. Lost in his ghastly past, he let loose again.

This time Gunter caught most of it – amazingly without any actual bodily harm. His father's woeful marksmanship had drawn a near perfect outline of his body. Looking down, Gunter noticed a telltale wisp of smoke. A round had passed between his legs, close enough to leave a smouldering hole in both his combat trousers and his leopard-print boxer shorts.

'Jesssuusss Popa, stop!' he frantically mouthed. His father, finally owning up to his diminished capabilities, sulkily heaved himself back into the car and wound up the window.

There seemed to be nothing that could stop Newton closing with the huge truck. Bennet steadied his aim at the truck's tyres, while Gunter Van Loop fired at the Citroën's front wheel. Suddenly the Citroën was spinning, bouncing off the old wall in a shower of sparks. The vicar and the scientist flinched, screamed, swore and prayed. Finally, after what seemed an eternity of impacts, they were at a standstill.

Game over.

Bennet and Newton peered through the receding dust cloud. They could only mutter choice four-letter words as La Senza's convoy whipped on into the distance.

# FAST CARS

The dust from the chase had drifted away by the time Newton and the Reverend Bennet finally eased themselves out of the wreck. Newton could only marvel at how they hadn't both died. The car was a festival of bullet holes, blast damage, dents and scratches. One whole panel of bodywork above the rear right wheel was missing altogether, exposing the suspension, and only one section of glass did not contain a crack.

Newton left Bennet fighting with the flat tyre and felt for his iPhone, frantic to call Jameson with an update. There was so much to tell him.

Too bad, then, that as Newton pulled the phone from his pocket, it fell cleanly in half. Various parts of its savaged exterior dropped into the dust at his feet. The glass was shattered; the tip of a bullet sat decoratively in the centre. For Newton, the oft-lamented phrase 'I couldn't live without my phone' was in this case literally correct.

'Looks like we're offline, Rev,' he said, showing Bennet what was left of the phone.

'So it would appear,' Bennet replied, heaving off the wheel and rolling it away. 'Looks like we're on our own.'

'Yep,' said Newton, lifting out the spare, which despite everything was still miraculously inflated. 'At least we know where they're going.'

'We do?'

'Has to be Bilbao. It's the nearest port.'

'I concur,' said the vicar. 'Do you suppose we can catch them?'

'Dunno,' said Newton. 'After that little altercation with the wall, the car might be a dead duck. Better get the wheel on and see what state she's in. Poor old Citroën – what a way to treat a motoring classic.'

The Reverend Bennet heaved the spare into place, dropped the car down off the jack, then grunted like a tennis pro as he tightened the bolts.

'You must let me know what you have for breakfast,' said Newton. 'It's clearly top notch.'

'There,' said Bennet, wiping his hands on a handkerchief. 'Want to see if she starts up OK?' Newton hopped in and put his key in the ignition. The car hesitated for a second before, cautiously, it seemed to regain its pre-accident mojo. Once again, they were greeted with the fighter-plane roar of the engine. Grinning like a schoolboy, Newton gave Bennet the thumbs up.

'What do you reckon?' shouted Newton through the window.

'I say we take the chance. I believe we could still head them off. At the least, we might hold them up.'

'Agreed,' said Newton, taking a deep breath. 'Hop in.'

After a few clunks and pops, the bruised old Citroën heaved itself up out of the dust and gripped the tarmac. With La Senza so far ahead, they were going to have to flog it to make up the distance.

'What the hell have they done to this car!' marvelled Newton, shouting above the roaring engine.

'Clever, isn't it!' the vicar shouted back. 'You know they offered to do the same to my moped, but I said no. Not sure I'd feel safe on it.' Laughing, they sped on past Tudela, Logroño and Miranda de Ebro, gradually clawing back La Senza's head start.

'If my damn phone was working we could check the ferry times,' yelled Newton. 'It would be helpful if you had a phone yourself Reverend.'

'I'm so dreadfully sorry. Can't be doing with the troublesome things.' Unable to talk without shouting, they pressed on until they finally reached the city limits of Bilbao at dusk. Newton swung fast around the ring road and entered the port.

The ship had just left the dock.

The huge blue and white car ferry was edging away from its berth, positioning itself to take the channel out into the Bay of Biscay.

'Bugger, bugger! Arsepipes!' yelled Newton, banging the steering wheel.

'My words exactly,' said Bennet. They watched the ship for a few seconds in silence. 'Hold on, give me the binoculars,' said Bennet. The vicar focused the lenses. 'Well helloooo ... look who's having a stroll on the deck!' He handed the binoculars back to Newton.

'Sorry?' said Newton. 'What am I looking for?'

'About two thirds along the first set of rails at the front.'

As Newton rolled the focus, a fuzzy figure sharpened into a somewhat erotically dressed nun.

'Bennet, you old dog you!'

'No not *her* Dr Barlow, really. Look who's with her.' Newton panned left.

'What? Is that him? That's La Senza?'

'I'm guessing yes. Quick, get back in the car, I've got an idea,' said Bennet, pointing. 'There's a mole out there in the channel; they have to go past it. I think I might be able to take a shot.'

'Gotcha,' said Newton. Without hesitation he charged the Citroën away and along the dockside as the ferry, massive in the harbour lights, turned to face the open channel. They were through the gates now and out onto the mole, charging along the narrow access road as fast as Newton dared, the harbour wall dropping sheer away into the black water. Running out of road, Newton slammed on the brakes and the car squealed to a stop, inches from the edge. Together, they clambered up onto the harbour wall as the ferry, a looming mass of lights, began to build up its speed as it pushed for the open sea.

Up on the high wall, the Reverend Bennet pulled out his Beretta and steadied himself. Through the binoculars, Newton could clearly see La Senza, his nun and Ascot McCauley looking out as Spain drifted away from them, a look of smug satisfaction upon their faces.

'Are you going to kill him?' asked Newton.

'Yep,' said Bennet, cracking his neck and slowing his breathing.

'Didn't think you could do that,' said Newton. 'Thou shalt not ... and all that?'

'Not a problem in this case,' said the vicar without emotion, as he pulled back the hammer.

'Why?' said Newton.

'Because he's already dead.' Bennet fired.

The small pistol was hardly the right weapon for a long-range assasination, but even so, Bennet's shot was impressively close to the mark. La Senza's small fancy dress hat whisked off the top of his head as if it had been pulled with a wire. Confused, the Cardinal looked up before Gunter, who had heard the crack of the bullet, grabbed La Senza and bustled him back into the hull.

'Bastard!' said Bennet, slapping the wall in frustration. 'If I'd had my hunting rifle I could have put it right between the bastard's eyes!'

They watched the ferry slip past them and away out to sea. In 24 hours it would be docking in Portsmouth and there was nothing they could do.

'So, what now?' asked Bennet. They leant wearily for a long five minutes against the wrecked DS until Newton broke the silence.

'Fancy a drive?'

'Where to?' said Bennet, putting the Beretta back into his jacket.

'Dieppe,' said Newton. 'It's about ten hours away if you drive sensibly.'

'And if we *don't* drive sensibly?'

'Seven.'

'I'm not even going to ask what our average speed will be,' said Bennet with a glint in his eyes. 'But I'm up for it if you are.'

'Get in,' said Newton.

\*\*\*\*\*\*

Free from interference, La Senza and his party could enjoy their voyage in relative serenity. Dinner was duly consumed in the cafeteria with La Senza eating an ungodly quantity of burgers and chips, inflicting on Baxter's lean and sensible body a wave of trans fat and salt it had spent much of its adult life avoiding. Once they were suitably sated, La Senza and Sister Wendy retreated giggling to their cabin, leaving Ascot McCauley and Van Loop senior to sit awkwardly at the table over some cruelly expensive spirits.

'So your family has been waiting since 1510 for this La Senza chap to come back then?' Ascot offered hopefully. Van Loop looked at him sternly.

'*Cardinal* La Senza, Mr McCauley, please. You must call our leader by his correct name. Anything else is disrespectful.'

'Cardinal, your worship, whatever,' said Ascot, sneering dismissively. 'Well, is he what you thought he'd be like?'

'I have to confess he's more annoying than I was expecting. I was prepared for him to be gloriously evil, but he seems a bit more adolescent than that, I fear.'

'He certainly has his moments,' said Ascot. 'More Dick Dasterdly than Darth Vader.'

'I just wish he'd say thank you once in a while, you know,' said Van Loop sadly. 'I mean, my family waited five centuries for him – from father to son we waited. Oh the endless centuries! And we kept his treasures intact. Even when the family hit the bad times, we never dug them up. We could have done, you know. Like at the end of the war, when I was hiding from those spiteful war-crimes people; life was really hard for me you know. I hated Argentina. The diet was all meat, nothing but meat!' He looked wistfully out of the window. After a long sigh, he turned and looked at the now-somewhat-ruffled Ascot, fixing him with his dead watery eyes. 'And you Mr McCauley, what do you believe in?'

'Money,' said Ascot standing. 'Look, I'd love to chat, but I'm in need of some sleep. I'll get to my cabin if it's all the same to you. Can you remind me what number I'm in?'

'Number 57,' said Van Loop impassively. 'Next to the Cardinal and Sister Wendy.' Ascot, pained, closed his eyes, all hope of a quiet night in serious doubt.

'Great, just great,' he huffed, and draining his brandy, he left Van Loop staring out at the lights as the boat pushed forward through the swell.

******

As the ferry sailed slowly through the Bay of Biscay, Newton and Bennet hacked north along the French motorways like a Japanese bullet train.

Around Poitiers it began to rain heavily and a steady stream of water came pouring down through bullet holes in the roof, leaving both of them shivering. Bennet flicked on the ancient heating system but it merely propelled warmish air away through the back of the car where it heated the empty motorway behind them.

By Le Mans, Newton's eyes felt like they had hornets in them. He blinked, then as he glanced in the rear-view mirror, he did a double take – the merest trace of Sixsmith's ghost was sitting in the back seat.

'Alex?'

'Hello,' said the ghost of Alex Sixsmith, his voice distant.

'Why are you so faint?' asked Newton, puzzled.

'Too far ... from ... my ... relics,' Sixsmith whispered, his voice fading in and out so much that Newton and Bennet were straining to hear him at all. 'We've not ... heard from you. What's ... happening?'

'Well,' said Newton, 'the safe new job you got me has resulted in me being shot at, and I'm afraid my phone took the bullet. And sadly, the vicar here hasn't got one of his own. Sorry.'

'Did ... you ... find ... anything?'

'I'll keep it brief,' said Newton. 'La Senza is getting help from the McCauleys. Let Jameson know. This bloody machine is on its way back to Portsmouth on the ferry – it'll probably be there in a few hours.'

'The McCauleys? Crikey! Are ... you ... sure, did you see them?'

'Very sure, one of them was trying to kill me at the time,' said Newton. 'Look, I'll make a full report when I get back to Newhaven and get my phone replaced.'

'I'm sorry,' said Sixsmith. 'I'm really ... struggling ... to hear all ... this. Can I ... suggest ... you send back a ... proper ... report from ... Newhaven? You ... can ... get a ... new phone ... there.'

'That's even better!' said Newton to the space left as Sixsmith finally faded out completely. Exhausted, Newton begged the reluctant Reverend Bennet to do the driving and after swapping places, they headed back out onto the motorway towards Dieppe.

\*\*\*\*\*\*

Newton awoke a few hours later frozen into a sodden ball by a near-fatal mix of wind chill, fatigue and damp clothes.

'Are we there yet?' he said, as he slowly sat back upright. He tried without success to defrost his hands in front of the car heater as if it were a warm brazier. 'You'd think that if they go to the trouble of souping up the engine and the suspension, they could have had a pop at the heater!'

'Cheer up,' said the vicar, yawning, a thin layer of frost upon his shoulders like severe dandruff. 'We're nearly at Dieppe. We'll find you a nice warm bench on the ferry.'

'Luxury,' said Newton, who despite the thrill of the chase was getting a tad frayed around the edges. It was nearly daylight now, and all the road signs were pointing to the Channel. With everything depending on keeping up the pace and catching the ferry, Newton and the Reverend Bennet streaked like F1 champions around Rouen and on to Dieppe.

\*\*\*\*\*\*

The alarm clock enraged Gabby for a good minute before she

remembered that it heralded a fun day out. She yawned and stretched then got up briskly as Viv clattered out a basic breakfast. It was still dark when they piled into the old Vauxhall and set off for distant Dorset.

'Boy, you can really yawn!' said Viv laughing, trying to stifle an infectious yawn of her own.

'Yawwwwwwwwww ... sorry,' said Gabby, fiddling with the heating. 'Sheeet, it's cold.'

'Sure is,' said Viv. 'We can warm up with a coffee once we get onto the M3.'

'Good plan,' said Gabby, yawning again.

'Stop that, you're making me do it too!' said Viv, as the pair yawned and laughed in good spirits. 'Anything from your dad on your phone?'

'Not a bean,' said Gabby. 'Probably busy,' she added from beneath a curled lip. 'He'll be gutted when he finds out where we're going.'

'He will!' said Viv. 'In fact, let's not answer if he calls. We can just send him a shot from the phone. Surprise him.'

'Yeah – radio silence!' said Gabby, as they swung west towards Heathrow and onto the M3.

******

For Newton and the Reverend Bennet, the queue for the Dieppe ferry had been interminable. They froze in the soggy squalor of the semi-derelict Citroën as the boat's ramp came down. Finally, the front cars in the queues were given the thumbs up and Bennet eagerly started the engine. As soon as they were parked up, the two half-frozen men hunted the boat for comfortable seats with full access to a hot pipe. With an out-of-order public phone finalising their isolation from the organisation back in Britain, they sat shivering until, utterly exhausted, they fell asleep. Not even the cacophony from the children's play area could have woken them.

Under a leaden sky, the ferry slipped its moorings. Despite the delays and La Senza's head start, the good guys and the bad guys were bound for an almost simultaneous landfall.

A long day was beginning.

## CHAPTER 32

# FUNNELS

Viv and Gabby bounced the fringes of Bournemouth, circled the expanse of Poole Harbour then swung down into the Purbecks. The landscape became noticeably more scrubby as farmland gave way to scraggly heathlands. With nothing but the occasional clump of pine trees, it took on a romantic windblown flavour, the winter sun finding hidden colours in the heather and gorse.

As they reached Langton Hadlow, a large dump truck pulled out in front of them, its bulk somewhat out-of-keeping with the village's sleepy ambience. Viv slowed to let it out. Around them, everything seemed strangely quiet. The windows of the shops and houses were dark, their neglected paintwork layered in dust.

'Hardly a jumping joint!' said Viv, frowning. 'Looks half dead.'

'Everything's been sold – seems a bit odd,' said Gabby. They carried on behind the truck to the village square, where Viv did a circuit around the war memorial, then pulled up and parked in the shadow of the old tank.

'Wow, a real ghost town!' said Gabby as they climbed out and stretched. 'All the pubs and shops are shut. Weird!'

'Hello ladies,' came a voice from above them. Looking up, they saw a door in the side of the tank creaking open. A man was looking down at them, a cheery smile on his face. 'Are you looking for something in particular?' He swung himself out from the hatch and climbed down, wiping his oily hands on a rag.

'Err ... yes,' said Viv. 'We've got an appointment with the curator at the museum. Not till later though. We're wondering if you can get some lunch here? All the pubs are shut down.'

'Yes, sadly they are,' said the mechanic, with a mixture of melancholy and resignation.

'Is that a real tank?' asked Gabby.

'It is indeed young lady,' said the mechanic. 'A real World War One tank. She saw action too – Cambrai 1917,' he said, pointing up at the machine guns poking menacingly out from the side cupolas. 'Guns are dummies, of course, the real ones are kept under lock and key, but other than that she's 100 per cent authentic. And she's a runner.'

'A runner?' asked Gabby.

'Yes, she still drives. Once a year we back her off this plinth and take her up the road to the tank museum at Bovington for their big display.'

'So where's the village museum?' said Viv.

'Well ladies,' said the mechanic, pointing down the once-picturesque street. 'The museum is just up there by the castle wall. It's easy to spot, it's the only building without one of those ghastly estate agent signboards.' He sighed. 'Poor old sod is still hanging on, bless him. Those developer bastards – they're hounding him round the clock. Same with us.'

'Developers? What ... in a place like *this*?' said Viv.

'Sadly yes,' said the mechanic. 'But that's the modern world for you. Anyway, I'd better get on. We might have to move this dear old warhorse soon and she needs a bit of prepping. Much as we'd love to hang on and fight the bastards, a garage with no vehicles to fix and no petrol tanks to fill is hardly a good business proposition. If we aren't here, who'll keep this old dear going? We'll just have to hand her over to the tank museum.' He patted the slab-sided monster as if it was a Grand National winner. 'Sad really. She's still got some fight left in her, even if we haven't.' He climbed back up and clambered through the hatch before popping his head back out: 'Have a good day ladies.'

******

The Reverend Bennet nudged Newton awake and handed him a coffee.

'Wake up Dr Barlow. We'll be docking in about thirty minutes.' Newton, who was dry on one side and still damp, be it warm damp, on the other, reluctantly grabbed the coffee and sat upright, blinking.

'OK ... hold on ... where am I?'

'On a car ferry. Wakey wakey!'

'Ah ... yes, I remember now,' said Newton, blearily. 'Funny, these days I find the lines between dreams and reality increasingly hard to discern. I was having a dream that was actually less surreal than real life. And it felt good.'

'I concur,' said Bennet, sipping from his cup. 'It's a funny old world to be sure, but then, that's what makes it interesting.'

'Spose,' said Newton. 'But I have to say there was something quite comforting about being completely and utterly wrong. Tell me Reverend,' said Newton changing tack, 'I've been meaning to ask you something. You're a man of God right?'

'I am.'

'So how does all this fit in with your beliefs? Not one of these ghosts or spirit guides has mentioned God. Not once. Not even obliquely. Doesn't that kind of throw your whole religion thing out of the stained-glass window?'

'Well,' replied Bennet after a thoughtful pause, 'it may be true that they haven't confirmed the almighty. But they haven't confirmed the non-existence of God either. It's much the same as here in the land of the living isn't it? It's still all about faith at the end of the day.'

'But the afterlife they describe hasn't got a God in it at all. It must mean he doesn't exist.'

'Prove it,' said Bennet calmly.

'I can't,' said Newton. 'You can't prove a negative.'

'But don't you see, in a way nothing has changed,' continued the vicar, clearly confident in his conclusions. 'There is no proof for or against God, and as many of the dead seem to be just as prone to belief systems as the living, well then, it's business as normal.'

'Don't you find it infuriating, though, that they won't tell you everything?' said Newton. 'I mean, they know something we don't, something massive and frankly it's driving me nuts.'

'My dear boy,' continued Bennet. 'Like most clergymen, I've spent my whole career encouraging people to be happy with faith in the unknown. I can hardly get impatient myself. I'm sure I'll find out eventually.'

'I'm a scientist, though,' said Newton. 'I need answers now. I don't do faith.'

'As I see it, they simply won't bend the rules. I'm afraid you'll have to just wait and see what happens when you croak, just like the rest of us.'

'Well as much as I'd like quick answers, I'd rather forgo the death bit for the moment,' said Newton resignedly.

Bennet stood up. 'Well Dr Barlow, I guess we'd better get organised. We'll have to hit the ground running.'

The coast was a grey smudge ahead of them and after looking briefly out from the passenger deck windows at the brightening day, they set off for the car deck. As the ferry docked at Newhaven, far away to the west Cardinal La Senza and his party were making good time. They'd left Portsmouth some twenty minutes earlier and were already skirting Southampton. The convoy was entering the New Forest when Hadlow Grange called in.

'Hello Epsom,' said Ascot wearily, La Senza's dribbling head weighing sleepily on his blazer shoulder.

'I've been on the internet,' said his brother smugly. 'You'll never guess what I've found.'

\*\*\*\*\*\*

Viv and Gabby walked in the bright winter sunshine up to the Langton Hadlow village museum, its old-world charm defiant amongst the estate agent signboards. The door wobbled on its aged hinges, a rusted metal bell rattling and jangling above them as they made their way inside.

'I'll be right there,' the curator called from the back room. Gabby and Viv looked around them at the eccentric objects along the walls and exchanged looks combining amusement and confusion.

'Blimey,' said Viv. 'Nothing like a well-thought-out public space, eh? Looks like Tutankhamen's tomb!' The curator was bustling his way out to the counter and he peered over his spectacles at the two of them.

'Aha, you must be the young ladies I was expecting. You've come a long way.'

'That's right, from London.' said Viv. 'We've come about the antique thing ... the figure on the box.'

'Ah yes. So tell me. What do you know about it?' he said hopefully.

'Us ... well nothing, I'm afraid,' said Viv.

'It's for my dad,' said Gabby, filling the awkward silence that followed. 'He's been looking for it, but cos he's away we thought we'd find it for him.'

'That's right,' continued Viv. 'We found your post online and thought ... hey that's it! So here we are.'

'Ah that's a pity,' said the curator. 'I was rather hoping someone would tell me something about the beastly thing. It's a bit odd, you see.'

'It's not just odd,' said Gabby. 'It's pig ugly!'

'Ugly, yes,' said the curator. 'But I'm afraid its looks are not the only problem. Do you know why your father is interested in it?'

'Not really,' said Gabby. 'He works for a place that does telescopes and stuff. Must be something to do with that.'

'Well,' he continued, 'I guess we'd better go and have a look at it then.' They followed him into the rear room.

The carved box sat alone in its cabinet. Viv and Gabby approached the case and peered cautiously inside. Unexpectedly they felt something uncomfortable wash over them like the breeze from an open refrigerator.

'Well there it is,' said the curator. 'Horrible, isn't it?'

'Isn't it just!' said Viv, shuddering. 'What do you know about it? Is there a story? I mean, why is it all covered in tape and wire?'

'Oh just a precaution,' the curator said without elaborating. 'It's got *something* in it.'

'Sorry, what do you mean?'

'Well that's just it, I'm not really sure,' he replied. 'However, regarding its origins, well … all I know is that my grandfather picked it up in Germany after the First World War.'

Gabby took out her phone and aimed for a photo, but Viv nudged her. 'Do you mind if we take a picture?' Viv said.

'Not at all. Please, feel free,' said the curator. 'You said your father knows something about it – perhaps he can shed some light upon its history. Personally though, I'd be pleased to see the back of it.' Gabby held up her mobile phone and after she was happy with one of the shots, she forwarded it to her father.

'That's great,' said Viv. 'Hopefully Gabby's dad can help you clear it up.'

'Actually, yours is not the only enquiry I've had,' said the curator. 'Funnily enough, I had another email this morning. Someone local, as it happens. They'll be over sometime today to have a look.' Even as the curator spoke, there was a rumble outside. The daylight that had poured brightly through the old window was suddenly blocked by a slab of white as a large lorry pulled up to the museum's exterior. The old metal bell above the door clanged again.

'Oh,' said the curator. 'I wonder if that's him?'

\*\*\*\*\*\*

In Newhaven, Newton ripped open the excessive packaging of his new phone and slotted in his old sim card. The phone immediately began chirruping and jangling with annoying ringtones. 'World and his wife have been after us,' said Newton, scrolling. 'Jameson, Sixsmith, Jameson, Sixsmith ... oh ... and there's one from my kid and my girlfriend ... whoops, I forgot about them!' Newton rang Jameson.

'Dr Barlow, there you are!' said Jameson, somewhat brusquely. 'Where the hell have you been?'

'Yes, sorry. Problems with the phone. Look, I don't know how much Sixsmith got through to you but here's the facts.'

'Go on,' said Jameson.

'First, the McCauleys are helping La Senza.'

'So I heard,' said Jameson earnestly. 'Well at least we know where they're headed then.'

'Where's that?'

'Dorset,' said Jameson. 'The horrible little creeps have their HQ down there. It's in an old mental hospital in the Purbecks, Hadlow Grange I think it's called. Nearest village is Langton Hadlow.'

'OK, gotcha,' continued Newton. 'But did you realise they've got the device, this bloody machine thing?'

'Oh no!' said Jameson. 'Really?'

'Yes really,' said Newton. 'It was hidden in a ruined chapel north of Zaragoza. They whacked it into a big eighteen-wheeler, then got it onto the ferry from Bilbao to Portsmouth. We got there just as the ferry was leaving.'

'We?' said Jameson.

'Yes, I'm here with the Reverend Bennet.'

'Ah ... you met. Yes, he's a good man in a tight spot is Bennet.'

'So I noticed,' said Newton. 'Anyway, they have some heavies working for them, really mean ones. Guns, lots of big guns.'

'I see ... OK, what else?' asked Jameson

'Well,' continued Newton, 'we reckon they've picked up considerable funds, probably in gold. That means whatever fun and games La Senza's planned can be financed without him begging for a loan from any of the high-street banks.'

'Yes ... I see,' said Jameson thoughtfully. 'His plunder could go into the millions.'

'Oh and we caught a glimpse of him on the deck of the ferry,' said Newton.

'Who, La Senza? What did he look like this time?' asked Jameson.

'Well, he was a long way off,' said Newton searching hard for a comparison. 'But to be honest, he hardly looked like an Inquisitor – he looked more like a thirty-something bloke in a red cape.'

'Ah, well that will be the body he's taken you see.'

'So it's a possession then?'

'Oh for sure,' said Jameson. 'These creeps must have set him up with a body donor. Some hapless sap with health but no brains.'

'OK, so what now?' asked Newton.

'Well I guess we can take it from here Dr Barlow,' said Jameson. 'You've done well, but it's a purely tactical effort from here on. No need for you to get in the line of fire. Can you put Bennet on? I'll be handing the operation over to him now.'

Bennet took the phone.

'Yes Mr Jameson,' he said, with a professional air. 'Yes I see ... No, that's not a problem ... Yes ... I can assemble them in a few hours ... There may need to be a cover-up afterwards, so we'll need cleaners ... you will? Excellent. I'll do my best ... yes ... you can count on me, Mr Jameson.' He listened intently again, then ended the conversation and handed the iPhone back to Newton.

'So that's that then?'

'Yes Newton,' said the vicar, smiling. 'I must say though what an absolute delight it has been.'

'Likewise Rev,' said Newton. 'It's been a blast.'

'It most certainly has. Well ... there's a train station up the road. I'll need to get going if I'm to get back to my parish in time for the briefing.'

'Of course,' said Newton, 'I'll let you get on.' They shook hands and the Reverend Bennet left his colleague standing by the car.

Newton watched the unlikely tough guy walk away in the crisp winter sunlight before finally turning back to the phone. Scrolling through the missed phone calls and texts he opened the message from Gabby. A sinister coldness began creeping up Newton's legs.

There was a photo of an old glass cabinet with Viv to one side and an elderly man with thick spectacles on the other. Slap bang in the centre of the cabinet between them sat a grotesque carved box topped with the vile figure of a 15th-century Inquisitor, his clawed hands gnarled like angry talons.

'Hi dad, viv and I found your funny box thing! At museum in dorset ... c u soon, gabbs xx'

Horror engulfed Newton. The implications chased each other around his writhing guts like fighting cats.

'BENNNEEEETTTTTT!' he yelled. With the mother of all sinking feelings coursing through him, he ran after the departing vicar like a Jamaican sprinter.

CHAPTER 33

# THE GATHERING

'I'm coming with you,' said Newton, the tone of his voice declaring no room for argument. He was frantically texting, calling and emailing Gabby and Viv as he spoke. Uncharacteristically, neither was picking up. Gabby in particular was never, but never offline; it wasn't looking good.

'I'm not so sure,' said the Reverend Bennet, shaking his head. 'This is going to be a real slugfest Dr Barlow. You don't even know how to use a gun.'

'I'll learn.'

'Look, I understand your feelings, of course, but it's better to leave it to the professionals.'

'*Professionals*, are you sure? No offence Rev, but you're a part-time ninja vicar, not the SAS. That's my daughter and my girlfriend down there!'

'What do *you* propose then?'

'The police, the real SAS, MI5 ... I dunno.'

'And risk the secrets of Purgatory leaking out into the mortal realm? No Newton. Dare I say it, there are more important things at stake here even than our loved ones.'

'With all due respect 007, that's easy for you to say. Bloody hell, anything could be happening to them! And what's more, it's my stupid fault that they're there in the first place.' Newton gave himself a self-abusive smack on his furrowed brow. 'Oh I've been such an idiot!'

'Don't be so hard on yourself, Dr Barlow, you weren't to know this would happen.'

'Yes, but it *has* happened. I was sloppy with my cover story and I got them into trouble. Period. Say what you like ... I've got to be there or so help me God, I'll break the story to the press myself.' Bennet looked aghast at Newton's biblically reinforced threat.

'You wouldn't!'

'I bloody would,' said Newton, knowing full well that no one would believe him if he did. Still, it seemed to shake Bennet, which was the whole idea. The vicar was wavering.

'If you did come down to the, err, combat area, would you stay out of the way?' Bennet looked into Newton's darting eyes. 'No heroics, Dr Barlow.'

'I promise,' said Newton, knowing that on all balance of probability, he was lying. Bennet looked at his watch and pulled a face.

'Look ... I can't pretend I like it, but we're wasting valuable time. First we'll go to my church in your car, meet up with the assault squads and get tooled up before we head down to Dorset. But I mean it Dr Barlow – no heroics.'

Newton nodded and crossed his heart in a very poor genuflex. The vicar rolled his eyes. Newton shrugged with a sigh of resignation as Bennet climbed back into the Citroën. Once again the two of them were back on the road, tearing out of Newhaven towards Bennet's parish.

It took them a mere thirty minutes to reach the church in the sleepy old village of West Belvingdon. The Norman church dozed amongst gravestones and gnarled trees, while Tudor half-timbered houses crowded against the churchyard's walls. Newton screeched to a halt by the churchyard gates. Bennet leapt from the car and dashed frantically up to the door, Newton close behind.

'Wait here,' said Bennet. 'I need to get some keys.' Newton rang both Gabby and Viv's phones again. Both were still dead. His teeth grinding, Newton no longer feared the worst, he positively felt it, all the way from his toes to the tip of his quiff. As he dialled again, without success, Bennet bustled back out with a large bunch of keys and beckoned Newton into the frosty graveyard. 'Here!' said Bennet. 'You'd better prepare yourself for this, might be a bit of a shock. Again, Dr Barlow, I must urge you to remember that you're sworn to secrecy – if this little secret got out, well, it would take a lot of explaining. They stood at the door of a large family crypt. Bennet fitted an old key into the lock and with a heavy push, the door swung back.

'OK, Dr Barlow, this is it. Let's get organised.'

There was a distinct oily smell in the gloom. Bennet hit the lights, then they descended some clean and modern steps into a lower chamber. In time, the low-energy bulbs gradually started to light up the cramped space; Newton stopped in his tracks.

The vault was packed with racks of powerful modern weapons, cleaned and ready in purposeful, organised rows. There were sniper rifles with huge sights, grenade launchers, body armour, mortars and light machine guns. There were two-way radios, flare pistols and claymore mines.

'What the hell ...' gasped Newton, flabbergasted. 'Is this legal? There's more weaponry here than in the whole of Afghanistan. What is this place?'

'Oh this is just my little arsenal,' replied the vicar cheerfully. 'Have to put it somewhere.' Bennet lifted an assault rifle with a laser sight and grenade launcher. He loaded a clip and pulled back the charging handle. He switched on the built-in targeting laser and moved it from point to point around him like a seasoned pro.

'Do you mind,' said Newton, as the bright red dot settled between his eyebrows. 'Oh gosh, sorry,' said Bennet. 'Force of habit! Actually, this isn't that good to be honest. It's two years old. The new ones have a far greater lethal range, increased muzzle velocity and they're 200 grams lighter – makes for a really nice action.'

'Looks pretty lethal to me,' said Newton, idly picking up a grenade. 'Do you get air miles on any of this?'

'Please, Dr Barlow,' said Bennet, rushing forward and plucking the sinister egg from Newton's hand. 'I must ask you to refrain from playing with the weapons.' He placed the grenade carefully back in its holder. 'They're not toys. This is a strictly tactical effort now, and you must consider yourself a civilian amongst soldiers.'

'OK, if you say so,' said Newton. 'But shouldn't I at least have a small hand gun, you know, for my own self-defence? How about that one there?'

'The Beretta Tomcat? Are you sure? A very popular gun with the fairer sex, that one. Hardly an assault weapon, but you'll probably be safer with that than something meatier. Here, let me show you the basics.' Bennet popped the small pistol open, loaded it and then pointed sternly to the small button on the side. 'That's the safety catch, Dr Barlow. Please keep it on unless you really mean to use it. Don't want you winging any friendlies.'

'OK, understood,' said Newton, placing the small gun inside his jacket pocket. He looked anxiously at his watch.

'Worried about the backup? Please don't, Newton, they'll be here. I've worked with these people before. They're the best we have. If anyone can sort out La Senza and his little minions, it will be this lot. Come on, let's go topside and see if they've arrived.'

They climbed back up into the cold bright air. On the road beside the dry-stone wall, an old minibus was pulling to a halt. On its side, Gothic letters proclaimed: 'Parish of St Vincent on the Marrow, Church of England'.

'Excellent!' said Bennet, slinging the rifle over his shoulder by its strap and switching on his field radio. 'The St Vincent's are absolutely first-rate. All dead-eye shots and exceptionally cool under fire.' Newton looked at the newcomers with a mixture of disbelief and horror. This 'first-rate' squad was nothing but a mix of paunchy vergers, overgrown choirboys and a woman who Newton was guessing did the flowers. 'Oh don't go by how they look, Dr Barlow,' said Bennet, noticing Newton's disbelieving expression. 'These people are fully combat-hardened. Trust me. They're as hard as bloody nails.' Newton noticed that one of the hard-as-nails squad seemed to be nursing sciatica in his lower back.

'I hope you're right Reverend, because these people may be the only way I'll see my daughter again.'

'Oh look,' said Bennet excitedly, 'it's the Catholics!' A new van stopped and disgorged another squad of unlikelies. 'Sacred Heart School, St Malden on the Weave', said the sedate typography. The priest in charge walked briskly up to Bennet and clipped his worn brogues together with a mild click.

'Well hello there, Reverend Bennet. It's been a while now!'

'Hello Father Finnigan,' said Bennet, shaking his hand warmly. 'It certainly has. Haven't seen you since that business up in Lymeswold!'

'So it was, Reverend, so it was. That was a fine old scrap, was it not?'

'It certainly was,' said Bennet, smiling at the memory. 'Please, Father, let me introduce Dr Newton Barlow.'

'Hello doctor,' said Father Finnigan. 'Are you not the atheist fella from the telly?'

'Yes ... er ... sorry,' said Newton sheepishly.

'Ah don't you worry now,' said Father Finnigan. 'This is hardly the place for a whole load of theological argy bargy. This is a time for action. Reverend Bennet, are the old Sikhs and Muslims here yet? We'll be needing all the firepower we can get on this one, so we will.' Bennet looked over to see two more vans rolling up to the church wall.

'That's them now,' said Bennet, checking his watch. 'All we need is the militant agnostics and we'll be ready to roll.'

'I'm sorry? How, er, why ...' said Newton, for whom the situation was fast becoming ridiculous and not a bit comforting. 'No forget it,' he said, changing his mind. 'I'm all bemused out.'

'Sorry, Dr Barlow,' said Bennet. 'I'm afraid this must all seem quite bizarre to you. Understandably so. But it is all rather typical for us I'm afraid. All faiths and no faiths are in on this one. La Senza is simply too ghastly to be allowed to continue his little enterprise. So we've had to call in all the battalions.' Bennet called over to his late arrivals. 'Hello Mullah Arani, Narinder. Help yourselves to some weapons. Radio frequencies set to two please. It's likely to be a night assault so dress dark and warm please. If you need to fill a thermos, please feel free to use the vicarage kitchen.'

Greeting each other warmly, the various faiths and denominations bustled away into the depths of the vault. Newton's gaze drifted onto an old lady cleaning away dead flowers not more than fifty yards away from the crypt, seemingly oblivious to the bizarre goings on. He debated with himself for a second whether he should tell Bennet that an outsider could see them. However, the woman knowingly answered his gaze and winked; opening her warm winter coat, she patted what looked like a magnum. Newton, incredulous, smiled back.

The squads were all pouring back up into the graveyard, tooled up and looking slightly more sinister now they were adorned in their combat vestments. Even so, it was a bloody long way from *Who Dares Wins*.

'Dearly beloved,' said Bennet, 'listen up.' Everyone gathered around him. One of the Catholics took out his hearing aid and turned up the volume. 'Now chaps, this is a tricky op from the get-go. You've been told what we're up against, so you'll know that we will need to be on our toes. Stay alert! We've got boots on the ground, and after they've done a proper recce of the target, I'll be able to draw up a proper plan of attack. Time now is ...' He looked at his cheap watch and they all followed suit, one with a fob chain. 'Thirteen hundred hours. Set your watches. Be advised we have friendlies in the target area, so go easy with the spray and pray stuff. Oh, and I don't need to tell you that God is on our side.' There was a murmur of agreement. 'We'll be setting off in a moment. If we get separated on the way down, just head straight for the village of Langton Hadlow – Finnigan here will show it to you on the roadmap. We'll rendezvous there. OK,' said Bennet. 'Good luck and good hunting!'

Everyone filed away to their minibuses. As Newton watched them, every bone in his logical body told him to phone the police, the army or even the Automobile Association, anyone other than this bizarre assault force.

'You really believe in these people, don't you Reverend?' he said doubtfully.

'Yes, Newton, I do. Don't worry. We'll find your girls.'

'I hope so,' said Newton, 'I really hope so.'

\*\*\*\*\*\*

It took the multi-faith convoy the best part of three hours to reach Langton Hadlow. The sun was starting to dip behind the surrounding hills, and it leant a deep orange to the bracken of the heaths extending west towards Juggin's Lump.

The minibuses pulled up to the war memorial and the squads piled out around the old tank. Frantic, Newton positively flew from the wreck of the Citroën and located the museum. The old door stood open. It was eerily quiet inside, and calling to his daughter and his girlfriend, Newton ran from room to room, but found nobody. But he found the case he had seen in Gabby's photo. It stood shattered and empty, and sickeningly, his daughter's mobile phone lay broken and dead upon the floor beneath it.

Newton realised that no matter how bad he had felt during his fall from grace, he had never felt as bad as this. Fear, dread and guilt gnawed and spiralled around his innards, bringing forth a first-class nausea that threatened to bring up the breakfast and dinner he hadn't eaten.

'I'm sorry, Dr Barlow,' said the Reverend Bennet, placing his hand on Newton's bowed shoulder. 'I'm really sorry.'

'The McCauleys have taken them, haven't they.'

'Yes, I'm sorry, I'm afraid they have. A couple of mechanics working on the tank saw them bundled into a Land Rover. Ascot McCauley and the Cardinal took them, by the sounds of it. Terrible bad luck.'

'It's not bad luck, though, is it Reverend?' said Newton, looking sadly at the shattered screen of Gabby's phone. 'It's my own bloody fault for leaving that damn silly picture out.' Father Finnigan came into the room, his assault rifle slung over his shoulder and a black vest over his thick jumper liberally stuffed with ammunition.

'Dr Barlow, Reverend Bennet, sorry to interrupt – it's just that the Baptists are back from the recce. You'll be wanting to hear their report, will you not?'

'Yes. Thank you Father Finnigan,' said Bennet. He turned back to Newton, whose eyes were staring out unfocused. 'Come Newton, the best thing for you now is action – let's get on with the operation, it will take your mind off things.' Gently, he ushered the bereft Newton Barlow back out of the museum. The assault team, fully armed and, at a push, dangerous, was gathering in the fading light.

The Baptists, swathed in shrubs and greasepaint, ushered Bennet and Finnigan over to an old pub table where they had spread a map.

'OK, here's a basic outline of the target buildings,' said their leader, his features hard to discern beneath his hand-knitted balaclava with appliqué foliage. 'There are two buildings, both surrounded by a high wall. It's a serious affair, a fifteen-footer, topped with a nasty range of sharp and pointy things. We'll need to rustle up some ladders if we are going to get over it.'

'Gates?' asked a heavily armed Sikh, as he applied boot polish to his cheeks.

'Only two that we could see. Both impossible to breach quietly, I'm afraid, and both are covered with machine guns. Our only option is to go over or through the perimeter wall.'

'Tricky,' said Bennet. 'Any *good* news?'

'Well there are a couple of tall trees outside the complex, so we can at least look down into the grounds.'

'Well that's something,' said Bennet. 'Pushpindar, Mullah Arani, Father Finnigan, can you have your best marksmen up in the trees to give us covering fire and keep us aware of any movements amongst the goons inside.'

'Right you are Reverend,' said Father Finnigan, nodding to his best men. 'Now then, did you fellas by any chance get an idea of just how many of these bad guys we're talking about?' The recce chief consulted his notes.

'We counted seven armed men patrolling the area behind the walls with an unconfirmed number inside the buildings. Could be as many as thirty.'

'Well, we'll have these recce boys here draw up a map for your squad leaders,' said Bennet. 'I'll issue you with complete tactical orders in the next hour or so. All we can do now is wait for the rest of the squads to arrive. I imagine we'll go in around midnight.'

'Midnight!' gasped Newton, incredulous. 'But but ... but it's only six now! We have to go in immediately – they've got my daughter and my girlfriend!'

'Now now, Dr Barlow, please!' said Bennet. 'We simply don't have the numbers yet. There are only thirty of us here. They'll pick us off like bargains at a jumble sale. We have to wait for back-up!'

'But ... but ...' protested Newton.

'Seriously Dr Barlow, I know it feels wrong, but he's right,' said Father Finnigan. 'If we go in half-cock, these fellas up at the Grange there will eat us for breakfast, lunch and dinner. We need the numbers.'

'Oh for God's sake,' snapped Newton in a rage of frustration and fatigue. 'I don't believe this!' He flounced away from the circle of warrior priests with his hands on his head like a footballer after a failed penalty, his troubled mind whirring away like a hacked electricity meter. Father Finnigan moved to calm him.

'No. Leave him be Father,' the Reverend Bennet said quietly. 'He's tired and emotional. We'll just have to try and do our best to help these unfortunate women for him. Now ... where was I ...' Bennet carried on with his eve-of-battle sermon while Newton, worn out, cold, damp and horribly worried about his loved ones, sat down heavily on upon the bonnet of the DS and dropped his head into his hands.

'Well, that's it for now,' Bennet said to his troops. 'Get some shut-eye, check your weapons and ammo. Make sure your walky-talkies are charged and set to the right frequencies. I'll get the verger here to see if he can rustle us up some sandwiches.'

'Excuse me Reverend,' said Father Finnigan, looking away from the group towards the departing blue and white rear of a classic 1974 Citroën DS. 'But where do you think Dr Barlow is going?'

\*\*\*\*\*\*

Newton wasn't thinking that logically any more. His swirling thoughts contained ghastly possibilities, things he didn't want to even start entertaining. With his foot hard down on the accelerator, he charged away from Langton Hadlow leaving Bennet's assault team staring after him.

'Newton! Stop!' said Sixsmith urgently from the back seat.

'Can it, Alex,' said Newton sternly.

'Newton, please. You have to do what they say. You can't do this alone.'

'Just watch me,' said Newton ignoring the vision.

Four heartbeats later he caught his first sight of Hadlow Grange. Dark and ominous in the fading crimson light, it stood clear of the surrounding gorse and heather in a sharp silhouette of Gothic architecture and gnarled trees.

'Please Newton, I beg you to reconsider.'

'Sorry Alex. I have to do this,' said Newton. He slammed to a halt facing the wicked metal gates, his heart pounding in his rib cage. Ignoring Alex's remonstrations from behind him, Newton eased himself from the battered old car and, indifferent to the brambles clawing at his fingers, pressed the buzzer.

The static crackle of the ancient intercom popped and fizzled then settled down to an awkward prolonged silence.

'Can I help you?' came the nasal answer. Newton swallowed hard as he leant in towards the microphone. There was no going back now.

'My name ... is Dr Newton Barlow. I've come to get my daughter and my girlfriend.'

There was another heavy, crackling pause before Ascot McCauley spoke again.

'You'd better come in.'

## CHAPTER 34

# MACHINE

The forbidding road into Hadlow Grange was lit only by Newton's solitary remaining headlamp. As he crunched fearfully along the gravel driveway, the beam caught Van Loop's mercenaries cradling their automatics and as he passed, they filed in behind him, their guns at the ready. Inexorably, he approached the offices of McCauley Bros, property developers, until finally, his headlamp lit Ascot McCauley standing arrogantly, his arms folded before him. Newton fought with a burning temptation to just run him over. Reluctantly, he stopped the car and stepped out onto the gravel.

'So Dr Barlow, we meet again.'

'I'm sure you don't need me to tell you that's an awful cliché,' said Newton, raising his hands as two thugs began a somewhat theatrical show of frisking him. 'The gun you're looking for is in my inside jacket pocket,' he said. One of the gunmen looked him malignantly in the eye and pulled out the pistol. 'I'm just trying to be helpful,' quipped Newton, now armed only with his sarcasm.

'That's a pretty little gun,' said Ascot. 'Didn't I see one like that on *Desperate Housewives?*'

'I had you down as more of a *Cash in the Attic* kind of guy.'

'Very good, Dr Barlow, very funny. You should be on TV,' said Ascot, as the hired muscle brought Newton forward. 'Oh I forgot, you were once, weren't you! How very tactless of me.'

'It's OK,' said Newton. 'I forgive you.'

'Right then gentlemen, I'm sure our guest is only too aware that he'll pay dearly and quickly for any foolishness. You can let him go.' The big meaty fists released their grip. Newton made a point of re-arranging his clothing, a somewhat cheap attempt at nonchalance despite the fact he was actually bricking himself. Arms behind his back, Ascot turned towards the house. 'Dr Barlow, if you please.' Obligingly, Newton followed Ascot into the Grange. The goons followed three steps behind, trigger fingers twitching.

'So, you feel comfortable about helping this nut La Senza, do you?' said Newton, as they turned down one of the oak-

338

panelled corridors.

'Comfortable? Business isn't about being comfortable, Dr Barlow. We are not cocooned academics. This is the real world. For us it is merely a business proposition. We scratch the Cardinal's back and he will scratch ours.'

'And how exactly is he going to scratch yours?'

'Oh it's simple enough,' Ascot continued. 'You see, the Cardinal is a very angry man. Absolutely livid. He isn't at all pleased about what they did to him, and like all angry little men, he wants revenge.'

'On the Church?'

'On just about everything, as far as I can tell, but yes, mostly on the Church.'

'So how does that benefit you? Do you hate the Church as well?'

'Oh on the contrary, Dr Barlow – I love the very ground it stands upon.' Ascot suddenly turned to face Newton and the thugs. Stopping in their tracks, they all piled up like cars on a motorway. Behind him, Newton felt the gun barrels nudge into the small of his back. Impassioned, Ascot's eyes widened. 'Do you have any idea just how much property the Church owns in this country, Dr Barlow?'

'I'm guessing I'm about to find out,' said Newton.

'It's worth about eight billion pounds. Let me say that again. It feels so nice when I say it aloud. Eight billion.' Ascot closed his eyes to savour the figures. 'Oh yes ... take St Paul's Cathedral. It alone stands on land worth some £84 million, a truly prime development site!'

'You want to develop St Paul's Cathedral ... *seriously?*'

'Of course!' said Ascot. 'What is it now? An empty shrine to some worthless, meaningless God – we would make it live and breathe!'

'How?'

'Offices, shops ... some upmarket restaurants. And it's not just St Paul's, think about it. All the minsters, parish churches and abbeys. There are some 50,000 churches in these islands. All empty, dead and useless! I haven't even started to add up all the synagogues, mosques and temples. Even the scientologists have a few dozen places we could scoop up. And that's just the buildings. There's also all the wonga in the offshore accounts and tax havens. But, one step at a time, we'll start with the churches.'

'Well,' said Newton calmly, 'that's nice, isn't it? All those beautiful buildings ... have you no soul, Ascot?'

'Why should you care? You're the big-mouthed atheist, not me. I'm not interested in anything but business. Business is pure, honest and clean, unsullied by superstition, and unpolluted by stark reason and moral considerations.'

'In what way is it honest?'

'Because Dr Barlow, it doesn't hide how cruel it is. And what do people like you have to show for your integrity, eh? The moral high ground?'

'Sure, but you know the problem with the moral high ground, don't you?'

'And what would that be?'

'The view is terrible.'

'I am immune to your smug criticisms Barlow, just as I am immune to your limp do-goodery. Nothing matters to us but our own material improvement and the removal of those who block it.'

'What a lovely sentiment. Remind me never to get trapped in a lifeboat with you,' said Newton. 'However, I'd feel somewhat remiss if I didn't point out that you're making a laughable mistake.'

'And what that would be?'

'You're trusting La Senza, one of the most evil, self-serving monsters ever to have walked the earth. A man who's trustworthiness can be measured in microns. He'd stab *himself* in the back if his arms were long enough. What on earth makes you think he'll keep his side of the bargain?'

'We know we can trust him,' said Ascot. He was keen to look like he meant it, but his Adam's apple went up and down like a blob lamp. Newton twigged that he had a knife worth twisting.

'Ha! You can't trust him at all, can you McCauley? Did you bother to do any research on La Senza by any chance?' continued Newton. Ascot hesitated. 'You didn't, did you – oh priceless! This is a man who would destroy his own family, his own supporters, innocents. He'll do you the first chance he gets. You scratch his back Ascot, and he'll use yours to make a lampshade.'

'We've thought of that!' protested Ascot angrily. 'He needs us. Without us he'd be doomed. Tied up forever in this Purgatory place they all keep banging on about. Your righteous friends would be all over him like chicken pox unless we were here and he knows it. Who do you think has paid for all this?' Ascot waved his needly finger around like a wand.

'Didn't the Cardinal's fan club chip in?'

'What the La Senza sect? Oh sure, they donated some funds ... but it was McCauley Brothers who put up the serious capital. We know a good venture when we see it. Anyway, that's not the point,' said Ascot, trying to reassure himself. 'La Senza *can't* do anything untoward. We've insured against that.'

'Really? And how have you done that then?'

'We've er ... got a contract.' Ascot's Adam's apple convulsed again.

'Ha!' said Newton. 'Well if you've got a *contract*, that's alright then!'

'Oh you can laugh all you like Dr Barlow,' said Ascot furiously. He turned on his heels and the party began once again to walk down the corridor. 'But, I should be careful just how much you laugh in a moment, because you will be meeting the Cardinal in person. Trust me, the only jokes he laughs at are his own.'

'Yeah whatever,' said Newton. 'Just take me to my kid and my girlfriend.'

'Your daughter ... yes ...' said Ascot through gritted teeth. 'A spirited child.'

'I like to think so.'

'Perhaps if you had been a better parent, she'd have been less inclined to bite.' Ascot held up his hand. A new bandage was wrapped around his thumb, a spot of red forcing its way through the gauze.

'Oh good girl!'

'That is not how children should behave, Dr Barlow. Our father would never have tolerated such a thing, never! And as for your lady friend,' Ascot hissed, 'she called me an arsepipe!' Despite the seriousness of the situation, Newton smirked.

They exited the rear of the Grange and Newton found himself face to face with the asylum. It reared up before him like a Victorian prison, its horrible detail thrown into stark relief by several powerful lamps. The big truck sat outside, empty.

'What a charming little spot,' said Newton. 'Does it still have all its original features?'

'The family bought it ten years ago,' said Ascot. 'It was a home for the mentally disturbed.'

'No changes there then,' said Newton, and Ascot threw him another withering glance.

'It suits our requirements admirably. It is large, remote and self-sufficient, and it has its own vegetable garden and generators. We can operate without any outside interference.'

'OK so you can grow your own potatoes. Doesn't stop it being a monstrosity.'

'Actually, McCauley Brothers have always specialised in the more unusual locations. Places that the squeamish, the sensitive and the thoughtful frankly wouldn't touch. More fool them. I don't expect you to understand.'

'I don't,' said Newton. 'You just sound a tad mad to my untrained ears as it happens.'

Ascot opened a small side door and they entered the asylum. The atmosphere was clammy and deeply unhappy. Newton kept his eyes upon Ascot's pin-striped back until finally they were in the atrium.

And there was the machine.

Its most shocking feature was the devil-like carved face, its mouth agape to portray the very mouth of hell itself. From its bloated blood-red jaws sprouted wicked, rapier-thin teeth in several cruel batteries, each as sharp and long as cavalry sabres. Above the gaping maw, two sets of evil eyes stared malevolently out at Newton, and as he was marched across the hallway he could feel its ghastly gaze following him. Lolling from its hideous lips there ran a primitive conveyer belt, looking for all the world like a horrendous tongue. The metal and leather belt was studded liberally by foul hooks and prongs, and spun around a series of old wooden wheels and rusted metal cogs like a caterpillar track.

Behind the monster's head, reptilian scales and bat wing flaps gave way gradually to a cathedral-like structure complete with flying buttresses and stained-glass windows. The coloured glass portrayed a chilling series of tableaus – there were scenes of awful suffering and eternal damnation, often both at the same time. It was a triumph of medieval flat-packing, constructed for expansion after transport; some of Van Loop's men were busy extending out towers or slotting mechanical elements onto the outside, increasing its dimensions even as Newton watched. There were gargoyles and bellows, wicked Gothic chimneys, wheels and pulleys. But its archaic lack of sophistication also gave it the air of an illustration by Heath Robinson. The hideous machine was now telescoping out, extending until it stretched on its huge wagon wheels all the way down the centre of the long atrium to a length of some 20 metres. All the while, Van Loop's technicians were measuring and photographing the exterior of the unique contraption as if it were a saucer at Roswell.

'So this is your little baby, is it?' said Newton.

'Not mine, Dr Barlow,' said Ascot, stopping by the monster's head. 'This is La Senza's device, and so it shall remain. We are not interested in the how and why of the plan, only the final accounting.' Newton walked up to the vast mouth and lay his hand upon the theatrical carving, expecting to feel something, anything, of the people that it had so utterly consumed. There was nothing.

Newton shuddered. No connections, no residue, no spirits. It had erased them like a dead hard drive and powdered them into packet soup.

'Dad!' Gabby shouted to Newton from the top of the stairs and he looked up to see his daughter, Viv and the old man in the photo Gabby had sent from the museum. They were restrained by the heavies but otherwise seemed intact.

'Gabby! Sweetheart!'

'Sorry, Newton! I'm so sorry,' shouted Viv. 'I had no idea.'

'Silence!' said Van Loop senior from their side. He looked down to Newton, sneering. 'Dr Barlow, you are very foolish coming here alone.'

'Frankly, I'd say I was foolish coming here at all,' said Newton. 'And who the bloody hell are you?'

'My name is Raymond Van Loop. I am a direct descendent of Ceferino de Lupero, my illustrious ancestor who loyally served the great Inquisitor back in the day.' Van Loop gestured to his men to take the hostages down the staircase and Newton, desperate to be reunited with his loved ones, instinctively moved towards them until a goon slammed the butt of his weapon viciously into the back of his knees; he buckled, wincing, to the floor.

'Newton!' yelled Viv.

'I'm OK love, it's OK,' said Newton, struggling back to his feet.

'Very touching,' said Van Loop. 'Now ... as I was saying, my family was entrusted by the great Cardinal to maintain his relics on earth, to wait until such time as we could safely re-activate them. There were five relics – each a finger from the hand of the great one himself. My forebears, with great care I might say, hid them all around Europe. So there were five chances to bring back our beloved Inquisitor. Five. In time, of course, there were problems. Some were lost to us, scattered by wars, misfortune and fate. But we retrieved those we could and for centuries, we waited.'

'What took him so long to come back? And why now?' asked Newton.

'The key, Dr Barlow, was the book.'

'What book?'

'The necromancer's handbook, of course.'

'Really? Is there such a thing?'

'Yes doctor, there is. We thought it had been utterly lost. It contained all that our Cardinal, praise be his glorious name, needed to produce this incredible machine that you see before you today.'

'But you lost it?'

'Yes ... regrettably we did. When the Cardinal was murdered by those primitive subhumans in Sierra de Luna, betrayed by the Church he hoped to serve and then totally dominate, well, the book vanished. One of our men, a gutless coward, had ridden away with it upon his person. My forebear searched for it for the rest of his life, but to no avail. It was gone. Without it, we were unable to retrieve La Senza's spirit and bring him back to us.'

'And then you found it?'

'No, not us, our colleagues here, the McCauleys, they found it at an auction.'

'I only paid two hundred pounds for it,' said Ascot, smugly.

'A snip!' said Newton.

'Oh it is not to be valued by its mere financial worth, Dr Barlow,' said Van Loop. 'The book is a key, a cipher. It enables one to talk with the dead, almost as if it were a telephone.'

'So Ascot,' said Newton. 'You made contact with the old bastard, did you?'

Newton was smashed down again and he winced hard as the pain shot through him.

'Show respect!' said Gunter from behind him, his gun held high for a second impact.

'To answer your question, Barlow,' said Ascot. 'Yes – we had a lovely little chat.'

'It must have been nice to hear a voice that wasn't in your head for a change,' said Newton.

'It was most informative. The Cardinal made us an offer, told us all about how the afterlife worked. Then, to get things moving, he helped us to link up with Mr Van Loop here.'

'And you all lived happily ever after?'

'Well we shall see about that,' said Van Loop. 'It is the Cardinal who will ultimately decide what will happen. It is to him that we look. Glory be his name.'

'So when do I get to meet this infamous Inquisitor?' asked Newton. 'I'd love to know what all the fuss is about.'

'Well, you're in luck then, Dr Barlow,' said Van Loop, as a door opened upstairs. 'For now ... he comes!' Right on cue, there was a swish of cheap fabric at the top of the great staircase. La Senza and Sister Wendy were strutting down like pantomime royalty. Epsom and Plumpton followed wearily, with trays piled high with snacks and drinks.

Despite the fact that he'd inherited a toned young body, La Senza's newfound passion for junk food was already beginning to tell; he was starting to display a paunch beneath his cheap party robes. The scene was made all the more tawdry by the po-faced respect the gathered acolytes around La Senza were displaying, bowing and scraping in a ripple as he passed. Van Loop senior caught Newton grinning; shaking his head, he nodded to his son and Newton once again winced at a blow from a gun butt.

'Oi stop that!' said Newton. 'You might break something.'

'Hail great La Senza!' said Van Loop. 'Cardinal, we have him, the agent of the council! The one who has dogged us all the way from Spain.' La Senza reached the bottom step and turned his gaze upon Newton.

'Kneel before the Cardinal!' said Gunter and he thrust Newton back down onto his knees.

'Ah ... how nice,' hissed the Inquisitor. 'Welcome Purgatorial scum, what is your name?'

'My name is Dr Newton Barlow.'

'A physician?' asked La Senza. 'Do you know anything about teeth?'

'No ... I'm a doctor of physics. If you want to get your teeth done, go to a dentist.'

'Physics? I have heard of that. Is that not the guild who can make fireworks that destroy whole cities?' La Senza's eyes widened at the idea. 'I have seen this on the tele-vision device upstairs. Make one for me!'

'A nuke or a tele-vision?' asked Newton.

'The big explosion thing,' said La Senza. 'I've already got a tele-vision.'

'Not a chance,' said Newton without hesitation. 'Even if I was willing, which of course, being of sane mind, I'm not, I wouldn't know where to start. I'm purely theoretical.'

'You look and sound a bit like a wizard to me,' said La Senza walking closer. He gazed into Newton's eyes. 'So, I understand you work for my mortal enemies up there in that other place.'

'Yes, I do,' said Newton. 'However, I'm here in a private capacity. I'd like you to let my daughter and my girlfriend go.' La Senza turned and looked to the two women. They stood nervous and small amongst Van Loop's gunmen. The frail old curator looked even smaller.

'Oh ... I see. It's a love thing, is it?'

'I would say so, yes. They've got nothing to do with this. Let them go.'

'Ah, but they were somewhat interested in the fifth box, were they not?'

'Come on. They didn't know what it was – I was the one looking for it.'

'Ah but that's just it, now they know all about me. And whilst I love the attention Dr Newton Barlow, I'm afraid a line has been crossed. The damage has been done.'

'Keep me and let them go.'

'Haha, very noble and selfless, but no, you're all staying. The more the merrier!' said La Senza, walking over to his machine and running his hands across its vile carvings as if it were a racehorse. 'You see, now that my beautiful machine is here, ready to be tested, well ... I will be needing subjects. Guinea pigs, if you will. Small piggies first of course.'

'You bloody wouldn't!' said Newton.

'Oh yes of course I would,' said La Senza. 'I am evil, you see. Everybody says so.'

'So I gather. Is that so important to you – the bad-boy image? I mean, you could just be ... *nice*.'

'Nice? NICE?!' La Senza looked at Newton again as if he were forty

346

miles beyond mad. 'Is that what you and your friends in Purgatory would prefer? For me to be ... nice?'

'Yeah, why not? Give it a try, you might like it.'

'I very much doubt I would,' continued the Cardinal, strutting away with his hands on his hips. 'I'd much rather be evil. Nice is for cowards, the scared and the weak. I am none of these things.'

'What are you then?' La Senza whirled back in response and leant forward at Newton, his tacky red silk glove ending in an aggressive pointing finger topped with an ostentatious ring.

'I am strong. I am very strong. I am charismatic, I am a leader. I have no pity, no remorse, no empathy. I am evil!'

'Oh very diabolic,' said Newton. 'Have you had too much coffee?'

'Ha! How do you think anything happens in this lousy, pathetic world? Do good things *really* come to those who wait? Eh? Of course not. They come to those who take.' He made an ostentatious grabbing motion with his gloved hand. 'No, my friend, the only thing the meek will inherit is more weakness. It is only the strong who will thrive.'

'And you don't have a problem with what that attitude will mean for other people?'

'Why would I? If you show pity, remorse or sympathy to the weak then they merely infect you with their weakness. Empathy, Dr Barlow, is a disease to which I am immune.'

'Hold on hard case, didn't you need other people to rescue you? Didn't they spring you from your little hole in Purgatory? I'd say that makes you a tad needy yourself.'

'No! I was betrayed!' screamed La Senza. 'Those weaklings in the Inquisition, they turned on me. They didn't have the first clue about terror, repression and horror. They needed someone really nasty to show them how it was meant to be done. Well *I* did that ... me! I was the greatest Inquisitor of them all. More sadistic than Torquemada, nastier and more petty than Mendoza!'

'So what went wrong?' said Newton. La Senza was strutting feverishly about, his cheap robes building up a crackling static.

'They got scared ... they allowed base fear and pity to infect the purity of what could have been a really fun Inquisition. *They* wanted to limit things to the Jews and the Muslims ... not me, I wanted to root out the Christians as well!'

'But you *are* a Christian. I know it's easy to overlook, but you are actually dressed as a Roman Catholic Cardinal.'

'Hahaha ... you mistake me for a believer! Oh how naive. You don't think I believe in God do you?' La Senza cackled out another wearisome villain's laugh; Van Loop and his toady supporters joined in until the Cardinal's gloved hand bade them stop. 'Even if this ... *God* person ... should exist, well, then I would merely consider him competition. A *nuisance*.'

'Delusions of grandeur aside,' said Newton, 'what's it all about though, this private Inquisition of yours – seriously, what's the point?'

'Point? Do I need a point? No! But if I must indulge your foolish curiosity ... I shall sum it up thus: fun!'

'Fun ... *fun*? That's it?'

'Certainly. You have fun don't you?'

'Yes, sure, but usually it involves a good movie and a bottle of Chilean Merlot, not torture, death and revenge.'

'Takes all sorts, I suppose,' La Senza mused almost thoughtfully. 'Well for me, fun is seeing people burning to death, begging for their lives in the torment of horror ... oh and reality tele-vision.'

'Wow, you really are a sick puppy!'

'I like to think so. Anyway, you Purgatorial idiot,' continued the Inquisitor. 'Who are you to decide what is sick and what is healthy? Why can't I have what I want? I am merely following my heart's desire like everyone else. In this case, it just so happens that my heart is as black and cold as frozen coal. I'm just being honest. Besides, your friends up there in that ludicrous council ... how dreadfully boring you all are. Is that what you'd prefer?'

'Do I look bored to you?'

'Oh don't worry, Dr Barlow, I'll soon make sure you aren't bored at all!' La Senza laughed and walked back to his machine. 'Do you have any idea what this machine can actually do?'

'I've read the reports.'

'*Reports*? Oh I'm quite sure they don't do it nearly enough justice. This machine is a triumph, a work of twisted genius. Here, let me give you a guided tour,' said La Senza. 'Let's start at this end.'

'The head?'

'Yes, excellent, let's call it the head. You will see that it is fashioned into the very mouth of hell. Nice touch I'm sure you'll agree. Now then, the conveyor here with its hooks and barbs drags the subject along towards the jaws. Once the poor darlings are caught on the hooks there can be no escape and struggling will only make them become fastened more firmly. Clever, eh? That was my idea.'

'It's very important to express your creative side.'

'It's a gift frankly,' said La Senza smugly, too vain to realise he was being mocked. 'Now, once within range of the teeth, the trap is closed, and at that point the real fun can start. I can't pretend to know everything about the design – I'm not very technical myself, I'm more of a hands-on-throat kind of guy, but I can tell you that once you enter this second area then you will receive your first injuries,' he added, proudly. 'There are batteries of knives and crushers. They're calibrated to revolve at just enough speed to really hurt you, but – and this is the clever bit – they won't actually kill you! After all, if you're going to go to the trouble of mechanising death and destruction, then why do it quickly?'

'So death comes later?'

'Oh yes, a lot later – there are acids and fires and all sorts of slicey fun still to come. But anyway, you'll see all that for yourself. I don't want to spoil the ending.'

'Did you think all that up on your own?'

'No ... I have to confess that I had some help. The concept was mine, though. You know, the whole preparation process.'

'Preparations for what, dare I ask?'

'For the death of the soul, of course,' said La Senza. 'If it was just about torture and death, Dr Barlow, then this would be a very, very expensive way to do it. No, the whole point of this little machine of mine is that it destroys both the soul and the flesh in one single, terrible process. I'll be giving you a demonstration shortly.'

'What's it like on a delicate wash?' asked Newton. 'Only I've got a pure wool jumper on.'

'Amusing ... however, the point is that once you enter the mouth of hell, then there is nothing, but nothing, that can emerge from the other end apart from dust. No soul to join your loved ones in heaven or hell – just dead, dead dust.'

'Nice!' said Newton. 'Have you thought about going on *Scrapheap Challenge*?'

'Haha ... I like it! I wager you have more spine than all these ghastly sycophants crowded around me combined.' He gestured to Van Loop and the McCauleys, all of whom looked somewhat insulted but were too scared to say so. 'It will be a shame to have to wipe you from the record, you entertain me. However, let's be realistic, if I let you live then you'll just mess up my little plan. Work must always come first.'

'Yes, I was going to ask you about the plan. Every super-villain has a monstrous scheme, don't they? Since I'm going to be killed soon anyway, you may as well tell me yours.'

'Yes ... yes, I see that, I may as well, I can't see how it can do any harm. Actually, it'll give me pleasure to describe it to fresh ears. It's such a good plan, you'll simply love it.'

'Try me.'

'Well, as you will probably know, those pious little souls in Purgatory are kept in their vivid state by the very relics that you and your chums go to so much trouble to keep safe and sound,' he said, looking closely at Newton to discern whether he already knew that. It was clear that they both understood the process only too well. 'That's right, Dr Barlow, I know all about them. The little relics that are hidden here, hidden there – well, I'm going to round them all up. Every shin bone, every trinket, every painting, every single object and their attendant spiritual connections. And, when I have them all, well, then they will enter the device.'

'OK, so what? You can get a few, maybe, but they'll stop you. These things are very, very well hidden. One nutcase with his little toy can't stop the good guys in Purgatory.'

'One?' said La Senza. 'You don't think I'll be happy with just one of these, do you? Even now, I have technicians upstairs drawing up plans for thousands of these things. Modern technology combined with the knowledge of the ancients – we'll have an army of machines, hoovering up the souls of the good and gracious until there is no one left to stop me. Not a one!'

'OK, so you wipe out all the nice folk – then what.'

'I was just getting to that,' said La Senza petulantly. 'Many of the most truly evil people – and I proudly count myself amongst them – are still trapped up there. Oh what a dreadful waste! All the twisted, the cruel and the heartless, waiting, just as I waited. Well, with the forces of good obliterated, I will liberate them. I'll make these dark souls the leaders of nations and armies. Every economist, mover and shaker will be one of my own kind. Imagine it – Saddam, Beriya, Himmler, Heinrich, Ivan the Terrible ... a veritable *Who's Who* of evil, running everything there is to be run. All the rapists, the murderers and the psychotics, directing traffic, running hospitals and organising prime-time programming schedules.'

'Are you sure they aren't already?' asked Newton.

La Senza paused and narrowed his eyes. 'Maybe ... I'm not sure, I'll have to check,' he said, making a note to self. 'But I'm sure you can see the potential, Dr Barlow – a world run *by* the evil *for* the evil. There will be nothing to prevent me bringing my unique style of Inquisition to the earth once again. Oh what fun we'll have! We'll burn and we'll brand, we'll starve and we'll hang – there will be no end to the suffering!'

'Impressive,' said Newton.

'Yes, well I did have a lot of time to think it through.'

'Too much,' said Newton glibly. 'Tell me this, Cardinal, I'm curious – what would your father have made of all this?'

'My father? What has he got to do with this?'

'Well, as I understand it, he wasn't that keen on you. I'm told you came a poor third to your two brothers. He dumped you on the Church while they got to see the world. Must have really stung.'

'What?! Such impudence! Why, I could kill you now.'

'You could, but wouldn't that only make you look a bit ... *over-sensitive?*'

'Over-sensitive? What do you mean? I don't ever have such feelings!'

'Oh come on, yes you do. I only had to mention your family and you started to go red in the face. Look, you're the same colour as your dressing gown.'

'This isn't a dressing gown!' railed La Senza. 'These are my robes of office!'

'Bollocks, that's from a fancy-dress shop, it's polyester,' laughed Newton. 'And as for your girlfriend, what's *that* all about?' La Senza's eyes were staring madly as if they were set to pop out.

'Sister Wendy is dressed in the manner befitting a nun.'

'If you say so Cardinal,' said Newton, his eyebrows raised. 'But she looks like a right bloody slapper to me.' Insulted, Sister Wendy hissed angrily. She brandished a whip with sharp, gloved fingers. Newton's sarcasm was starting to bite.

'Wendy, ignore him!' said La Senza. 'He's trying to rile us.'

'Wendy, that's a nice name ... how much does she charge per hour?' asked Newton. The nun shrieked in anger and cracked her whip in the air. 'Ah' said Newton. 'I take it she's fully booked then?'

'My dear doctor, I can kill you angry – or I can kill you calm. It's all the same to me. So please, don't waste your time and mine,' said La Senza, changing the subject. 'Truly, Dr Barlow, I admire your spirit for coming here alone to rescue your daughter and your girlfriend.'

'You do?'

'Well no, not really, but anyway, here you are, and given that I need a few test subjects for the machine, it's nice to have the extra numbers. It's been in storage a long time and it's probably a bit rusty, so I can't promise it will make a clean job of you. But, my technology people have had a good look at it and they assure me it's all ready to go. It's a beautiful bit of craftsmanship actually. Here, let me show you it in action. It was designed so that it could be powered by a train of oxen, a windmill or a water mill, but tonight we shall be using something a bit more modern. Gunter, the gen-er-a-tor please.' From behind the machine there was a rattle as the power kicked in.

La Senza popped open a small door above the control panel to reveal an array of pulls and buttons, somewhat like the controls on a church organ. After cracking his fingers ostentatiously, the Cardinal dropped a lever.

The machine twitched, very subtly, like a dissected frog in a biology class. Gradually, an internal glow began to spread along its foul length. Flickering gold, blue and green flames danced up behind the stained-glass windows. On the roof, large leather bellows began to wheeze asthmatically, their ghastly sulphurous breath fanning the growing flames. Above the hiss and cackle of the fires, there was a clang of metal against metal as sharp knives and toothed wheels inside the monster started to grind against each other.

'That's the blades, Dr Barlow!' shouted La Senza, above the cacophony. 'I had the boys give them a bloody good sharpening ... razor sharp now, hahahaha!'

The symphony of hate and malice pouring out from the beast was near deafening. Newton fixed his eyes on Gabby and Viv, his mind frantically trying to find an angle, anything that could stop what was beginning to look inevitable. La Senza was flipping and switching buttons manically like a crazed Count in a black-and-white movie. Then, chillingly, he pointed to Gabby. Newton was in a panic; to his horror, his daughter was being dragged forward. She was fighting hard to break free, her big Dr Martens slamming down on the henchmen's army boots with pathetically little effect.

'Let me go you wankers!' screamed Gabby, trying unsuccessfully to sink her teeth into one of Gunter's men. Just as Newton was about to make a last-ditch attempt to break free of La Senza's goons and throttle the Inquisitor himself, something popped up in the back of his grey matter.

'Wait!' shouted Newton. 'I'll do you a deal!'

La Senza turned to look at him and cradled his ear, grinning, the noise of the machine swamping Newton's desperate plea.

'I SAID I WANT TO MAKE A DEAL!'

La Senza stopped the machine. It waned and puffed, coughed and clashed a few times then growled to a standstill. Its menacing jaws closed. La Senza closed the control panel and walked with slow deliberation back to Newton.

'Go on, Dr Barlow,' said the Inquisitor, slowly. 'Impress me.'

Newton was panting like an excited dog. 'You want to wipe out the good and the godly ... right?'

'Oh yes,' said La Senza, smiling and closing his eyes. 'I most certainly do.'

'Right, so ... you know where these relics are?'

'The relics?'

'Yes,' said Newton. 'You'll have to find out where the relics are if you're going to destroy them. Do you *know* where they are?'

La Senza thought for a second, his eyes looking from side to side beneath a furrowing brow.

'Van Loop,' he said, finally calling to his dark champion. 'We know where all the relics are, don't we?' Van Loop senior, normally very self-assured, suddenly looked a trifle unsure of himself.

'Er ... the relics? The good relics?'

'Yes,' snapped La Senza. 'The good relics. We know where they are hidden, am I correct?'

'Er ... well ...' said Van Loop, nervously. 'Not yet we don't, er ... but it won't be long I'm sure.' La Senza closed his eyes wearily.

'Van Loop, dear loyal Van Loop ... just how long has your family been party to my dark ambitions?'

Van Loop shrugged pathetically.

'I'd say around five hundred years!' La Senza snapped, keeping his eyes on Newton as he began to realise that his captive might be onto something.

'Er ... yes, that's about right,' said Van Loop.

'So, what we're saying here is ...' continued the Cardinal. 'My beautiful, diabolic plan to take over the world might, just *might*, be slightly hampered because of one tiny detail, namely ...' he drew breath. 'Namely, that we cannot take over Purgatory by destroying the reliquaries of the good guys because ...' Now he started to scream. 'You haven't had the fucking bloody bollocking good sense to find out where the bloody things are buggering hidden! Is that right?!'

'Er, well ...' said Van Loop, shuffling awkwardly from foot to foot as if he needed the toilet rather badly, which by now he probably did. 'When you put it like that, I have to admit it does sound a little remiss.'

'IS THAT FRIGGIN WELL RIGHT?!' yelled La Senza, sending a rain of burger-tainted spittle into Newton's eye. The entire room was looking numbly at Van Loop and he sagged, knowing only too well what was probably about to happen.

'Sorry great Inquisitor, I'm so sorry. You see, it was just that I was so busy trying to get you back on earth, I must have sort of ... overlooked it. I was under pressure, you know. I'm not a young man anymore.' Van Loop's lame excuses were not making an impact upon the Cardinal.

'Dr Barlow, we will discuss your "deal" in a moment,' said La Senza. 'But if you will forgive me, I need to inform one of my employees of the outcome of his annual appraisal.' With that, he walked slowly back to the control panel and reopened it. He gestured to the gunmen to seize his admirer.

'What?' screamed Van Loop, as the gunmen held him firm. 'NO! Dear, great, wonderful La Senza! Please no. Didn't my family help you all these centuries ... didn't we bring you back? Oh, your great cruelness ... show me some pity. I'm your biggest fan! Cardinal, *please!*'

It wasn't that the Inquisitor was deaf to Van Loop's desperate pleading – it was more that he was getting off on it. La Senza pointed to the end of the belt. Old Van Loop, struggling pathetically, was hauled towards the machine.

'OK,' said La Senza, buoyantly. 'On you go!' The old man was thrown unceremoniously onto the conveyor.

Dazed, he tried to raise himself back up. Straight away, he felt something snag upon the left sleeve of his jacket. Looking down, he could see one of the evil thorn-like metal barbs catching the material.

He reached down to try and detach himself.

'Oh dear,' he panted. 'Oh dear, oh dear, I seem to be stuck on something.'

As he tugged at the barb, his other sleeve caught firmly on an equally wicked hook. Secured like a fly on a spider's web, each desperate movement seemed only to ensnare him further. Frantic, he looked towards the demonic figure of La Senza. With a horrible almost slow-motion movement, the Cardinal switched the machine back on.

'Oh no ... oh no! My great one, please no!' Towering above him, the jaws of hell began to widen; they bared their wicked fangs as ahead of him down the track, like a sinister echo of a tacky fairground ghost train, the inside of the monstrous contraption erupted with blue, yellow and orange flames. 'No please, La Senza, I'm sorry, I'm sorry, I'm soooooooo sorry! I'll make it up to you, I promise ... I'll do lots of unpaid overtime.' He looked over towards his only son. But Gunter was strangely blank and unmoved by his father's predicament. 'Gunter help me, please. Help your poor Popa!'

'I'm sorry, father,' he said in a dead, emotionless voice. 'You always brought me up to obey the great one. You told me that when he returned I was to follow his commands no matter what. This I am doing now.'

'Gunter, I was wrong ... it was a joke! Just a little joke. Be a good boy and help your poor father off this nasty thing!'

'No.'

'Gunter PLEASE! I am your daddy!'

'What a disobedient boy your young Gunter is,' said La Senza smugly. 'I blame the parents.'

The belt shuddered forward. Van Loop's eyes were now as big as hubcaps and he tugged frantically at his stuck clothing, each feeble thrash making him more immobile and impotent than the last. 'Oh God ... no ... no, no!'

Now he was passing through the wicked jaws, the razor-sharp blades hanging like the teeth of an anglerfish, slicing his clothes through to the flesh. Van Loop's frantic begging and pleading were drowned out as he passed like a log into a sawmill. Occasionally, he would appear at one of the colourful glass windows, desperately banging and begging for mercy, before the hooks dragged him deeper still into the ghastly interior.

It took but three minutes before the horror of Van Loop's passing was thankfully, mercifully, at an end. From the rear of the machine there came a subtle whirr and then, flatulently, the beast emitted a whoosh of gas mixed with a fine dust containing all that was once the very being of Raymond Van Loop. A pair of mangled, broken spectacles clattered red-hot to the stone floor where, in a puddle of rainwater from the broken roof tiles far above, they briefly hissed. The body and soul of Van Loop were gone forever.

La Senza switched the machine off and wiped his hands on his cheap robes. The great atrium was deathly silent now, so silent that drips from the roof could be heard splashing to the floor in rooms beyond. He walked back towards Newton.

'Now then. About this deal of yours?'

Newton hadn't had long to formulate his gambit. He wasn't even sure if La Senza would bite at all. However, if his gamble didn't work, at least he'd bought some time and made La Senza sacrifice one of his own.

'Well. You need to know where the relics are,' said Newton, in the most nonchalant voice he could muster. 'But you don't.'

'So it would appear,' said La Senza. 'Go on.'

'Well as it happens ... I know where they are.'

'You do? Wonderful. Tell me.'

'No,' said Newton firmly.

'I'm sorry? Did you just say no to me?'

'Not unless you let the girls and that man from the museum go free.'

'Haha ...' La Senza laughed, with practised theatre. 'How about I edit that slightly for you. Tell me where the relics are or I'll kill them. Yes, that sounds so much better!'

'Kill them and you'll have to kill me. Kill me and I'll definitely never tell you anything.'

'A good try ... but ... if I let them go, why would you tell me anyway? Are you going to tell me that you are a man of your word or something?'

'Oh good lord no, Cardinal. I fully expect you to torture me eventually either way. But trust me, I'm never going to tell you anything if you don't let them all go. I can cope with the pain if I have to.'

'Oh everyone says that ... at first. What makes you so sure *you* can cope?'

'I've read a lot about pain. It's merely a question of disabling pain receptors using the process of voluntary synapse disassociation. I'm sure you've heard of it – plenty of people have had pain-free surgery like that.' It was a bad lie. Newton was counting on the gathering being free of neurologists.

'He's lying,' said Gunter. 'There's no such thing.'

'On the contrary, young fellow m'lad,' said Newton, bluffing. 'The mind can cut off the way that neural transmitters send pain signals to the frontal lobes of the cerebral cortex.'

'Bullshit!' said Gunter.

'Surely you've heard of people walking on hot coals? Same thing. You'd be surprised what you can do under pressure. But even then, it's worth pointing out that most torture is utterly pointless anyway. As an Inquisitor you should know that.'

'Well, I have to admit I did it more for fun than profit,' said La Senza, wistfully. 'I didn't care whether my victims were guilty or not, to be honest.'

'Precisely,' said Newton. 'You just make the poor sap tell you what you want to hear. Anyway, you won't know whether or not I've told you the truth until you've wasted months, if not years, chasing around after these relics like a big bunch of arseholes.'

'We have drugs,' said Gunter defiantly. 'Sodium pentothal.'

'Oh that old chestnut,' said Newton. 'That will just make me drunk. Only works in films. You might as well get me pissed up on fifteen pints of Stella.'

'I say we just kill him,' said Gunter. 'He's bluffing.'

'Sure,' said Newton. 'Pop me in if you want. But then you'll have a real problem finding the relics. I happen to know just how well they're hidden. Spread out in the most unlikely of places, precisely so the likes of you will never get your hands on them. I hid a lot of them myself, recently. Eric the Greek, for instance – I moved him to new premises not two weeks ago.'

'The Greek? You know where the relics of that pathetic little paper pusher are?'

'Oh you know him?'

'Know him?' raged La Senza. 'He's the vile little creep that had me trussed up these last five centuries. Where are his feeble bones? TELL ME!'

'Nope ... not a hope. Let them go.'

'I must know! He imprisoned me, strung me up like a dead chicken, such degradation, such shame for a truly great and evil man like me! To be humiliated in such a way! TELL ME WHERE HE IS!'

'No, no and a whole dollop of no! Release the girls and the old guy and we can discuss it.' Newton returned La Senza's bulging gaze with a calm, cold exterior, quite at odds with his increasingly warm and liquid interior. Infuriated, La Senza bellowed like a wounded bull and stomped impotently around in a lather.

'Arrggghhh, you drive me to distraction wizard! I will not stop until I get what I want, you should know that!'

'Well, I can be a stubborn bastard myself,' said Newton blankly. 'But that's the deal, let them go and I'll give you the Greek, the council, anyone you want. If you don't release them, you get nothing. Zilch, nada, zip.'

His hands clenched in frustration, La Senza turned away from everyone in the room and bowed his seething head in silence. He was taking deep breaths of indecision, any trace of logical strategy fighting hard with a stronger irrational need for fast visceral revenge. Newton was gambling on the bile and the malice.

Finally, La Senza spoke.

'Release them.'

Gunter, who up to this point was willing to obey the Cardinal without question, was open mouthed.

'What?' he gasped. 'With the greatest respect, my great Cardinal, are you *sure*?'

'With the greatest respect, Gunter, shut the fuck up. You heard him, he can give me the council and the Greek. I want them. I must have them, do you hear me?!'

'But my lord, surely ...'

'Shut up!' yelled La Senza in a cloud of spittle. 'Release them now! I want these bastards as soon as possible. I want to see Eric the Greek's smug little face as I crush and smash his brittle bones into a pulp. I must have revenge on that little bureaucratic worm. Resist me, disobey me and you will share the fate of your wretched father ... do you hear me?!' La Senza's fury and vengeance was unstoppable, and like all successful tyrants, he ensured that no one could give him a second opinion, even if it was in his best interest. Gabby, Viv and the curator were allowed to walk.

Unsure, nervous, they drew level with Newton. He winked at Viv as subtly as he could and nodded towards the door. Viv held Gabby's hand tightly as if she were her own daughter and walked towards the entrance. They waited as Gunter reluctantly pulled back the bolt and the door swung wide open. A blast of cold air entered the atrium. Outside a mist was starting to form, hanging in thickening clouds amongst the rose bushes and statues. Viv and Gabby looked back at Newton, reluctant to leave him in the old asylum. Firmly he nodded to them again and with a heavy heart the girls turned back towards the darkness beyond.

Ill-timed, inconvenient, and totally out of whack with Newton's desperate gamble, this was the moment that the Reverend Bennet chose to launch his assault.

## CHAPTER 35

# ASSAULT

As Gabby, Viv and the curator reached the open air, a crackle of gunfire erupted at Hadlow Grange's perimeter.

'Oh no, not now Bennet,' Newton grimaced. 'Not now!' He looked at La Senza, then at Gunter. 'RUN!' Newton shouted, very, very loudly at the girls. 'RUN!'

They didn't really need to be told. But run to where? It was either out into the cold goon-infested grounds, or back into the dark labyrinth of the asylum. Viv looked at the curator and hesitated.

'Go, go!' he warbled. 'Save yourselves!' With mixed feelings, Viv grabbed Gabby and they bolted past two of Gunter's men and away down a gloomy side corridor.

'No!' wailed La Senza after the departing hostages. 'Sister Wendy ... fetch!' The weirdly clad Wendy Dryer, or what was left of her, flared her nostrils and clattered away after Viv and Gabby on her cheap stilettos. Gunter's men turned their guns back onto Newton, who shrugged and grinned unhelpfully. 'I don't need to tell you that the deal is off Dr Barlow!' barked La Senza.

'Who's attacking? Give me numbers!' Gunter yelled into his radio.

'Front gate sir,' crackled the reply. 'Unknown number of armed men approaching the entrance – we're returning fire.'

'So they haven't breached the perimeter?'

'Doesn't look like it, sir. I've sent men to all the possible weak points.'

'Who are they?' asked Gunter.

'It's dark, but Olaf swears he saw a couple of, er, priests.'

'Priests? Oh no, it's them, it's the Purgatorians!' said La Senza, hissing through his clean white teeth. 'They've come for me!' He turned wild-eyed to face Newton. 'Betrayal! You, you led them to me,' he snarled.

'Nah ... I just got here first, Cardinal,' replied Newton. 'Don't flatter yourself. Hanging out with the McCauleys, you weren't *that* hard to find.' La Senza narrowed his eyes and cast a glance at Ascot, which he would have been better off not seeing.

Suddenly there was a sharp crack. A bullet whacked into one of Gunter's men. Well-aimed, it hammered into his leg and dropped him like a skittle.

'Argghhhhh, I'm hit,' he wailed. Everyone scattered. Everyone except Newton, who was rather hoping the marksman could see him nice and clearly.

'Sniper ... get under cover!' yelled Gunter, and with well-oiled efficiency, the gunmen took up positions, their weapons at the ready.

'Barlow, are they really your Purgatorian friends?' said Gunter, from behind a pillar.

'Yes, I expect so. They're a bit odd I grant you, but they are dreadfully keen,' said Newton gleefully. 'Oh, and they outnumber your lot by about three to one.' Newton hadn't a clue whether his arithmetic was accurate or not, but it sounded good.

'See these men?' said Gunter, pointing to his hired muscle. 'These men have fought everywhere there is to fight. Chechnya, the Balkans, Central America, the Philippines. Do you really think a bunch of whackos with a few BB guns are going to impress them? We'll wipe your priests out in fifteen minutes.'

'We'll see,' said Newton, not wanting to agree with Gunter's pre-match assessment, but erring horribly close to it in his heart.

As each side tried to assess the other, the gunfire slowed and then abated. An electric silence fell upon the battlefield, disturbed only by the occasional crackle and pop from Gunter's radio.

'Gunter,' came a report. 'This is section three, on the western wall. We can hear something.'

'Something?' asked Gunter 'What kind of *something*?' There was a pause as the gunman tried to interpret the noise.

'Not sure ... sounds like an engine. Clanking ... I'm really not sure. But whatever it is, it's getting nearer.'

'Sections four and five,' Gunter yelled into the radio. 'Get to the west wall, NOW!' He pointed to Newton. 'You lot, keep your eye on this bastard. And make sure nothing happens to the Cardinal.' Using whatever cover he could find, Gunter dashed away towards the threatened perimeter.

'I hate you Barlow,' said Ascot, cowering on the floor behind a packing case.

'I love you too, Ascot darling,' said Newton, looking down at the property developer, squirming in discomfort below him. 'You all right down there? Want me to get you a cushion? Cold stone can give you terrible haemorrhoids.'

'You've ruined everything, damn you. It was all going so well till you stuck your pompous nose in.'

'Poor lamb,' said Newton. 'Did we count our chickens a little too optimistically?'

'Arrgghhh ...' Ascot McCauley's patience had thinned then finally snapped, and he suddenly burst out from behind his box and flew at Newton, his hands out before him like the claws of an enraged tomcat.

'Wooaaaah. Get off me you prick!' said Newton, recoiling. He jumped away, regained his wits and with a distinctly unpractised left hook, he popped Ascot straight in his weasely chops. Stunned, the property developer careered backwards. Newton nursed his academic hand. He hadn't had a fight since he was eight years old and that had lasted a mere twenty seconds. Now he had a real fight on his hands, this time with an angry dandy who resorted to everything from biting to kicking and spitting.

'Get him Ascot!' yelled Epsom, who was taking refuge up the staircase with Plumpton. 'Give him a good drubbing!'

'Yeah, come on Ascot,' taunted Newton. 'Let's see what you've got!'

Seething with his lost ambition, Ascot flew up from the floor, boiling and fizzing like a firework. With a tennis player's grunt, he landed a punch into Newton's guts. Winded, Newton buckled forward. Ascot then brought his bony knee up and into Newton's jaw, flipping him over onto the floor where he skidded along on the damp tiles. 'Oucchhh.' Fighting dirty, Ascot didn't wait for his opponent to get up – he lunged at Newton as he lay dazed and prostrate.

But Newton was waiting. As Ascot swung his Oxford brogue towards his head, Newton rolled, shot out an arm and grabbed McCauley by his thin leg. Heaving it away, he threw Ascot completely off balance making him collapse onto the floor in a mess of pinstriped limbs. Discarding his sense of fair play, Newton jumped up and then stamped on the property developer's belly. His foot landed like a falling bookshelf.

'Gummphhh!' yelled Ascot.

But Newton did not possess a killer's instinct. Unable to go in for the knock-out blow, he stepped back to give Ascot time to reconsider. 'Had enough?' asked Newton.

\*\*\*\*\*\*

Gabby and Viv were tearing fast through the building. Occasionally, the rooms were lit where Gunter's men had been at work, but for the most part, the building was forbiddingly dark. Frantic, they crunched over the glass and sodden paperwork, desperate to lose their pursuers.

'Up here,' shouted Viv, leading Gabby by the hand as they clambered up a service staircase towards the upper floors. They tore away from the guttural shouts of Gunter's men and the occasional shrieking hiss from Sister Wendy, hunting for them in the corridors below.

\*\*\*\*\*\*

Gunter arrived at the western wall. The mist had matured into a fog, and dazzling beams from the arc-lights made the whole place look like a cheap 1980s pop video. Gunter listened for a moment to the approaching clanking sound. Out beyond the wall, something was moving, something mechanical. It squeaked and squealed, rising and falling as it drew nearer. Spooked, the gunmen looked to Gunter.

'Top floor ... come in. What can you see?'

'Nothing Gunter – this damn fog mun, we can't see shit,' said the radio.

'OK, keep looking, and if you see anything, I wanna know.' The noise suddenly died. It seemed to be throttling back. Gunter looked to his men; in full combat order, hidden behind cover, they had their weapons at the ready. 'Steady boys. Keep tight.'

With a roar, the engine sound burst explosively back into life. There was a huge thump and the wall collapsed, shards of wire, broken glass and masonry showering Gunter's helpless gunmen. Through the ragged breach came a tank. Fresh from its recent overhaul upon the war memorial plinth at Langton Hadlow, the World War One veteran was forcing its way into the grounds. As Gunter's men scattered, its Lewis machine guns – each lovingly and illegally restored despite every sensible regulation – spat lead at La Senza's private army.

'Get back ... fall back!' screamed Gunter. Recoiling from the shock of the tank's unexpected arrival, they retreated back to new firing positions behind the statues and gazebos. Safe for the moment, they returned fire, but their low-calibre slugs merely sang as they pinged ineffectually off the tank's heavy steel plate.

Inside the tank, the mechanics were reliving their glory days, whooping like schoolboys as they advanced defiantly into the grounds. From behind the safety of the steel monster, the Reverend Bennet and Father Finnigan looked at each other and nodded.

'Are you ready, Reverend?' asked Father Finnigan, manfully. Bennet cocked his assault rifle.

'One was *born* ready, Father Finnigan, one was born ready! OK chaps,' he yelled. 'Charge!'

Bennet and the Purgatorians poured into the breach.

\*\*\*\*\*\*

As the battle erupted at the broken wall, Newton and Ascot's grudge match was warming up nicely. With his brothers shouting encouragement from the banisters far above, Ascot was back up on his feet and in no mood for capitulation. He grabbed a crowbar and launched himself at Newton, poison in his beady eyes.

'Die, you anti-business bastard!' he shrieked. Newton, who had foolishly turned his back on the developer, was dealt a glancing blow to his left arm, and stunned by the sudden pain, he fell heavily against one of the machine's giant cartwheels. Ascot rushed to exploit his advantage and jumped onto Newton, hysterical with hate, ramming the metal bar hard up against Newton's throat and pinning him to the ground with his bony knees. Alarmed and immobilised, Newton simply couldn't heave Ascot off his chest, and as pain burned in his windpipe and his breathing faltered, he began to panic.

There was a crack of a bullet in the wheel above them. Newton and Ascot looked up, first to the splintered wood, then out of the big open doors to the battlefield outside.

One of Bennet's snipers had chosen his moment to intervene.

'Look out Ascot!' shouted Plumpton from the staircase. Ascot yelped in alarm.

With his attacker distracted, Newton took his chance and he heaved Ascot over onto his back. Ascot lay confused and inert for a second, until another round from the sniper flashed in a spark upon the floor between his shiny shoes. Shrieking, he scuttled away into cover behind a stone pillar. Emboldened by anger, Newton went after him.

The gunmen around them were thoroughly enjoying the fight; Ascot and Newton were hardly action-movie material and each scuffle only seemed to generate more amusement. Two of them seemed to be taking bets.

For want of anything more tactical, Ascot then slung the crowbar at Newton. The revolving iron spun and slammed into his chest. In agony, he crumpled to the ground.

'Bravo Ascot!' shouted Epsom excitedly. 'Now finish him off!'

Choosing to ignore the sniper, Ascot dashed at Newton as he nursed his bruised rib cage, the intensity of the impact leaving him winded and wincing, his vision blurred. Immobile, there was little Newton could do to stop Ascot's frankly playground assault. The developer fell upon him with a whirlwind of kicks and punches, Chinese burns and bites that had Newton merely shielding himself, unable to strike back. High in one of the pine trees, Bennet's sniper was following the action with his crosshairs, frustrated that there was nothing he could do. Ascot either stood over Newton, making a double kill inevitable, or else the scuffle was so confused that the marksman couldn't discern just whose body parts he was about to maim. He held his fire.

Ascot had Newton by the hair now. He was trying to land another series of girlie kicks to his guts when Newton finally broke free – just enough to swing a hand into McCauley's groin. He grabbed his assailant's family jewels and twisted them wickedly. There was a high screech. For good measure, Newton then twisted equally hard in the opposite direction. Ascot, unprepared for this eventuality, immediately dropped Newton's quiff and shrieked again. Passing quickly from tenor to alto, Ascot doubled up.

Newton, battered but not bowed, struggled back up onto his feet and locked his arm around Ascot's head. Taking a deep breath Newton charged forward, Ascot's head aimed directly at a stone pillar.

******

Reaching the top floor, Viv and Gabby were in near-complete darkness, running fast down the blackened corridors looking for a place to hide. From cell to cell they dashed, but each tiny room looked more of a trap than an escape. Behind them, they could hear their pursuers crunching up the stairs. They kept running.

There were occasional fire exits, but they were all well secured so Viv and Gabby were forced to move on after each futile attempt to batter their way outside. On they fled. Their hearts pounding, they rushed on deeper into the foul guts of the asylum.

Sister Wendy was bounding after them along the corridors like Catwoman, her trashy rubber habit catching chinks of light as she advanced relentlessly onwards. Cackling, she cracked her whip for intimidating effect. Despite the muffled gunfire from outside, Viv and Gabby could hear it only too clearly.

Unknowing, they were being driven into a trap. The corridors were funnelling Viv and Gabby towards the deadest of dead ends.

******

The old tank shook off the collapsed masonry, trundled onto the once-ornate lawn and stopped. The thickening mist and the darkness were making things equally difficult for both sides. For the mechanics inside the old tank, it was worst of all. The evil fumes of its ancient engine were making their eyes stream and its deafening clatter assaulted their ears as they scanned for targets amongst the statues and shrubs.

Gunter's men were mere dashing shadows, fleeting targets that ran from cover to cover. The tank's machine guns spat after them as they jumped up to fire before ducking back to safety behind the masonry and vegetation. Determined to hit back at the behemoth, Gunter loaded a fresh clip and swung out from behind a statue of Athena, dispatching a stream of rounds that rippled across the tank in a shower of sparks.

'On the right!' screamed the driver spotting the muzzle flashes.

'Oh bugger,' said Gunter, as returning bullets pounded into the masonry around him. He threw himself back behind Athena. Neatly, clinically, a bullet severed the goddess's head and it rolled promptly off her mythical shoulders. With a dull ghastly thud, it landed on Gunter's head. 'Argghhhh ... bastard, bastard, bastard!'

Bennet's assault teams were pouring into the grounds. Taking cover behind the tank, statues and fountains, they exchanged fire with La Senza's thugs. The warrior priests may have looked ludicrous and ineffectual, but just as Bennet had promised, they fought with a cool professionalism. Gunter's men, baffled and to an extent rather insulted by their adversaries, looked to each other for reassurance as wave after wave of archdeacons, vergers and priests of every denomination imaginable came at them like tigers through the shrubs. Tracer scythed through the neglected rosebushes, while grenades erupted in great clods of frozen mulch.

Dominating the exchange, the tank was wheeling back and forth, its twin Lewis guns sending streams of lead into the low walls and balustrades where Gunter's men crouched, bewildered.

'Retreat!' shouted Gunter. 'Back to the asylum!'

******

Ascot's thin leg tripped Newton just before he could slam the property developer's head into the pillar. His balance compromised, Newton barrel-rolled and slid across the floor. As he raised himself back onto his feet, Ascot, wasting no time, was up and onto Newton's shoulders like a monkey. Locked onto his back like a rucksack, he flailed away at Newton's face.

Frantically Newton tried to rid himself of the pounding, scratching McCauley. He spiralled them both around the big hallway, the two of them bouncing and ricocheting off the columns, but Ascot, in for the kill, was not to be budged. Newton's face was soon a mass of bloody scratches.

'Go Ascot!' yelled Plumpton.

'Kill him, brother! Kill him!' screamed Epsom hysterically.

Newton frantically struggled to rid himself of his attacker. Ascot had one finger up Newton's nose and a thumb in one of his eyes. Ignoring the highly amused gunmen around them, Newton staggered from side to side until finally the two of them went sailing fast across the room like ballroom dancers until finally, they crashed hard into a low obstruction. Winded, they lay still briefly, waiting for the stars to stop spinning.

Newton was the first to look down. Ascot, struggling to get up himself, followed Newton's gaze. They were both stuck on the machine's conveyor belt. Newton looked at Ascot; Ascot looked at Newton. Alarmed, they both looked at Cardinal La Senza.

The Inquisitor was giggling, laughing to himself, clearly thinking something they were both rather hoping he wasn't.

******

Viv and Gabby were heading down their final corridor. With Gunter's two henchmen hard on their heels, they tore along the top floor heading nowhere in particular. Luckily, they were moving too fast and too nosily to hear or sense the sad spirits that had so freaked out Christopher Baxter. Their eyes were focused only on a distant chink of blue-white light. It wasn't much, but with death at their heels, they ran for it with a crazed desperation.

Galvanised by the sight of the two goons close behind them, torches on the ends of their gun barrels, Viv and Gabby rushed on, eventually reaching a fire escape. They frantically pounded and pushed at the door until finally, their fingernails cracked and bloodied with the effort, the door began to give way.

'Please ... please!' Viv muttered breathlessly. 'Come on!' But the desperate hammering had also alerted the gunmen, and as Gabby looked on in horror, the distant torches suddenly started accelerating straight down the corridor towards them.

'Quick!' screamed Gabby, and together the two of them threw themselves in panic at the troublesome exit.

The gunmen were just a few yards away when the door finally burst open. In a bundle of arms and legs, Viv and Gabby tumbled clumsily out through the door onto the fire escape. Sliding, Viv sent out her arms and legs until she snagged an upright. She stopped just in time to see Gabby slide through a broken railing and begin a plunge towards the dark unknown of the asylum's rear.

'Help!' she screamed, and Viv, desperate, thrust out her hand. Mercifully it closed on one of Gabby's big black boots, just in time to prevent her vanishing towards Plumpton's ghastly body pits far below. Straining, Viv pulled Gabby back bit by agonising bit until finally, the two of them lay panting and crumpled on the metal stairs.

Like death, the torches fell upon them.

'You ...!' said one of Gunter's men. 'Get up!'

'I can't!' lied Gabby. 'I've broken my leg.' She looked at Viv and winked.

'She can't move!' said Viv, cautiously, picking up the ruse. 'You'll have to come and help us.'

'Oh for fugs sake,' said the first gunman. 'Here, take my gun,' he said to his colleague. He looped the assault weapon off over his thick neck, and handed it to his pal. He began to walk down to the girls.

With the extra weight, the fire escape started to creak horribly. Instantly, the gunman changed his walk from a practised swagger to something more vertigo-induced, but keen not to display anxiety, he continued edging forward until he was halfway down the first set of steps. He reached down to grab Gabby by the scruff of the neck.

Viv and Gabby exchanged glances, and Gabby, whose teeth were increasingly her weapon of choice, plunged her gnashers deep into the goon's rubbery fist. The stabbing pain shot through the man's hand with all the intensity of an impacting bullet, and he recoiled backwards, screaming. With nothing to stop him, he fell away through the broken railings and down into the mess of cadavers and detritus below, landing with a cacophony of breaking glass and snapping bones, not all of them his own.

'You leettle fucking betch!' yelled his pal. Furious, he threw off his colleague's gun; cradling his own, he sent a entire magazine of bullets streaming out at the girls. Sensibly, they ducked back down behind the metal steps as a cloud of sparks erupted amongst the rust and paint flakes. But the gunfire also drew the attention of one of Bennet's snipers. A round came righteously out of the night, hammering hard into the man's gun, sending it clattering away useless into the darkness below. Even then, the gunman didn't hesitate. As the sniper rounds hissed around him, he leant down, unsheathed a commando knife from his boot and leapt forward to attack the girls, crouching powerless beneath him.

The rust and ice were his undoing. His meaty bulk and his angry momentum made him slip in a ghastly, uncoordinated loop, and yelping like a scolded dog, he slipped arse over Kevlar. Clanging hard against the metal work, he sailed shrieking past them.

Desperately, he shot out his arm, and just in time his sausage-like fingers clamped onto the perforated metal. The fire escape groaned in protest. Clouds of rust flew out into the darkness. Frantic, he tried to pull himself up, but his combat couture was working against him. His body armour had ridden up badly and no matter how hard he tried, he couldn't bring his dangling left arm up towards the staircase and he was left hanging like a one-armed monkey. Knowing he couldn't climb up alone, he began to panic. The staircase lurched again.

'You ... woman,' he said to Viv. 'Help me.'

'You've got to be joking,' said Viv, standing. 'Come on Gabbs, let's go.'

'Please ... help me!' he persisted, pathetically. Viv and Gabby clambered furiously up the steps. They looked back as the goon dangled and swung beneath the creaking fire escape. Summoning a last burst of energy, he abruptly freed his arm and it shot out to grab the metal; he looked up at the girls and laughed. Then he noticed what was hanging from his index finger. In the darkness, he couldn't be sure which of the grenades the pin had come from, so he was then obliged to flail away at his chest until the last of them fell away and landed in the body pit below. Again, he looked back to the girls and grinned malevolently. He was still grinning as the grenade burst in the gloom below him. It was at this moment that the fragile fire escape finally lost its argument with gravity. Squealing and groaning, it plunged towards the ground with the hapless gunman still attached. The crunching metal and screaming merged into one long cacophony before finally falling silent. Gabby and Viv backed away from the precipice and into the dubious safety of the building behind them.

Back inside the building, the two women lay breathless and crumpled on the filthy floor trying to gather their wits. They didn't have time.

Sister Wendy was upon them.

******

The Purgatorians were advancing steadily across the grounds towards the asylum. Although they'd lost five or so of their number to Gunter's marksmen, they were forcing La Senza's private army to fall back under their assault.

'Onwards, onwards!' yelled Bennet. Rushing from cover, he and Finnigan led their men in a frantic charge at Gunter's uncomprehending militia as they recoiled in disorder.

The old tank was now right on top of the gunmen, crushing decorative fawns, nymphs and goddesses beneath its massive steel tracks as it drove the thugs back towards the asylum. But Gunter's men were not spent. Out of nowhere, a round hammered into Father Finnigan and he was slapped like a crash-test dummy onto the frozen ground.

'Father Finnigan!' yelled Bennet.

'Don't stop Reverend! Keep going. Give 'em hell!' yelled the mortally wounded priest. Heroically, with the strength ebbing away from his torn body, Finnigan urged the Purgatorians on. With a heavy but proud heart, Bennet turned, wiped a tear from his eyes and then raged forwards, firing from the hip. Buckling under the vicar's fury, two of Gunter's men were scythed down as all around Bennet the return fire chewed up the hydrangeas.

The tank pitilessly flayed Gunter's men as they retreated, leaving many of their number wounded and broken amongst the shrubberies. The survivors, with bullets dancing at their feet, regrouped at the asylum's big entrance door. They rolled combat-style into the hallway and threw themselves into cover, firing back at the priests and vicars as they inexorably closed in on La Senza and his machine.

******

Newton and Ascot wriggled like fishing bait on the conveyor belt, their clothes hooked irretrievably. La Senza, clearly enjoying himself, moved the shuddering belt slowly forward towards the guts of the monster, switching it on and off, giggling like a cruel child.

'Ascot! We're coming!' yelled Epsom and Plumpton, finally bolting down from their safe zone on the staircase. Newton, not expecting help, was faster on his wits. He frantically slipped off his leather jacket and undid his belt as fast as his numb fingers would go. The two men were getting uncomfortably close to the jaws of hell. Ascot was watching Newton with some incredulity as he got down to his underwear. Now only in his pants and socks, Newton was able to jump up from the belt towards the huge fat top lip of the devil itself where he swung like a surprised lover outside a bedroom window. Epsom and Plumpton dashed towards their brother.

'Get me off ... pull me off this bloody thing!' Ascot howled. With panicked clumsiness, they tried to pull their ensnared brother off the conveyor as he lay there, barking instructions. It was a fatal mistake. Epsom looked on in horror as his own clothing hooked, snagged and then dragged. He leant towards Plumpton, who, seeing where things were going, tried hard to back away from both of them. It wasn't going to work that way. Epsom and Ascot grabbed at the third brother in a

371

frenetic last-ditch attempt to get off the conveyor.

Plumpton joined them on the belt.

'Cardinal! Shut the bloody thing off!' shouted Ascot.

'Hahahahaha NO!' laughed La Senza. With vile exuberance, he turned up the speed, and the triplets, howling, lurched forward.

'Don't! You can't! Stop!' yelled Ascot. 'You simply can't!'

'No such word as *can't*,' shrieked La Senza.

'But ... but La Senza, you bastard, we've got a contract!'

La Senza's laugh was childish, pathetic and juvenile, but it did a fine job of making it blatantly clear to all three McCauleys that life was about to change, and not for the better. Like wasps on flypaper, they thrashed pathetically as they inexorably approached the jaws. Plumpton, always the most emotional of the three, whimpered like a toddler at a bad circus. In desperation, a frantic hand, probably Epsom's, reached towards Newton's dangling foot. As it got near, Newton quickly pulled the leg out of range and clambered up and over the machine's vile head until, finally safe at last, he stood upon the monster's roof. The hand below, its fingers grasped pointlessly around Newton's sock, was then whisked away into the machine, and with it, the rest of the McCauley brothers.

Gunter crashed back into the entrance hall.

'Gunter ... get the Purgatorial bastard!' screamed La Senza pointing. Gunter looked up, and without hesitation, fired. Amongst the splinters and sparks, Newton dodged and weaved through the Gothic embellishments looking for cover. All around him, gargoyles were losing their ears and noses as Gunter's bullets flayed the woodwork.

For the McCauleys, there were to be no such second chances. Deep inside the throat of the devil, the first fires were reaching out as they were simultaneously racked and sliced by the first wave of blades, spikes and wires. The doomed McCauleys were toasted, cut, sliced, grilled, burnt and then ground like peppercorns, while above them, dancing like a nudist on hot tarmac, Newton dodged the gunfire.

'Close the damn doors!' yelled Gunter, ramming in another clip. 'You lot, guard all the exits and entrances, we can hold them off for a while. We need to buy time!' As the bullets perforated the heavy oak, the big doors were slammed shut. They piled obstructions against the door and with their guns levelled at the barricade, they backed away.

Outside, the gunfire abruptly ceased.

The screams and the pleading inside the machine were all anyone could hear. The triplets were writhing in a torment of flame, slashing blades and crushing grinding wheels. Newton had the worst seat in the house. Beneath him, separated by only four inches of medieval woodwork, the agonies and soul-destroying torments were that extra bit vivid. Lying flat to avoid the attentions of Gunter's laser-sighted assault weapon, Newton could hardly ignore their death throes. Even in their last moments, the triplets bickered and squabbled amongst themselves until finally, in a grim choral crescendo, the family argument swelled into one appalling scream. Mercifully, it then ceased.

At the rear of the infernal machine there were three puffs of inert empty powder. They rose in three distinct clouds of sickly beige dust. As they drifted away into the gloom, the sterilised, soul-free signet rings of Ascot, Epsom and Plumpton McCauley plinked and sizzled as they fell one by one onto the cold stone floor.

## CHAPTER 36

# THE END OF THE AFFAIR

Newton could still smell whatever had happened to Ascot, Epsom and Plumpton McCauley. It drifted up from the machine in wisps of purple and sickly yellow and floated away in the still cold air.

'You can't stay up there forever Dr Barlow,' giggled La Senza. 'Why don't you come down and have a little chat. You must be freezing.'

'Nah, you're OK,' said Newton.

Outside the shooting had stopped and the tank's engine was clucking away as it sat idling, awaiting orders.

'Cardinal,' said Gunter, 'I'm afraid we are going to have to attempt a break out.'

'What!' shrieked La Senza. 'You mean we are going to abandon my machine?'

'It's not as bad as it sounds great Inquisitor,' continued Gunter. 'We've got all the drawings and plans. We can create new ones whenever we want. But if we stay here then we're in big trouble.'

'Certainly looks like it,' said Newton from the top of the machine.

'Shut up Purgatorian scum!' snapped La Senza. 'Break out you say? But how? We are surrounded are we not?'

'I've been working on that,' said Gunter. 'The McCauleys gave me a guided tour of the place before you "processed" them. Seems we can get out through a service tunnel from a kitchen on the south side. Cardinal, can you be ready to roll in five minutes?'

'But Sister Wendy! My love, my plaything, my little angel! She's off hunting those ghastly women! I can't go without her!'

'Oh how touching!' said Newton. 'You do have a soft side after all.'

'Silence dog! No I don't.'

'Yeah ya do lover boy. You're a big woos.'

'Ignore him Cardinal,' said Gunter. 'We are running out of time. They won't sit out there forever, we have to get going. We need to get to the plane and get you out of here!'

'Oh it's a toughy!' laughed Newton, ducking as Gunter sprayed the woodwork.

'You have the book?' asked La Senza.

'Yes Inquisitor,' said Gunter. 'I have the book, the money and the plans. The relics also.'

'Yes,' said La Senza, 'we have to plan for every eventuality. Just like before. If they should get me, you know what you must do.'

'Yes great Inquisitor. We will bring you back, just like before. I swear to you.'

'Yes ... this is most important,' said La Senza. 'Mind you, I am dreadfully worried about Sister Wendy.'

'That's not very evil,' said Newton. 'You're starting to sound empathic. You'll be sending greetings cards next. Then it's a slippery slope towards charity work.'

'Nooo ...' hissed La Senza. 'It's an *evil* kind of love.'

'How can you have an evil kind of love, you moron!' said Newton.

'It's a love *born* of evil!'

'Yeah right ... if you say so.'

'Ignore him Cardinal, we are running out of time,' said Gunter anxiously.

'Oh it's such a dilemma isn't it?' mocked Newton. 'Save yourself or rescue the missus!'

'He's right Gunter. I can't leave her!' wailed La Senza.

'Cardinal – snap out of it! He's playing with your mind. You're evil, you have to forget her and save yourself.'

'I can't,' said La Senza. 'She's so lovely!'

'A girl like that only comes along once in a lifetime,' said Newton sagely. Gunter's frustration was reaching fever pitch. A stream of bullets chopped their way up and down the woodwork.

'Look at me Cardinal, look into my eyes. You're evil, remember ... *evil.*'

'Evil, yes ...' said La Senza. 'Yes that's right.'

'And heartless, unthinking, cruel, mean. That's what's so *good* about you!'

'It is?'

'Yes great Inquisitor! It is, that's why we all follow you. Don't throw it all away ... for ... LOVE!'

'Evil ... yes I am,' said La Senza, wavering. 'I am, aren't I?'

'Nah, you're a love-sick puppy!' said Newton, who was rewarded with an instant bullet that sung off a nearby chimney.

'Yes you are evil,' insisted Gunter. 'And that means you have to ignore any feelings you might have for the nun, no matter how lovely she is, and come with me. We have to get you out of here. If you stay, well ... then you'll end up back in Purgatory.'

La Senza shrieked. 'Not that again, it was so terribly boring up there!'

'Exactly,' said Gunter earnestly, 'and that's why we have to leave and get you to the plane.'

'Yes, yes you are right,' said La Senza reluctantly. 'I *must* go.'

Outside, there was a roar and a squeal of tracks.

'The tank Cardinal, they are about to use it on the doors! We have to go now.' He turned back to his militia. 'OK men,' shouted Gunter. 'There is only room on the plane for the Cardinal, myself and three bodyguards. The rest of you will have to fight your way out. Once we get to safety we can regroup.'

'How will we find you again?' said Olaf.

'I'll let you know on Facebook,' said Gunter.

'But I'm not registered on Facebook, sir,' said Olaf. 'I find it a bit ... *creepy*. Can you text me?'

'Surely you're on Twitter?' called Newton. 'Or Linkedin?'

'Text, tweet, whatever the fuck, look we'll work it out later,' said Gunter, exasperated. 'Jeez.'

'Yes sir! Good luck!' Olaf saluted.

'Thank you Olaf.' Gunter gestured to two men nearby. 'You two, Kurt, Norman – come with me. Grab the money and the plans. I'll guard the Cardinal. As they began to file quickly away towards the service tunnel, Gunter turned, and in one swift movement, lobbed a grenade. Up it went, spinning through the air until it clattered onto Newton's hiding place. As the bad guys melted away into the corridors, the grenade rolled, gently fizzing, up to Newton's face.

******

Sister Wendy approached Gabby and Viv like an aging runway model. Tottering on her hooker's heels, she clicked forward across the lino like a praying mantis until she stood a mere whip's length from the girls in the blue-grey light, and halted.

'Well hello ladies,' she hissed.

'Whatever,' said Gabby.

'Time to go girls,' said Wendy. She cracked her whip and it landed on Viv's thigh with an agonising slash.

'You bitch!' she yelled angrily.

'Leave her alone you ugly tart!' yelled Gabby, who grabbed a chunk of wood and heaved it at La Senza's girlfriend. But the nun deftly dodged the missile before sending out a second whip crack that coiled tightly around Gabby's arm. Wendy pulled hard and Gabby began to slide forward. 'Viv! Help me!'

Viv grabbed Gabby's legs and pulled. The nun's strength was phenomenal. Viv had to wedge her foot against a door stop, but even then she was fighting a losing battle.

Thankfully they were not alone.

Viv was the first to notice. She saw Sister Wendy's face change from dominatrix to mortified child in a heartbeat. She dropped the whip and staggered in dread, falling against the wall for support. Her gaze was fixed above and behind them in abject horror. Viv, her hair prickling and her skin creeping, gradually turned to look back at what really ought to have been an empty space. Instead there was a pair of semi-transparent sensible shoes and two veined stockinged legs. Shuddering involuntarily, she followed them upwards.

'No, no, please ...' whimpered Wendy, her fist rising up to her horrified mouth.

There was no doubt what it was – it was one hundred and fifty per cent ghost. From the see-through body to the locally plummeting temperature, what else could it have been? All it really needed was staring eyes, a malevolent expression and a radiating sense of mortal dread. Viv checked; it had all of these.

'Mother ... no, please!' said Wendy.

'Oh you've been a naughty girl Wendy Dryer, a very naughty girl,' said the spirit, completely ignoring the women at her transparent feet.

'Mother ... no, let me be ... I'm grown up now.'

'Grown up? How dare you! You'll *always* be my little baby,' continued the spirit. 'My *naughty* little girl!'

'No mother, no! I'm a grown woman. Leave me be!'

'You're what you always were Wendy Dryer – a dirty little tart. Thinking your dirty, smutty little thoughts. A bad and a naughty little girl.'

'I'm not naughty, I'm a normal girl. A *woman*!'

'You ran from me, when those sick naughty people killed me, you ... you stayed away. I haven't forgotten,' continued the ghost. 'You never came to see me. Well, I'll *never* let you go now – not this time!'

'Mother please no!' Viv, hypnotised as she was by the ghostly confrontation, pulled her wits together.

'Gabby, come on, we've got to go!' They stood up and dashed past the dumbstruck figure of the nun. As they raced past her, Sister Wendy did nothing to stop them.

'Look at you,' said the spirit of Matron Dryer. 'Look at you, you filthy little slut. What do you look like? You and your dirty friend. I've watched you – I've seen what you do. You dirty little harlot!'

'No Mother no! Don't say that!'

'I'll never let you out of my sight now, you cheap little slag. No more naughty girl.'

'But I'm not naughty,' said Sister Wendy. She slapped her hands over her ears and turned, staggering away a few tottering steps.

'Oh yes you are. Like all the young women nowadays. That's what you are! A naughty girl.'

'I'm not naughty, I'm not naughty!' screamed Wendy. 'I'm not naughty.'

Viv and Gabby ran on and away from the macabre family reunion, but soon, in the total darkness, they were utterly lost. Horribly lost. Staggering and stumbling along they could not work out where they were or where they were going. Gabby, tired and stressed, began to lose her teen coolness, and as she held on to Viv's hand, her bottom lip began to tremble. But as they panted and hugged in the darkness, they began to sense a change in the light, a faint blue glow appearing behind them. Viv turned and saw a vague shape grow closer and more defined, condensing into the figure of a young girl, no more that fourteen or fifteen years old.

'Follow me,' said the spirit.

\*\*\*\*\*\*

Newton bounded back over the top of the machine and was in mid-air when the grenade burst. The resulting cloud of medieval shrapnel showered down around him, but mercifully, it left him unscathed. He landed heavily and rolled to a halt in his pants and sole remaining sock, wondering what on earth was coming next.

It was the tank. It came through the big oak doors like a punch, splitting and tearing the thick wood into matchsticks. Once in the hallway, it shuddered to a halt, its machine guns swivelling back and forth looking for targets. Satisfied that Newton was alone, the tank clattered to a standstill.

The Reverend Bennet, grinning through his goggles, emerged from the hatch and looked down.

'Newton, my dear boy. Where are your trousers?'

'They're in that bloody thing!' said Newton. 'It was either me or the Levi's I'm afraid.'

'Oh dear, you must be freezing.'

'I'm getting there.'

'So *that's* the machine is it?' said Bennet, climbing down as the assault teams joined them in the atrium.

'Yup. Nice eh?' said Newton. It was still running and Bennet was strolling a little close to the barbed conveyor belt for Newton's liking. 'Hold on Vicar, I'd stay back if I was you – it bites. We'd better try and switch the bloody thing off.' Newton opened the control panel and pulled at the various levers until thankfully, after a few roars, groans and slashings, the beast ground to a halt.

'Well at least La Senza had to abandon it. I'm guessing he's done a runner?' said Bennet, cautiously looking into the jaws of hell.

'Yep, we'll have to get after him pronto, there's a tunnel apparently, out from the kitchens. And don't think it's over – they've got blueprints of this monster, they intend to build more.'

'Oh dear,' said Bennet. 'That's not good. What about the McCauleys?'

'Smell that sort of smoky bacon thing?'

'Yes,' said Bennet.

'Well that's the McCauleys.'

'Oh dear. How very unfortunate.' He turned back to his team. 'OK lads, time to get after the blighters. Pair up and start a search of the upper floors. Father Finnigan's team, you come with me, let's find this damn tunnel.'

'Where *is* Father Finnigan?' asked Newton. Bennet looked down.

'Father Finnigan ... he ... he didn't make it.'

'Oh I'm so sorry,' said Newton sadly.

'He died doing what he loved,' said Bennet. 'So let's remember him by carrying on his work. Let's get after the bastards!' There was a defiant roar from the warrior priests, which tailed away awkwardly.

The priests began to split up. They melted away into the side rooms and up the stairs as Newton, Bennet and Finnigan's bereaved team dashed along corridors looking for the kitchen. Bennet finally found it and opened the trap door to the exit tunnel.

'It's in here,' he shouted, peering down the stairs into a dark cellar.

'Oh great, another dark enclosed space,' said Newton wearily. Cautiously, they descended the steps and hurried off along the tunnel.

******

The spirit girl led Gabby and Viv down the stairs and back into the atrium. The old tank sat there, clinking and popping as its engine cooled, the mechanics by its side. Oiling and fixing, they stopped to look up as the two girls descended the staircase, the blue-white ghost of the girl in front.

'Bloody hell!' said one of them, his jaw dropping open to release his rolled cigarette.

'You are safe now,' said the spirit. 'The bad people, they've gone. You can trust *these* men.'

'Thank you,' said Gabby. The spirit turned to leave. 'Hey, wait!' Gabby shouted as the spirit drifted back up the staircase. 'Where are you going? Why don't you come with us – can't we help you?' The girl looked back.

'I'm sorry, no. I can't leave as long as this building stands. I'm trapped here. I died here and that means I'm part of the fabric of the place. I will be ... forever.'

'What? Really? But that's terrible,' said Gabby. 'Surely we can help you, there must be something we can do.'

'Thank you, but no, it can't be. I've been here too long. I cannot leave. I am its memory, and my memory is embedded within *it*. We are trapped, the building and I. As long as it remains I cannot be at peace.' With that she drifted away, and with a heavy heart, Viv held Gabby back. 'Sweetie please. We've got to leave.' Gabby had huge tears running down her cheeks.

The mechanics rushed towards them.

'You alright ladies?' one asked warmly. 'Quite an evening! Come on, let's get you out. Safest place is in here I reckon.' Carefully they all clambered into the tank. Inside the curator sat small and nervous, warming his hands against the pistons. Shivering from cold and stress, they bustled up against each other like baby blue tits. With a spectacular growl, the mechanic opened up the engine and backed the old tank out of the hall, down the ornate steps and into the grounds.

******

Bennet's torch caught the movement just before the gun fired. One of Gunter's rearguards had been waiting for them.

'Look out,' said Bennet, and he pushed Newton hard back against the dirty old wall and out of the line of fire. The bullet flashed past them. Crouching, Bennet fired back. There was a horrified scream followed by a dull thump. Rushing forward they found the gunman sprawled; he wasn't dead, Bennet had made sure of that. A neat wound had opened up in his exposed shoulder and he was lying stunned by the shot.

'Thou shall not kill,' said Bennet.

'Amen,' said the holy men behind him.

'Newton – grab his trousers and his jacket while he's too limp to fight back.'

'I'm not sure he's my size,' said Newton, pulling at the man's belt.

'He'll do,' said Bennet. 'And you may want to check for a weapon.'

'I hope you mean what I think you mean,' said Newton dryly as he slipped off the man's trousers.

'This is no time for innuendo, Dr Barlow,' said Bennet disapprovingly. 'Get those clothes on fast, they can't be that far ahead, judging by this joker.' Newton threw on the trousers, boots and jacket. The wounded gunman was lying shivering on the floor. 'Don't worry about him, we'll pick him up later. Come on, let's go.'

Soon they were nearing the end of the tunnel. It abruptly emerged into a boiler room, part of the greenhouse heating system. Guns at the ready, they cautiously climbed up into the glasshouses. Instantly, there was a ripple of gunfire and a shattering of glass. Bennet's men fanned out and returned fire.

'OK chaps, come on now. Get them suppressed.' The fire fight flared and Newton crouched down in alarm as broken glass cascaded down.

'Bloody hell!' he screamed above the cacophony of gunfire.

'Quite,' said the Reverend, who popped up over a potting table and sent out three well-aimed shots, each rewarded with a yelp, a scream and a profanity.

'Jesusssss!'

'Really,' said Bennet. 'Why do they have to blaspheme every time I shoot them?'

'Maybe you just converted him!' suggested Newton helpfully.

'I strongly doubt that,' said Bennet reloading. He shouted to his team: 'I make that three down. Any others?'

'I don't think so Rev.'

'OK then. Brethren – up and at 'em!' Dodging from cover to cover, they moved through the old kitchen garden until they came to the open gates. Beyond them the heath lay open. La Senza, Gunter and his men were clearly visible in the distance running frantically towards the distant Antonov, its engine idling in the straggling mist.

'There they are!' screamed Newton.

La Senza was having enormous trouble running in his cheap fancy dress robes and he was forced to hitch them up high to free his legs. The bag containing the relics beneath his arm only made matters worse, and as he staggered along, he struggled to lift the clothes up from his shoes.

'Gunter, help me!' he shrieked.

'Come on Cardinal!' yelled Gunter looking back. 'We are nearly there!'

The pilot, who had been smoking nervously as he waited for the party, dropped his cigarette as they approached, stubbing out the butt upon the frosting grass.

'Gunter I'm ready ... where are we going?'

'You're not going anywhere,' said Gunter, knocking him down with his rifle butt. 'C'mon Cardinal, I'll fly this bird. Get in!'

'Oh Wendy, my sweet dear Wendy,' whimpered La Senza as they clambered aboard. 'I'm sorry my dark love. Forgive me!' He looked back forlornly towards the Grange.

'No time for that,' said Gunter, and as soon as they were all safely aboard, he slammed the hatch and dashed for the cockpit. 'Buckle up. They're coming after us, it's going to be a hot take-off.' Dropping into the pilot's seat, he threw the switches and the anachronistic Russian biplane wheezed as it came to life. Wasting no time, he slammed open the throttle and the old Antonov began rolling away across the rough grass.

'Dammit, fire at the buggers,' yelled the Reverend Bennet. The vicar dropped to his knees and began firing short controlled bursts at the approaching aeroplane. Gunter could see the rounds cracking off the cowling in front of him. Racing, the biplane scattered Bennet and his men as it charged between them. Frustrated, the Purgatorians fired at the departing bulk of the plane as it spliced the gathering mist, their bullets punching holes in the fuselage as it climbed away.

But the Antonov had more trouble in store. As the murk parted, there, suddenly, was the green-grey mass of the World War One tank, crawling at its pitifully low top speed into the path of the roaring biplane. Gunter desperately pulled back hard on the stick. The Antonov, screaming on the edge of a stall, reared up, clawing for height.

Lurching like a closing-time drunk, the plane howled, its throttles to the wall as it jumped over the tank. Gradually it was fighting its way into level flight, but by the time Gunter regained control, another obstacle was looming out of the mist – this time a line of straggling pines just seconds from impact. He threw the Antonov over to the right, jinking through a gap in the trees and then pulling up once again, whooping ecstatically like an Apache with the exhilaration of a close escape.

Not this time.

Jittery from the firing and alarmed by the approaching mass of the Antonov, Hadlow Grange's resident rooks exploded babbling and cackling out of the pines. There was nothing Gunter could do to avoid them. He threw his arm across his face as the first of the oily black shapes smashed through the windscreen, filling the cockpit with a wet mess of blood and feathers.

Blinded, he lost control.

The Antonov was as good as pilotless. It plummeted to the ground, smashing through the perimeter wall of the Grange and careering in a mass of metal, canvas and wire across the overgrown lawns. It barrelled on through the shrubs and statues, emitting a sickening squeal as the fuselage was torn to pieces. Finally, it hammered into the asylum. Hissing and steaming it lay there inert.

Bennet, Newton and the warrior priests ran forwards towards the crash site. But before they could close with the wreck, there was a ghastly flash of yellow and red. The plane erupted into a fireball as the full tanks ignited. With an intense boiling roar, the clouds of burning petrol engulfed one whole wing of the asylum in an incandescent mushroom. In no time, the entire building was ablaze.

With the mist mingling with a toxic cloud of smoke, visibility at the crash site was reduced to mere feet. Fighting his way through, Bennet reached the wreckage. There was not much to see.

'Dead, they're all dead,' Bennet announced, holding the Purgatorians back with his arm. 'No, don't. It's not pretty.'

Behind them the tank drew up to the hole in the perimeter wall. Excited, Gabby and Viv were instantly out of the tank and running up to Newton.

'Dad!'

'Gabby, my love ... thank God! You're OK! And Viv ... I was so worried!' They hugged ecstatically, but the relieved reunion was cut short. Roasting in the fire, Gunter's private arsenal began cooking off.

'Better move back chaps,' said Bennet.

The asylum was a sea of fire. Hypnotised by the inferno, they were transfixed as the blaze leapt from window to window at breakneck speed. Thus preoccupied, they understandably failed to see the flash of red behind them.

The bloodied figure of La Senza was staggering, singed, through the shrubberies. He limped desperately towards the hole in the wall, clutching the book and his bag of relics. And he was oh so near to escape when he heard her. The voice sailed out from the flames and he stopped. Wendy was calling to him.

'Balthazar!'

La Senza looked back, torn pathetically between selfishness and need.

'Balthazar!' came the longing, desperate voice.

He could not ignore her. The nun could be clearly seen on one of the building's high verandas, her habit silhouetted in the light of the rapidly approaching flames. But Sister Wendy was not alone; behind her lurked the spirit of the nurse, the hideous spectre of her controlling, maniacal mother.

'Balthazar ... my love, my only love,' called Wendy, her voice floating in and out of the flames. 'Don't leave me here with *her*. Please, Balthazar, take me with you!'

But Matron Dryer wasn't going to let her daughter go anywhere ever again. Bound by a weld of guilt, duty and subservience, Wendy stood stock still in front of her as the flames closed inexorably in on them. In life, in death, there never would be another separation.

Gabby was the first to spot them; they all looked up at the two figures as all-consuming flames framed them upon the balcony.

'Oh my dear sweet Wendy!' sobbed La Senza loudly, his black heart breaking.

Everyone turned.

La Senza, tears streaming down his face, realised his mistake immediately. There was but a second's grace as they all exchanged bewildered glances. Then, as Wendy finally sagged and dropped amid the flames, La Senza bolted.

'After him!' yelled Newton.

The fog and the smoke pouring from the Grange had mingled into an evil soup, suddenly full of fleeting shadows and dashing figures as Bennet's men ran helter skelter across the heath in pursuit. Further and further Newton and the Purgatorians radiated until eventually, as they distanced themselves from the crashing timbers and roaring flames, the air carried nothing but their urgent voices and rustling vegetation. In the echoing mist, it was soon hard to tell where the panting and shouting was coming from. Confused, both the hunters and the hunted passed mere feet from each other without making contact.

Suddenly, Newton found himself separated and alone in the fog. Bennet, likewise, was also out on his own and he advanced warily through the gorse bushes, his arms outstretched with the Beretta before him. To make matters worse there were sheep snuffling and running chaotically through the heather. As they edged dangerously close to the cliff tops of the south coast, the crash of waves added their roar to the concerto.

Just then, a cold gust of wind blew in from the sea. It was enough to roll back the mist as Newton, edging cautiously forward into the clearer air at the cliff edge, finally found his quarry. Facing him, with his back to the sheer drop, was Cardinal Balthazar De La Senza in all his self-appointed glory, cradling the necromancer's book and his sad little relics in his bloodied arms. Defiant, he hissed at Newton like a Komodo dragon.

Keeping his eyes on the Cardinal, Newton called out to his colleagues.

'Over here, he's over here!'

Bennet, Viv and Gabby caught up.

'Don't come any closer!' hissed the Inquisitor defiantly. 'I'm warning you!'

'Oh come on La Senza mate, for pete's sake, give it up,' said Newton. 'It's over.'

'*Over?*' said La Senza, his eyes wide and staring in defiance. 'Oh that's what you'd like, isn't it. Well what will you do ... if ... I ... jump?'

'Jump?' asked Viv. 'What good will that do you? You'll die.'

'I've done it before!' said the cornered Inquisitor. 'There's nothing to it. I'll come back again, and again and again. If I jump I'll take these with me – the book, the relics. They'll all come with me. You won't know where they'll turn up. Someone will find them. Some lousy beachcomber, a child, I'll take them over, I'll possess them. I'll return.'

'Hold on. *Can* he do that?' asked Newton sceptically.

'Errr ... sadly yes,' said Bennet, his face grim as gravel. 'Yes, he can.'

'I'm not scared of death! Don't you see! I know it's not a permanent state of affairs,' laughed La Senza.

'It might hurt a bit,' said Gabby.

'*Hurt?* Ha! It's nothing, stupid girl. You've no idea what pain is until you've been torn into pieces by Spanish peasants. You think I'm scared ... what, of *drowning*? Ha! It means nothing to me! It's an easy death. Nothing!' La Senza backed closer to the precipice, wobbling dangerously on the edge of the drop.

'I'll grab him,' Bennet muttered. 'You get the bags.'

'If you say so,' said Newton doubtfully. They began to edge forward.

'Don't come any closer,' warned La Senza, 'I mean it!'

The Cardinal was balancing very unsteadily, the crashing of the waves below him a constant roar. He was either going to fall or jump, and Newton tensed at the prospect; the idea of fighting with a possessed nutcase on a cliff edge contained no appeal whatsoever. Luckily for Newton, the moment never came.

Disturbed in their nocturnal cliff-side roosts, a cloud of seagulls suddenly exploded up behind La Senza like a flock of angels, their white feathers flashing in the darkness. The cause of their disturbance was now appearing at La Senza's feet. Two gigantic filthy hands were clumping and clawing up the very edge of the precipice. Rising up from the abyss came the Bonetaker. Huge and sodden from a long journey across the English Channel, the giant heaved his seaweed-draped mass up behind La Senza and paused. Terrified by the vision, a couple of Bennet's men dropped their weapons and ran shrieking away into the mist.

La Senza was still blissfully unaware of what was directly behind him, and both baffled and insulted that his dramatic finale was losing its momentum.

'Whaaat?' said La Senza, suddenly crestfallen. 'Whaaaat?'

'What the hell is that?' said Newton.

'Bonetaker,' said Bennet. 'It's OK, he's one of us.'

'One of us? Are you *sure*?' said Newton, as Gabby edged behind her father.

'Kind of a freelancer,' said Bennet. 'Long story.'

The Bonetaker was fully upright now, almost double the Cardinal's height and twice his width. A mackerel flapped off his old leather hat and dropped wriggling onto the grass.

'What's going on?' asked La Senza. 'Why are you all looking at me like that?'

'What makes you think we're looking at *you* at all,' said Newton. 'You might want to turn around.'

La Senza, his face confused yet uncompromising, weighed things up. He wavered for a second, wondering whether it was a ruse or not. Then the Bonetaker's right hand landed hard on the Inquisitor's shoulder and clamped shut, pinning him in place. La Senza turned his head very, very slowly and looked up. Hanging over him, a ghastly display of mangled facial features and seaweed, was the Bonetaker. La Senza let out a low whimper.

'Nooooooo, nooooo.'

'EVIL!' said the Bonetaker, his voice a low rumbling boom that Newton could feel in his belly. 'Evil, bad!'

'No ... I'm not,' begged La Senza pathetically. 'I'm not a bad Inquisitor. I didn't mean to hurt anyone ... please nooooo.'

But the Bonetaker was not to be deflected in his mission. He'd followed the scent of La Senza's evil back and forth across the Channel and his programming was so deep and so strong that there was nothing that could have distracted him from his target. He grasped La Senza like a fat child picking up an action figure, and with his other shovel-like fist, he scooped up La Senza's ghastly possessions. Then he pulled the Cardinal over the cliff into the abyss.

Newton and the Purgatorians waited for the splash. There was nothing, only silence. Puzzled, they crawled forwards and peered over the cliff edge to look down to the sea far below.

On a ledge some fifty feet beneath them, the Bonetaker had landed with his prey. Babbling in sheer terror, the Inquisitor was pinned like a butterfly under the monster's huge sodden right boot as the Bonetaker plucked at the flaps of his oily coat, retrieving the tools of his ancient trade. As Newton, Viv, Gabby and the Purgatorians watched from above, the Bonetaker arranged his bowls and powders. In a low muttering incantation, he began to prepare his ghastly subject for oblivion. With La Senza weeping in terror beneath him, he started to crush the carved boxes. One by one he lifted them from the bag and mashed them against the rocks, picking amongst them until the grinding bowl was filled with nothing but the fragments of La Senza's previous fingers. Missing nothing, the Bonetaker reached down and tore the trinket with the remaining bone from La Senza's neck. It joined the others.

As the huge form continued its incantations, a ghastly purple aura began to form around La Senza. It grew into evil little wisps and as he stared at the beginnings of his own annihilation, the vile little man began his last desperate pleas for forgiveness.

'Please, I'm not guilty. I was only obeying holy orders! I'll be good now I promise, just tell me what you want, I'll get it for you. You can join me ... I dunno ... just don't do this to me ... please ... PLEASE!'

It was a pathetic and hypocritical display. Just as so many had begged and pleaded to this same Cardinal for mercy, so now he did the same. And just the same, it fell on deaf ears. Programmed to seek and destroy evil in all its forms, the Bonetaker was unstoppable. Like a machine, he continued unmoved by the Inquisitor's pitiful begging. As he ground the relics, mixing in his blood from a fresh cut he had slashed in his own hand, the glow around La Senza and his relics built, flowing in ghastly spiralling fingers. Amazed and horrified, Newton and the girls watched as the Inquisitor, his eyes pleading towards them, began a horrible twitching spasm. Driven by the incantations, the soul of La Senza was about to be evicted from the stolen body of Chris Baxter.

'Nooo ... I beg of you. Show me mercy!' La Senza beseeched.

'No,' said the Bonetaker, his refusal booming like a foghorn.

'Please, have you no pity?' said La Senza finally, doing his best to look vulnerable and misunderstood. The Bonetaker stopped.

On hearing the words, he paused in his grinding and his huge head turned slowly and deliberately until the old tired eyes looked directly into the eyes of the Inquisitor.

'Pity?' he asked in a deep bass baritone.

'Yes ... please ... show me pity!' begged La Senza, hopefully. The Bonetaker took what felt like a lifetime to reply.

'NO,' he said bluntly, and turning back to his work, he ground hard into the mess of bone fragments. The blue flames intensified as La Senza spasmed one final time, his ridiculous party robes bathed in a vortex of purple tendrils. They rose in a coiled representation of a human figure for one last second before, with a rushing roar, they flew into the Bonetaker's bowl ... and fizzled out.

All that was Cardinal Balthazar De La Senza was gone.

Gone for good.

Beneath the Bonetaker's boot lay the bruised and battered body of one Christopher Baxter, salesman. Poor Baxter looked up in mystified horror at the Bonetaker then down at the crashing waves below him, and he did the only sensible thing he could.

He fainted.

## CHAPTER 37

# AFTER THE FIRE

It took all night for the asylum to burn to the ground. For hour on hour it crackled, roared and hissed, the flames charging down the long corridors consuming all before them. As the blaze took the building there was a symphony of tumbling masonry, tortured girders and splintering glass. Finally, the vile edifice died, the walls falling in upon each other until there was nothing left of the building but a Stalingrad-like wreckage of toppled brick. At 4am, the firestorm jumped the short distance from the asylum to Hadlow Grange. By the time the pale wintry sun finally rose in the east, both buildings and all their questionable contents had been consumed.

Despite the late hour and the stressful day, Newton, Gabby and Viv didn't have the slightest desire to sleep. They perched on the roof of the tank some 200 yards from the conflagration, hypnotised as they watched the pyrotechnics and in their awed silence, the blaze warmed them like a fan heater.

Jameson and his clean-up squad arrived with the dawn. The motley collection of pre-war ambulances, antique fire engines and anonymous removal vans fanned out across the grounds until the entire site was swarming with stern-faced Purgatorians, busying themselves amongst the ruins in the search for anything that could raise awkward questions in the cold light of the new day. It soon became clear that La Senza's ghastly contraption, tinder dry after centuries in the arid Spanish climate, had gone up like balsa wood. Like its creator's dark ambitions, it had been utterly obliterated. As an extra bonus, the blaze had also taken all the other foul, evil-soaked artefacts so beloved of the late McCauley brothers.

Dawn had also seen the last of Van Loop's henchmen located in the surrounding heathland or holding out in the castle at Langton Hadlow. Bloodied, broken and most definitely bowed, they offered no resistance to Bennet's irregulars. Ahead lay an intensive few years in what from the outside, at least, appeared to be a religious retreat off the west coast of Scotland. Here they were to be thrashed into a more benign frame of mind through round-the-clock workshops in basket weaving, pot throwing and transcendental meditation.

There was a reunion between Eric the Greek and the Bonetaker, which was brief and bittersweet. They sat with each other alone for a while before the Bonetaker, his shoulders impossibly hunched and weary, ambled away into the last of the smoke and vanished. It took half an hour for the smell to clear.

Poor Christopher Baxter meanwhile was in an understandably lamentable state. For the one-time plastics salesman there was much therapy ahead, but for now it was as much as he could do to keep down the hot sweet tea and sympathy. Shivering in Cardinal La Senza's cheap robes he rocked slowly back and forth, whimpering to himself and dribbling.

Needless to say, considering the scale of events, there was a mountain of Purgatory-related paperwork in the offing, but Sixsmith thankfully persuaded Eric the Greek to let it wait until Monday morning. However, Jameson insisted on making sure that the witnesses to the night's events were to be trusted with what, one way or another, was a bit of a big story, so after a short induction course he sternly swore in Gabby, Viv, Baxter, the mechanics and the curator of the Langton Hadlow village museum. With these formalities duly observed, Newton was finally able to lead his daughter and girlfriend back to the battered Citroën. After saying his farewells to Bennet, they headed home.

\*\*\*\*\*\*

Two weeks later, Newton pulled up gingerly in front of Rowena's Cambridge town house to collect his daughter for the weekend. The Citroën had now been beautifully restored; from the chrome bumper to the leather seats, the crystal-clear windscreen and the fresh tyres, there was no trace of the car's recent misadventures. At Newton's request, even the heater had been given an overhaul.

He rang the bell.

'What time do you call this?' hissed his ex-wife, looking out to Viv in the passenger seat outside. 'Gabriella!' Rowena barked up the stairs. 'Your father is here.'

'Hi,' said Newton hopefully to his ex-wife's friends gathered around the antique kitchen table. It was not returned. There was a scramble of oversized boots on the stairs and Gabby huffed and shrugged her way down to the front door.

'A word,' said Rowena sternly. 'I've got a bone to pick with you, about last time.'

Newton felt a cold sweat pass through him like a late train. 'Yes?'

'Frankly, Newton, I don't think you're making enough effort.'

'I'm not?'

'No you're not. Gabby complained that she was bored out her mind,' Rowena declared sharply with a raised eyebrow.

'Bored?' said Newton confused. 'Did she, did she really? Bored?'

'Yes bored,' said Rowena, waving a manicured digit. 'Newton, look, you are her father. I really think you should try harder.'

There was a ripple of tutts from the table.

'Oh I'm sorry,' said Newton. 'My bad.'

'Be a better father,' said Rowena with her eyes narrowed. And with the nodding reinforcement from the table endorsing her, she bustled Newton back onto the street where Gabby was sullenly slouched against the wall. The door slammed loudly behind them.

'Have you considered a career in the theatre?' asked Newton discreetly, his eyebrow raised.

Gabby subtly returned her father's wink and then flounced away to the car, throwing herself onto the back seat and folding her arms in perfect imitation of teenage sullenness. With Rowena's gaze following them from the front window, they pulled gently away down the narrow street, into the suburbs, then out towards the ring road.

'Right then,' said Newton to his passengers as they finally dropped the theatricals. 'What we got?'

'Let me see,' said Viv, consulting the job sheet. 'Haunted hotel in the Peak District.'

'Peak District eh?' said Newton, shifting the gears. 'Well, we'd better get a move on then.'

The Citroën purred, whined and finally found its voice once again. There was a surge of pistons, a throaty roar of carburettor and the scream of the supercharger. And then, like a spitfire roaring off the runway, the old car carried them away like a rocket to the north.

## AUTHOR'S NOTE

If you can spare a couple of minutes to write a review on Amazon/Goodreads that would be great, and if you'd like to subscribe to my newsletter, which will include updates on my next book, please email me (t.j.brown@theunhappymedium.com). You can also follow me on Facebook and Twitter.

## ABOUT THE AUTHOR

Born in Dorset, T. J. Brown studied fine art and sang in bands before eventually settling into a career in publishing, designing and illustrating science and aviation titles for some of the UK's biggest publishers.
He lives in Kent, dangerously close to two pubs.

## ACKNOWLEDGEMENTS

For being kind enough to read the story in an embryonic state
yet not laugh and point at me until I cried, I'd like to thank:

Tim Benge, Loz Biggs, Pete Cane, Mark Conroy, Dave Edwards,
Tanya Featherstone, Stephen Finnigan, Robert Forsyth, Olive Gilhespie, David
Gurdon, Mark Harrison, James Hart, Stephen Heard, Nick Jenkins, Andy Knight,
Duncan Mallard, Emma Marsh, Jimmy Muir, Lucian Randall, Bridget Rankin,
Nick Ratcliffe, Joel Sassone, David Saxton and Marston York. Special thanks to
Kaleesha Williams, Denny Henke and the Eels.

For being good sports and allowing me to include them in the pub scene
at The Two Crowns, thanks to Jackie Jenkin, Pete Mckenna, Bill Rankin
and Scott Robson.

Many ideas in the book were inspired by speakers and general chat at a
UK Skeptics meeting at Muncaster Castle in Cumbria.
For that, many thanks to everyone at the friendly gathering, particularly
Jason Braithwaite, Chris French and castle manager Peter Frost-Pennington.

My mother Joy Brown listened to me read the chapters as I wrote them, a great
help as the book took shape. Chris Rowan encouraged me to write in the first place,
while my colleague Giles Sparrow has instilled some semblance of grammar and
punctuation in my thick skull over the past fifteen years.
Eduard Llena Portell advised on Spanish terms and Elly Truitt elaborated on
medieval automata.

Big thanks to all of them.

While writing this novel I found myself thinking a lot about two old school friends
who are sadly no longer with us – Roger Davies, who introduced me to comedy a
very long time ago, and Neil Torrible, who so wanted to write.

Most of all I'd like to thank and dedicate this novel to Hazel Muir.
No Noggin no novel. xx

Printed in Great
Britain
by Amazon

31678418R00234